PRAI

MW01258395

"In this beautifully written story of an old crime, a secret has shaped a family for generations, until one woman goes in search of the truth that will allow her to reconcile the inherited traumas in her life. Celebrated author Boo Walker deftly explores the curious power of genetic memory in a modern American family . . . *An Echo in Time* vibrates at the sweetest frequency and pulls gently at just the right heartstrings."
—Kimberly Brock, bestselling author of *The Lost Book of Eleanor Dare*

"*An Echo in Time* is a beautifully written, emotionally powerful story of a young woman's journey to break the cycle of generational trauma . . . I found myself cheering for Charli at every turn and smiling at the deeply satisfying and nuanced ending."
—Yvette Manessis Corporon, international bestselling author of *When the Cypress Whispers*

"*An Echo in Time* is a captivating novel about the generational legacy of secrets and shame and one woman's journey to love herself by righting the wrongs of the past. Walker has crafted a beautiful and moving tale of loss and healing that is part love story, part mystery, and all green lights."
—Melissa Payne, bestselling author of *A Light in the Forest*

"Walker dazzles . . . The characters all earn the reader's emotional investment, and the pacing is perfect. Readers will fall in love."
—*Publishers Weekly* (starred review)

"Walker's attention-grabbing and surprising plot highlights the engaging characters in this tale of second chances. For fans of women's fiction such as Nicholas Sparks's and Kristin Hannah's work."
—*Library Journal*

"A heartwarming read."

—Historical Novel Society

"Boo Walker is a true talent, and his latest novel is a captivating tale of one man's journey to reconcile who he used to be with the person he's becoming. *The Stars Don't Lie* is a beautiful reminder that sometimes returning to the past is the best way to find your way forward."

—Camille Pagán, bestselling author of *Good for You*

"Boo Walker has written a book with a tender heart . . . a great story of redemption that carted me away."

—Barbara O'Neal, bestselling author of *When We Believed in Mermaids*

"The perfect mix of character-driven, heartstring-pulling drama and sharp-witted humor. Clearly Boo Walker is an author whose time has come."

—Julianne MacLean, *USA Today* bestselling author

"I love books with breathing characters you can root for, a narrative of human life to which you can relate, a conclusion that can stop the heart, and an author who can bind them all together with passion and soul. Boo Walker proves he's that kind of writer."

—Leila Meacham, bestselling author of *Roses* and *Titans*

"If Nicholas Sparks and Maeve Binchy had a baby, he might sound a lot like Boo Walker."

—Jodi Daynard, bestselling author of *The Midwife's Revolt*

"I was swept away by Boo Walker's deft storytelling and incredibly complex characters. Soulful but also full of sharp dialogue and humor, [this] is exactly the sort of book you get lost in, then mourn when it is over."

—Suzanne Redfearn, #1 Amazon bestselling author of *In an Instant*

THE SECRETS OF GOOD PEOPLE

ALSO BY BOO WALKER

An Echo in Time
The Stars Don't Lie
A Spanish Sunrise
The Singing Trees
An Unfinished Story
Red Mountain
Red Mountain Rising
Red Mountain Burning
A Marriage Well Done

Writing as Benjamin Blackmore

Lowcountry Punch
Once a Soldier
Off You Go: A Mystery Novella

THE SECRETS OF GOOD PEOPLE

A NOVEL

BOO WALKER

WITH PEGGY SHAINBERG

LAKE UNION
PUBLISHING

Published by Lake Union Publishing, Seattle

www.apub.com

Amazon, the Amazon logo, and Lake Union Publishing are trademarks of Amazon.com, Inc., or its affiliates.

ISBN-13: 9781662523700 (hardcover)
ISBN-13: 9781662523717 (paperback)
ISBN-13: 9781662523694 (digital)

Cover design by Caroline Teagle Johnson
Cover Image ©Jean-François Brière / Plainpicture

Printed in the United States of America

First edition

For Peggy, Leigh, and Lynn

Chapter 1

THE SHUTTERS OF HIMSELF

February 21, 1970
Day 1

Catherine Overbrook stirred drowsily and extended her arm to touch her new husband. Here I lie, she thought, listening to the sweet song of the Gulf of Mexico outside my window. *My* window! Only yesterday, I was Catherine Thomas, afraid to venture out alone from my third-floor walk-up in Chicago, where angry drivers mashed their horns as their cars kicked gray slush onto the slippery sidewalks. This morning, I will look out the window of *my* house and see pines and palmettos and wondrous turquoise water. I will stroll on the beach, visit friends—real friends, *real-live* human beings who do not scurry past on dark city stairs, wary and watching with a fearful look in their eyes. There will be no traffic or sirens, no raucous street voices. For the first time in my life, I will be swept away by the music of the waves, hypnotized by the *swoosh* of palm fronds dancing in the breeze. I will be refreshed by the crisp salt air and the sweet scent of Cape jasmine, the fragrances of my new life.

Her fingers explored the empty pillow beside her. Frank was not there. Catherine opened her eyes and raised herself on one elbow. Had he not come to bed at all? The pillow was unrumpled, the sheets and blanket straightened to hotel standards. Or perhaps he'd managed to make his side without disturbing her. She was still getting to know his habits, but it would be just like him to make the bed with her in it.

Puzzled, she reviewed the night before, which was not an easy task, what with the fogginess in her brain. The party at Dr. Sandy Westerling's. Frank's displeasure with her behavior. Last night—an occasion warranting celebration—was her first taste of Champagne. They were all so welcoming, so loving, and so insistent! They toasted and toasted and toasted, their wonderful new neighbors.

Though hazy, Catherine could remember waltzing home along the beach at midnight, clinging gaily to Frank's arm. She had, she recalled, stopped halfway and said, "Look at me! Would you believe I am merry? I've never been merry before, Frank. I'm thirty-seven years old, and never in my entire life have I ever been merry!" She'd giggled unsteadily. "I've always been 'gloomy Catherine.'"

Balancing herself gently, she rolled out of bed. Her head pounded. In the bathroom, she pulled on the sink tap, noting the lack of evidence that Frank had been there earlier. No damp towel, no shaving gear. Tasting again the joy from the previous night, she smiled at herself in the mirror. He couldn't possibly be mad, could he? Her rare bit of joy was something to celebrate. In Frank's case, a celebration might not be a toast or even a pat on the back. A nod would have been sufficient, but it wouldn't be fair for him to berate her. For goodness' sake, they'd just begun this new life. He was probably out on a beach stroll. The salt air and sand between his toes would be so good for him.

Refreshed after a shower, she made a happy clatter in the kitchen—measuring coffee, unwrapping frozen sweet rolls and sliding them into the oven. The glare of the brilliant Florida sun set the drums to work in her head once more. Everything has a price, she thought wryly. Even being happy. If he's truly upset, he'll have to forgive me this once. Every little animal, when set loose for the first time, dashes wildly to be sure it is really free.

Frank wouldn't understand, though. From what she'd gathered, he would never do such a thing—lose control. Not even for a minute. Last night, he'd accepted one polite drink, then stared disapprovingly at the guests giving toasts, as though he found them silly and abhorrently effusive. He'd been rude to her new friend Miriam Arnett too. She had given him a welcoming hug, and he'd backed away like she was a leper. He didn't like being touched. Of course, Miriam wouldn't have known that. Miriam's husband saw it, too, and given his smile, apparently enjoyed the awkward moment. What was his name? David? He sat there in his wheelchair, looking at them under thundercloud eyebrows, grinning like a boy who'd tied a can on a cat's tail. Catherine could hardly believe her eyes.

Once the rolls were ready, she arranged them on a tray along with napkins, two cups, a pot of coffee, a small bowl of sugar, and a carafe of cream. Carrying them out to the deck, she called toward the beach, "Frank! Breakfast!"

The planks of the deck felt warm and smooth on her bare feet. How delicious it was, when only ten days ago, she was pulling aside the curtains to see the gray of another Chicago day. No matter how angry Frank might be, nothing could touch the euphoria she felt on this bright-blue morning.

Catherine placed the tray on the glass tabletop and sat in a wrought iron chair facing west. The only thing missing might be a newspaper. Did they deliver out here? Frank seemed like the kind of person who liked to keep up with current events. In fact, he'd had strong opinions on Nixon and had shown interest last night when Dr. Westerling had told him that most of the Chicago Seven had been sentenced to five years in prison for crossing state lines to incite a riot.

Deciding she'd look into newspaper delivery later, she poured a coffee and helped herself to a roll. They were far better while still warm, and the first delightful bite caused her to sit back and soak in more of her surroundings. Bright rows of pink and white periwinkle flanked the boardwalk stretching down to the beach. The flowers nodded to her in the breeze, and she waved back.

I'm going mad, she thought. Waving to flowers! The only flowers I ever saw in the city were in florists' windows, wires around their stems, standing in wads of green sponge. These are *my* flowers: growing in dirt, bending, alive, not wired to stand at attention. Why shouldn't I wave?

If she told Frank that she had waved to the periwinkle, he might have her committed. She could see the headline: Doctor Certifies His New Bride Is Insane.

Was he really going to miss breakfast? Fine then. She would take her art box down to the beach. Frank would like it if she did that. Be useful. Create. Work. Earn her keep. "Enjoyment is for the animal kingdom," he liked to say.

Enough! she reprimanded herself. I am grateful that I'm skilled with a pencil, pen, and paintbrush. My art is what separated me from the sleet and loneliness. Frank might never have found me if it weren't for the effort I put into growing my talent.

The first time Catherine met Frank, she'd been standing beside her display at the medical conference in the convention center in Chicago. Her field, medical illustrations, was highly specialized, and she was more familiar with every corpuscle of the human body than the average physician. She'd spent the morning discussing her services with potential clients such as textbook publishers, doctors trying to write books, and drug-company representatives.

Frank studied her drawings with focused intensity. If she had sketched him that day, he would have been Ichabod Crane from *The Legend of Sleepy Hollow*. He was tall, with frail skin stretched over bone. Shoulders stooped, he bent forward at the waist like a man nursing a pain in his back. His hair was the color of dried leaves and trimmed close to the scalp. Catherine guessed that Ichabod had twenty years on her.

"You drew these?" he asked, inspecting her art closely. "What fabulous work." He plucked a business card from her display. "I'm writing a book and looking for an illustrator."

Catherine read the name on his convention tag: FRANK OVERBROOK, MD. BURBANK, ILLINOIS. "What is your specialty, Dr. Overbrook?"

Frank looked at her, and his eyes closed. Not his actual lids but the shutters of himself, the part of him that allowed others to look in.

"Excuse me for prying," she mumbled hastily.

He gave a weak smile, then tucked the card into his pocket and marched abruptly into the lecture hall. Though she didn't know why, she felt like she'd offended him.

⁓

After the convention, Catherine returned to her life in a one-room apartment full of easels, canvases, and the smell of turpentine. She drew up a schedule of commissions and set about her solitary work. Out of her pencil and onto paper flowed fingers, feet, jawbones, and intestinal tracts, which she would then bring to life with ink and paint. Thursdays, she went to the supermarket. Saturdays, she researched in Chicago's downtown library. Working at home, she had no office acquaintances, no telephone calls, and no neighborhood visitors. She was completely isolated in her frozen tundra.

Summer passed, then autumn. She hardly noticed Christmas except for the transition from bone sketches to the blood-chemistry drawings that were due. When her doorbell rang on an impossibly frigid February day, her paintbrush clattered to the floor. Chicago had gone wild with the trial of the Chicago Seven, and everyone was being especially careful. Suspicious and afraid, she pushed the spring lock in place and eased the door open on the chain.

Ichabod Crane said, "Miss Thomas? We met at the medical convention last summer. I am Dr. Overbrook. Pardon me for the surprise. Your address was in the conference catalog."

Frank sat in the only chair she had while she perched on a stool at her drawing board. He scarcely seemed to notice the turmoil of the room: the haphazard stacks of books, the jars of pens and brushes, the boxes spilling over with tubes of oils. She was, for the first time, acutely aware that there was nothing womanly in her apartment. No flowers or fake-fruit bowls or pillows or afghans or souvenirs of happy times.

She tried to see herself through his eyes in the cold, unwelcoming room. Her painting smock, old friend of eleven years, was stiff with the remnants of oil and gesso. The only time she used the mirror was once a day, when she combed her long, brown hair in the morning, which had been hours ago.

"I'm sorry," she said. "I must look a fright."

"As a matter of fact, Miss Thomas . . ." He looked away, awkward with words. "You are exceptionally beautiful. You must know that."

"What? No one has ever said that to me."

He probably believed her. And it *was* true. In the countless foster homes of her past, not once had anyone told her she was beautiful. He sat examining her so objectively, enclosed inside those foggy eyes, that he did not seem to be there except for the body that housed him.

"I've wanted to call, but I—I . . . ," he stuttered. "I had a meeting downtown and thought I'd come by and see if you might be interested in dinner. It's last minute, I know . . ."

There it was, then. The deliverance. *The Miracle on 34th Street.*

"Are you sure?" she asked. Perhaps he'd confused her with someone else.

A spark of confidence ignited within him. "If I'm not overstepping—"

"No, no. I mean, yes, I'd like to go. You're not overstepping." Catherine took a deep breath. She had no social self, no small talk, no courting clothes. This was all new to her. "Do you mean tonight?"

He gave a smile that was nearly handsome. "If it's convenient."

While he took a stroll, she found a dark dress and a brooch that a drug company had sent as a Christmas promotion. She owned no makeup, or perfume, or shoes with slender heels. No bright scarves, beads, earrings. Somewhere in her dark infancy, her ears had been pierced, and there had been little diamond chips there. When she was six, though, her foster mother had taken them from her, saying that only cannibals punched holes through their skin.

Catherine and Frank went to dinner in a hotel dining room. The menus had velvet covers with gold tassels. She, who dined nightly with soup and tea balanced on a drawing board, marveled at the fancy lettuces, the crusty sourdough bread, the grilled prawns.

Frank ate quietly and quickly. *Enjoyment is for the animal kingdom*, she would soon learn, was his most quoted adage. He pleated his linen napkin into intricate shapes and watched from somewhere deep inside himself until she at last set down her cup.

Embarrassed, she said, "I'm not much of a conversationalist."

"I like people of few words," Frank said. He smiled, a strange, stiff smile, as though the muscles were not sure where to go.

She did want to know him, though—to understand him. "Are you still writing your book?"

A glow rose in his eyes. "I am, indeed. And I do hope to enlist your services—if you're interested."

The topic of his book created an aperture into his otherwise closed demeanor, and he spoke about how he had recently shuttered his practice to put all his efforts into the project. "My hope is this will be a standard text in medical schools throughout the country."

It didn't take long for her to ascertain his brilliance, and she thought that this book would indeed make a difference. Though the conversation remained sparse, he sifted through her own life story with a series of genuine questions.

"Do you think you'll be in Chicago forever?" he asked.

"Oh gosh, I suppose so. I could stand to get away from the protests, and this time of year is not my favorite—but where else would I go? I don't have any family anywhere else. I've barely traveled outside of Illinois, other than to visit conferences for work. Maybe one day I'll escape these winters and go south."

Despite his moments in which he seemed to close himself off, Frank listened with incredible attunement and care, more so than any other person she'd ever met. He might have been different to some, but she found his shyness and modesty, paired with his intelligence, to be incredibly alluring. Even the longest of their pauses in conversation wasn't altogether uncomfortable. Ultimately, there was a beautiful sense of raw humanity that lingered among the two introverts as they worked their way toward a connection.

Growing braver as dessert came, Frank asked, "You never cared to have children?"

Catherine let a bite of sherbet melt on her tongue, savoring the bits of pineapple, and then responded, "I've never met someone I'd want to have children with." She set her spoon down. "How about you?"

"There was a time when I wanted kids." His entire body fell into a frown. "Actually, I was married before, but it didn't work out. That would have been my chance." He scratched his head and stared into the untouched carrot cake the waiter had brought him.

Other women might have had a problem with his previous marriage. Not Catherine. All she heard in his melancholy tone was more of his own humanity escaping, a man who had been fighting his own battles.

Afterward, he helped her into her coat, steered her out into the street, and escorted her patiently up the three flights to her door. "Lunch tomorrow?"

"I'd be delighted."

He was unable to hide the pleasure in his eyes, and her heart danced at the idea. As she heard his footsteps echo down the stairs, she rushed to look in the bathroom mirror. Pale face, straight dark hair drawn back and tightly pinned. She could not find the person he called *beautiful*.

A few dates later, as they sat at lunch, he announced, "I'm moving to Florida next week."

Her throat tightened, and an empty feeling invaded her chest. She had *finally* tasted what it was like to have a relationship. She had listened with giddy anticipation for the ring of the telephone and waited eagerly for the doorbell. She hadn't known she was so lonely until he appeared. A picture ran fleetingly through her mind: Two cups on the table. Menus with tassels. Shy glances at herself in the mirror.

In a heartbreaking turn of events, the drug-company brooch, with its bent clasp, would now return to the soft cotton bed of its gift-box coffin, much like Catherine's heart.

"My former roommate from medical school needs someone to take over his small practice," Frank said, "and it will be the perfect way for me to continue seeing patients while working on the book." Frank, who had touched her only through the elbow of her heavy coat, reached across the table and put a dry hand on hers. "Marry me. Go with me."

"Next week?" Catherine felt thick-tongued, nearly stupid. She had been locked in a silent, lonely world for too long to say more.

"Yes." He withdrew his hand. "I have to go back to Burbank tomorrow to finish packing and meet the movers. I could pick you up on Thursday."

The world spun around her. Someone wants to marry me? Is this truly happening? Who is this extraordinary man who has come to set me free?

"I know it's . . ." He cleared his throat. "I know it's spur of the moment, but . . . I've not felt like this in a long time, and I thought that . . . perhaps you shared similar feelings."

If she didn't say anything, he'd take it as a rejection, but her words were caught in her throat. The most she could muster was a series of nods as tears pricked her eyes.

Catherine went about preparing to abandon her city life. She settled her lease and withdrew money from her accounts. There was no one to call and notify that she was leaving, only the clients who had commissioned illustrations. She sent letters informing them that she was returning their retainers and could not commit to further work until she was settled. Frank sent movers to collect her books, art supplies, and what few clothes would work in a tropical climate.

On departure day, Catherine opened the door to Frank at precisely 8:40 a.m. He had warned her that there could be no dillydallying if they were to marry, catch their flight, and reach the island by late afternoon.

The apartment loomed empty behind her. Her luggage was the only trace of the Catherine who had lived there. She stood in a new pink linen suit and flushed as he stared. Then he did it again—that look that indicated he had cut off the view inside himself. But only for a short moment this time, as if he'd caught it and forced himself to come back to her.

Allowing a smile to form, he picked up her bags. "I have a taxi waiting. Let's go get married."

Something close to fear hovered over her as she closed the door on Catherine Thomas. There was not a vestige of her former self left behind. It felt as if she'd cut away a cankerous sore . . . that lost, lonely Catherine.

When the two of them locked eyes at the courthouse and read each other their vows, she also made a promise to herself: This is the start of my new life. I will never return to the woman I was before Frank broke me from my cocoon and gave me wings. He may have been strange, but she was far from normal. He may have been slightly stiff, but she wasn't exactly loosey-goosey.

The evidence of his love and his hope for their future could be found in the shake of his voice when he made her his wife and the tremble of his hand when he slipped a lovely gold band with diamonds onto her finger. As she admired the diamonds sparkling on her band,

and as she gazed up into her husband's eyes, she wondered if she might have breathed life into him as well.

They were perfect for each other.

As the newlyweds climbed aboard a Pan Am flight and flew away from O'Hare, watching Chicago disappear below, the caves of Catherine's past closed and fell away.

~

Frank had previously arranged the purchase of a car in Sarasota—a Plymouth sedan as angular as his personality. After a quick taxi to the dealership and the signing of papers, they were finally able to slow down as they drove southward along the Gulf Coast.

Wearing what Catherine thought might be a look of satisfaction, Frank looked out at the expanse of blue-green water and murmured, "I like to fish. It's the one recreation I allow myself." Catherine made a mental note to learn about fishing. She would buy a rod and reel and somehow find the stomach to run a hook through an icky worm.

Then he said, "Though I suppose it's still categorized as work. Many of my best ideas for the book came to me while I was out there alone on Lake Michigan. We'll see if I can tolerate the Florida heat."

Catherine took his note about solitude to heart. No . . . do not buy a rod and reel. Unpack your art supplies and give him his space!

They drove south past Naples, turned off the highway onto a marl road hemmed in by walls of lush growth. Some miles in, they passed a sign that boasted PARADISO, POPULATION: 2,405.

"Better make that 2,407," Frank muttered.

Catherine dared not peek over at him. Had he just tried his hand at humor? There was hope yet.

Paradiso wasn't much more than a fishing village. A brief row of unpainted stores and scattered houses lined Main Street. Wooden piers jutted into the water like rotten teeth. Not that it was unappealing— the scene was stunning in its own way, a slice of what had to have been old Florida. But the evidence of the town's lack of wealth was hard to ignore.

At the center of Main Street stood the Paradiso General Store, the post office, and then the doctor's office, a gray building suffering from disrepair. A small sign read SANDFORD WESTERLING, MD.

"Is that going to be your office?" Catherine asked.

"Don't judge by outward appearance," he said. "Good medicine can be practiced in a jungle."

Of course Frank did not judge by outward appearance. If he did, he could never have chosen her.

The winding road that led them out of the village soon approached a narrow and primitive wooden bridge.

"Here we are," he said. "Osprey Isle."

The car bumped across the rickety platform and onto a small clearing paved with broken shell. Behind them, the bridge still shuddered from the weight of the car. Ahead, there was a thicket of dense foliage. He pointed to a post hammered low in the center of the clearing. A board was painted with crude arrows and names.

Catherine read aloud from top to bottom: "Carter, Arnett, Westerling/Greely, Nye, Overbrook. Someone has added our name!" She flushed with pleasure.

He drove in the direction indicated by the *Overbrook* arrow and negotiated a twisting, shelled pathway. Suddenly, the foliage ended in a burst of sunlight. The house spread wide before them, encircled by verandas. Red bougainvillea spilled across the tile roof. Star-studded white jasmine twined the walls. Rows of polished windows winked reflections. Buzzing with excitement, Catherine raced up the steps to the porch and peeked inside to see a sun-flooded living room with direct views to the Gulf. Frank followed with a faint look of satisfaction breaking through his frown.

Like a child, Catherine ran through the big rooms, caressing the massive old wicker couches and chairs, kissing the sprawling potted ferns, peering out every window at the white beach and blue water below. "I can't believe it. I keep thinking I'll wake up back in Illinois." She could not contain herself and threw her arms around him. "I simply love it!"

Frank looked lighter than ever. "I think we'll be happy here."

She stared into his eyes, and he was present now, more handsome than he'd ever been. A young boy's blush came over him. Was he about to kiss her? She would allow it. No, she'd love it! She waited, letting him work through whatever mental blocks he may have had.

Something seemed to click, and he finally moved his lips to hers. She closed her eyes as he gave her a timid peck. Despite the kiss's lack of romance, she bathed in what she knew would be a relationship that would soon grow into something incredibly beautiful. Some people have walls, and those walls take time to come down. It was the case with both of them, and that was okay. As their lips parted, she committed to breaking down his walls and allowing him to do the same for her.

A smile nearly lifted him off his feet. Ichabod had turned into Prince Charming. "Thank you," he said.

She rubbed a smudge of lipstick off his bottom lip. "'Thank you'? What for?"

"For being you."

Prince Charming might have enjoyed more than a kiss if not for the interruption of a great voice bellowing from the porch: "What a rumpus!" A boisterous bald man about Frank's age—midfifties—bounded through the door, his face alight with joy. Freckles rose above his bushy, red eyebrows and spread down into thick muttonchops in front of his ears.

He thumped Frank on the back and dragged Catherine into a crushing embrace. "Welcome to Osprey Isle, Catherine! I'm Sandford Westerling, but everyone calls me Sandy. I'm the lone doctor of Paradiso who desperately needs your husband's help. Speaking of"—he gestured to include Frank—"congratulations to you both on your matrimony. Everyone on the island looks forward to celebrating tonight."

Considering their similar ages, it was rather strange that Frank had moved down to eventually take over the practice. Sandy looked too young to retire. To each his own, though. It wasn't anything to worry about.

～

Catherine pushed away the coffee. It was cold now, as were the rolls. Where could Frank be? When he returned, she would fix a brunch. Melon and scrambled eggs and strawberry jam. He would learn what *enjoy* means. It might take time, but the sun would thaw him. The warm Gulf water would wash over him and—

A scream pierced the air, rattling the scattered palm fronds and drowning out any sign of the surf. "Help! Somebody! Anybody!"

Catherine dropped the tray and ran, heedless of the potential splinters from the planks of the boardwalk. She slid to a stop at the top of the short flight of steps that led to the sand.

Sylvie, the blind woman whom they had met at the party the night before, knelt at the tide line, poking her white cane at the trunk of a sodden body tangled in seaweed. "Somebody's dead down here!"

Catherine stood frozen, her eyes locked on the body, her heart spilling from her chest, her life falling to pieces.

Her Frank—her miracle—lay face up on the sand.

Chapter 2

'TWAS THE NIGHT BEFORE MURDER

February 20, 1970
The Day Before

The previous evening, Dr. Westerling—or *Sandy*, as he kept insisting to Catherine—presided over a lobster pot sputtering with boiling water as Frank and Catherine arrived for their welcoming party.

"Greetings!" Sandy roared, lifting a lobster that frantically clawed at the air. The doctor swayed his hips to the swing music that played from a portable radio resting on a table otherwise occupied by bottles of wine, liquor, and mixers.

"Can't leave the pot," he called. "Pour yourselves some bubbles and introduce yourselves around."

Champagne in hand, Catherine took in the vision of Sandy's backyard. A driftwood fire kicked sparks; a circle of torches lit up the approaching darkness; a long wooden table spilled over with serving dishes of food; and her new neighbors mingled barefoot in the patchy grass against the backdrop of a sunset streaked with purple and gold. What a wonderful life they'd stepped into.

A young blond woman, likely in her early thirties, called over to Catherine and patted the chair next to her. "Come join me. I'm Sylvie, your neighbor one house north."

Catherine squeezed Frank's hand and left him to fend for himself. As she sat down, Sylvie said, "Sandy tells me that you're an artist. A real, honest-to-goodness artist that gets paid. I haven't been able to sleep, making plans for us. There's a place in my studio for you. You can splatter and leave a mess, and absolutely no one will care."

"I like you already." Catherine took a nervous gulp. "What's your medium?"

"Sculpting. I'm great with mud pies." Her grin was mischievous, though she seemed shy about making eye contact. "We're going to be such wonderful friends; I feel it in my bones. It can get lonely here on the island. All of us are so glad to have you."

"Isn't that the truth," said an approaching brunette clinging to the stem of a martini glass. She was maybe a decade older than Catherine and moved toward them like a dancer of the questionable sort, smoothing the clinging jersey of her dress. "I'm Miriam Arnett. I have absolutely no talent, but maybe we can be friends too." She tossed back the rest of her drink and then flung the leftover olive over her shoulder.

"Miriam!" called a sharp voice. A man tore forward in an electric wheelchair.

She rested a hand on his shoulder. "This is my husband, David. Believe it or not, he can be sweet when he's not being a curmudgeon."

David Arnett wore a beige leisure suit with a royal-blue stripe running up the sides. His hair was combed back with perceivably obsessive effort and glistened from Brylcreem. His tanned face was shaved clean, showing a man who'd likely been handsome in his earlier years, though his appearance was bogged down by a scowl. His stout trunk, strong arms, and skinny legs indicated paraplegia.

He glared at his wife's hand on his shoulder. "I'm always sweet."

"Uh-huh. The truth is, he doesn't approve of me having fun." Miriam turned her empty glass upside down. "What can I say? My glass has a hole in it." She gave a girlish shrug and turned and wandered toward the lobster pot. "Sandy, your glasses have holes in the bottoms. My martinis keep disappearing!"

"We can't have that, dearie!" Sandy called.

Feeling uneasy in the tension, Catherine put her focus on the changing colors over the water; a strand of autumn orange had appeared. She wondered if one day she might try her hand at painting such a sky. "It's so perfect, it doesn't seem real."

David maneuvered his wheelchair in between Catherine and Sylvie. "They never get old, and I've been watching them since I was a kid." He had a firm and deep voice, clearly charming when he wanted to be.

Catherine said to Sylvie, "You have to take off your glasses to see all the color. You're missing out!"

"Of course she is!" David exclaimed. "She's blind, for God's sake!"

"You rude oaf!" Sylvie snapped, then turned apologetically to Catherine. "David has the manners of a warthog."

"Entirely too weak an acclamation," he retorted.

"I thought you knew about me," Sylvie said, talking right past David. "Please don't worry about it." Only then did Catherine notice the white cane resting against her leg.

Sylvie fumbled with the arm of David's chair. "Where's the start button on your wheelchair? I want to run you right into the water. The nerve, trying to shock our new neighbor."

"My goodness, why is everyone so sensitive?" David touched the control, and the chair whirred away.

"Don't dislike him for that," Sylvie whispered to Catherine. "He enjoys unsettling people. As a matter of fact, I appreciate his authentic nature. He never pretends things are different, and I don't have to pretend with him either."

Catherine sat dumbly, twisting the stem of her empty glass. Her impression of parties was people loving one another, laughing, being kind—like books and the movies portrayed. These exchanges had been upsetting and even troubling.

"Are you frowning?" Sylvie asked. "We're a motley bunch until you get to know us. At least, all of us but Sandy—"

"What are you saying about me?" Sandy asked, appearing out of nowhere and dragging a canvas chair in front of them. A spattered white apron was wrapped around his squat, round body. He used a corner of it to swab the sweat from his shiny, bald head. "You know I love to be gushed over."

"Have you shaved that mess off your face yet?" Sylvie asked him, likely referring to the thick sideburns that nearly reached his chin.

"Why don't you see for yourself?" He guided Sylvie's hands to his muttonchops.

"They're getting gray. I can tell. They're stiff."

He slapped playfully at her fingers. "There is no advantage to not seeing, my dear, if you can *feel* gray."

"Is gray such a bad thing?" She let go and nestled back into her seat.

Sandy stretched out his legs and dug his feet into the wild grass. "It's just that I thought you were the one love of my life who would always see me young and handsome. I hoped I might be able to fool you."

Catherine thought that these two people were marvelous, and they helped drown out the discomfort from her interaction with David earlier.

"Oh, but I do see you young and handsome," Sylvie said, "even if your sideburns are gray."

The doctor patted his cushy belly, and his laughter bubbled over and spilled out in great gusts of merriment. One by one, the others joined them, circling about, drawn by his happiness.

At the doctor's request, Nurse Glenna shuffled over with a Champagne bottle. She was a contradiction: thick-boned and slightly heavyset, yet she had the muscular features and upright posture of one who had a steady workout routine. Her cropped hair was the color of cigarette ash. Judging by the clumsiness with which she filled their glasses, she didn't seem to be the kind of nurse who would be gentle when administering a shot.

They made toasts: To bald doctors with muttonchops. To girls who wore glasses at night and men who made passes. To disappearing drinks. And to electric chairs for people too lazy to walk.

The fire spat and flared red in the twilight, and the hilarity of the crowd grew. Catherine watched everyone from a world away, feeling the Champagne work its way through her timid edges. Sandy drew these people together. He made their faces glow, their gaiety real. They clung to him, each of them, as they toasted. Look at me, Sandy. Look what I can do. Listen to me, Sandy. Hear my funny words.

Suddenly, Sandy tore off Catherine's shoes and sent them flying toward the dunes. "Go native, love."

She jerked her feet back, tucking them out of sight under the chair. They looked too white, too vulnerable, too personal.

He shook his head. "Native, Cath. Doctor's orders."

She thought it over carefully, going to war with her hesitation. Tapping into the looser part of her, she finally raised her glass as she had watched the others do. "Am I *Cath* now? Do I have a new name?" It felt lovely to have a new name to go with this glorious new life.

She waved her Champagne flute. "I have a toast. To new names . . . and new friends."

"Hear! Hear!" hailed Miriam, followed by the others. Catherine felt giddy as the idea of being accepted by this new community settled into her.

She twisted her head to find Frank, to see if he might feel the same. Not in her way, but perhaps he showed a twinge of excitement at this new adventure. To her dismay, he stood hunched over and forlorn by the dunes, the last of the sunset sneaking by him unnoticed. Catherine caught his eye, and he raised his glass and offered a microscopic smile. Seeing even a modicum of joy on his face filled her heart, though, and Catherine wondered if it might be her destiny to find a way to bring even more of that out of him. Was it possible to draw light out of the darkness?

Glenna pushed through the circle bearing a platter of steaming, spiny lobster and bowls of melted butter. "Lobsters are ready, Doctor." She was a woman on a mission, likely an exceptional nurse in that regard.

Sylvie quietly explained to Catherine, "Glenna never stops being Sandy's nurse. If she were belly dancing and Sandy called, she'd drop her finger cymbals and say, 'Ready, Doctor.'"

Although she tried, Catherine could not conjure up pictures of Glenna belly dancing. To see her stiff gray crewcut of a hairdo beaded with spangles and feathers, her mighty legs stomping, her powerful arms writhing above her head, her heavy wristwatch catching the light, her little black eyes darting like flicks of a snake's tongue.

Catherine rose unsteadily. "Another toast, everyone. To belly dancing and lobsters as red as fire trucks and to having entirely too much to drink!" She tapped Sylvie's glass with her own, and they dissolved into laughter.

A bit delayed, Miriam raised her glass, sloshing her fresh drink onto the grass. "Hear! Hear!"

Sandy took the platter of lobsters from Glenna, his voice tender. "How could I hold the world together without you, Nurse? You are my one and only true love."

A guarded smile graced Glenna's lips.

"Sandy Westerling!" Sylvie pouted. "You told me I was your one and only true love."

"You *are*, darling girl," he whispered. "On Tuesdays."

After a good round of laughter, everyone found a seat around a long table full of delicacies and began to fill their plates. Catherine squeezed onto the bench next to Frank. "Everything okay?"

"Yes, of course," he said. "Just a long day, that's all." He patted the back of Catherine's hand.

Assisting Sylvie, Sandy cracked a lobster, pulling the sweet pink flesh from the shell. "Straight from the Keys, Cath and Frank. These little devils don't have delicious claws to pick apart like their cousins in Maine, but their tails are"—he gave a chef's kiss—"delectable." He piled onto the plate a corncob with an overly generous cut of butter, several halved new potatoes, a helping of bright-green broccoli florets, and a couple of cubes of ripe pineapple and melon. Then he set a bowl of butter down and guided Sylvie's fingers as she located each item in front of her.

Sandy does love them, Catherine thought. He loves them all, and they love him back. Whatever the reason for his early retirement, Sandy was leaving big shoes to fill.

⌒

Thirty minutes later, Glenna began to clear the table with efficiency and determination. Someone had changed the station on the radio to rock 'n' roll—maybe the Beatles, though Catherine wasn't much of a music aficionado. Everyone helped carry the dishes inside, then drifted back out to face the Gulf. Glenna extinguished the torches and broke up the fire, and they sat in starlight, letting the evening die. Over the dunes, wet sand left from the falling tide shimmered.

Frank sat in a chair with Catherine on the grass next to him. If he were a toucher, she mused, I could lean my head against his knee. Tentatively, she tested the waters. He grew rigid and shifted his position. Why is he so cold? Both his demeanor and his skin. If only she knew a way to break through to him, to raise his temperature.

David's wheelchair whirred to a stop beside them. "We're calling it a night. Frank and Catherine, I hope you've had a good time." He grinned at Frank's dour expression. "Don't think too badly of this crew, Dr. Overbrook. You'll get used to us."

Catherine clutched Frank's hand and replied to David, "This has been the most wonderful night of my life."

"Mrs. Overbrook, you're an old-fashioned lady," David said, making it sound so intimate as to exclude Frank. "A rare species. That is my

A-number-one compliment, now and forever." Then he yelled over his shoulder, "Miriam! Come hop on. I'll drive you home."

She came over in an unsteady walk, balancing herself with each careful step. "G'night, all," she mumbled.

"Give Sandy back his glass," David commanded.

"But it's a long way home."

He shook his head in frustration, then gripped the joystick on his chair and spun away without another word.

Miriam glanced at Catherine. "Don't let us spoil your evening."

Catherine waved a hand in the air as if she hadn't been affected at all, but a sick feeling passed over her as Miriam followed David around the house.

Sandy placed a hand on Catherine's shoulder. "Don't go yet. A party is no good unless there's someone who wants it to go on and on. Isn't that right, Frank?"

Frank gave a grunt that might have been intended to be cordial. "Actually, I thought we might speak about work before we head home."

Sandy's shoulders heaved in a resigned lament. "Frank, Frank! You confuse social activities with the heavy-handed business of making a living. Your first night here was to let you see the island and to look us over." He sighed. "But if you must, come inside. We'll talk in my study."

"Is there anything else I can do, Doctor?" Glenna asked, popping up from her seat.

Sandy waved his hand. "No, thank you, Mary Liz—I mean . . . Glenna."

Glenna's eyes grew wide.

"Pardon me. This old brain is running on fumes. *Glenna*, please come along with us. You know all the answers better than I. Cath, love, take a tour of my house while we talk. Look over every niche. I want you to make this your second home."

The three began to walk away as Sandy said, "This is the lady, Frank, who keeps my office and my life in order. Without her, I would wear one red sock and one green. I might give whooping cough shots for broken legs."

Lingering on the patio, Catherine gave herself up to the serenity of the quiet night. The stars shone vividly in the cloudless sky, causing the sea foam of the surf to sparkle as it rolled over the sand. The waves sighed as they drew away, and the pines murmured in answer. She felt as though she could sink into the ground and sleep forever. But Frank would be disappointed in his new bride. She shook herself vigorously and went into the house.

The air in the small parlor tasted sweet with the faint scent of gardenias. A Victorian love seat was half-covered with a carelessly tossed shawl of blue wool. A china teapot painted with pink dogwood blossoms and its matching cups rested on a tea table. Near the window, a velvet chair faced a needlepoint frame. The work, partially completed, held a needle threaded, ready for the next stitch.

Catherine examined the rows of watercolors on the wall. All flowers. Magnolias; camellias; forsythia, japonica, and bachelor buttons. Their execution, unlike her own precise linear drawings, seemed hazy. Liquid impressions with a dreamlike quality. Each one was signed in the lower corner with hair-fine initials: M. E.

Sinking down into the velvet chair, Catherine cupped her hands over the soothing texture of the armrests and closed her eyes and lost herself in the scent of gardenias and the dizzying buzz of overindulgence . . .

"Dr. Overbrook is ready to leave."

Catherine jumped from the chair with a gasp and found Glenna staring down at her. "You startled me."

"My apologies," Glenna said. "Your husband seems eager to get home."

"How long have you guys been in there?"

"Just a little while."

Catherine looked at one of the floral watercolor paintings. "What does *M. E.* stand for, by the way? They're lovely pieces."

Frank emerged from the office before Glenna could reply. "Come along, Catherine." He clutched her arm and led her toward the front door.

Descending the stairs, she stumbled, but he gripped her tightly.

"Look at you," she said, "my knight in shining armor. Dr. Frank Overbrook, my wonderful new husband. Are you taking me to bed now?" She was seized with giggling, her head light from Champagne and happiness. "Look at me, Frank. Gloomy Catherine. I'm actually *merry*! Take your merry wife to bed, Frank. Our new bed!"

Chapter 3

When the Call Comes

At a table in the back corner of the Salty Pearl, Detective Quentin Jones perused his cards and reached for the burning cigarette balancing on top of the overflowing ashtray. After a puff, he blew the smoke in a broken circle toward a ceiling decorated with articles of underwear and weatherworn dollar bills. The place had been around for fifty years, and by now, the bounty must have added up to a few thousand bucks. There had definitely been more than a few who'd guzzled their beers with their eyes on the cash, plotting a theft.

Of course, a potential criminal would have to get by Betsy Cable over there behind the bar. She'd bought the place a decade earlier, along with the shabby house next door, and she was not afraid to show her shotgun to drunk compadres on the edge of causing trouble.

Her restaurant stood on stilts on the water about twenty-five minutes from Fifth Avenue in Naples—that's *if* you navigated the bumpy dirt road by car. Half the people, including Jones, came by boat. His Boston Whaler was tied up out back. No matter where they came from, they came *for* the fried-seafood plates, the strong cocktails, and a view that kept even the natives satisfied. Nothing captured the Salty Pearl better than the slogan that hung above the row of blenders on the back bar: A Sunny Place for Shady People.

Jones had pocket sevens. By the looks of the other three gentlemen at the table—all more than twice his age—they didn't have a thing.

Just as a Four Tops track kicked in on the jukebox, Hugo set down the river: a seven of spades. Keeping his excitement to himself, Jones scrutinized the other two players, looking for tells. Mac wasn't swallowing, his Adam's apple staying put. Salvaje was avoiding eye contact.

"Let's get to it, Jones," Hugo said, tapping his wedding ring against the table. It had been six years since he'd turned over in bed to find his wife had passed in her sleep.

Jones lowered his aviators to the end of his nose. "What are you in such a rush for? This is Florida."

"Because I refuse to die at this table looking at you three clowns."

"Fair enough. I raise you boys ten." Jones tossed in a couple of chips and let them splash before enjoying another puff of his smoke.

Salvaje folded, dropping his cards with fingers that trembled from the Parkinson's that was slowly taking him away. He went after his own cigarette as though he'd earned some alone time with it.

"Mac," he said, "you ought to fold too. What'd I tell you? That boy can see through cards."

Mac, a retired detective, met Jones's bet. "I think he's full of it."

Jones allowed a confident smirk to rise on his face as he showed his set. Mac cast down his losing hand with a curse. Salvaje said, "I told you so."

In slow motion, Jones raised his arms across the table and dragged the pot his way. "Good game, gentlemen." He stubbed out the cigarette and polished off his Pabst Blue Ribbon. "Now, if you'll excuse me, I'm going to go throw a hook in the water and see if I can find a sheepshead for dinner."

"You know, Jones," Mac said, "if I were you . . . what? Almost thirty? Those Brando looks. I wouldn't be worried about fish. I'd have my hook out trying to lure one of those beach bunnies over there. They've been watching you the whole time."

Jones peered through the broken screen to the deck, where a pack of women sunned themselves like alligators. One of them was indeed looking his way, and he whipped his head back toward the table before their eyes locked.

"Yeah, well . . ."

The thing was . . . cards, he understood. Angie over there, he didn't. Because there was no truth in that wild feline of a woman.

"The brunette, what's her name?" Hugo asked.

"Angie."

"That's right. Angie. Son, if I was—"

Jones pinched his mustache. "Is this how you punish me for taking your money? Giving me a hard time?"

"What you need to do is stop hanging out with us geezers and go land a good woman."

Jones took in the three men whom he'd come to know as his friends—maybe his three fathers, or the three wise men. Larry, Curly, and Moe. Good men who were also good examples of how things can go down in flames.

"You three are the biggest wrecks in South Florida, maybe the state . . . but you're *my* wrecks. Someone's gotta take care of you. Besides, I like beating you fellas and taking your money. Makes me feel good about myself."

Salvaje coughed out a laugh. "Don't exclude yourself from this ring of bozos, Jones."

"Hey, I come for the mahi-mahi and coconut rice. You happen to always be here."

"Keep telling yourself that," Hugo said.

Betsy Cable's sharp voice cut through the air. "Quentin, you got a call!"

Jones turned and looked across the restaurant. Most of the tables were taken. Betsy was waving the phone at him. "Don't I love being your secretary."

He popped up. "Excuse me. My day off just got cut short."

With one hand pouring rum into a shaker, Betsy stretched the cord and handed him the phone. Jones squeezed in between a man with an eye patch who smelled like whiskey and an agitated blonde who seemed glad to use Jones as a divider.

"Detective Jones here."

The gruff voice of his supervisor—the infamous luminary known as Detective Melvin Wycoff—came back at him. "Jones, I need you to work today."

"I should have figured." He couldn't deny the sudden sense of purpose that ran through him, though he'd been looking forward to sitting out in the sun with a line in the water.

"Body washed up on the beach on Osprey Isle, off Paradiso."

Just like that, it began. A new body, a new chapter, another reason to get out of bed. "Let me run my boat back home. I'll take the patrol car over. Be there in about forty-five. Can you have Challa meet me?"

"He's already on his way."

Jones hung up the phone and slapped some cash on the bar top. "Betsy, I'll pick up the tab for Tom, Dick, and Harry over there."

"I'm sure it's their money anyway."

Jones cracked a grin but came up empty with a response.

She leaned in, and as she took the cash, her gold earrings dangled. "Be careful out there, Quentin. Collier County isn't like it used to be."

"No, it's not, is it?"

Before he could escape, Angie—the top gator out there on the deck—broke away from the pack and stopped him. It had been a week since he'd seen her, and she hadn't gotten any less appealing. She was all woman, every bit of her. Thick, wavy hair. Long, smooth legs easing out of cutoff jeans. Cowboy boots that Jones had slid off a time or two. A tight shirt that made life seem unfair. Of course, she was more than that, and that was the problem.

"Where you going in such a rush?" she asked, her gravelly voice carrying some attitude with it. He wasn't all that good with women, but he knew when one was mad at him.

"Headed into work," he said, knowing he was about to catch some heat for his recent behavior.

She chewed on her lip. "I was hurt you didn't call me back."

Oh, here we go. Angie needed to go to the back of a long line of ladies who were mad at him. He wasn't good like that, being a companion of any sort. If he had a dollar for every woman who'd called him out on it, he'd have more dough than what hung from the ceiling.

Angie took his silence as an insult. "You don't think you own this place, do you? Like I can't ever come back to the Salty Pearl, because it's where Detective Quentin Jones hangs his hat. That's not the way it works."

He raised his hands, then ran one through his short, brown hair. How the hell was he going to get out of this one?

As if she had another personality, she stepped closer to him and unfastened one of the buttons of his Hawaiian shirt, drawing something on his chest afterward. "What are you doing later?"

Jones smiled. "Now, that's not fair, is it?"

She inched closer. "What's not fair?"

"You're using your female powers against me. In your case, you've got them in spades." He resisted the urge to lower his eyes and take in what he'd let go.

She wouldn't break eye contact with him. "Seriously, what is it with you? You take me to your pad and ravish me and then leave me to find my own way home in the morning. What kind of treatment is that?"

Jones drew in a breath. Unlike that poker game back there, there was no winning this one. "Angie, I'm not the kind of boat you'd want to cross the Atlantic with, if you know what I mean. I'd take you right through the Bermuda Triangle. I'm best for a quick jaunt to the Keys and back."

"I'm not boat shopping," she said, clearly irritated. Her shoulders drooped. "Don't do that—smile like that. Trying to charm me. Who are you, Q? What are you so afraid of?"

He knew what she'd like to hear, which also happened to be the truth. "I'm afraid of hurting someone who doesn't deserve getting hurt."

"Yeah, well, too late for that."

His mouth flicked a smile. "I have to get to work."

"That's what you said last time."

"I wasn't lying then, and I'm not lying now."

The other side of her flared up again. She stepped back and gestured for him to pass by her. "Then go." She raised her voice, drawing the attention of the patrons nearby. "Go run away . . . from the best thing that could have ever happened to you!"

"That could be true." Jones glanced at the old-timers back inside. They were all looking at him with shit-eating grins. They loved being spectators in Jones's world.

"Angie," he said, twisting back to her, "trust me, I'm not the kind of guy you want to keep waking up to."

She narrowed her eyes at him, trying to strangle him with a deadly look. "Don't come crawling back."

"I wouldn't insult you that way."

She finally broke away from the stare down and shook her head in disgust as she moved away, not unlike a gator slipping back into brackish water.

Jones got out of there quickly, walking fast down the dock and pulling the line off the cleat. He didn't dare glance back as he eased the Whaler out into the middle of the bay and headed toward the Gulf.

⌐

At a house on Osprey Isle, Jones rolled up the window of his patrol car, then climbed out and stuffed his holstered Smith & Wesson .38 Special revolver into the waistband of his shorts. You never knew with these island yahoos. He still wore his flowery shirt, and it was unbuttoned halfway down his chest. His trusty Sperry Top-Siders covered his feet. Though every supervisor he'd had in his ten years on the force had yelled at him for working out of uniform, he'd learned that as long as he kept successfully solving homicides, he could get away with it.

Some folks were good at building houses, others practicing the law. Quentin Jones hadn't been much good at anything until he'd set foot into the police academy after high school. It turned out he'd simply been looking for the right thing to put effort into. He'd also proved to have a knack at solving crimes. Probably because he'd never been one for following the rules. Stepping into the mind of a criminal was easy for him.

Challa, one of the overworked evidence technicians, got out of the other patrol car. A camera swung from his neck. His thin hair was cut short, putting extra attention on eyes that looked like they could fall out of their sockets if he sneezed.

"It's too pretty out here for dead bodies," Jones said, looking at the house and the expanse of blue beyond. He would kill for a view like that. Well, not *kill*. Then he'd have to investigate himself.

With a heavy sigh, Challa said, "'Pretty' doesn't make much of a difference when it comes to these things."

"I guess not." Jones gestured toward the steps. "Shall we?"

As he started to knock on the door, a woman pulled it back. She tried to give a welcoming smile, but her lips weren't having it. She stared at both of them, her face overcome with disbelief. Had to be the victim's wife.

"Good morning, ma'am. I'm Detective Quentin Jones, Collier Sheriff's Office. Behind me is Officer Challa. We received a call about a . . . a body?"

She closed her eyes, as if to shoo away the word. "Come in."

As they followed her inside, Jones asked, "What's your relationship to the victim?" Voices came from farther inside—surely friends who were there to comfort her.

She turned back and stopped. "He's my—*was* my—husband. I'm Catherine Overbrook."

"I'm so sorry."

Another futile attempt at a smile.

Accustomed to the sun-bronzed skin and careless hair of seaside girls, Jones studied her fragile, icy beauty. What was she hiding behind those sad eyes? Guilty or not, she was obviously torn up inside.

"When's the last time you saw him alive?"

"Last night. Before midnight. We walked home from Sandy's house and . . ." She pressed her eyes closed.

Jones folded his hands at his waist. "I'm sure you're not up for much talking and probably need to sit down. If you could point us to the crime scene, we could talk afterward?"

Not that I'll give you a choice, he added to himself, knowing even the seemingly most brokenhearted of spouses could be guilty—*if*, in fact, foul play was involved. One of the first lessons he'd learned when he joined the squad was that you treat every dead body as a homicide till proved differently. In an investigation, every second counts.

Mrs. Overbrook drew in a big breath through her nostrils. "You can go out this way." Jones glanced at the crew sitting in the living room and offered a nod, but he was already focusing in on the scene. The rising sun was hitting hard, cooking the body, burning off evidence.

Jones and Challa pushed through the back door and onto the deck. A table had been set with breakfast for two. Jones kept an eye out for anything that seemed off. He preferred to see things for himself before he questioned people. Because half of them told lies, even when they thought they were telling the truth.

At the end of the boardwalk, the bloated body came into view. It looked like the tide had brought him up. The man was on his side on wet sand, about twenty yards from the water. His head was twisted face up.

A chubby, bald man with thick sideburns stood nearby, his arms crossed. When he noticed Jones, he hurried toward him. "I wondered how long it would—"

"You're messing up my crime scene," Jones called out, descending the steps to meet him.

"Just keeping the birds off of him."

Several different footprints led to the body. "Do me a favor and move directly toward me, staying right of the rest of the prints there."

The man did as he was told.

Once he was close, Jones asked, "Who are you?"

"I'm Dr. Sandy Westerling. I live two houses up. Frank was a friend of mine. It's such a shame."

"If you'd wait inside," Jones said, "I'd appreciate it. I'll be up shortly to ask questions."

"Happily," the doctor said, kindly passing by them.

Jones turned to Challa. "I can tell from here there's some marine damage. Crabs, fish, sharks . . . He definitely fed a few animals out in that water."

"I'd say so." Challa pressed his eye to the viewfinder of his camera and started snapping shots.

Once he'd taken a few, Jones walked in Sandy's footsteps and approached the body. Strands of seaweed poked out of a white button-down shirt dyed with blood. The vic, who was quite older than his wife—probably in his fifties—wore pleated khakis. One of his leather shoes was missing. One thing was for certain: he hadn't been out for a voluntary pleasure swim.

The man's skin was pale, like he'd avoided the sun at all costs. A white foam bubbled up from his mouth. His big nose hung like a closet hook, and his cheekbones pushed out below his eyes. What in the world was a pretty woman like Mrs. Overbrook doing with him?

Marine life had indeed had its way with the body, along with the salt water and sun too. The scratches and scrapes were likely the result of rolling back and forth on the sand all night, brushing up against shells and debris. A gash—picked at by crabs and fish—showed above the collar of the victim's neck and was likely the cause of the blood. It was potentially a stab wound, though it could have happened in the water. But the way the blood had settled onto the shirt made it look like the bleeding had started before the body hit the water—before his heart had stopped beating. Foul play was highly possible.

Three different sets of footprints led to the body, two of which looked like women's. There was a set of knee prints too. Someone had gotten down close in an attempt to revive him.

When Challa was done taking the initial shots, Jones popped on gloves and went to work, talking to himself as much as to Challa. "I'm guessing the vic is in his fifties." Jones pried the arms up; the body was in full rigor. "I don't see any obvious defense marks. Potential suicide, though that's a rough way to go." He searched for any other wounds. Nothing.

Jones looked out to the Gulf. It had been calm, barely any drift. "He was out in the water for a few hours at least. Someone might have dragged him out to sea, not counting on the waves washing him back up." He eyed the stretches of sand in both directions. "It's a shame it was low tide. Perfect spot to commit a murder. The whole crime scene's probably washed out to sea."

After taking a moment to think, he said, "Challa, shoot every footprint on this beach, leading up to every house and leading around the bends there. Keep an eye out for cigarette butts, bottle caps. Anything that doesn't belong. Make sure you go up into the dunes too."

"You got it," Challa said in between clicks.

"It's a small island," Jones continued. "I'll put in a call and get some officers to sweep the whole place, see if someone tried to bury or burn evidence."

Back to the body, he murmured, "What'd you do to upset somebody? You left your wife up there to sort things out for herself. Or did she do it? What can you tell me?"

Jones reached into the pockets and found Overbrook's leather wallet. One credit card, a license. Several bills adding up to forty-eight dollars. A few business cards. He was a doctor with a practice in Burbank, Illinois. A Polaroid picture of his wife had nearly been destroyed by the water.

"You loved her then, huh? Or did you keep the picture for another reason?"

The *click click* of Challa's camera sounded from the dunes.

Jones poked at the wound ever so slightly. He couldn't tell if it was a slice from a blade or something with a point.

He stood up, lit a cigarette, and looked down at what was left of Frank Overbrook. "Did someone kill you, Frank? Who kills a doctor?" Jones turned back to the house. "Was it one of them? Or some stray that came upon you out here? I guess you're not too worried about it now, are you? Let's see what the medical examiner says."

～

The slam of the ambulance doors brought Catherine back to the present. She watched the van carrying Frank's body roll through the archway of trees toward the rattling, protesting bridge. They would pass the general store and the Paradiso Post Office and drive to Naples, where they would take Frank down a hall and into a tiled room to begin their dreadful work.

She ran through the rooms of her mind, closing doors, fleeing from the image of that big wicker basket the men had carried from the beach and around to the front of the house. She'd watched them from the doorway, seeing the basket rock from side to side as they walked. Don't think anymore, Catherine!

Returning to the living room, she looked at her houseguests, still strangers to her. Dr. Sandy, who was the heart of the island, and his devoted nurse, Glenna, who was reserved and awkward but not mean; then Sylvie, who seemed overly eager to be a friend. Had Catherine moved into some nightmare neighborhood where newcomers were murdered? Were they part of an evil scheme?

"I wish I could do something, Cath," Sylvie said in a friendly tone. She sat on the wicker couch, her cane laid across her knees. Though her eyes were covered by glasses, her face still evoked concern. "I want to help you if I can. I want to be a friend, Cath."

Before she lost her footing, Catherine retreated to a chair and mumbled a thank-you.

"Let's give you something to take the edge off," Sandy said, nodding to Glenna, who snapped to attention from her stance by the window.

Glenna opened the black bag and produced a syringe. As Glenna prepared the sedation, Sandy tore the edge off an alcohol packet and reached for Catherine's arm. "Get some rest, and you can face what's coming later."

Catherine submitted meekly as Sandy dabbed her arm and Glenna slipped the needle into place with perfect precision. Catherine barely flinched.

Detective Jones came in from the front entranceway and put his eyes directly on her. "Mrs. Overbrook, I'd like to—"

Sandy waved the detective off. "She's in no condition to talk to you now, Detective. I've given her something to calm down. Please come back in a few hours."

Jones looked at the syringe. "The medicine could have waited until I had a chance to ask some questions."

"She's fragile," Sandy said. Catherine's eyelids were already losing their strength.

"That may be so," Jones said, coming closer, "but there's a killer on the loose. The more I know, the safer y'all will be."

Sandy lowered the volume of his voice. "We're grateful for that, but Catherine has just lost her husband. Let her sift through her shock."

Sylvie suddenly sprang to her feet, stirring Catherine from her drowsiness. She rushed forward, her arms outstretched. Her cane rolled from her lap and clattered across the floor. "Quentin?" She reached for him and put her hands to his face.

He looked at her uncertainly. "Miss Nye?"

"I'd know your voice anywhere, Quentin Jones. Is my art student all grown up and now a policeman?"

Catherine felt herself falling away from reality. The figures bending over her floated into a remote misty tunnel. Her tongue was thick, her limbs grew heavy. Sandy lifted her to her feet, arm around her waist, and supported her down the hallway. The bed was still unmade, exactly as she had left it, with Frank's smooth pillow beside her head.

After Sandy pulled back the covers, she did her best to slip inside despite her muscles giving way. She pressed her head into the pillow and . . .

"I'll stay with you until you fall asleep," Sandy crooned, smoothing her hair. "Go to sleep, now."

⌒

"What are you doing out here?" Jones's pulse hammered through his body. The woman who'd first captured his heart was suddenly standing in front of him. He hadn't seen her in ten years. If that wasn't enough, he was trying to grasp with his mushy mind what the white cane and dark glasses suggested.

"Isn't that a story?" Sylvie mused. "I'd need all day." She was looking toward him but not directly at him. Her thin body was encased in ragged jeans and a loose work shirt knotted carelessly at her small waist. A cascade of golden hair fell across her shoulders.

He shot back through the years, recalling exactly the wedge he'd found himself in as a troublesome senior in high school, knowing love for the first time with a woman he could never share it with—a teacher five years his senior. She'd been the only woman who had ever left a mark, and here she was, right back in front of him and dredging up every bit of what had faded in the last decade.

"Quentin was once my student," Sylvie explained to the other woman, who wore a plaid robe over a wet black bathing suit. "The first year I taught. I was barely old enough to teach . . . and he . . ." She swatted a hand through the air and redirected her attention to Jones. "I can't believe it."

"The small world of Florida," Jones barely uttered. Rattled to the core, he wasn't quite ready to continue with her, and instead turned to the other woman. "Who are you?"

"Glenna Greely. I'm Dr. Westerling's nurse."

Jones tried to sharpen his mind by returning focus to the investigation. "I'm assuming you were in the water when the body was discovered, Miss Greely?"

"I was snorkeling when Sandy came running up the beach, calling for me. I tore off my mask and fins, grabbed my robe, and ran after him."

The doctor reappeared with his black physician's bag, and Jones asked, "When will I be able to talk to her?"

"A few hours," Sandy said. "She was in shock. A sedative was the right thing to do."

Jones didn't want to give Catherine time to work on her alibi or story. And he wasn't particularly fond of the doctor trying to play top dog, but he'd let it slide for now.

"Glenna and I need to get to the office—we have patients waiting on us—but someone should stay with Catherine."

"I'm free today," Sylvie offered, "but I need to run home first. I left the coffee on, I think, and need to cover some clay so it won't dry. Could I do that?"

"I'll see you home, Miss Nye. I can hear your story on the way."

"My story?" Her delicate eyebrows lifted above the dark glasses.

"Hear what happened," he amended, then turned back to Sandy. "Can you give us about thirty minutes? I'll give her a ride home and take a statement."

"We can do that." Sandy inched closer. "Was it a murder?"

Jones met him square in the eyes. "Yet to be determined."

Once Sylvie and the detective had gone, Sandy turned to Glenna, who was stiff with worry, her gaze cast out toward the Gulf. "Glenna . . ."

"Yeah?" She didn't turn to him.

"I . . . I think it would be best . . ." Speaking about it proved incredibly difficult. "He seems like a sharp detective. He'll do some digging."

She let out a sigh and finally twisted his way. "What do we do, Doctor?"

Sandy stood and went to her, setting a hand on her shoulder. "We don't say a word."

Chapter 4

Long Time No See

"My patrol car's straight ahead," Detective Jones said to Sylvie as he guided her down the steps of the Overbrooks' house.

She tapped the cane on the next step. "My house is only one north. We could walk. Driving disorients me."

"I'd like to have the patrol car, just in case."

"In case of what? Am I your prime suspect? Are you going to cuff me and throw me in the back?" A sly—dare he even think, *flirtatious*—grin eased onto her face.

"Of course not." Distracted far more than he liked to be, Jones helped Sylvie into the car and slid behind the wheel. He found himself tongue tied as he returned to the clearing and took the next driveway up, one far less manicured. Underbrush scraped the sides of the car.

Breaking a long silence, Jones asked, "When did you move out to Osprey Isle, Miss Nye?"

"We call it Lollipop Island . . . a private joke . . . because of the shape. The bridge is the stick, and our houses are in a semicircle along the beach. Other than the Overbrooks, I'm the newest to the island. It's been three years now."

At the end of the drive, Sylvie stepped out and tapped lightly at the ground with her cane. "Aha! You took me to the right place. Feel the pine needles? I call it Sylvie Spongy Avenue. At the Overbrooks', the path is broken shell. Very crunchy. When I walk over there, I say, 'You have arrived at Greely Crunch.' Well, now it's *Overbrook*, since the sale."

He slung the canvas bag containing his recorder over his shoulder and circled the vehicle to her side. "When was the sale?"

"Recently. Within a few weeks. The Overbrooks arrived yesterday, can you believe that? One day in Florida and it comes to this."

He led her to her house, a wide, rambling frame of weathered boards. Most of the windows stood open. Sea oats lined the entry, and a breeze from the water stirred the wooden rockers on the front porch. Inside, the smell of wet clay filled the air. The rafters held macramé hangings. Sisal twined with shells and driftwood waved lazily from the ceiling. Mounds of clay wrapped in wet cloths decorated every surface. Clay figures of pelicans and gulls soared and sailed; dolphins leaped from slate squares; sea creatures cavorted and swam through every workspace.

"Is everything topsy-turvy?" she asked. "I'm a lousy housekeeper."

"It looks fine," he assured her, walking over to a long worktable where cans spilled over with carving tools, finely pointed chisels, and sharp scrapers.

"You have a lot of dangerous objects," he said, searching the blades for blood.

"The tools of the trade."

He glanced at a clay starfish on the table that could almost be confused for the real thing. "You were always so gifted. Do you have a kiln here?"

"Oh no. I'm afraid I try not to play with fire these days. Miriam takes me to a studio on Marco Island when I have a batch ready for firing."

Jones noticed two fettling knives poking out of one of the cans; he remembered using one in her class. Several scalpels rested next to a stack of ribs and scrapers. Frank's deadly wound could easily have come from a blade on this table.

"Find a place to sit," she instructed, waving a circle around the room. "If it's dirty, find another. Miriam comes over occasionally and checks me out for crud on the surface. She looks at my laundry and tells me what's presentable. Disinfects me, so to speak."

He was half listening, distracted by the sharp objects in her possession and by the idea that he couldn't let himself be fooled by her. His uncle had taught him how to find the truth, how it was a song that you could hear once you let go of the other noise. Sylvie made the noise so much louder.

"This Miriam person sounds like a kind individual," Jones said, taking in Sylvie's beauty and telling himself he could not let his attraction to her get in the way.

With relative ease, Sylvie rose to her tippy-toes and located a pull chain above the chair and activated a ceiling fan. A tinkling wind chime strung with shells turned with the rotating blades. She ran her hand across the seat of a rocker, found it empty, and said, "Voilà! A place that isn't brimming over. Here. Sit."

As he did so, she said, "Miriam is a lovely person—takes me to the grocery store, takes me shopping for clothes or art supplies."

As Jones imagined this life of hers, his heart ached. After he'd graduated in Sarasota and gone to Tampa for the police academy, he'd dreamed of her thin hands guiding his own over the clay in the classroom, bending above him so her hair brushed his face as she explained angles or textures.

"It's in there, Quentin," she would say. "In the clay. Something is waiting for you to find it. Sink your thumbs into it like this." She would press his hands into the cool surface, digging, smoothing, shaping, while he sat enamored.

"I haven't shut up for one minute. Did you notice?" She found the coffeepot and unplugged it, busy, darting about the room. She was on familiar ground. "I've wanted to ask you something for a long time," she continued, standing before him, her beauty as evident as ever. "Who was Brooke?"

The name grabbed him. He wiped his damp palms on his trousers, remembering the notebook he had lost. Reams of juvenile verse on blue-lined essay paper . . . about a sprite named Brooke. How had Sylvie known?

He was unable to answer, and was thankful Sylvie could not see him flush.

"Did you marry Brooke?"

He cleared his throat, afraid his voice would betray him. "I'm not married, Miss Nye."

"I found your notebook," she said softly, satisfying his curiosity. "The poems were rather good. It was childish of me to keep them, but I was a child then too. Want to hear a confession, now that it doesn't matter anymore?" She crouched beside him, peering up, her eyes hidden behind the black lenses. "I wanted to be Brooke. I had a crush on you, truth be told."

Jones held his breath.

"She must have been special. May I touch your face?" Sylvie placed her hands on his face, totally absorbed, and traced her fingers across his closed eyes, his cheeks, his chin. A round of shivers washed over him. "Why, you grew a mustache! Look at you, all grown up. I remember you being such a troublemaker. How in the world did they let you be a police officer?"

"They probably wouldn't have, had they known me in high school." He couldn't think of those days without a level of guilt creeping into his psyche.

"You did have a reputation, didn't you?"

An image of a younger Quentin popped into his mind.

~

A degree of hope lingered in the Jones household for years after Quentin's father had been classified as MIA by the United States Army Air Forces. The hope could be compared to how a family felt when a kidnapped child has been missing for far too long or when a loved one has been trapped in a coma for years.

One has trouble letting go in these situations, begging the question: Is the tragic finality that accompanies the news of death better than the horror of white-knuckling a fading hope?

For Quentin and his mother, Alice, the answer came thirteen years after a B-17 bomber piloted by Lieutenant Timothy Jones was shot down a few miles west of Dresden, Germany, during a bombing campaign on February 25, 1945. He was twenty-nine years old—a year older than Quentin was now. A pilot in one of the few surviving planes had reported seeing two parachutes open shortly after Jones's plane took a barrage of enemy fire that tore off the starboard wing.

Alice and Tim had taken over her family's thirty-two-room motel called the Sea Turtle on Camino Real in Sarasota a year before Quentin was born. Alice had managed the staff and front desk while Tim ran the business side of things, but she'd taken it all over when he'd decided to enlist. His father had been an aviation enthusiast and had taught a young Tim how to fly a small prop plane all over Florida, so despite Tim being older than most who were enlisting, he felt like his flight skills could be put to good use against the evil brewing in Germany.

In the months and years to follow, Alice clung to the idea that it was her husband who had been attached to one of the two parachutes. Quentin's earliest memories were of watching Alice race to the phone when it rang or to the door when the bell chimed, hoping to find her husband standing there.

A renewed sense of optimism ignited once the war ended. Countless stories in the newspaper and on the television told of MIA soldiers finally returning home. They were being released from POW camps or coming out from their hiding places, where resistance fighters all over Europe had been assisting them. Tim Jones was not one of them.

Alice found strength in the hope that Tim was on his way back to her. She worked long hours with a toddler either on her lap or at her feet and rarely showed any signs of grief. Looking back now, Quentin thought she'd been delusional, not accepting on any level that Tim was likely dead.

The loss didn't hit Quentin until he reached double digits. Though many men hadn't come home, there were still a lot of fathers who were there to throw balls with their sons in the neighborhood. Or build sandcastles. Take a boat out. Go fishing. Alice tried to fill the void, but Quentin grew distant from her, as if she'd been the one to shoot down his father's plane.

In 1958, two air force officers finally gave Alice the knock she'd been waiting for, but it wasn't with the news she'd hoped. Tim's remains had been found by German grain farmers plowing a new field. The officers presented Alice and Quentin with Tim's dog tags and assured them that Tim's body was en route back to the United States for a proper burial.

Hope died that day. Alice sank into a deep depression, leaving Quentin to fend for himself. By the time high school came around, Quentin had established himself as a troublemaker, the kid the other parents talked about. He owned the role well, and with each year, he'd test the limits of his rebelliousness by taking his mother's car without permission, smoking a joint in the school bathroom, skipping classes for days at a time. She told anyone who would listen that being his mother was like trying to put out a fire while it rained gasoline. Unable to control him, Alice enlisted further help from Tim's brother, Hank, who was a homicide detective for the Sarasota Police Department. Hank had tried over the years to connect with Quentin but had yet to succeed.

It had all changed when Quentin started breaking laws with drug use and truancy. Hank enlisted the entire police force to notify him if there was trouble with his nephew. His efforts only proved to upset Quentin, who rebelled harder, running away from home, hanging out with dropouts, testing harder drugs.

During the summer before Quentin's senior year, Hank tried a different tack. He started taking Quentin into the station to let him shadow some of the officers for a day. The teenager showed surprising interest. Though Quentin wanted to ride with his uncle on homicide calls, Hank wouldn't let him. Still, Quentin got a hard look at the underbelly of Sarasota: the petty crime, drug running, bribery, and the organized crime. Then the unexpected happened.

Quentin had found his calling. If his mother would have let him, he would have skipped his last year of high school and gone straight to the academy. Thank goodness she won, though, because it was his senior year when Jones walked into his pottery class and experienced flickers of love and desperate attraction for the first time.

Jones joined the force soon enough and, within four years, reported directly to his uncle in the homicide division. The thing Uncle Hank taught him above all else was the importance of justice, how a good cop must live by it. Bending rules was one thing, especially if it was in the name of getting at the truth. Searching a premises without a warrant, telling a few lies in an interview, or even pocketing some weed during a bust were acceptable breaches, but there was no gray area when it came to justice.

"Quentin," Uncle Hank told him more than once, typically sticking his big hand around the back of Jones's neck, "you just keep chasing justice. That's where you'll find your meaning." Dammit if Hank hadn't been right. Finding the bad guy was the most addictive and fulfilling experience he'd never known, and it never lost its punch.

Folks now called Quentin an old soul. He'd attributed it to having wrung out every last bit of his youth in his first year in homicide, but it was also when he found exactly what he was supposed to be doing with his life.

~

"Quentin?" she asked. "Are you still there?"

"I'm here, Miss Nye," Jones responded, thinking hope wasn't always a bad thing like what he and his mother had felt waiting on his dad. Sometimes good could come from it.

47

"For a minute there, I thought you'd gone away. I'm babbling because I'm glad to see you." She started to the kitchen, speaking to him over her shoulder. "Remember that *awful* bust of Lincoln you made in class?"

"Oh, I do." He smiled, impressed by both her memory and how gracefully she moved. What a challenge it must have been, learning how to interact with the world all over again.

"All in all, though, you were one of the best students I ever had. Have you dabbled since then?"

He shook his head. "I'm afraid my artistic sensibilities were left in your studio."

"What a shame." Sylvie foraged in the refrigerator and put together a tray of cheese and fruit. "We can eat first, can't we? Even policemen eat." Without waiting for an answer, she found plates and forks and bread. She filled tall glasses with ice and placed them on the table, then took a seat. "I'm showing off. I may not keep a tidy house, but I have learned to feed myself with the greatest of ease."

"It's extraordinary," he said, unable to peel his eyes away from her. All of her was extraordinary. "When did this happen? Your eyes?"

Sylvie stabbed a piece of cheese with a serrated bread knife and extended it toward him. "It was one summer about four years ago."

He took the cheese, unsure if he was prepared to hear her story. Also acknowledging that she was handy with a knife. There would be no crossing her off the list of suspects yet. She ran the knife deftly into the heavy bread crust, speared a slice, and set it precisely in the center of his plate. Could she take a man's life just as easily?

"Boating accident," she said. "I got a chunk of money out of it, by the way. But my family came apart. They couldn't stand to watch me banging around, falling on my prat. It hurt them too much. I took my money, came south to Lollipop Island, and bought the beach house. Here, I can fall and spill and let loose the occasional outburst, and"— she lowered her voice—"not make anyone pity me. I can't stand pity,

Quentin. It happened, and that's the way it is, and there's nothing I can do."

"May I ask about the accident?"

"I don't particularly like revisiting it, but . . . I was scalloping with a friend on Crystal River, and another boat blindsided us. They'd been drinking. My head hit the trunk of a fallen tree."

Jones winced at the visual. "I'm—"

"Don't apologize, if that's what you were going to do. Everyone feels a need to apologize. I'd rather you not be one of them."

Jones did not confirm or deny his intentions. Perhaps it was best to discuss the accident later.

She offered a polite pause before continuing.

"I'm happy now," she stated. "I love the island and everyone on it." She shook one of the glasses filled with ice; the cubes clinked together rhythmically. "Ready for tea, Detective Jones?"

He watched with apprehension as she poured from the pitcher. At exactly the right moment, she stopped.

"Amazing!" he blurted out.

She laughed with delight. "It's my parlor trick. I hold the glass just so and balance the pitcher against the rim. When it touches my thumb, bingo! I stop. It took, well . . . at least fifty practice attempts to figure that out, but it makes me look impressive at parties."

He was tickled to recall her lovely sense of humor. Then he wondered if her blindness might be a hoax, an impish joke. Either way, she was throwing him off his game.

She laid aside her glasses and sat, returning his stare, a mild grin quivering on her lips. He lifted his hand soundlessly and fluttered his fingers close to her face.

"You saw that old black-and-white Charlie Chan movie, right?" she asked. "The one where he catches the murderer by proving the man was not really deaf?"

Foiled, he snatched back his hand in surprise. How mortifying.

"The air is still and hot in here, Jones. You waved your hand in front of me. I felt it. You were testing me, weren't you?"

"Yes," he confessed. "I was testing you. You're so sure of yourself. You're impressive."

"I am impressive, I agree, but I'm not a murderer. That's what you were wondering, isn't it? We have to talk about it, don't we?" A deep sigh rose out of her. "Do we really, though?"

"Yes, ma'am."

"Such a southern gentleman. Not many of those left in Florida, you know." Sylvie poured tea into her own glass, stopping at the perfect moment. She took a short sip and then tilted her head to one side. "I guess you know the real reason I keep yapping . . . to keep from talking about it. I'm not particularly fond of murder. I suppose no one is. Other than homicide detectives."

"I don't know that I'm fond of it, but it's the world I live in. And you're right, we do have to talk about it. I'll be far more at ease once I can zero in on what happened."

She raised a finger. "First . . . you must tell me about you. A cop? Is that what you've been doing all this time?"

He nodded before realizing a physical response wouldn't cut it. "Yes, I went straight to the academy in Tampa after high school."

"You must have seen some awful things since then."

Another nod before catching himself. "That's right."

"What else is out there for you, then? You're not married. How about a girlfriend?"

"No."

Jones thought he saw a flicker of pleasure as he answered. It had been ten years since they'd seen each other, but they were falling right back into this flirtatious space like it had been only a day. He had enjoyed watching her unabashedly as she spoke in front of the class. He could study her face, her expressions, without her questioning his interest. Teachers were used to that sort of attention. Now he was doing the same thing.

"I think we should focus on—"

"Oh, c'mon, Quentin. Ten years. Surely you can tell me what has become of you. Why are you single? Twenty-eight isn't exactly old, but still. What is the life of the man that once drew my heart? That's right, I said it. After the accident, I've become less afraid of speaking my mind."

He felt a strong kick from his own heart and had to clear his throat to make sure his words didn't spill out in a jumble. "I don't remember you ever holding back."

She smiled and her eyes almost found his.

"Miss Nye, a man is dead, possibly murdered."

"So you're not sure?"

"The autopsy will be the final word on the matter. For now, I'm treating it as one. Let me focus on ensuring that everyone on this island is safe. Afterward, we can catch up."

"When is the autopsy? Must I hold my breath?"

"Let me worry about that." Hopefully today, he thought. Autopsies were always best done within twenty-four hours of death.

Her head dropped in surrender. "Tell me how to begin."

Jones reached into his bag and pulled out the Norelco recorder and a pad and pen. "Is it okay to record? Just so I don't have to take a bunch of notes. I never can read my handwriting."

She hesitated, as they all did.

"Don't worry. I'm not trying to get you into trouble."

"Okay, then. Guess we have to get down to business, then."

He set the microphone on the table and pointed it in her direction. As he pressed record, it clicked to life. "Begin with this morning. How did you find Dr. Overbrook? What were you doing there?"

She clasped her fingers together and then pulled them apart nervously. "I go for a beach walk most mornings, very early. *And* most nights, for that matter. Sometimes south, sometimes north. As you can imagine, time of day doesn't matter. In case you're wondering, I count my steps and use different landmarks and sounds to guide me."

Tilting back in the chair, he allowed her to approach the events in her own way.

"The tide was up this morning," she continued. "The beach was narrow. I walked with my feet in the water; that's how I know my way. Just enough water to cover my toes."

He cracked open the pad and jotted down notes as she spoke.

"Today, I went south and fell over something. I thought a dead manatee had washed up. They do, sometimes. They smell up the whole island when the sun comes out. I reached down and felt a human hand and started screaming." Sylvie shuddered at the memory but found her pace and continued for a while.

"What can you tell me about Dr. Overbrook, Miss Nye?" Jones asked once she'd run out of words.

She stretched out a hand, imploring. "Can't we drop this 'Miss Nye' thing? Can't I be Sylvie to you now that you're older?"

He glanced at the recorder. "I don't think so. No." He could only imagine the snowball effect of letting her into his private life. No, everyone here—every suspect *always*—had to be less human to him. Formal, if not distant, relationships were required in order to seek out the truth. Especially with this one.

She slumped back crossly.

"Dr. Overbrook?" he reminded her.

"All right, Detective No Fun!" she said. "I only met him last night. Sandy had a party to introduce them to everyone on the island."

"Who is 'everyone'?"

"The Arnetts, Glenna, Sandy, me. Everyone but the Carters. They're a younger couple who stick to themselves. I'm sure Sandy invited them, but we don't count on the Carters for any of our get-togethers. They're so young, you know. Practically teenagers."

"Did the Overbrooks know anyone here before last night?"

"Only Sandy. He and Frank were roommates in medical school in Gainesville. He was moving here at Sandy's request, to help with the practice."

Jones frowned. "He has that many patients to need help? In Paradiso?"

"He hasn't been well."

He let the explanation stand, unremarked upon. "Did you walk the beach last night after the party?"

"Yep, after the party."

"Could you have . . ." He stumbled. He'd almost said *seen.* "Did you hear anything out of the ordinary last night?"

"I'd say something, wouldn't I, Quentin?"

"I'd hope so."

Apparently agitated, she stood and began to clear the table with economical, efficient movements. He watched with admiration as she stored the food and rinsed the dishes. She tucked them neatly into a drying rack and wiped down the tabletop.

"We'd better get back," she said firmly, closing the interview as if she had brought down a gavel to dismiss the jury. "Can you please shut off the recording?"

He did so, wondering about the abrupt change of mood, what she might be hiding. Of course, anyone who'd discovered a dead body would not be themselves later in the day. Deciding he'd get more from her another time, he relented and pushed away from the table.

"Everything turned off?" he asked, glancing around the hodgepodge room. He reached for the pull chain and stopped the rotating blades.

"It doesn't really matter that much," she said. "My electric bill is always low. I only use light bulbs for guests, you know."

"Shall I close the doors and lock up?" he offered.

Sylvie found her cane beside the door and pushed open the screen. "It'll be the first time they've been locked since I moved here. It's safe."

"It wasn't safe for Dr. Overbrook," Jones commented. "I'd keep it locked going forward."

"Yeah, well . . . I guess it's getting harder and harder to avoid evil."

"Sadly, I think you're right."

They made the short return trip back to the Overbrooks' in silence as she sat moodily withdrawn. *I can't call you Sylvie, Detective Jones* reasoned to himself mutely. *I am a police officer, not your art student. What if that hole in Frank's neck was made by one of the tools of your trade back there? What then?*

Sylvie was out of the car almost before he stopped, cane out in front, making her way over the shelly drive, up the porch, and into the living room. During their absence, Glenna had changed from her wet suit and now wore men's khaki shorts and a brown, shapeless striped shirt, hastily buttoned awry. Her rubber flip-flops slapped heavily against the terrazzo floor as she rushed to meet them.

"Thank God you're back!" Her bright black eyes glinted at Jones. "The doctor isn't feeling well. He should go home at once."

Sandy sat slumped on the wicker couch, his elbows on his knees, hands covering his face. Beads of perspiration glistened on his bald head. He raised himself, mouth trembling, and tried to stand. Glenna ran to brace him as he fell back, his face drained of color.

"He needs an ambulance," Jones said. "I'll radio for—"

"No!" Sandy's voice burst out, unexpectedly adamant. "I won't have an ambulance."

"He only needs to go home," Glenna commanded, holding fast to Jones's arm to detain him. "I know what to do for him. He'll be all right."

Sandy struggled to his feet, clinging to the back of her shirt for support. They stood, an immobilized trio, each locked determinedly in position to keep him upright.

"Do what she tells you, Jones," Sylvie said urgently. "She can take care of him."

Together, they wrapped Sandy's arms around them and half carried, half dragged him out the door. The doctor gasped sharply with each step, and the sounds made a bizarre staccato rhythm in counterpoint to the thump-slap of Glenna's flip-flops as they guided him to the car. He shook convulsively, sweat streaming from every pore.

Chapter 5

THE AGILE ONE

Before Detective Jones could even get the patrol car into park outside Sandy's residence, Glenna vaulted out and ascended the ramp with a fierce, lunging momentum. He'd scarcely had time to step out and open the door where Sandy was slumped and shivering when Glenna careened down the ramp, thrusting an ornate wheelchair in front of her.

The chair seat and back were fatly cushioned in a faint-green silk. The back above the headrest was silvered cane, woven in patterns of butterfly wings. On each side, book pockets of the same delicate cane design rested above the soft, soundless rubber wheels. It must have come from a museum, handcrafted for royalty.

Together, Glenna and Jones lifted Sandy into the chair. The doctor's eyes were closed, but as his hands touched the armrests, he struggled to rise. "Not this chair," he protested. Glenna pressed him back and released the brake, shoving the chair forward and up the incline. Jones followed, confused by Sandy's comment.

Dr. Westerling's interior, unlike the sprawling, airy rooms of the Overbrooks' or Sylvie's, gave no indication of beach living. They passed through rooms hidden in semidarkness, the sun blotted out with heavy maroon draperies. The stiffly formal furnishings seemed transported from a Victorian parlor, miles away and years ago. Carved mahogany. Velvet. Needlepoint. Marble.

The bedroom held massive carved furniture and window coverings that shut out light and air. Jones threw off the crocheted coverlet and lifted the doctor's trembling body into a great four-poster canopy bed as Glenna disappeared into the study. She returned bearing a hypodermic needle and quickly plunged it into Westerling's limp arm. With her blunt fingers against his pulse, she put her complete attention on the second hand of her watch.

Gradually, the strenuous breathing slowed. His shuddering subsided and he lay quiet, eyes closed. Jones saw tears squeeze out from under his lids and slide down into the shaggy red-and-gray sideburns. Finally, the doctor slept, his chest rising and falling in easy cadence. Only then did Glenna release his wrist and beckon Jones to follow her out of the room.

"Will it be safe to leave him?" Jones cast an uncertain glance at Sandy's ashen face. "We really ought to call an ambulance or get him to the hospital."

She closed the door firmly. "He'll be all right now."

"What is it?" he asked. "His heart?"

"You surely know, Detective, that I can't discuss a patient's condition."

She had backed him into the parlor as they spoke. He stopped, unyielding. "Circumstances alter cases, Miss Greely. I need to talk with Dr. Westerling."

"Tomorrow."

She was in total command and stood her ground as confidently as a white-coated surgeon. There would be no conference until she pronounced her patient fit. Considering she'd also run a sedative through Catherine's veins, it was almost as if Glenna didn't want anyone to talk.

Sounding as sweet as he could, Quentin asked, "Would you mind if I ran out to the car and grabbed my recorder? Just to take a quick statement."

"Not without my consent," she said sharply.

"That's why I'm asking." He held a long staring battle with her.

"Fine," she finally said. "I'll let the office know the doctor won't be coming in till later."

He hurried to grab his bag before she changed her mind. Back inside, he positioned himself on the damask sofa and rested an elbow on the carved rosewood arm.

Seated in the chair by the phone, Glenna finished her call, then folded her arms and glared at him to demonstrate her defiance. "I really don't have much to offer."

"This is all just protocol." It was almost entertaining to see people squirm as they attempted to outsmart him. Setting the mic on the coffee table, Jones pressed record and sat back with his notebook and pen to face his adversary.

"It was you who discovered the body?" Jones watched her expressionless face for a revealing flicker.

She stared back, contemptuous. "I'm sure Sylvie told you it was her who found him."

Ah, Glenna was above trickery. There was a better way, though. He studied her carefully. What did she like? What did she pride herself on? What would break the antagonism between them?

He attempted a friendly smile, folded the notepad, and returned it to his pocket. "Look, Miss Greely, you seem to be the one that all the others turn to for help." He hoped his face did not betray the outrageous lie. "I was hoping to be able to do the same thing."

The knotted muscles in her arms relaxed perceptibly. Still seeming suspicious, she said, "You're new to your job."

He laughed, thinking he'd heard about everything in the last ten years, but he ran with the ruse. "You've found me out! I am kind of new, and I'm learning, and I need all the help I can get. Preferably from you because I believe you wouldn't betray me to the others."

He had found it—the key. She liked to be thought of as both an authority and a person of discretion.

All of her seemed to relax. "What are your questions?"

Jones started lobbing them her way. Keeping her answers short, she spoke about her morning and how she'd arrived at the scene.

After a while, Jones asked, "Dr. Westerling and Dr. Overbrook were long-standing friends, I understand?"

She bristled up like a blowfish under attack. "You're saying, are you, that Doctor knew him . . . therefore, Doctor killed him?"

"Of course not. I'm simply vying for the facts. Did any of the others know the Overbrooks before last night? Did you?"

It took her a moment to collect herself. "I got the impression . . ." She shook her head, her face impassive again. "Never mind."

"You got what impression, ma'am?"

"Nothing," she muttered. "I was mistaken."

"Please don't conceal information, Miss Greely. It might be dangerous for you. Something you heard or observed might—"

"I said it was nothing!" she snapped.

Jones didn't push too hard yet, making a mental note to follow up instead. People up against a wall clam up, and he wanted everyone comfortable and yappy. It was the same reason he wasn't collecting potential murder weapons.

"Then tell me about last night, if you will. What was the party like? Who was there?"

"Doctor wanted to introduce the Overbrooks, to get them off to a good start." She paused, reflecting. "He even asked the Carters, but they didn't come, of course."

He glanced up, interested. "Why do you say 'of course'?"

"They keep to themselves."

"How long have they been on the island?"

"A few months."

"How old would you say they are?"

"Early twenties—but again, I don't discuss clients."

"I'm not asking for their medical history. What's been the interaction? What do they do?"

She seemed to weigh where these questions fit into her medical oath. "They're the artist-hippie type. They don't leave the island much, don't even have a car. On occasion, I see him riding his bicycle into town for groceries. He does his best not to engage with anyone."

"Seven miles round trip to the village and back with groceries?"

"He's in good shape."

"So they want nothing to do with anyone else on the island. What in the world are they doing here?"

"They're younger, that's all. Most of us are more than twice their age."

Jones turned this information over in his mind. He'd get to the Carters soon enough.

"Will that be all, Detective?" she asked, after another ten minutes of questioning.

"Just a little more, Miss Greely. How long have you lived on the island?"

Her chin lifted and jutted forward. "I was born here. My parents once owned the entire island but sold it off one chunk at a time." She paused, then: "I'm the one who sold the Overbrooks their house."

"Oh. You didn't mention that earlier."

"You didn't ask."

"I asked if you knew him prior to his arrival."

"I didn't. We worked through a real estate attorney. I never once even spoke to him on the phone."

"He bought the place sight unseen?"

She nodded.

Jones eased back his aggression. "That's amazing, your family owned the whole island. Is there anything left?"

"No. Papa had sold off everything else a long time ago. The Overbrooks' house was the last of the holdings, but it was too big for me. Now I'm staying in the doctor's guesthouse."

"That must have been hard, severing your family's ties to the island."

"It was sensible. Dr. Overbrook needed a place for Catherine and him. Having a house on the island was an enticing part of the package. We really wanted to get him down here."

"That puzzles me, ma'am. Paradiso has just over two thousand residents. Why would there be a need for two doctors?"

Glenna's eyes were guarded. "Doctor hasn't been well, as you can see. He wants to make sure his patients are taken care of."

Jones gave his warmest smile. "You think highly of him, don't you?"

"Naturally."

"Would you inherit his place after he passes? Is that part of the plan?"

A defensive glare rose in her irises. "That has nothing to do with it."

"What is your plan, then? You had to have thought of one, considering you've liquidated your holdings on the island. Did you intend on continuing with Dr. Overbrook? Did you find him personable?" Jones decided to push. "Was he not the kind of person you expected?"

Stiffness clung to her jaw. "I had planned to leave."

"Ah." Jones leaned in to the silence until she continued.

"I've never traveled before. I'd like to see the world."

This woman was full of surprises. "Then you were waiting for Dr. Westerling to pass?"

"I'm not waiting. I'm serving him until he retires. Selling the house now sets me up for my eventual departure."

"I see." Jones thought he'd better slow down her pulse. "Traveling the world is something I'd like to do. My father was stationed in both England and Italy."

Glenna glanced at her watch.

"We're almost done," he said. "How long has Dr. Westerling been on the island?"

"Doctor and his wife came about seven years ago. From South Carolina."

"Were you and Mrs. Westerling friends?"

"You're getting a long way from Dr. Overbrook's death, aren't you?"

"I am," he admitted, feigning incompetence. "Excuse me."

She waited a thoughtful moment. "Well, yes. Mary Elizabeth and I were good friends. At night, I came in to play rook with her." She handed him a silver-framed photograph from the marble table.

Detective Jones examined the fragile heart-shaped face and the gentle doe eyes of Mary Elizabeth Westerling. He visualized the scene: Glenna's powerful square hands shuffling and slapping the cards down with authority . . . the delicate woman in the picture picking daintily at the deal, fanning a shallow arc like an old-fashioned painted fan.

"Dr. Westerling was a fortunate man," he remarked. "You're a nurse, but also friend in the bargain."

She raised startled eyebrows. "Though everyone calls me *Nurse*, I'm not actually licensed. Well, I *know* as much about nursing as anyone. My parents were both invalids for years. That's why I stayed on the island. They were old before I was born. By the time I could have left, they were like babies. Babies to be fed, dressed, and tended . . ." Her voice trailed away.

He waited, silent and attentive.

"When they died, I began to assist Dr. Westerling. It seemed too late to leave here by then. Start a career, I mean. My parents were my career. Since nursing was what I knew best, Doctor asked me to work for him and began to teach me what I didn't know."

Her speech held no self-pity. She merely stated the facts, staring at him intently as she did, measuring her words on him. He found his friendly encouragement more valuable than any questioning.

"You must get lonely here on the island," Jones said. "How do you pass the time?"

"I'm a woman of the water. I swim, snorkel, scuba dive, and spearfish."

"I'm a lot like you in that regard. I also grew up near the water. But my hours lately don't leave me much free time. I spend the daylight either searching for clues or looking through the windshield of a patrol car."

Her countenance was now shining, enthusiasm in every muscle. "It doesn't have to be daytime. Night waters are beautiful too. Did you ever watch the phosphorus lights on the waves? Like melted silver rolling onto the beach." She laughed. "It gets on your skin . . . like neon lights on your body. Doctor used to amuse Mary Elizabeth that way."

Glenna glanced about the somber room, recalling her friend, the frail, wasted woman who had transplanted her belongings but could not sink her own roots into the alien soil. The woman who had withered in the brilliant sunlight; who had drawn the drapes and looked out only at night, when the pine thickets might transpose themselves into fragrant magnolia branches if one pretended enough; who had painted the watercolors in the dim, shady rooms.

In Glenna's mind, she could see Sandy rolling and tumbling in the night waters, rising to flap his arms toward the house, spelling out *I love you, Mary Liz* in letter spirals that glowed in dazzling green phosphorus against the black sky.

Mary Liz, in the silver cane wheelchair on the beach, had lifted a weak hand toward him, whispering, "Watch over him, Glenna. Protect him for me." All the while he romped and played and flung himself about in the sparkling, ghostly, shiny green of the waves. To keep Mary Liz from thinking of pain. To remind her of life. To invite her to struggle harder. To fight. To cling to a tenuous thread of life.

He would run to the house, lumbering and loping, drops of glistening water clinging to his ears, and he'd fall at her feet and ask, "Did you laugh, love?"

She would stretch out a transparent white hand and, with the energy she had saved for him, say, "Sandy, you're my one and only true love!"

Glenna craved a love like that but had accepted that such a connection was far out of her reach. She'd missed her chance years ago, and now she was too old for marriage, too old to have a baby.

Catching herself, Glenna stopped abruptly. "Forgive me, Detective, I forget myself when I talk about the Gulf." And about Sandy, she added to herself.

Changing the subject, Detective Jones asked, "Have there ever been intruders on the island?"

"No." She gestured in the direction of the clearing. "If an intruder came from the land, they would have to cross the bridge. From the clearing, they would have to go down one of the paths to reach the beach . . . a path to someone's house. It doesn't happen often, but sometimes people bring their boats up to the beach. I haven't seen any visitors in a long time, though. We look out for one another."

"It's nice to have such attentive neighbors."

She nodded, trying to be patient with his questions, making sure she didn't give him any more than he asked.

"Working as a nurse—albeit unlicensed," he observed, "you must be a good judge of character. What can you tell me about Dr. Overbrook? Your impression of him."

"He was dignified. Serious. Not used to social life, I think. He didn't like it at all when his wife got drunk."

"Drunk?" he queried quickly.

"Not drunk—tipsy," she amended. "She was . . . well, she was getting loud and gay. He had to lead her home." Glenna caught herself digging her finger into her palm. Just a little longer, she told herself as she set her hands on her thighs.

The detective closed his notebook and then pressed stop on the recorder. "I think that's it. Thank you for your help, ma'am. If you need me, call the station."

Glenna attempted to hide her delight as she sprang up. "You sure? If you need anything else, you know where to find me." The pitch of her voice was much higher than she'd intended.

He offered a gentle and handsome smile in return, then retrieved his things and headed for the door.

Chapter 6

An Unharmonious Couple

Out at the clearing, five officers waited around two patrol cars. Four of the five puffed on cigarettes, creating a tobacco halo over their heads.

"Thanks for coming out, fellas," Jones said, well aware of his casual dress compared to their uniforms. There was something too stiff about walking around in those blues. It was Florida, for God's sake. The tropics. But these guys were mostly fresh out of the academy and had to do what they were told, which meant dress properly and race over for an evidence walk when volunteered by a higher-up.

"I don't know exactly what we're looking for yet," Jones said. "The coroner is with the body now. There was a wound on the neck, so maybe something sharp. The tide wasn't moving too quickly last night, so if a crime was committed, I'm guessing it didn't take place too far from where we found his body. Look for disturbances in the sand. Places that have been dug up. You know the drill. Mark it off and find me, all right?"

Being the youngest detective in Collier County, Jones wasn't much older than these guys, but he could see the respect they had for him in their eyes as they all nodded and offered *yes, sirs*.

Once the men had disappeared into the brush, Jones went to find the Arnetts. Their driveway was wide and smoothly paved. Jones inched along, however, as it twisted and spiraled among the dense Australian pines and rampant flame vine. It seemed the islanders had taken great precautions to hide themselves from each other.

The house beyond the trees was a low Spanish stucco, sparkling white with mica chips, hugging the wild grass and sand. A convertible Pontiac GTO was parked on the left side where the driveway widened. The windows and doors of the house were concealed behind gracefully arched courtyards and broad walkways shaded with a red-tiled roof. A wheelchair ramp descended from the main entrance.

Canvas bag over his shoulder, Jones left the car and took a quick peek into the Pontiac and into the trash can. Following the sound of music, he went around back and climbed a set of steps to an open terrace. A well-maintained pool spanned the length of the house. Umbrella tables, deck chairs, hammocks, and chaises were scattered across the expanse of a bright Spanish-tile floor. Another wheelchair ramp sloped down to the sand.

"Anyone home?" he called out over "Suspicious Minds" by Elvis drifting from a radio player near the house.

A slim, bronzed woman glistening with suntan oil raised a languid hand to lift her sunglasses to her forehead, then surveyed him quizzically. Stretched out on a lounge chair, she wore a black bikini top and a purple sarong.

"Well, well! Look what the day hath wrought!" She swung her slender brown legs over and assumed a seated position, then lifted the straps of her bikini top into place on her shoulders. "Can I help you?"

"I'm Detective Jones, ma'am." He proffered his badge and ID, noticing freshly painted toenails the color of red roses.

She accepted the wallet and read each line with mock gravity. "Howdy, Detective." Standing, she lifted the cover of a large metal cooler, found an ice pick, and chipped expertly at the frozen block inside.

She dropped the hard chunks into two glasses and grinned. "How about something to cool you off?"

"No, thank you." He would have loved something, but he had to keep his head clear. "You're Mrs. Arnett?"

"You win the prize, Mr. Detective, sir." Her smile was dazzling, her teeth white against her tanned, perfectly oval face. She poured herself a drink that looked like boozed-up lemonade.

"Is Mr. Arnett at home?"

Over her shoulder, she called, "David! We have company."

Jones looked in that direction and noticed a couple of video cameras perched above the doors. This couple took their privacy seriously.

He and Miriam Arnett talked about the weather till a man in a wheelchair motored onto the terrace. David Arnett eyed her sparsely clad figure, his face venomous. His powerful body, trapped in the confines of the chair, was as tense as a caged animal's. "Go get dressed, for God's sake." He shook his head at Jones. "I swear, she'll be the death of me."

Miriam tilted the glass in a clinking salute. "Take him to the pokey, Officer. Whatever the charge, he's your man. I'll testify."

David fixed on her a stare so full of savagery that Jones studied them with interest. The woman chuckled a private joke to herself as she turned her back to them. She refilled her glass, humming lazily under her breath.

After introductions, Jones asked, "You and Mrs. Arnett were at Dr. Westerling's last night?"

"What the hell does a dinner party have to do with the sheriff's department?" David demanded irritably.

His wife, wriggling into a voluminous terry robe, paused. "It wasn't an orgy, Officer. Just a plain old lobster boil. Did you steal the silver, David?"

Jones frowned, watching carefully for tells. "One of the guests was killed last night."

"Killed?" they echoed in unison. "Who?"

Jones thought he recognized a flicker of fear in the woman's face, but it passed so quickly he wasn't sure. "Dr. Overbrook was murdered."

"Murdered?" David burst out. "Who'd want to kill a cautious stick like him? A rock has more personality."

Miriam's hand paused in midair. "Did you set up this joke?"

"It's no joke, Mrs. Arnett," Jones said. "In fact, I'd like to take your statements with my nifty recorder here." He pulled it out of his bag. "Do you mind?"

"I don't see why not," David said.

"That okay with you, Mrs. Arnett?"

"Sounds like good fun to me."

Sliding the recorder back into the bag, he pulled out the small microphone, then hit record. "Did either of you know Dr. Overbrook previously?"

"We only met him last night." David's answer was directed at Miriam, imprinting the words like visual instructions.

Jones watched the sidelong glance cast toward the woman. "Did it seem to you that anyone else at the party might have known him before?"

They both reflected carefully. "No."

"Can you tell me how he acted last night? Did he seem troubled about anything?"

"I'll tell you how he acted," Miriam volunteered. "Like a stick-in-the-mud . . . or sand, I should say. He mostly stood around disapproving of us."

"For once, I have to agree with my wife," said David. "Believe me when I say that is a landmark statement. He hung around on the edge of things, looking disagreeable. He hardly spoke a word to anyone."

"Yes, he did," Miriam said. "He talked to Glenna while she was tending to the lobster pots."

"That must have been one hell of a conversation," David said with a heavy dose of sarcasm. "Two bores boring each other. Strikes me as a good arrangement for everybody's sake."

"Could you hear their conversation?" Jones asked.

"Who wants to eavesdrop on two plow horses like that?" he scoffed. "We couldn't have heard it, anyway. The rest of us were a pretty noisy crew."

"You have a strong opinion of the man, considering you didn't know him."

"I know his type—another outsider thinking Florida is the answer to everything."

Jones tried another direction. "You must have been surprised that Dr. Westerling was bringing someone else in. Osprey Isle is small for two doctors, no?"

Miriam searched the depths of her empty glass and wandered back to the cooler. She picked up the ice pick and began to chip slowly. Her back was turned to them, her shoulders tense with waiting. The air was charged with unspoken trouble.

"You are implying," David countered finally, "that Dr. Westerling did not need a partner . . . that he enticed his friend here for the purpose of murdering him. Is that what you're saying?"

"That could be one angle to the murder, Mr. Arnett."

"No way, Detective!" Miriam yelled as she slammed the cooler shut.

Jones shrugged. "He seems to be the only one who knew the victim."

David rolled restlessly to and fro in his chair, tapping nervously on the armrests. "I assure you, Sandy's motives are pure. He's a widower with a disease that's slowly eating away at him, but he's fully devoted to making sure the people of Paradiso have good medical care."

"What does he have?"

"Lymphoma. A slow-growing type, but deadly. He's been refusing treatment, but we're hoping he'll come around. I know Glenna is pressing him. It's just that the side effects can be as deadly as what he has now."

"I see." Jones waited for more, but David had made his speech. "What did he have to say about this new doctor coming to town?"

"Your turn, wife dear." David folded his arms and stared into the distance.

Miriam picked up the recital. "He said he had an old school chum who wanted to come to Florida. He said . . ." She faltered. "He said the man was a fine doctor. That was about it."

Jones took out his notepad and consulted the pages briefly. "Were either of you on the beach last night after the party?"

David turned his malevolent grin on his wife. "If Miriam had gone down to the beach, you might have had two corpses instead one. She would have drowned. She was sloppily drunk, sir."

"How about you, Mr. Arnett?"

"Perhaps you didn't notice," he snapped, "but I don't travel on foot. This vehicle, unfortunately, sinks in the sand. If I had been on the beach, I would still be sitting there waiting to be rescued."

Jones made note of the potential lie, given the ramp that led down to the sand. Officer Challa hadn't mentioned finding any tracks from a wheelchair along the beach. Jones would have to follow up with him back at the station.

"Forgive me for the invasive question," Jones said, "but how often do you leave the island, Mr. Arnett? Are you able to ride in the Pontiac?"

He shook his head. "Fortunately, I don't have many places I need to be, other than medical appointments, for which I hire a private ambulance service. I'm lucky enough to have Miriam run all the errands. She even picked me up a sausage-egg-and-cheese this morning."

Jones made a note. "What a lucky guy. Mrs. Arnett, what time did you go out this morning?"

She shrugged matter-of-factly. "Oh, eight or so. After coffee. I needed something to soak up all the alcohol from last night. If you haven't eaten at the general store in town, they have great biscuits."

"Great sandwiches too," David added.

"I'll make sure to give one a try." Jones returned to the matter at hand. "There was nothing then . . . *nothing* that you noticed, either during the party or afterwards? A quarrel? A disagreement of any kind?"

David's lip curled in a cynical smile. "Not unless you count any conversation that takes place between Mrs. Arnett and me. We maintain a running disagreement and exercise it faithfully." His restless hands plucked at the white duck trousers covering his motionless legs. "Ask anyone on the island. Our unharmonious relationship is the chief diversion here."

"What he's saying is, you're looking in the wrong place, Detective. If David or I committed murder, it would most certainly be one of us you found . . . not a man we had just met."

She was, Jones observed, more sober than she pretended to be. She moved into the shadow of the colonnade as she asked, "How was he killed?"

"He was found on the beach, ma'am. Puncture wound in the front of his neck."

Her back was turned, voice muffled, as she asked, "What made the puncture?"

"We haven't found the weapon," Jones said, moving his gaze to the cooler, where the ice pick was stored. "Something small and sharp. We'll know more soon."

They both retreated in silence as Jones turned off the recording and stuffed the microphone back into his bag. "Let's talk again soon. In the meantime, please don't go far without telling me. If you remember anything helpful, give the police station a call."

They ignored him as he made his way down the steps and around the house. Once he was out of sight, he lingered for a moment, listening intently.

Though Jones couldn't make out the words, he heard David say something in an angry tone. Miriam responded, "You will never ease up, will you?"

Jones waited for more but heard only the buzz of the wheelchair as David went back inside.

⌐

Miriam pulled clear plastic wrap across the salad, covered the tray of sliced ham and turkey, and stacked the cake and fruit into the hamper. David appeared beside her, whirring to an abrupt stop, inches from her feet, forcing her to jump aside.

"Going on a picnic?"

She was dressed now, wearing a plain white shift and sandals, her dark hair tied back with a scarf. There was not a trace of the woman who'd sat drinking on the terrace a short while before.

"I'm going to the Overbrooks'."

"Bearing gifts?" he said with a snort. He flipped the napkin to inspect the contents of the basket. "Taking arsenic for the widow, maybe?"

She closed her eyes tightly and leaned forward against the sink until she controlled her trembling hands. This was not the time to heighten their own war. "This is what you do for neighbors. Think how alone Catherine must feel." She bent down toward him, brushed the top of his head with a kiss, and laid her cheek against his hair. "Come with me."

"And spoil your plans for her?" he sneered, disengaging himself. "You may be right. I *should come along* . . . to protect her." Setting the chair in motion, he sailed out of the kitchen.

Biting her tongue, Miriam listened to the wheels chatter against the uneven tiles to the far end of the terrace. Why had he lied about the wheelchair? Though it wasn't as speedy, he had no problems moving on the wet sand after a high tide. He only had to wash it down afterward before rust set in.

Miriam heard the cooler lid slam against a bench and the savage *chip . . . chip . . . chip* of ice. His anger was a sharp point itself, stabbing her every time, reminding her what she'd done to him. She blinked back tears. Strange, she thought, that I can still cry . . . or even feel. Shouldn't a well finally run dry? Will the day come when all this will seem like nothing? When will I not cry because I will not care?

No. Never. If he suffers, I suffer. That is how guilt works.

~

Those first days and nights after the crash, it seemed that nothing, ever again, could be so painful. Miriam climbing out of the driver's seat unharmed to watch the men with crowbars and torches cut David's mangled body free from the wreckage. Sitting day and night beside him in the small, inadequate hospital a thousand miles from home where he lay, more dead than alive, swathed in casts and pulleys. What pain could surpass that time?

She knew the answer, she reminded herself. Agony of the spirit could surpass that time. She could see David's pale face when he had drifted back to awareness, when he had discovered that his legs no longer moved, that he would not stand again, that a rolling chair would henceforth be his prison, his cradle. Once it had registered, he had screamed . . . and cried . . . and screamed again, and then they had made him sleep.

After the days of sedation, there was nothing but silence. Miriam sat in the hospital room while they ministered to his body, shaving, feeding, bathing, and rehabilitating him. He watched her every move, his eyes secretive and malignant, never speaking. Any time she stirred, however slightly, his eyes fastened on her and stared steadily till she had to drop her gaze or turn away.

Eventually, the physician signed a discharge sheet, saying, with forced cheerfulness, "You can take him home today, Mrs. Arnett. I have written instructions for you outlining home care. He'll need continued physical therapy several times a week." David gave no indication that he was listening. "If you follow the program faithfully, with your help and support, he will find that there are many things he can learn to do for himself."

The doctor left. Miriam busied herself with packing her husband's things. She laid orderly rows across the hospital bed: his shaving gear, slippers, watch, ring. He had kept such lizard-like stillness that his voice, when he finally spoke, jolted her, and the objects in her hands clattered to the tiled hospital floor.

"Are you wishing you had married someone else?" he asked.

She ran to him and tried to embrace him. "Oh, David." She pressed her cheek against his. "Thank God! I was afraid—"

"You left the brain intact," he said. "I bet you were hoping I'd gone dumb. Then I couldn't report you."

"Don't talk like that, David," she said, petting his face. "Have hope. We're going to be all right."

He pushed her away. "Oh, are we? I can read your mind, you know. I hear you wondering how long you will have to stay tied to me while other men line up in waiting."

She listened in shock, inarticulate misery, as he indulged his story, growing more spiteful as the days dragged by. Her temptress image grew in his fertile imagination. She was a seductress, larger than life. Every man, he thought, was her prey. That youthful husband, so dim in her memory, was everything he could no longer be. She wept; she argued, reasoned; and finally she ceased to answer, ceased to struggle. She made a discovery in the years that followed. She found that drinking softened the virulent sounds, blurred the sharp edges, and made the day start later and end sooner.

His jealousy and obsession extended to all men. Until he'd met Sandy Westerling. Sandy had been the lifeline. Fat, bald, funny little Sandy, who could not fish and did not know a baseball bat from a hockey stick. His consuming passion for chess, however, pulled David back into the land of the living.

Sandy played ruthless, bloody games and lost his temper when he did not win. He cursed David for laughing at him. He stayed away, pouting, then came back with a gruff, unapologetic "I want a game to get even." He gave David a way to excel, to outwit, to triumph. The gift was so subtly delivered that David did not know.

Even Sandy's attentions to Miriam did not disturb David. The man was so obviously in love with his Mary Elizabeth, so devastated by his grief during her long, torturous illness, that he never entered David's fantasies about her. He never grew into a rival.

Miriam had happily looked forward to meeting Sandy's new associate, Dr. Overbrook. Another couple on the island would break the monotony. Perhaps David could make a new friend. Perhaps he would be the same kind of gentleman as Sandy. But Frank hadn't fit the bill, and David hadn't taken to him well at all.

Though he'd certainly behaved awkwardly around Catherine, David didn't seem to mind so much. Only Miriam could know that his odd behavior around the newcomer was his childish way of attempting to connect. Miriam found it interesting how Catherine blossomed from restrained to nearly gregarious as the night went on and the Champagne flowed. Perhaps that was what had made her husband fall in love with her in the first place, and Frank was indeed in love with her. Miriam could see that twinkle of care in his otherwise vacant eyes.

After turning the tap full force, Miriam held her wrists under the cold rushing water. She splashed her cheeks and pressed a towel to her eyes. Then she ran a dishcloth across the spattered counter, picked up the hamper, and called out, "*David*, I've left a sandwich for you."

As she turned to leave, she heard his chair coming from behind. He whirred around her, blocking her way to the door. He sat hunched, menacing.

"I know there's something you're not telling me," David said. "Something that started long before last night. I know that you sneak away, claiming to go on long walks or to take Sylvie to town. Where is it you go, little wifey? I have my eyes on you."

"Will you *stop* it?" Miriam said, crushed by the prison of her own design. "I've done nothing but be loyal to you."

"Oh, I don't know about that."

The color drained from her face. She gave a sharp cry and plunged around him, dashing out the door with the basket bumping heavily against her. Life would have been so different had he not woken up after the crash.

Chapter 7

THE DRIFTERS

Detective Jones sat parked in the circular clearing by the wooden sign. The other officers were still out there combing for clues. Riffling through the pages of his notepad, he was reminded of Lieutenant Snyder's words warning him that law enforcement is "facts and figures, Jones; intuition does not solve murders."

Absently, he tapped his teeth with the pencil. Four o'clock. The winter sun was nearly done with its work for the day, sending only spidery slivers of light through the pines. He studied the names on the sign from south to north: Overbrook . . . Nye . . . Westerling/ Greely . . . Arnett . . . Carter.

Levi and Amber Carter. None of the other island residents seemed to know them well. Why the need for seclusion? No visitors. No automobile.

Jones understood the need for privacy, the refreshment of a lonely day with only the sound of surf and gulls. Sometimes on his days off, he sought such isolation. He withdrew from noise, traffic, voices. It would be nice to be a Scotsman, he thought wryly, wandering the moors. Herding sheep . . . falling asleep under a tree, eating off the land, bumping into someone every few weeks. Maybe the Carters were simply of a like mind. It was time to go find out.

Climbing out of the car with his gun and canvas bag, he moved into the tunnel of trees, pushing aside the arms of moss that clutched his sleeves. The path, once a driveway, was overgrown with seedling pines and water oak, leaving room for only the width of his body as he pressed through. Long snakelike cactus tongues slithered about the trees, twining and coiling underfoot.

Halfway in, a stack of fallen trees attempted to block any passage. Wooden signs nailed to the trunks read: **PRIVATE PROPERTY! KEEP OUT! NO VISITORS! THIS MEANS YOU!**

Jones pushed aside low branches and maneuvered around the obstruction. As with other paths on the island, this one ended in a burst of late-afternoon sunlight. The glittering Gulf water momentarily blinded him after the dim approach. He stopped at the edge of the trees, allowing his eyes to adjust. The house was raised high on stilts, bleached by sun and salt to a soft, porous gray. The windows all stood open, white blinds flapping inside. Under the house, a red bike lay on its side.

In the shade of a set of steps in the back, a woman—presumably Amber—sat cross-legged, bent intently over some handwork. A round belly pushed out from her otherwise skinny frame. Nurse Glenna and Dr. Westerling had clearly chosen not to disclose her pregnancy.

The mother-to-be couldn't have been much older than twenty, a face sharpened with intent eyes. Her hair, a loose braid tied with twine, was the same color as her tanned skin and the garment she wore. She could have easily melted into the earth.

Around her, scraps of cloth, weighted down by shells, were spread out on the sand to dry. Unaware of Jones's presence, Amber drew out a miniature awl from a metal toolbox and began poking holes in each shell, stopping frequently to wipe the shining awl point on her skirt and to blow away any grit. It seemed every woman on the island was handy with sharp objects. Task completed, Amber ran a macramé cord through each hole, keeping the shells in place with a knot. At last, she tied off the ends, held the necklace up for inspection, and then set it aside.

Before she moved on to the next piece of jewelry, she lifted her arms high above her head and stretched, showing swollen nipples rising from her flat chest.

There was something familiar about her.

Startling Jones, she abruptly leaned forward and clutched frantically at the folds of her dress. "Levi!"

In an instant, a slightly older man vaulted down from the deck overhead and landed beside her with the lightness of a cat. His body was cut lean and muscular, his sandy brown hair scraggly like he'd leaped off a bus leaving the Woodstock festival. He was still handsome but in a weathered way. Where hers was gentle, his face said that he'd seen a lot of the world and a lot of the bad in it.

He tried lifting her to her feet. She shook her head from side to side, moaning, refusing to change position, as she let out short, gasping yelps. He tried to comfort her, but she curled into a tight ball—her arms wrapped around her bent knees—and rolled sideways away from him.

Jones ran out from under the house. As his shadow fell across the sand, they froze. The crying stopped as precipitously as it had begun.

"Do you need a doctor? I have a car in the clearing."

"Who the—"

"Pardon me. I'm Detective Jones from the Collier County Sheriff's Office. I came to ask some questions and heard her screaming."

Levi put his focus back on Amber. "Are you okay, honey?"

She seemed to be coming back to life as she unfolded her body and began to press up. Levi tried to help, but her knees gave way, and she collapsed onto the sand, clawing the air and knocking over her toolbox as she went down.

"Labor pains?" Jones asked quickly as he drew closer, wondering if he should get her to the hospital. There were as many emergencies on the island as potential murder weapons. At this rate, they should have kept an ambulance on standby.

Amber glanced at him in naked terror, then hid her face and rocked from side to side. Levi gently picked her up and started for the house.

His bare feet grasped the plank steps as he steadied himself at every rise until he had carried her inside.

Detective Jones moved into the shade to wait. From where he stood, he heard frenzied whisperings. The young woman sobbed. Levi paced from one side of the little room to the other as he talked. His words, indistinguishable, hummed with fear.

With their distractions, it would be hard to read their faces when he revealed news of the murder. He began playing through possible scenarios. It felt ridiculous to think of Amber as Frank's attacker, considering her condition. That Levi, though. Physically, he had the ability to best anyone else on the island.

The Carters looked like those countless drifters wandering aimlessly along the highways: restless, ragged, glazed eyes on masked faces. He saw them every day, packs strapped to their backs, lifting their arms in hopeless gestures as they flagged the passing cars, trying to escape from God knows what.

Jones spun a story in his mind. The Carters had approached Overbrook on the beach, demanded drugs . . . and then threatened him? No good. They wouldn't know the doctor had arrived on the island. Yes! They did know. Sandy had left an invitation in their mailbox. Remember to ask Westerling if he mentioned that the newcomer was a physician.

His eyes fell on the contents of the overturned toolbox. He crouched and began to gather the instruments. Though he saw no blood, the collection of awls gave him a surge of relief. Sylvie was not the only one working with such tools. Though women were never likely murderers, he wasn't ready to count anyone out—including Amber.

He looked up to find Levi staring down at him from the porch. "Is she all right?"

"Yeah."

Jones stood. "Will you come down, or shall I come up?"

The man hesitated, then reluctantly descended.

"Is this your property?" Jones asked, coming face-to-face. Levi had a couple of inches on him.

"No."

"Rented?"

"Rent-free."

"How'd you arrange that?"

Levi stood tense and still. Only his eyes moved to squint against the late-afternoon sun. "I take care of the place."

"Do the owners know you take care of it?"

"He knows. We have an arrangement."

"Who is 'he'?"

"A guy named Barry Gatt. He lives up in Sarasota."

"He sure has put a lot of trust in you."

Levi pulled his long hair behind his ears. "He just wants to keep some of the Paradiso teenagers from sneaking around and having their way with the place."

"Hence the signs out front, I suppose."

"That's right." The young man crossed his arms. "May I ask why you're here?"

"I'm getting there. Do you have any identification?"

Levi lifted his shoulders in a gesture of denial. "It's out there in the Gulf. Lost it while working on a fishing boat."

"That's inconvenient. How long ago?"

"Last week," he said. "How about you? How do I know you're a cop?"

Jones flashed his badge. "I'm a detective."

"Detecting what?"

"Could I see your wife's identification?"

Levi smiled lazily. "What do you think she might have? She doesn't drive, she has no driver's license, and she's never had a job." It was his longest speech. Probably realizing this, he swiftly withdrew.

"I understand you were invited to a party last night. Dr. Westerling left a note in your mailbox."

Levi watched the seagulls sail and swoop overhead. "He always does that."

"You don't have any interest in participating?"

He blew out a gust of air. "They're a bunch of squares, man. Amber and I do our own thing."

"Weren't you curious about meeting your new neighbors?"

He shrugged. "I don't know how it's much of my business."

"Did Sandy mention that one of the newcomers was a doctor?"

"I'd heard."

What in the world was this kid hiding? Jones kept his patience. "Did you get a chance to meet them yesterday?"

"Caught a glimpse of them in the clearing. We didn't talk."

Jones drew in a long breath, searching the eyes of the young man for the truth, letting the seconds stretch out and cleanse the air. Then he dropped the hammer. "He was murdered on the beach last night."

Levi's head jerked. "Murdered? Someone was murdered here on the island?" His astonishment seemed genuine. He stole a furtive glance toward the window. The young woman was crouched there, listening, but as Jones followed his gaze, she disappeared.

"How was he murdered?"

"You tell me."

"No, no, no. I had nothing to do with anything around here. We mind our own business. Why the hell would I go out and murder someone, especially someone I don't know?"

Jones regarded the inscrutable face. "If you don't mind, I'm going to record the rest of our conversation." He extracted the microphone from the bag. "I have a disorganized mind, so I'm just trying to keep it all straight. That okay?"

Levi shook his head. "I'm sure you'll think I'm guilty if I say no."

"I try not to make assumptions, Mr. Carter." As Levi relented, Jones reached his hand in the bag and clicked record, then held the microphone low so as not to intimidate the kid.

"What are you doing here on Osprey Isle?"

"Just livin', man . . . like I said. Minding our own biz." He matched Jones's calm. "Look, Detective, we came here to be left alone. To leave everyone else alone. Don't drag us into something we know nothing about." His words came out as practiced.

"That's a lot of privacy to expect," Jones said. "May I ask what you do for a living? Or do you have an alternate source of income?"

Levi jammed his big brown hands into his jean pockets and shifted restlessly in the sand, his bare feet scraping semicircles and rubbing them out. He eventually sighed. "Okay, I'll give it to you straight: we're on the lam like you think. Amber's parents hate my guts. They want their little girl back home."

"This is the plan? Raise your baby out here, keep hiding from her family?"

"For now."

"How'd you come upon this perfect gig, watching a beach house with a view that folks would kill for?"

"Amber and I were hitching down Tamiami Trail, and we turned off the highway to bed down out of sight with our bedrolls. The next morning, we wandered into Paradiso General Store, and *bingo*. There's a small poster: HELP WANTED—LOOKING FOR A CARETAKER."

"Lucky you," Jones remarked. "So grocery money comes from a great little smuggling operation, right? Or are you living off fish and swamp cabbage?"

Levi touched the cloth bundles with his big toe. "We make junk for tourists to buy. Tourists love that stuff, you know. I take it to the general store. You can check it out . . . All honest and legal."

"You're going to pay for the baby by selling trinkets?"

"I'm working on finding something."

"All honest and legal, I'm sure."

Levi squinted angrily. "Naturally. I'm hoping Charlie at the general store will hire me before too long. I've been asking."

Signs of them planning on staying, Jones noted. "Levi Carter. Is that your real name?"

"Are you kidding?" He smirked. "Is anyone really named Levi Carter?"

"Okay. Your name?"

"Stanislaus Ostrowski."

"I feel like you're making this more difficult than it needs to be."

He pinched his beard. "I just don't appreciate people coming to bother me when I've done nothing wrong."

"I have to say . . . you seem beyond disinterested in the fact that a man was killed right down the beach. It doesn't worry you that there's a murderer somewhere around here?"

"Of course it does."

"Then let's quit this game you're playing, and shoot me straight. Where'd you come from?"

Levi hesitated, clearly still trying to decide how to play this conversation. "Detroit."

"Service record?"

He laughed. "I don't fight other people's wars."

"Work record?"

"Dishwasher. Janitor. Busboy. Odd jobs. I never stay anywhere long. Just get some green in my pocket and move on."

"Name some places," Jones said.

"Well . . ." He wrinkled his forehead. "Bud's Café somewhere in Mississippi. The Central Café in El Paso. I was a cherry picker in Michigan. Dug potatoes in Wisconsin. Picked cotton in Tennessee."

"In other words, you're telling me you don't leave tracks. That's not good enough, whatever your name is."

"It really is Levi Carter." He waved toward the beach house. "Look, we had nothing to do with a murder. We aren't hurting anyone. Just leave us out of it."

Jones shook his head and cracked a grin at the absurdity of the request. "A man has been murdered not far from this door. Until we catch the murderer, your life will be an open book, like everyone else on the island. You won't have a secret left."

"Levi," the young woman called plaintively.

"I need to go in," Carter said, kneeling down to collect her tools and jewelry. "It's getting dark."

"I'd like to talk to your wife."

Levi stood back up with his hands full. "Unless you have a warrant, it's time we part ways. Like I said, we haven't done a thing. And I'm not saying another word with that device running."

"Is that how you want to play this? You're going to make me go bother a judge right now? I can come back later with a team and knock the door down."

Levi's defensiveness softened. "Can't you see she's not feeling well? She's due any day. How about we do this tomorrow?"

Jones sighed. Everyone on the darn island kept trying to push off questions. He needed to be easy with this one, though, if he hoped to get everything he needed to know. "I'll be back tomorrow to take official statements. You and your wife think hard about last night. What you saw. What you heard."

Carter nodded a dismissal and ascended the steps.

"Don't leave town, Carter," Jones called out, ending the recording.

Levi nodded, then vanished through the door.

Jones left the way he came, going under the house, poking around some, then exiting along the overgrown drive. He glanced back to find Levi watching from the window.

The kid was hiding something.

As he continued on, Jones decided it was time to check in. Time to sort his thoughts. To set inquiries in motion about Dr. Frank Overbrook, formerly of Burbank, Illinois, and Catherine Overbrook of Chicago. Time to turn the countless pages of a book and look for a face like that of Levi Carter. Time to pull criminal records and connect with the medical examiner.

~

"We just zipped him back up," Rush Parker, the medical examiner, said in a nasally voice as he led Jones down a hall to his office. "We can always walk back to the cooler if you need to see anything else. You're right: He got picked and pecked apart, didn't he?"

"Yeah, I'm hoping you were able to get a decent read."

"I know what killed him, if that's what you mean."

Rush was five foot nothing and wore glasses as thick as a frozen lake up in Michigan. Wild gray hairs sprouted from his ears and the top of his bald head. His office was a short drive from the police station, right next to a burger joint called Jesse's. The ceilings were low, and the floors were made of linoleum. The place smelled like formaldehyde.

Rush reached for a pot of coffee on top of a file cabinet and poured a fresh cup. "You care for one?"

"Nah, I'm okay."

After sitting down at his desk, Rush dumped several packets of sugar into his mug. Jones watched with wide-eyed surprise as one, two, three, four, *five* went in before the man finally stirred it all and took a sip.

"You want some coffee with that sugar?" Jones asked.

"You sound like my wife," he said before taking another sip. "You definitely got yourself a homicide. Death by exsanguination. Stab wound to the neck. Hard to tell with the damage. He was gushing blood, basically chumming the water and turning himself into fish bait. As you know, the skin around the neck is extremely elastic, so it pulled apart. I pinched the flesh back together. The incision is maybe a quarter-inch wide, three or four inches deep. As for the weapon, your guess is as good as mine. But something sharp."

"I was hoping for more." Jones sat back and crossed one leg over the other, letting his mind absorb the information. "I've already seen some pottery knives, an ice pick, a few awls."

"It could be any of those things. The wound really isn't saying much. Your killer was either someone extremely familiar with human anatomy or someone with a whole lot of luck, because they hit the carotid like a dart on a bull's-eye. You find him, I'd get him to buy you a lottery ticket before you lock him up. Dr. Overbrook bled out pretty quickly, though he was still alive in the water."

"How do you know?"

Rush gulped his coffee and smacked his lips with delight. "The froth in his mouth, the water in the sinus cavity and trachea. His heart was still pumping when he went under. But barely. It's the bleed-out that killed him."

"You're saying the killer stabbed him and then dragged him out into the water while he was still kicking?"

"I doubt he was kicking. Just some agonal breathing and the last beats of his heart. He sank within an hour. Tide changed and started rolling him back toward shore, which explains all the cuts and bruises. I'd say he died between midnight and three, give or take."

Jones smacked his knee. "Dammit, I was hoping you could give me more on the weapon."

"I'm good but I'm not *that* good, Jones. The range of possibilities is wide right now. I wouldn't even want to venture a guess."

"What if I bring them in?"

"If you bring them in, I can see if something fits, but I'm not promising anything."

Jones rubbed his face and spoke into his hands. "I'll lose any camaraderie I have with them. If it comes to that, I'll let you know." He crossed his arms. "How about the angle of the attack?"

"Hard to say definitively with the damage to the body, but it looks like a downward angle—struck from above."

Without much to go on, it was going to be a long few days. He was out of there fifteen minutes later and went to check in with his supervisor, who'd made him the primary for the case. Next, Jones tracked down Officer Challa for some follow-up and then put in requests for information on everybody on the island. They were so damn far down in South Florida that it felt like they were on another planet when it came to intel. After addressing a few pressing concerns with other cases, he hit play on his recorder and went to work poring through mug shots, looking for Levi's face.

It was going to be a long night.

Chapter 8

When Day Falls to Night

Catherine sat with Miriam and Sylvie in the living room, watching the last slender log crackle and fall into the glowing embers below, sending out sparks in dancing patterns across the wide tile hearth. The doors to the patio were open wide, with only screens left to protect them from the mosquitoes. The wood hissed, sighed, and settled with a final burst of yellow flame.

"I always wanted a fireplace," Catherine murmured. "I used to watch the snow from my window in Chicago . . . or the sleet . . . and imagine what it would be like. The sound, the feel, the sight." She extended her hands to the dying fire.

Sylvie stirred on the couch. "I bet you never dreamed you would have one in sunny Florida, with the doors flung open at the same time. February is like that here."

The three women fell silent again. They'd sat through the interminable afternoon, mostly avoiding the one subject that had brought them together. All through the meal Miriam had prepared, they stumbled their way into flurries of conversation, skirting what was uppermost in their minds: Frank . . . lying cold and still, somewhere miles away.

Now the sun had fallen, painting the windows black. Miriam stretched her long, beautiful legs and pushed herself up from the chair. "Think you can sleep, Cath?"

"Sleep?" Catherine complained. "When things go wrong, why must we sleep? So we can't think?"

"Exactly," said Sylvie. "Save it for tomorrow."

"I do have a lot to think about, you know," Catherine mused. "I don't even know if Frank has a family. He told me that he was married before. That's all I know." She spread her hands in a gesture of apology, wondering if they could understand the impulsive marriage. She thought not. Not these two beautiful people with families and friends and neighbors, part of the tight community of the island.

"The water's probably boiling." Miriam moved to the kitchen door, interrupting the awkward moment. "Let's have a cup of tea and then I'm calling it a night. We should all get some rest. Unless you want me to stay with you and Sylvie?"

"You must go home," Catherine said. "Both of you." She leaned forward earnestly. "I'm not afraid."

"Who says I'm staying to protect you!" said Sylvie. "I'm staying for company. Anyway, a fine lot of protection I'd be! I'm a good fighter," she added wryly, "but I can't see exactly where the nose is to punch."

In the kitchen, Miriam listened to the hum of voices from the living room as she prepared tea for the three of them. Her mind was heavy with thought.

"Need help?" The voice was inches from her shoulder.

Miriam jumped back with a sharp intake of breath. Sylvie stood at her elbow, staring at the far wall. Her eyes without glasses were curiously bright and blue.

"You just took ten years off my life, Sylvie!"

"Oh, Mir, I'm sorry." She sounded genuinely concerned. Her eyes turned from the wall to the sound of Miriam's voice. "We're all jumpy. I should have thought of that. I only came to see if there was something I could do."

"You ought not to creep up on people like that."

She grinned impishly. "Maybe I'll put a bell around my neck." She raised her arms in a ballerina pose. Dropping them back down, she said, "Funny. I always thought of myself as noisy and clumsy. Now you tell me I'm silent as a swan. Gives me a whole new image of myself."

"Stop acting like your usual crazy self," Miriam said, giving way. Being churlish with Sylvie was like scolding a sunny, happy child. She turned off the burner and lifted the kettle. "Don't move. I'm coming by you with a teapot." She filled three cups and stirred in a bit of sugar and milk with a trembling hand. "Go sit with Catherine. You can't carry cups of hot tea, can you?"

"I could have carried them empty," Sylvie argued. "You could have filled them in the other room." She followed Miriam into the living room. "Hey, would it be too much to ask for another piece of your cream cake?"

"Yes, but I'll bring you one anyway." Miriam set the cups on the table before Catherine. "Drink up, Cath. Don't let it get cold."

"I really don't want it."

"Drink it anyway."

Catherine relented, lifting the cup from the saucer and taking a sip. "It's bitter. Everything tastes funny to me tonight. It's as if my taste buds are numb." She glanced up quickly. "That wasn't kind of me after you brought such a lovely supper. It was good of you, Miriam. It's only that I—"

"You don't have to explain. I knew you couldn't enjoy it. I only wanted you to eat and drink something."

"It's uncouth to say this," Sylvie chimed in, her face mischievous, "but I enjoyed it enough for both of us. Excuse me, Cath, don't judge my sympathy by my appetite, but my cooking is limited. When I luck onto something special, I give it all my attention. You must admit, Mir is a fantastic cook."

Catherine laughed unexpectedly. "Sylvie Nye, I have never known anyone quite like you."

Sylvie tilted her head, sending a spray of golden hair across her shoulders. "My mother always said I was one of a kind. I'm hard to take, you know." She stretched luxuriously toward the fire, then reached for her tea. "When I came to the island, Cath, I was a mess. I might have even been a tad angry at Mir for dragging me here. I sat on the beach day after day, wishing the waves would wash me out to sea. Mess, mess, mess . . ."

"What changed?"

"One day, the Wizard of Oz came by. He asked me what I was waiting for. I said, 'Tomorrow.' Know what the Wizard said?"

Miriam bowed her head, whispering in rote, "My one and only true love . . ."

With a grin, Sylvie said, "Yes. He said, 'Sylvie, my one and only true love, tomorrow may be worse.' I thought about that for a long time, and he waited. He didn't try to explain or enlarge the idea. Finally, I said, 'Damn! You could be right.' I stopped right then and there waiting for tomorrow. What if it turned out to be worse? Maybe no cream cake tomorrow."

"There you go," Miriam said. "He and Mary Elizabeth both had the gift of always knowing what to say."

"Oh, that's who *M. E.* is," Catherine said. "What was she like?"

Sylvie smiled and fell back through the years. "Sandy said it best: She was ninety pounds of dynamite . . ."

⌐

Shortly after Sylvie had taken up residence on Osprey Isle, she was sitting in a chair on the porch of her newly purchased beach house, rocking listlessly, when Sandy bounded in on the creaking planks and announced that she must come and meet his wife. Sylvie refused. Despite Sandy's cajoling, she would not leave her chair.

Finally, with an angry roar, Sandy picked her up and lumbered down the steps. He wheezed and gasped as he grappled with his burden. It was ludicrous. Eventually, she had to laugh. This madman would break his back for her.

"You win!" she yelled as they drew near the clearing. "You win! You win!"

He set her down and sucked his lungs full of air. "I wish you had said that fifty feet back."

"You are a crazy man! Do you know that?"

"Mary Elizabeth tells me that every day."

Sylvie raised her hands in defeat. "All right. Let's go and meet her. I'd like to know a woman who could tolerate such a loon."

Sandy led her the rest of the way, grumbling at the trouble she had caused. He said he was having a heart attack and it was her fault. He was no John Wayne. Why couldn't she have been a polite little girl and come along without all that commotion?

Inside his house, he pushed her forward and said, "Mary Elizabeth, this is your new neighbor, Sylvie Nye."

"I'm glad you're here," the faint voice welcomed. "I was going to have tea." She directed Sandy to seat Sylvie close beside her. With her delicate hand closed over Sylvie's, she touched the cup, the plate, the fork, locating each item with wordless efficiency.

"The muffins are blueberry," Mary Elizabeth said. "I'm sure your nose has already detected that fact."

Sylvie did not like being there. It was worse than she'd anticipated. She could not use a fork in front of these strangers or slop the saucer with tea. She sat still, sniffing the air as animals do when danger signals.

"Don't be kind to her," Sandy grumbled. "She's going to be a pain in the neck. Such a disposition she has, Mary Liz!"

"Go away, Sandy," his wife said; then, to Sylvie: "I like a fiery woman! My great-grandmother had fire, Sylvie. She lived in the South, and this tea set belonged to her. During the war, when she heard the Yankees were coming, she buried it. Never touched dirt in her life until that day." She gave a tinkling laugh. "But that wasn't all. She ran to the pasture and gathered cow dung to cover the hole, in case they saw the fresh-turned earth and dug up her teapot. I use it every day to remind myself . . ."

Sylvie's curiosity won. "Remind you of what?"

"That all is not lost if you really put your mind to it. A battle maybe, but not the war."

"Oh, I don't know about that . . ."

Mary Elizabeth gave a soft grunt. "Another muffin?"

Sylvie realized that she had consumed the sweet and had drunk the tea without fumbling or creating a mess. She nodded yes to another helping.

"I want to commission some work from you," Mary Elizabeth said. "Sandy said you're a clay artist. I want a bust of Sandy . . . made of native clay."

"Ha!" Sylvie felt her lifeless eyes widen. "You think it'll look like him? Even though I can't see?"

"I suspect it will look exactly like him."

Sylvie tried to puzzle together this act of seeming kindness. "You want to give me busywork. Useless nonsense to keep me occupied. I don't need that."

"No." Mary Elizabeth clasped Sylvie's forearm. "*I* need it. I want to give my husband something special for his birthday this year. Something lasting. It's to be a surprise. Will you do this for me?"

"Who wants a bust of his own head?" Sylvie asked. "At least make the bust of yourself."

"No," Mary Elizabeth said. "I wouldn't like leaving pieces of myself when I go. This must be of Sandy. As I describe him to you."

The fragile hands sought Sylvie's arm again as she said, "I'm very tired, dear. Would you come back tomorrow?" She sounded exhausted as she added, almost whispering, "Save every day for me, Sylvie. Every day at three with Miriam and me."

Sylvie pondered Catherine's question: *What was Mary Elizabeth like?* "She was like Sandy."

Chapter 9

THE LOLLIPOP ISLANDERS

After saying good night to Sylvie and Catherine, Miriam hastened in the dark along the boardwalk toward the beach. As she descended the steps to the sand, the specter of Frank's body erupted into her consciousness. She shuddered, braced her shoulders, and plummeted down the remaining steps, then ran until she'd passed Sylvie's property.

From Sandy's house, a faint light glowed from the study. God bless Sandy. Of course he would be awake, holding up the world for them. She often passed his house as she walked during sleepless nights and saw him through the lighted window, sitting motionless in Mary Elizabeth's parlor, poised as though waiting for his wife to speak or appear in a doorway. Did he never sleep?

Glenna's small cottage, nestled behind Sandy's big house, was unlit. Around the curve, her own house was dark. David was probably long since asleep. She could only hope.

Needing a moment to think, Miriam set down the picnic basket and sat on the bench Sandy had dedicated to his wife. A small placard read IN LOVING MEMORY OF MARY ELIZABETH WESTERLING.

What would become of them now . . . the Lollipop Islanders? There was a time when she had been hopeful. There was even a time when she had dared to believe Mary Elizabeth's assurances.

"Nothing lasts forever, my dear Miriam," Mary Elizabeth had said to her as her graceful hands busied themselves over the china tea service. "Life has its seasons." She would slip in the sugar cubes with silver tongs and add them to the cups so gently that even the surface of the tea was not disturbed.

Miriam had met Mary Elizabeth in the worst of her own seasons. She had sought refuge in her new friend's semidarkened parlor every afternoon at three—a regular visit that Sylvie would eventually join. In that tranquil room, she could find a haven from their frightening new life. Come to think of it, it was surely Mary Elizabeth's kindness that helped draw such foreign emotions from Miriam, causing her to take Sylvie under her wing. Her former self would never have considered doing such a thing.

Perhaps it had started in the wake of the crash, when Miriam had become conscious in the car—the burned smells of rubber, the odor of gasoline, the sharp pain near her elbow—and realized what she'd done. A spark of light had hit her nearly as head-on as the tree they'd smashed into, and nearly as hard as the guilt that had come once she'd learned that David would never walk again.

In the following days, as David wrestled himself back to life, as the doctors fought to see if they could bring feeling back to his legs, Miriam had sought refuge in the hospital cafeteria. She would stay huddled in the corner, waiting for news, hoping that she might get a second chance to become a better person, someone so different from the father and mother who'd barely raised her, who barely deserved parental monikers.

On one of those days, Miriam had been hiding at a table in the corner, and all the guilt and sadness had finally brought her to her knees. She was folded over, her head resting on the cast around her arm, and she was bawling badly, letting out days and months and even years of repressed emotions.

A soft voice asked, "May I join you?" A young woman with blank eyes stood at the end of the table with a bandage over her bruised head and a white cane in her hand.

Miriam's first instinct was to tell the blind woman she was obviously busy, but imagining the young woman's troubles tipped the scales toward kindness, Miriam nodded consent—then realized her error. "Yes, if you'd like."

Sylvie introduced herself and plopped down with far more clumsiness than she would now. "I could hear you from across the cafeteria and thought I'd check on you. I'm new to not being able to see, but they're right when they say your other senses awaken dramatically. Above all the sounds, the sirens, the beeps, the utensils and plates clanking against each other, it's your crying that stood out. I don't mean to barge in, but I could hear exactly how I feel in your cry, and I thought that maybe we could cry together."

Sylvie reached out a timid hand. If ever there was a moment when Miriam's icy heart melted, it was then, and she took Sylvie's hand, and they cried together, then talked, then cried some more. After an hour, maybe more, they laughed, and a friendship was born.

It was the fall of 1951 when David and Miriam met. Some might have seen Miriam hanging around the bars of Coral Gables as a woman down on her luck who sought a break in the form of a man with wealth. They would have been right. She'd picked Coral Gables because it was a city of tremendous wealth, a place where handsome gentlemen of means grew on trees and offered hope for those born on the opposite side of the tracks.

Miriam's childhood in Evansville, Indiana, was a blur of broken roads, a life so far from the American dream of youth and opportunity. She'd grown up fast in a home drowning in alcohol and abuse and poverty, and she'd promised herself she would not keep living like that forever, even if it meant marrying a man she didn't love. That man turned out to be her first husband, a man she'd left in the night, setting her sights on a new life in Florida.

When she first set eyes on David and fell into easy conversation, though, she forgot about her rational desire for security. In its place came a genuine sensation of wanting, both physically and emotionally.

She'd been hanging around Coral Gables long enough to have established a friend group. Among them was an amateur matchmaker, who had told Miriam, "You must meet my friend David. He's recently single and delightful . . . and rich. I've told him all about you."

A day later, David had called to ask if she'd like to have lunch and visit the zoo in Key Biscayne. The zoo! she thought. What a fun and disarming idea for a blind date. As they enjoyed fresh cuts of fish, roasted rosemary potatoes, and julienne vegetables at the Coral Gables Country Club, David had charmed her in a way no man ever had. A thousand pounds of baggage lifted off Miriam, leaving in its place a cinder of possibility.

Heir to a grocery store chain, David was indeed charming, gregarious, and funny. She couldn't remember ever laughing so hard in her life, especially once they got to the zoo. He bought her a silly pink flamingo hat, and they pranced around talking to and emulating the animals. "Mr. Lion, what do you think of Miriam's hat? Makes her look tasty, you say? I tend to agree!"

In a flash, David and Miriam were in love and married, and he'd drawn her into his life—one of trust fund luxuries she never could have imagined. Within a year, she was hosting cocktail parties on the family yacht, taking tennis lessons with other young wives, and flying in private planes to tiny islands in the Bahamas.

Though she'd had to make tremendous sacrifices to get there—sacrifices she couldn't bear to recall—Miriam felt like she'd finally broken free of her awful childhood.

Of course, David was not perfect, a fact that came out more as they descended deeper into their marital abyss. She'd learned that David's father had famously run around on his mother, and she could see how it had given David trust issues. He was always worried that his brother was trying to outmaneuver him in the family business. Apropos their marriage, he didn't like Miriam going out with her girlfriends and would make unfunny jokes about how he would beat up any man who looked twice at her. Strangely, Miriam found David's possessiveness and paranoia endearing.

"You're my everything," she'd promise him, patting his head like he was a puppy. "I'm yours and yours alone, David."

No one was perfect, were they? *Life* was not perfect.

But it was close enough.

⌒

When David left the hospital, he had no interest in returning to his luxe Coral Gables life. "That life is over," he said. "That David is dead." Though he didn't say it out loud, he was too embarrassed to return to the same circles in which he'd been living. His brother had stepped up in the family business while David had been gone, and David didn't have enough fight to reclaim his throne. Instead, he was fine living off his inheritance and staying a long way from the life he'd once had.

Miriam took it upon herself to find a new life for them, and as she worked her way through the real estate ads across Florida, she found the house for sale on Osprey Isle and knew it was meant to be. Many years before, she'd come across a brochure for Paradiso and had thought it would be a dream to live there. Nevertheless, as a hater of sunshine and salt air, her grumpy and lifeless first husband had wanted nothing to do with the idea.

Their graceful old Osprey Isle house featured vast rooms and cool colonnaded porticos wreathed in orange trumpet vines. The view of the Gulf was the answer to a prayer Miriam wouldn't have even known to have from her devastating life in Indiana as a girl.

While she tried to make sense of her new life, David occupied himself immediately with an architect, refining the house for his convenience. He plunged into renovation plans with maniacal zeal, learning how to interpret sheafs of drawings and electric diagrams. He penciled notes with mad intensity, sometimes pausing to smile and nod in secret satisfaction as he reviewed the black and red lines. It was progress, Miriam thought, if he could lose himself in work. This house, this island, might be their salvation after all. He was so caught up in this project that she kept diffidently in the background, never questioning.

The workmen poured a wheelchair ramp to the driveway and paved a smooth path to the clearing. On the seaside, they laid a ramp from the terrace down to the beach. David wheeled his chair from one side to the other in optimism; it was the longest span of mobility he had experienced since the accident. He'd added thicker wheels to his chair so that he could roll down onto the sand when it was firm after a recent high tide.

From the ramps, the workmen progressed to the interior of the house. They polished the terrazzo floors to marble brilliance. They electrified the sliding-glass doors so that David had simply to touch a button to open. In David's bedroom and wing of the house, they built shelved walls from floor to ceiling. Here, he installed his books, a stereo, and his treasures. They added chair lifts around the perimeter of the room so that he could reach every shelf. His room, in all, was a self-contained kingdom entered only by the pool boy and the sullen village girl who came to clean—and even then, he sat in the doorway supervising.

Their work was almost finished. The last step began with drilling holes in the ceiling. They worked under his relentless guidance as he careened from room to room. He pointed, commanded, and drove them as they fed endless complexities of cable into the holes they had made.

"Is this air-conditioning, David?" Miriam asked timorously.

He looked at her with contempt. "Something much better," he said and wheeled away.

She learned the answer to his preoccupation too late. Intercom boxes and video cameras were installed in every room so that he was constantly aware of her every movement—a way for him to both watch her and torture her. When she emptied ice trays, his voice would chide from the hidden speakers, "Another drinkie, Mir?" When she turned in her bed, far from him in another wing of the house, the speaker above her pillow roused her: "Not sleeping yet, wife dear? Think pretty thoughts. Think how things used to be, before you drove us off the road, before you married me. Or how you could be with someone else."

She was terrorized, but she could not leave him. It was she who had done this terrible thing to him, who had maimed him until he bore no resemblance to the confident charmer she had married. She was the driver of the car, which meant she could not leave him, so she drank.

~

Miriam would never forget the day she dropped one of Mary Elizabeth's precious violet teacups and watched it crash, leaving the golden tea to creep across the bare floor. She had shattered a cup that weathered war, a cup that had been cherished by generations of women.

Mary Elizabeth paused only momentarily, picked up another cup from the tray, and poured. She added sugar and placed another spoon on the saucer. "Nothing lasts forever, Miriam."

For a while, it seemed that Mary Elizabeth's words might be true. Then perhaps there was a way through the darkness. She learned a great deal from Mary Elizabeth, and from her new friend, Sylvie, with whom she corresponded on occasion.

A year later, when another house came up for sale on Lollipop, an idea came to her. Sylvie had written and spoken to her on the phone about how difficult her life had become with her family, how she felt that she was dragging them down, how she could never become anyone other than the former teacher who'd been the victim of a boat crash.

Miriam called and said, "I'm picking you up. Come spend a few days on the island." As Sylvie enjoyed the smells and sounds and sweet tastes of a future on the island, Miriam imagined out loud what it would be like for them to become closer friends, and then she'd taken her to the house for sale, allowing her to stroll out onto the deck and soak up the tropics. With the sun splashing on her and the breeze tickling her skin, Sylvie found a sense of hope for the first time since her accident.

When Sylvie moved to the island, after some cajoling from Sandy, she joined each day at three for Mary Elizabeth's "afternoons." Sylvie brought her madcap, irreverent conversation to break the tedium. She tested herself against them with impudent buffoonery until Mary Elizabeth interceded, "You are an enfant terrible, Sylvie. It's time to go on with other things."

Sylvie slammed the floor with her cane. "Terrible? You'd be the same way had this happened to you."

"Indeed I would," Mary Elizabeth agreed with serenity. "But I would not be forever."

Sylvie had paused for a long time to consider her words. "By damn, you're right!" She folded her hands primly in her lap and with mocking gentility. "Two lumps and a lemon, please, Mrs. Mary Elizabeth."

The newcomer took a dainty sip, touched her lips with a tea napkin, and announced, "I will spare you ladies my worst temper from now on." Airily, she added, "I think I'll save them for your awful husband, Miriam. David and I can have mean contests." She gave them an impish grin. "I'll remind him that he's not the only one who's had his life ripped away."

Sylvie proved to be good for David. A kinship grew between them as they parried insults. They exchanged words no one else on the island would dare to speak. They laughed together in secret complicity about grim jokes only they could share.

The days passed. Sandy and Mary Elizabeth gathered their nets and captured even the struggling, resentful David. "You are an ass," Sandy would shout as he leaped to his feet and dumped the chessboard into David's lap. "Furthermore, you cheat!" He would storm away, across the ramp, muttering deprecations, while David shook with laughter.

Gradually, the islanders had evolved into a tentative community, each with a function solely their own. Summers melted into winters with no marking of days. Sylvie blossomed and worked under Mary

Elizabeth's discreet tutelage. David's malediction evolved into a cheerful optimism as he battled Sandy at chess or sharpened his wit with Sylvie or turned courtly in the presence of Mary Elizabeth. Miriam relaxed and grew golden in the sun, full of hope.

Little by little, Mary Elizabeth's "afternoons" grew shorter, and it was as if a gray cloud settled over Lollipop. Glenna began to visit. She left Sandy's office early and arrived to plant herself protectively behind Mary Elizabeth's chair, where she anticipated every move, fetching, carrying, bringing things within reach.

"I seem to be sleepy . . . Would you excuse me now? I'll see you tomorrow at three." Her voice would trail away as she sank, exhausted, against the pillows that Glenna had added to the chair.

Miriam remembered how she'd found out about Mary Liz's illness with dazzling sharpness, how she had turned back one day for something she had left in the parlor and how the sound of her friend's voice trickled out of the house. Miriam had stopped, uneasy, before she reached the door.

"I can't endure much longer," Mary Liz had whispered to Glenna.

Miriam leaned forward, still hidden from their view, to see Glenna lift Mary Elizabeth's slight body and carry her to her bed. She glimpsed that stark face as it fell against the uniformed shoulder and saw Mary Elizabeth's eyes black with longing for release.

Like Sandy now, Mary Elizabeth did her best to hide her dying from them, patrician and proud. She welcomed them each afternoon. She was best when Sandy was present. On those days, she would lift her arms to him and chatter prettily in her faint, soft drawl and assure him that she was "better today." She would press whatever gift he'd brought to her heart and flush with pleasure.

Miriam realized what Mary Elizabeth feared most: that Sandy might not be able to handle life without her. He might just snap.

~

Miriam stood and picked up the basket. She tasted salty tears on her lips. Enough! Life has its seasons! She kissed her hand, then touched the metal placard, wishing she had Mary Liz to guide her now.

Back at her house, she tried to slide open the back doors. They were locked. She knocked loudly on the glass, calling David's name.

No reply.

As her heart picked up its pace, she circled the house to test each door. All locked. She tried each window, clawing her way through the hibiscus bushes that grew high and thick, forgetting in her alarm that rattlers sometimes scuttled from their hiding place there. Everything was bolted. Dear God, David could be lying inside hurt, unable to answer.

Running to the garage around the north side of the house, she flicked on a light and frantically searched for a tool to break the glass door in the back. Her glance caught the heavy tire iron on the workbench. Back on the terrace, she raised the iron high and was about to crash it through the glass when bright light suddenly flooded the interior. The tool fell from her hands and hit the tile with a loud bang. Inside, David sat in his chair, pressed up against the glass door she'd been about to break. An ugly and spiteful grin rose on his face. In his hands, he held a glass of what looked like whiskey on the rocks. He saluted her and then took a long sip.

"Why are you so mean to me?" she asked.

I can't hear you, he mouthed silently through the glass.

Turning her back to him, Miriam stomped to the cooler and lifted the lid. She ran her hands along the side of the box, groping for the familiar handle. Most of the day's ice had melted, and the pick lay somewhere along the bottom.

David activated the electric door and rolled outside. "We're too burglar-proof for an ice pick, Mir. You could never open these doors with that."

Her hand met the pick, and she gripped it tight, anger swelling inside her. She lifted it out of the cooler and held it in front of her as it *drip, drip, dripped* stale water at her feet.

David rolled closer and asked, in a controlled and affable tone, "Or are you considering stabbing me? Wouldn't that be something? Go ahead, finish what you started, Mir."

She turned to him. The grin still hadn't left his face. "I give you everything, David . . . but you treat me this way."

"That's what we do, Mir. We thrive in our own dysfunction. We stew in a cauldron of our own wonderful witches' brew. You'd be bored, otherwise, wouldn't you? We're both so utterly unlovable, and yet we manage to find a way to love each other. And I do love you. You know that. I love you so much, I'd kill for you."

She knew he was speaking the truth. Despite what she'd done and how difficult she could be, he did love her. That's what mattered. Her fingers loosened, and she dropped the pick back into the cooler with a splash.

"There you go, my love," David said, his mouth stretching wider.

Brushing past him, Miriam retreated to the chaise. She stretched out and closed her eyes, hoping to drift away.

He followed her over. "Want to tell me about it? About Frank. Did he ignore your advances?"

She kept her eyes shut, wishing him away.

"You'll feel so much better confiding in someone. What did you say to the grieving widow?" His face was so close that she felt his breath on her cheek.

After a long beat of agonizing silence, Miriam looked at him. He was curved over her, his nose pointed up as if sniffing her.

He curled her hair around her ear. "Did you think we could vouch for each other tomorrow when the detective returns? That may be good for you, wife darling, but it means nothing to me. You don't think for one minute that I would *ever* be a suspect? There would be tracks in the sand, wouldn't there? Besides, I couldn't have put that hole in Frank. Not with the condition you put me in! Do you actually think Detective Jones would entertain serious thoughts about me as a murderer?"

"If he knew you well, he'd reconsider," Miriam said. "I wouldn't be surprised if you're the one who killed him. That chair did *nothing* to stifle your evil."

He scowled, and she wondered if he might implicate her just to spite her. Their bedrooms were separated by the vast living room. He could tell Detective Jones that she easily could have slipped out into the night without rousing him.

"I saw the way Frank looked at you when they arrived," he said. "I saw him push you away."

"He pushed me because I was drunk."

"You were trying to whisper to him. I saw you."

"I was telling him that I was glad they came to the island. I wanted them to like it here. God, your paranoia knows no end."

"Oh, I do believe you're glad they came. He could be your new cut of meat. Prime rib for the lady!"

Miriam thrust herself upright, and David's chair jolted backward. "Do you want to drive me crazy, David? Is that it? You're doing a great job, if that's the case. I'm going mad!"

He stared at her, his face empty of expression.

Miriam shook her head helplessly and lay back. She closed her eyes and tensed her muscles against the tics that assailed her. He sat quietly, watching and teasing her, humming tunelessly under his breath.

Disappearing inside herself, she feigned sleep for what felt like hours.

David eventually tired of his nasty game. The purr of his chair whirring away delivered sweet relief. The door closed behind him. At the sound of the lock sliding into place, she peeled open her eyes. The tide was going out now, hissing as it withdrew. Night birds called from the darkness. Ominous clouds drifted past the spidery outlines of the pines and palms.

Thoughts made a fearful carousel in her head. Think. Plan. Anticipate what David will say tomorrow. Sure, he loves me. But his hate comes in equal measure. Could he hate me so much that he'd frame me for murder? Just for fun, just to see what happened? Sadly, it was possible.

—

A while after Miriam left, Sylvie asked, "Do you want me to sleep in the room with you or in the guest room?"

"In the guest room," Catherine replied. "I'll toss and turn and keep you awake." They continued to sit, each wrapped in their own thoughts, the quiet broken occasionally by the weary sigh of the dying fire.

Catherine's eyes wandered over the comfortable old furnishings, the dim firelight, the moon-washed deck, the Gulf only steps away. "How could Glenna give this place up?" she asked, breaking a long silence.

"Number one," Sylvie said matter-of-factly, "this house doesn't hold the happy memories that you might imagine. She was trapped here by two sickly parents. Number two, if Sandy said, 'Sleep on the shells; I want to give your house to my friends,' Glenna would snap to attention and say 'Yes, Doctor.' It's that simple."

"How strange we all are," Catherine said through a yawn. Deciding it was time to call it a night, she pressed up but struggled to raise herself from the deep cushions. "It's the weirdest thing. I slept all day, and yet I can hardly sit up. I'm not sure I can make it to the bed."

Sylvie was quickly by her side, supporting her, bearing her weight as she moved on leaden feet. "That must have been some super-duper sedative Sandy gave you."

"I was wide awake a while ago, though. All of a sudden, I feel like I've been hit with a baseball bat."

"I'm tired too," Sylvie said. "What a long day."

The bedcovers were still turned down. Sylvie eased Catherine onto the bed, and she fell back against the pillow. Her eyes closed as her feet were lifted to the bed and covered.

What a nightmare this had become.

~

Jones pulled back into his house about midnight. *House* was a strong word. It was more a fishing shack that the owner had put up in the fifties after his wife chased him out of the house. Staple some dollar bills to the ceiling and Jones would have himself a restaurant. But it was on the water, and that's what had caught his eye when he moved down from Sarasota two years earlier.

On the water and a *long* way from civilization. He definitely understood the Carters' own interest in hiding from the world.

Jones pushed open the door and flicked on the light. The housekeeper hadn't been in yet. Probably because he didn't have one. A photograph of his father in his bomber jacket standing next to his B-17 was the sole piece of art hanging on the wall, a reminder of where he'd come from—even if his memory of the man was nearly vacant. What was not lost on Jones was that in May, he would turn the age his father had been when he was shot down. Sometimes when he looked at the picture, Jones wondered if he'd even make it to twenty-nine. It felt like there was some sort of timer ticking down the days to his potential demise.

He set a stack of case files down, shucked off his clothes, and grabbed a towel. Under the light of the moon and an army of stars, he traversed the path that wound through the mango groves to the water. He reached the edge of the dock where the Whaler was tied, looked around for the eyes of gators glowing in the moonlight, and dove in.

The cool water hit him in all the right places, and when he came back up, he felt renewed, the water as energizing as sunshine on his soul.

Back in the house, he put a record on the player, something he'd been hearing in his head all day, and sat back on the couch and closed his eyes. A few seconds later, O. V. Wright was singing to him. He focused in on the music, thinking that there might be no safe place in the world other than being lost in a good tune. It was nice to take his head away from Paradiso for a moment.

When he'd first joined the force, his uncle had always said, "You gotta step away sometimes to really get inside."

Stepping away wasn't easy for Jones, but just about everything his uncle had taught him had proved true.

When the needle hit the end of the record, Jones popped up. He hadn't eaten a thing since Betsy Cable's fish plate, so he rumbled around in the fridge. White bread, mustard, a slice of bologna, and some lettuce. What else did a man need? He put together a sandwich and cracked open a PBR.

As he took his first bites, the case came back and started clawing at him. The search of the island hadn't brought up a thing. Across the entire beach, the tide had risen all the way to the dunes, wiping the slate clean like an Etch A Sketch. There were no fresh holes in the dunes or in the woodland, at least none that those young officers had found. There were no recent firepits where someone could have burned evidence.

But all the evidence he needed was in the words, gestures, reactions, and post-offense behavior of the people of the island. He hadn't been able to shake what Glenna had said—or started to say—about Dr. Overbrook knowing an islander other than Sandy. Then there was Catherine. Of course she was grieving and knocked off her tracks, but something else was going on. He saw demons in her eyes. The Arnetts weren't any less troubling. Then the Carters. Levi was a classic candidate to be a murderer, but was it too obvious? It takes a lot of nerve to play hardball with a cop. Would he have been able to do that had he killed a man in cold blood the night before?

If Jones kept pressing, one of the islanders would crack. He didn't *need* to go to Frank's hometown. Though it would help, he didn't *need* a murder weapon. He simply needed to ask the right questions and set the right traps.

Sylvie could not guess how long she'd slept. It was not yet morning; she didn't feel the sun. Her senses tensed against some break in the rhythm of the room. She lay still, trying to recognize the intrusion, her eyes open but unseeing, her mind scrambling to fight through the sludge of exhaustion.

She heard something . . . a scampering whisper of papers shuffled, a drawer sliding cautiously, more papers and delicate rummaging.

"Cath?" she whispered, hoarse with fear. There was no response.

Furtively, she slipped out of the bed and felt her way along the wall, out of the bedroom, and into the living room. A light breeze smelling of the sea pushed through, and she wondered if they'd missed closing one of the windows.

Sylvie paused, listening. Nothing. Not a sound.

Hands in front, she crossed the long living room. She felt heat from the fireplace. That meant the fire had not yet grown cold. She had not slept long. At the entrance to the study, she sensed another presence and extended her arms, barring the door. "Cath, is that you?"

The only response was quiet breathing, in and out.

Sylvie tightened her fists in a guarded position. "Who's there?"

Someone shoved her hard as they hurtled past her. Sylvie fell forward, striking her head against a sharp edge as she went down. In that infinitesimal time of falling, she felt blood gather on her temple, but then it was lights-out.

Chapter 10

A Storm on the Horizon

February 22, 1970
Day 2

David dreamed he was falling, and as he awoke, he was sliding out of the chair. Savagely, he heaved himself back into position and pressed his fists against his sleep-swollen eyes and cheeks. A stubble of beard gritted his knuckles.

The chaise outside was empty. All those hours last night when he'd sat watching Miriam through the glass doors as she twisted and turned. The times he had dozed, then jerked upright as his head dropped forward and awakened again. It was all for nothing. He hadn't had the pleasure of seeing her get up and make a second attempt to get inside.

He unlocked the sliding door and rolled onto the terrace. Miriam was nowhere to be seen. The wicker basket she'd taken to Catherine's stood open beside the chaise. Ants left crumb-strewn trails in their wake as they carried away the leftovers.

The wind was rising. He lifted his head to watch fast-moving clouds obscure the rising sun. A welcome storm was on the way. One that would wash the island, pummel the beach, pound the dunes, and make everything new again.

David steered himself back inside and into his office, where he took his place at the console. He flicked his fingers over the control panel and turned up the volume for the intercom system. Ah, yes, he could hear her muffled breathing from her bedroom. Resourceful Miriam had found a way in. Drinkie winkie blurred her vision, blotted her judgment, but she had made it inside. She could take care of herself when the chips were down, a fact that made David smile.

From this soundproof room, he could listen to every sound in every crevice of the house. He could see people approaching outside. He could play music in nearly every room. He could unlock every exterior door. He was the automated man, dependent on no one. The leading lion in his pride. He glanced over at the drawer where he kept his gun. He was still captain of his ship, by God.

Little did she know, his reach extended far beyond these walls. He had eyes on her even when she left the island. Though the reports were that she was being a good girl, David knew that could change in an instant.

Turning, he smiled an acknowledgment to himself in the mirrored wall. She thought she had outwitted him, finding a way in, but a superior opponent is always a step ahead. She was where he wanted her to be, his wife being moved as carefully as a chess piece in his games with Sandy. "David, you dolt, what's a move like that going to accomplish?" Sandy would wink in false triumph but then watch with wide eyes as his castle walls tumbled in the series of moves that followed.

David's last move before falling asleep in his chair had been unlocking one of the windows on the side of the house. Good for her, she'd found it. He would have enjoyed watching her wiggle through, though.

Time to check on the ol' gal now. David propelled the chair out of his office and down to the far end of the hall. Outside her door, he paused as she whimpered. She slept with one hand curled against her cheek. He sat motionless, waiting until she, too, was still.

Her makeup had dissolved and left black rivulets that she had not troubled to wipe away. The satin comforter had slipped off, and she had curled into a fetal position, seeking warmth. He quietly drew near, picked up the coverlet, and spread it across her shivering body. Careful not to touch her, he drew it over her bare arms and shoulders. She stirred but did not wake.

David seldom came into her bedroom; certainly never when she was there. It had been a long time, months maybe, since he had investigated her room full of little treasures.

The room was elegant and graceful, much like Miriam when she was at her best. The bed had a tall headboard of white wood painted with blue flowers. They had brought it back from Europe, excitedly promising it would host their many guests in their place in Coral Gables, in their life that no longer existed.

It hurt too much to think of their old house and their former life. He turned to the dressing table, to Miriam's filigreed tray of perfumes and cosmetics. He touched the monogrammed silver brush, his second gift to her after their marriage. She'd hugged him tightly and told him that it was beautiful. "And you're beautiful, David," she'd added.

"Don't tell a man he's beautiful! Men aren't beautiful. I'm a stallion, if anything."

"You are." She had pressed her fingertips against his lips and traced the lines at the corners of his mouth.

He could not think of that either!

There were pictures everywhere. Snapshots framed in an assortment of silver ovals, squares, and rectangles. They covered her dressing table, the bureau top, and the nightstands on each side of the bed. He began to pick them up, one by one.

His favorite was the day they'd met. It was a blind date, and his friend felt they would be a perfect match. They both stood laughing in front of the hippos at the zoo in Key Biscayne, and right as a passerby who'd offered to take their picture clicked the shot, one of the hippos opened his mouth wide enough to push a basketball into it, creating the appearance that he was laughing too! Likely at the pink flamingo hat David had bought her.

In this one, she was plunging down a snowbank, her red scarf flying, her mouth a perfect O of surprise, as the camera caught one ski flying skyward away from her. In a photo taken the next day, she sat before a blazing fire, her leg encased in white plaster, with his hand offering a stein of steaming cider.

David picked up a photo featuring *Sweet Surrender*, the sailboat his father had given him. With a broken heart, he'd quickly sold it after the accident, but the wonderful memories lingered. Miriam had called to him at the helm, "Do something daring, Captain Lafitte," and he had hung upside down from the jib for her. "Not enough," she had said, and brought a steak knife from the galley for him to hold between his teeth. Pirate David, as silly and daring as ever, a side of him that she could bring out with merely a flash of her buttery smile.

Another shot captured them mountain climbing. Only a small rock face, true, and only once had they gone, during a trip to Switzerland. After they'd made it to the top, their guide had poured them coffee in bent copper cups and encouraged them to say *"Proscht!"* as he snapped a shot with the Alps in the background.

David's eyes swept over to the cut-glass decanter and the careful array of bottles on the tea cart beside her door. Since his last foray through her room, she had discarded the mixers, and he wondered how many times during her restless nights she'd lifted the decanters, not bothering with glass nor ice. No, she was too fastidious for that. To the bitter last, she would drink from a glass, pause to appreciate the beauty of the amber liquids; even alone and trembling, she would be a lady.

He bent close to her again to examine her face. There were lines now. Sharp slices between each brow and finer lines beside her lips. Little pockets were forming on her jowl. She looked old and sad in unguarded repose.

She changed position and buried her face in the pillow, almost as though she knew he was near. The cover slid to the floor again. He retrieved it and laid it back over her.

"Are you awake?" he asked softly.

No answer.

David wished he'd been better to her, *wished* that he could be better to her now.

He left the room, checking the time on the hall clock as he passed. Detective Jones would come by again today. If the officer was sharp—and he seemed to be—he must have gathered a great deal of information already.

Hopefully, he wouldn't dig too deep.

~

The sleet scratched the window as Catherine held her eyes tightly closed. I won't even get up today, she declared silently. The apartment is never warm enough for a Chicago winter, and I must be coming down with a cold. My head feels like a big lead ball swinging from side to side. But the nerve and muscle drawings are due to Precise & Accurate Illustrations on Monday. I'll have to get up. Their textbook goes to the printer on Wednesday. I feel awful, awful, awful!

Still keeping her eyes shut against the slate day, Catherine fumbled for the blanket to pull over her face. Her exploring fingers found only a thin sheet. No wonder she'd caught a cold. Feeling drunk and disoriented, she opened her eyes cautiously and inched her way back to reality.

She bolted upright as her eyes focused on the open window, where a damp wind blew jessamine vines against the screen. There was no sleet, no rumble of city traffic below, no smell of turpentine or wet brushes. There was warm air and the heady scent of jessamine! They were in Florida! On Osprey Isle! Frank, we made it!

Clutching the sheet, she looked at the empty space beside her and was stabbed by fear.

Yesterday had started exactly like this. For a moment, she clung to the hope that she was in the midst of a nightmare and that shortly she would hear the shower running or see Frank come through the bathroom door, his long face stern with disapproval as she lingered in bed.

It's not a nightmare, she admitted as she recalled her staggering trip to the bedroom last night with Sylvie. All this is happening.

I have to tell Sandy how I felt last night. My legs seemed unable to bear my weight. The shot he gave me must have been too potent. I slept all day, woke energized enough to sit with the ladies, and then collapsed for the second time. It was an unpredictable, immediate need to drop then and there.

Warily, she raised her head. It felt detached from her body, as if it hung somewhere in the air above her, a heavy balloon poised to fall with crushing weight. She touched her feet to the floor and held the edge of the bed as she stood upright and steadied herself. Using one hand to brace against the wall, she negotiated her way to the bathroom.

She pulled the shower taps open to full force and dropped her clothes in a heap, moving them aside with one foot as she clung to the sink in a fit of vertigo. Stepping inside the shower carefully, she felt the hot water pound against her neck and shoulders. Her brain felt thick and muffled. She moved the temperature setting to Cold. Ice needles stung her awake and slammed a heft of reality down upon her.

My husband has been murdered. The life we could have had is gone. That policeman will come to ask me questions today. And a funeral? Dear God in heaven, I will have to plan a funeral for Frank. I've never even been to a funeral. I've never even known anyone well enough to share such an intimate ritual. I'll have to go through all of Frank's belongings. He would never tolerate alien hands pawing and disarranging his orderly possessions.

As she dried off, she took in the tidy bathroom. The toothpaste was capped. His brushes had been lined up precisely. His razor had been dismantled and dried and returned to its case. His robe hung neatly on the door hook. How like him. The dark, uncompromising garment was hung properly suspended by the cloth loop provided for exactly that purpose. It was not Frank's style to joyfully fling aside a robe or to leave a mirror streaked with steam or a wet mat crumpled out of shape. A place for everything, everything in its place. Even the razor blade he had discarded was safely wrapped in tissue and deposited neatly in the wastebasket.

Guiltily, she rescued her peignoir from the floor and hung it over his robe. She adjusted the silk folds, pleated them to their original shape, and rethreaded the satin sash through the belt loops. She dried the gelatin from the melted soap and placed it back in the soap dish. She spread the wet towels straight and neat on the bar, then took a dry towel and polished the mirror. This would suit him. He would be gratified by her private observance of his rules and wishes.

As she polished the mirror, she reviewed the contents of her closet—all bright, new trousseau clothes—and wondered what to wear. What are widow's weeds? She turned away from the glass in embarrassment. Frank would clamp his thin lips in distaste at the frivolous, disrespectful thought. To consider the decoration of her body on the first day of widowhood. Abhorrent! His austere presence was as strong as if he stood beside her. Shaken, she returned to rubbing down the mirror, trying to avoid her own eyes.

Finished with her chore, she checked the unspotted surface. Her reflection stared back at her, white and solemn in the harsh light. With slow deliberation, she drew her hair tight and coiled it into a bun. She leaned forward, whispering, "I know you. You're Miss Lonely Hearts from the third-floor walk-up. When you wake again, you will see the sleet fall on the pavement below."

Two spots of color flooded her cheeks, and she saw, for a fleeting moment, the Catherine Overbrook from before Frank's death, the woman who sipped Champagne. Who bent over shells washed in by the tide. Who greeted bright-faced periwinkle along a path.

In the bedroom, she opened her closet. Her shopping spree through the bridal shops of Chicago had emptied her wardrobe of black and brown and all the colors of mourning. Florida was to have been a celebration of life, of color, of flowers. There were no provisions for death in the white satin shops.

She slipped into a blue long-sleeved, button-up dress. Frank's starched white shirts and gray and black coats rebuked her mutely from their waxed hangers. When she had buttoned the last button, she closed the closet doors like an obedient child and made the bed to smooth perfection.

It was barely dawn. She stood at the window, absorbed in the colors sizzling on the horizon and trying to reconstruct last night. Sylvie must still be sleeping in the other bedroom. Perhaps Catherine would make coffee and cinnamon toast and take breakfast to her in bed as a thanks.

Catherine moved into the hall. "Sylvie?" she called as she rapped softly on the guest room door. No reply.

In the living room, a turbulent Gulf breeze swept papers past her. The pages spun crazily through the air as the wind lifted and whipped them around. Puzzled, she bent to retrieve two sheets as they brushed her cheek and swooped toward the floor.

They were pages from one of Frank's drafts, marked up heavily with red pen. This was the first time she'd ever been so close to his work in progress. Copious notes handwritten in cursive filled the margins. Each letter was precisely the same size and same depth of color. No change in the pressure of his pen had altered the sharp lines. His penmanship was as rigorous and immovable as the man who'd written them.

The papers swirled about her, some sucked against furniture or draperies before they fluttered away. The back door stood open, admitting the sea breeze. How careless of Sylvie and her to leave it unlocked after all Detective Jones's cautioning. She moved swiftly to close the door.

Only then did she glimpse the inert figure sprawled by the study door at the far end of the room. She gasped and nearly lost her footing as a dizzy spell rushed through her.

Cautiously, she made her way closer until she recognized Sylvie's bare feet thrust askew across the sill. Her heart stopped. At once, she saw flashbacks of Frank's body in the sand. Death. Death. *Death.*

"Somebody help!" she called, realizing only afterward that there was no one else in the house.

Composing herself, she knelt and reached out to find a pulse. It was there, the light throb of life! Sylvie wasn't dead, thank God. Catherine's heart began to beat again.

Sylvie's left temple was clotted with blood, though. A cluster of red had straggled along her cheek. One of her hands extended in the direction of the desk.

Catherine sat back on her heels and looked around. Someone had broken in and ransacked Frank's desk. A mess of both typed and hand-written papers littered the floor. Every drawer gaped open. The top of his briefcase was peeled back. What had the intruder been looking for?

She stood, found Sandy's number, then lifted the desk phone and dialed. The phone rang again and again. With each staccato burst of sound that went unanswered, she wondered if Sandy had made a night call. He could be delivering a baby or . . .

"Yes?" His voice was muddled with sleep. "This is Dr. Westerling."

"Sandy," she said, "Sylvie's hurt. She's unconscious in Frank's study. I think she fell."

"Don't touch her. I'm on my way."

It wasn't long before Catherine heard fast footsteps approaching. She rushed out to the back deck and pulled open the door. Against the backdrop of the Gulf, Sandy and Glenna both came into view, racing along the boardwalk. Sandy's short legs pounded the wooden planks as his black bag thrashed wildly against his knees. He had not delayed by dressing. He wore cotton pajamas printed with flashes of green-and-yellow diamonds. Glenna ran close at his heels, her strong legs cutting the air. The wind caught the robe she wore and made broad flapping wings as she leaped.

They bounded past Catherine without acknowledging her presence, and when she joined them, they were already at work, performing with skillful efficiency. They cleaned the wound, then checked her pulse, blood pressure, and breathing. When Sandy lifted Sylvie's eyelids, she murmured inaudibly, glancing about with bewilderment.

Sandy and Glenna moved Sylvie to the couch and propped her up with pillows.

"What happened?" Sylvie leaned forward and wrinkled her forehead. "Ouch! That hurts."

Sandy pressed her back against the pillows. "You're the only one who can answer that, little love."

Sylvie closed her eyes and lay still as they waited, watching her with worried frowns.

"I heard something last night." She squinted her eyes, struggling to recall. "It sounded like someone rustling paper. I thought it was Catherine. I called to her. She didn't answer, so I went into the living room."

She tried to raise herself on one elbow. "Ow! That wasn't a good idea." She fell back. "Yes, I'm sure that's what it was. Papers. But the person wouldn't answer me." Her eyes widened. "Oh my God, was it the murderer? What were they looking for?" Without waiting for a reply, she said quietly, "Whoever it was knew me. They knew I couldn't see, because even when I spoke, they went on scrambling around. It wasn't till I got close that they tried to get out."

Catherine fastened her eyes on the floor to hide her fear from them. If Sylvie was telling the truth, the intruder had to be one of the islanders. What could they have wanted so desperately? Frank had only just met everyone. Unless there was something he hadn't told her. She shivered, unable to share this jolting insight with the three in the room.

"Feeling nauseous?" Sandy asked.

"Not nauseous," Sylvie replied. "Just a jimcracky of a headache. What a skull I must have." She raised a hand and explored the bandage on her temple, touching it gingerly.

"No permanent damage, little love. It would take more than a knot on your head to stop that sassy tongue of yours, but please take it easy."

Catherine turned to find Glenna rummaging through the papers on the floor. "What are you doing?"

Glenna turned to stone. "I . . . I'm collecting them before they blow away."

"Blow away? I closed the door."

"I was trying to—"

"Don't touch anything," Catherine said. "I'm about to call Detective Jones. He should see this as it is."

Glenna's eyes lingered on the last page that she had placed on the table.

Catherine strode across the room. "Why are you *looking* at them? It's none of your business!"

Glenna stood with raised hands and backed away. "Forgive me."

Can that be my voice? Catherine wondered in amazement. Never in my life have I been brave enough to give an order. I have spent all my energy staying in the shadows, letting people tell me what to do. Cowering, afraid, and angry inside, meek outside. "Don't make waves," they'd always told her when they transferred her to the next foster home. "Be invisible. If they don't notice you're there, they won't send you away!"

But this is my house. Those are my papers now. I have a home and a name, and I do not have to be invisible anymore. I have broken out of the chrysalis. I have spread my wings, and they cannot ever be folded flat enough to return to the person I was.

Catherine went to the phone again, tapped in the number for the sheriff's office, and asked for Detective Jones. The operator said she'd locate him and send him right over.

After the call, Sandy stepped toward Catherine and took her arm. "How are you feeling, dear?"

"Good, I guess. I'm still exhausted from whatever you gave me yesterday. I don't want any more of that."

"No, I don't think it's necessary again. Perhaps some Valium if you're feeling overwhelmed. Just let me know. I always have samples in my bag."

"I think I'll be fine." She raised her eyes and looked into his. "What's strange is that I woke in the afternoon and felt normal—or as normal as possible. I had dinner with Sylvie and Miriam. Then it was like the drug came back into effect. I could barely make it to the bed."

Sandy let go of her and nodded knowingly. "I'm sure it's exhaustion. There's nothing wrong with sleep. Perhaps it's the best thing you can do right now. Call me any time today; the next few days will be bumpy."

Catherine gave her best attempt at a smile. "Thank you, Doctor."

"One more thing." He paused. "When I lost Mary Elizabeth, the whole world came crashing down. I wasn't sure I'd ever recover. You know what helped? More than talking to people and visiting her grave? I wrote her a letter. A long letter, telling her how much I loved her, telling her that I'd never forget her." His eyes turned red. "Telling her I was sorry for some of the things that I'd done, the times when I could have been a better partner. I don't know, something about putting pen to paper healed the broken bits inside of me. Might be worth a try."

Catherine couldn't imagine writing a letter to Frank, not now, but she tried to be cordial. "Thanks for the advice."

Sandy gave a sweet smile and turned away.

Chapter 11

INTRUDERS AND LONELY WIDOWS

Detective Jones and Officer Challa offered a brief greeting to everyone and listened as Catherine caught them up.

Then Jones approached the couch. "Sylvie . . . Miss Nye, I mean. How are you?"

"I have a hell of a headache." She raised her hand to gingerly touch the gauze dressing.

"I bet you do. I'm glad that's the extent of it. Do you know who hit you?" He caught himself as he was about to ask *Did you see them?*

"No one hit me. I fell. Someone pushed me—shoved me, really—and I banged my head on something as I went down."

Jones looked at the empty bookshelf, noticing the sharp edge where she'd likely hit her head. "Did you get a sense whether they were male or female? Anything that you can recall to help me identify them?"

"I think it was someone on the island. Or at least someone who knows I'm blind."

Jones made a mental note. "What time did it happen?"

She turned restlessly, trying to make herself comfortable.

"Miss Nye?" he asked again.

"No idea—and I wish you wouldn't call me Miss Nye, Detective Jones. I am not your grandmother, nor am I a maiden aunt." She kept her eyes closed as she talked. "Make them give me my sunglasses, will you? I don't like everyone staring at me to see if I happen to look in the right direction."

"No one's staring at you, you vain vixen, you," Sandy said with a warm disposition—the kind that would likely allow him to get away with *anything*. He leaned forward to touch her arm. "Where are your glasses?"

"They must be on the chair by the bed in the guest room."

The doctor gestured to Glenna, and she left the room to retrieve the glasses as if she'd been sent on a mission to locate the Holy Grail.

"Miss Greely and I really need to leave," Sandy said to Jones. "We have patients stacking up."

Jones raised his index finger. Enough dodging interviews around here. "I need to speak with you both," he said. "I'll stop by your office shortly."

"Yes, that's fine."

Once Glenna had handed Sylvie her glasses, the doctor and his nurse exited the back door, both oblivious to the spectacle they made, what with him in his flashing green-and-yellow pajamas and her in a rough brown-plaid robe, striding behind him on the boardwalk, matching her steps to his.

"Sylvie," Jones said, "will you please hang tight till after I talk to Catherine? Then I'll run you home and do a walk-through to make sure you're safe."

"You think they're coming back for me?"

"I don't know what to think yet, but I do want to be careful. Lay back and rest your head. I'll check on you in a few."

As she did so without protest, Jones followed Catherine into the study, where there were clear signs of it being ransacked.

"I thought you would want to see it like this," Catherine said, indicating the raided briefcase, the scattered manila folders, and the open drawers in the study desk. "He was working on a medical book. This is everything he brought down on the plane."

She rested her hand on a neat stack that had been weighted with a chunk of broken coral. "Miss Greely gathered up a few sheets. Otherwise, nothing has been touched."

Jones nodded approval and glanced at Challa, who went to work taking photographs.

"Do you mind giving us a few moments, Catherine? Then I'd love to sit down and talk with you."

"Sure. Can I offer you two a cup of coffee?"

Challa politely declined, but Jones said, "Yes, I'd love that. Perhaps we could visit on the deck in a few?"

Catherine agreed and left them to their work.

After Challa had taken his photos, Jones snapped on a pair of latex gloves and began to rummage through the papers, taking in medical jargon that was far beyond his understanding.

"I didn't get this far in med school," he said.

"You went to med school?"

Jones grinned. "No. I thought about it for a minute, though."

Challa rewarded him with a slightly forced laugh. "Good thing you found another calling."

"That's true. The world needs detectives like me."

"I was more thinking that I wouldn't trust you to put a Band-Aid on me."

"Ouch, Challa. That one stung."

Challa let out a real laugh this time as he set down the camera and drew out his fingerprinting materials. "I'll hit all the surfaces and go through every page. See if I can find anything other than Dr. Overbrook's prints."

"As you go through the papers, see if there's anything that stands out. I know they need you back in town, but take your time with this one."

"I gotcha," Challa said.

Out on the deck, Mrs. Overbrook waited at the glass table with a steaming pot of coffee and condiments. Her delicate profile was turned west, her gaze fixed along the boardwalk.

She startled as Jones pulled up a chair. "Oh, yes, sit down, please."

Taking a seat, he pulled the microphone from his bag and waved it like a white flag. "I'm going to get my recorder going, if that's all right."

"That's fine. Whatever it takes." She was either devastated or a master of playing it cool.

He reached inside his bag and mashed the button with the red circle, then asked again what had happened. Catherine began, speaking slowly and carefully. Jones sensed some hesitation as she spoke. Perhaps whatever information she was withholding would come out unguarded later.

Once she started slowing down, Jones asked, "Why would anyone want to search your husband's papers, Mrs. Overbrook?"

She met his gaze directly. "As I said, he is . . . *was* . . . working on a book. A medical treatise. That's what brought Frank and me together. I'm a medical illustrator, and he consulted me about drawings."

Jones poured himself a cup of coffee and stirred in some cream. "Forgive me, but what exactly is a medical treatise?"

"It's a formal medical book that offers a variety of diagnoses and related treatments. His would have ideas that he's furthered in his years as a physician." She almost sounded like she was reading from a script.

"Would a half-written medical text cause all this?"

"The appeal would definitely be limited."

Jones inched toward her, trying to break through. "He must have brought old office records. Medical charts or correspondence? Something worth breaking and entering."

She splayed out her hands. "Maybe. I haven't gone through everything yet, but it seemed to all have to do with his book. Most of his things are with a mover headed this way."

That was going to be one of his next topics. "When will they be here?"

"I have no idea. I don't even know who he used."

She was really throwing him for a loop. What a hard woman to understand.

"Have you read what he was writing?"

"Only what I've looked over today." She let out a slow, controlled breath. "He was . . . how can I explain it to you . . . an *exceptionally* private person. I was going to start my drawings once we settled in."

Jones wondered at her lack of curiosity. Could she be faking? A new bride would ask questions of her new husband. Doubly so if she intended to collaborate on those very documents. He would have shown them to her, asked for suggestions and ideas. Yet even now she showed no eagerness for reading the scattered pages.

As if she had read his mind, she said, "If you had met Frank"—she lowered her eyes, speaking to herself almost—"no explanation would be necessary. We talked so little about personal things. We barely knew each other and only married *two* days ago, before taking the plane from Chicago to Florida." Her hands fluttered in brief apology. "We hadn't broken our walls of privacy yet. Maybe I didn't even know him at all."

Jones was taking it all in. He reached for his cup and dragged it his way. "You were married in Chicago, then were able to get down here in time for the party—all in a day?"

"*Before* the party, even. We were here in the late afternoon. Frank is meticulous; he had the logistics well planned. Married at the courthouse, then raced to O'Hare to fly to Sarasota. He'd already bought our car and had it waiting at the dealership. Once we got here, we were greeted by Dr. Westerling and Miss Greely. That's when we found out about the party. They wanted us to meet the other islanders."

"I see. Sounds like an exhausting day. What did you do in between your arrival and the party?"

She cast a look over his shoulder to the house. "Unpacked, explored the nooks and crannies of our new place, ran to the store, walked on the beach. We didn't have much time."

"Did you see anyone else before the party?"

Catherine considered, searching her memory. "We saw the Carters—at least, I'm pretty sure it was them. Later in the afternoon, Frank and I went to the grocery store. On the way back, we passed them in the clearing. They seemed to be reading the new name on the sign. We all stared at each other for a moment."

"What did they look like?"

"He was tall, young, brown from the sun. Long hair and beard. Barefooted. Wearing cutoff jeans, I think. The girl looked like she might be pregnant. They turned away pretty quickly, disappearing down their drive. I laughed and said we must have scared our new neighbor, but Frank didn't answer. He seemed bothered. Maybe because they looked a little . . . suspect? Once we got back to our house, he retreated to his study to work, and I was so happy to be here that I completely forgot about it."

"You think seeing this couple upset him?"

"Oh, I wouldn't know."

Jones was still getting a pulse on her. "Did you and Dr. Overbrook have a prenuptial agreement or make wills before you left Chicago?"

"How did I know this was coming? We didn't have any agreements in place or make wills." She contemplated Jones's question, her expression somber. "I have no idea what his finances were. I was lonely, not money hungry. I would have held on to him forever."

"And he to you?"

"I think so, yes." Her pronouncement was detached, as though she were a scientist giving a verdict after examining a slide specimen.

"But you barely knew each other. Tell me what led to your speedy wedding and move."

She explained their meeting at a conference, Frank's reappearance at her door the following year, and the few days afterward leading to their marriage. She stated only the barest facts, offering no explanation, injecting none of her own thoughts about the situation.

Jones sat leaning forward, listening intently, attempting to put some color into this black-and-white drawing of a woman. It was going to take more than this session to get it all out of her.

When she had finished, he packed his things and rose. "Thank you, ma'am. Officer Challa will stay here a bit longer and keep an eye on you and Miss Nye."

Catherine stood. Something else was on her mind. Her fingers absently brushed at a wisp of hair. "Who do I talk to about a funeral?"

Jones snapped out of work mode and found her eyes. "I can get you some names. Give me a day."

When they came into the living room, they found Sylvie sitting up again.

"How's your head, Miss Nye?" Jones asked, moving closer. Sylvie was still on the couch, still as a bird. Her dark glasses were propped up on her nose.

"Better, thank you," she answered, "but what did I tell you about calling me Miss Nye?"

"I'll try to remember."

"Uh-huh."

Jones sat beside her and said gently, "Can you stay with Mrs. Overbrook for a while? I need to go talk to the doctor, and then I'll be back to take you home." He turned to Catherine. "Is that okay?"

"Of course," Catherine replied, though Jones thought he saw disappointment in the look on her face.

"Great. Officer Challa is still in the study if y'all need anything."

~

It was hardly an island, Jones mused as the patrol car clattered over the hundred feet of boards that spanned the water. Osprey Isle was a shallow circle of a point, a key, until the high tide cut a swirling gully across the road. Some enterprising pioneer had flung a ramshackle bridge across the pass, and subsequent residents had kept it in barely sufficient repair.

He watched the rearview mirror as the signpost in the clearing disappeared behind him. Five houses of residents. All strangers to the murdered man except for Sandy and Catherine.

Would Westerling entice Dr. Overbrook to the island only to do away with him less than twenty-four hours later? Could they have had a sudden angry disagreement about their partnership arrangement—a clash so violent that Westerling struck out in a moment of rage?

Jones constructed the possibilities in his mind. Mrs. Overbrook had told him that the two men had a long conference in Westerling's study after the party. Perhaps they'd arranged to take a break and pick up the discussion later on the beach. That meant the disagreement was too deep to wait for the next morning. Then Westerling would have had to come prepared to carry the object that made the lethal hole. That meant that Westerling anticipated trouble so serious that he had arrived armed.

Westerling and Overbrook must have had extensive correspondence or telephone conversations. There had to be written contracts for Dr. Overbrook to travel fifteen hundred miles to a village in Florida. Maybe Westerling had not lived up to his promises and Overbrook had threatened legal action.

Dr. Westerling had admitted that his health was poor and needed Overbrook's help. He had gone to a great deal of trouble to locate him, and probably had made many concessions to convince an established physician to make such a change. Westerling would have stood by his agreement. Unless . . .

Suppose Overbrook arrived. He saw the situation firsthand. It was not what Westerling had represented. He saw the opportunity to demand more than he was promised. No. Westerling could simply refuse. Then Overbrook would have to be the angry figure. Overbrook would strike out. There was a struggle. Westerling disarmed him and delivered the deadly stab.

If not Westerling, who else?

Mrs. Overbrook. She illustrated medical texts and knew anatomy.

Miss Greely. A nurse with a profound sense of duty and knowledge of the weaknesses of the human body.

Could Sylvie have anything to do with it? Icy sweat crept into his armpits. As a sculptor, she also understood the human form. She would know where to stab him for a quick and certain death.

How about the Arnetts and Carters? So many possibilities. But the thought of a random island intruder was fading for Jones after the developments of last night.

Jones reached Paradiso just as storm clouds gathered overhead. Unpainted houseboats bobbed and sent clotheslines dipping and flapping against oil cans and bait buckets. On one deck, a swarthy woman, her head bound in a bright-pink covering, pushed listlessly at a broom, shoving the debris ahead of her and into the water. A man mending nets lifted his head to stare as the patrol car passed.

Jones slowed the vehicle to twenty-five miles an hour, cruising past scattered shacks that lay half-hidden in the water oaks, palms, and pines. Then the general store, the post office, and the concrete-block building that was Westerling's clinic appeared. He pulled the car onto a square of struggling grass beside the building and sat for a moment.

He watched the rearview mirror as two men emerged from a floating dock. They settled themselves on a plank porch and glared back at him, their faces closed and hostile. One of the men drew a vast sputum into his mouth and spewed it insolently over the railing.

Jones left the car slowly, feeling their bold stares follow him. Over the stench of fish and crumbling piers and salty nets, the men could surely smell trouble.

Paradiso was law outside the law, and the officialdom accepted that. Rarely was there a call for help from the villagers. If laws were broken, the villagers cared for their own. They found the culprit, delivered their own swift justice, and the city boys in brand-spanking-new uniforms were none the wiser. Jones had heard all the tales. If a fisherman disappeared, he had "fallen overboard," and no hours of questioning unlocked their secrets or changed their distant faces.

Now things were different. The foreigners, those Lollipop islanders, had called the other law, the county, the state, into their midst. There would be prying and comings and goings, and the villagers would become restless.

Chapter 12

Hardly an Island

Detective Jones pulled the squeaky door shut behind him and stepped into the reception room. It was furnished with plastic chairs on pitted-chrome legs. The furniture was arranged in random groups, as though dragged into conversational patterns by waiting patients. Overhead, a propeller-blade fan spun, lazily flicking the pages of ancient *National Geographics* and *Outdoorsmen* and *True Story* magazines. The walls featured children's paintings: leaping dolphins, starfish, shrimp boats, and crabs. A metal rolling cart overflowed with containers of paint and mason jars of turpentine and coffee cans stuffed with brushes and stained bits of rags.

"How do you like their work?" Sandy stood in the dark hallway. "The first time my young patients visit a doctor," he continued as he came over to meet Jones, "they're sick or hurt or afraid. I tell them that the day they feel better, they can come back and help me decorate my wall."

He touched a purple sailboat low on the wall. "This is Amy Dearden, age six. Broken arm." His hands moved across the mysterious landscape to a blue pelican. "Joey Campbell, thirteen years old. Fishhook in his cheek." He sighed. "Even the older ones paint sometimes. They're sheepish about it, but we get a cheering squad going, and they're soon working away."

Sandy lifted his arm to a graceful conch high on the wall. "That one is Tony Alladono, twenty-seven, gangrenous foot. He stuffed the wound with wet tobacco for three days so he wouldn't miss a shrimp run. Tony's proud of that conch."

"It's a great idea, Doctor."

Sandy nodded without reply and beckoned him to follow as he started down the hall. In his office, he pointed toward a chair and sat down himself in the opposing one on the other side of his messy desk. His medical credentials and one of his wife's watercolors hung behind him on an otherwise-gray wall.

Jones went through his spiel about his recorder, and the doctor didn't protest.

"What do you think happened to Dr. Overbrook?" Jones asked, resting the microphone on the desk. "You were the only one other than his wife who knew him. And one of the last to see him alive."

Sandy's freckled hands clasped and unclasped as he thought about his answer. "I'm stumped, Detective. Of course I had no reason to hurt him." He sighed and turned his chair so that he faced a window that looked out over the street. "He was stepping in when I needed him, helping me make sure the good people of Paradiso wouldn't go without care."

Jones wondered why he had looked away.

"Doctor?" Glenna Greely stood in the doorway with a stack of cardboard folders. A nurse's cap sat crooked on her head. "Is it all right to file these now?"

"Come in, Glenna. You won't disturb us." He waved a hand in her direction. "You know Miss Greely, Detective. Otherwise known as my right arm around here."

She gave Jones a crisp nod and turned to pull open a drawer from the metal file cabinet. She began to slip the papers into place, her wide shoulders straining against the stiffly starched uniform.

Jones didn't want to get off on a bad foot, but he decided to protest. "I would prefer to talk to you in private, sir."

Glenna's activity stopped, her entire being poised and alert. If Jones poked her with his finger, she might have popped. Sandy followed Jones's curious gaze. "I don't keep secrets from Glenna," he said. "Everything I might tell you, she's heard before. She's helped me through rougher times than these."

The nurse kept her face hidden, but Jones saw her dip her head in imperceptible agreement. Her ears seemed to redden with pleasure, but she busied herself again as though she had not heard.

"Glenna nursed my wife through a terminal illness and has kept my life together ever since. Believe me when I say that we could never have made it without her, neither Mary Elizabeth nor me. As I said, I have no secrets from Glenna." He tilted back in his chair and locked his hands around the lower curve of his round belly.

Jones held his ground, not saying a word. He'd wait all day if he had to.

Sandy's cheeks swelled. "All that's neither here nor there. If you really need a private interview—"

"That would be best."

"You heard the man, Nurse."

Glenna set the remaining folders on top of the cabinet and disappeared into the hall, pulling the door closed with indignant firmness. The two men sat quietly, listening to her march away.

Sandy adjusted in his seat. "She doesn't like being left out. Now, where were we?"

Back to business, Jones thought. "Tell me how you became friends with Dr. Overbrook."

"It was *loooong* before you were born, sonny. We met way back in medical school." A smile teased his lips as he gave a quick shake of his head. "Such a long, long time ago."

Friends? Could he call it a friendship? Sure, he could. They were friends the only way Frank knew how to be a friend.

Sandy had first met Frank when they were partnered up in the dissection of a cadaver during their first year attending the College of Medicine at the University of Florida. Sandford Westerling III brought with him a world where nothing unpleasant ever happened. He had money to spend and, with a quick, bright wit and a secure affirmation of his place in the community, plenty of friends sought his company. But he was by no means the most promising student.

Frank was the top of the class—brilliant, methodical, and precise— and there was no one who doubted that he'd go on to do great things. But his social skills were nearly nonexistent. He had an inability to filter his words, and he seemed to lack sympathy. To someone who didn't give him the benefit of the doubt, he came off as arrogant.

As Sandy came to know him, he saw how Frank suffered from bullying. His heart broke when fellow students would insult or play tricks on Frank. It seemed more rooted in their own insecurities than anything else. No matter the reason, Sandy always stood up for Frank and made it a point to attempt to break through his icy exterior—a challenge as daunting as any Sandy had ever known.

In their second year, two events occurred coincidentally. Sandy was summoned to the dean's office. He was being dropped. The board had recommended that he leave his struggling pursuit of medicine and go home to take over his rightful place as executive vice president of Westerling Industries—a story not unlike that of another islander: David Arnett.

Sandy emerged from the conference with the dean in stunned disarray. The receptionist flashed her dazzling smile. "Don't look so downcast. There are worse things than going home to play with your polo ponies."

"I don't have polo ponies," he told her, grinning despite himself. "And I want to stay . . . what could be worse than being booted out of the only thing you ever wanted to do?"

"Well," she retorted smugly, "at least you're not leaving because you couldn't pay your fees. That ought to be some consolation. Frank Overbrook might like to be in your shoes."

"Frank's leaving?" he asked in astonishment.

"Got his notice this morning." She leaned forward conspiratorially, the smile changing to a satisfied smirk. "If you think you're upset, you should have seen Frank's face. He walked out of here like a zombie."

Sandy left the administration building and wandered aimlessly through the campus, eventually forming a proposition in his mind. When he was satisfied with it, he sought out Frank's drab dorm room in the lower part of the quadrangle.

Frank was packing, creasing his meager garments with meticulous care, filing his belongings with surgical precision into a worn footlocker. Sandy sank onto the edge of the bed, disarranging the tight sheets. Frank glared at the disorder, then shrugged and silently resumed his task.

"Will you do me a favor, Frank?" Sandy asked. "I need you."

"What could I have that you need, Westerling?" His bony hand rested for a moment on the scarred trunk. "You're the golden boy who has everything." It was rare to see Frank emote, and Sandy saw through the insult to the pain.

Sandy's round face grew earnest. "You're right. I do have money. It was money that bought me into school. All those super microscopes you use were a part of my entrance requirements. But money won't save me this time." He laid his hand on the locker to stop the packing. "Listen to me, Frank. I was never heavy in the brains department. I can't make it on my own."

"What could that possibly have to do with me?"

"I can help you," Sandy said. "I can buy you in."

"Like Dr. Frankenstein, I invent a brain for you?"

Sandy, good humor ever near the surface, laughed. "Something like that. I need you to help me pass."

Frank's eyebrows lifted in contempt. "What would that help consist of?"

"Just help me study. That's all I ask. Help me understand and pull me along with you."

"No."

Sandy sprang to his feet, upsetting the carefully packed locker. "I want to be a doctor, Frank. I *really* want to be a doctor, more than anything I've ever wanted in my life."

Lines creased Frank's forehead. The profession held tremendous weight for him. "Why?"

Sandy faltered, embarrassed, wringing his freckled hands in agitation. Frank continued to pin him with scornful pale eyes.

"Look," Sandy said, his heart open wide. "I know you like the challenge, using that big brain of yours to restore order and solve the mysteries of the human body. I don't have your knowledge or acumen. I won't ever be the doctor you will . . . but I do want to help people. I love human beings. Simple as that. It doesn't have to do with what my family expects of me—if that's what you're thinking. I want to serve people. That's my purpose."

They sat in uncomfortable silence. Frank stared at the wall above his head, his expression speculative. Sandy felt like a curious specimen under the lens of Frank's microscope.

Finally, he said, "You'll pay all my expenses? And a tutoring fee?"

"Agreed."

"There will be no cheating. I will not tolerate dishonesty."

"Of course not." Sandy's face crumpled with relief.

"If you can convince them to let you stay, then I agree." Frank opened the fallen footlocker, righted it, and began to unpack. "Don't sit on my bed," he said coldly. "I don't like wrinkled sheets."

Sandy's father and his wealth had proved convincing, and together, Frank and Sandy made their arrangement work.

Sandy found that Frank was not an *unpleasant* companion. He was not sullen. He was, rather, an *uncomfortable* companion. He had no life outside his studies or work. He lived exactly as he ate and drank . . . sparingly and without joy. He was a demanding and relentless taskmaster as he led Sandy through the maze of chemistry, biology, anatomy, and physiology, and yet he never turned away in impatience. He never showed exasperation. Frank kept to their agreement with a dogged, determined concentration.

Keeping his side of the bargain, Sandy applied himself to all Frank instructed and tried mightily. Together, they made it to graduation, then parted with a solemn handshake. There were no pledges to keep in touch, no promises to get together again. It simply ended.

～

Sandy rocked forward and rested his arms on the desk. "I'd kept up with him over the years, read his articles in the trades. When I decided to bring someone else in, he was the first that came to mind."

"Paradiso is tiny. You must not have a busy practice."

He took a handkerchief from his pocket and swabbed his forehead. "I haven't been well lately. I'm thinking ahead."

"You thought of Dr. Overbrook right away? That seems unusual. You say you haven't heard from him since you were in school together."

"I'll tell ya, Detective, it isn't easy these days to find a man who would be willing to come to a village like Paradiso. Young men want to go where the money is. They want to specialize. They like to charge big fees and work long hours. You won't find any of that here."

"What made you think Dr. Overbrook would leave an established practice, then? Were you such good friends that he was willing to drop everything and come when you called?"

Sandy shook his head quickly. "No, he was already closing his practice. I'd phoned him up to set the wheels in motion, and that's the first thing he'd told me. That he'd taken on this book and that he wouldn't have any more time. Attempting my hand at persuasion, I suggested that he'd have time to do both, as we'd be working together with a much smaller client load."

Jones was searching for any indications of Sandy steering away from the truth but was coming up empty. "How'd you find him, anyway?"

"I wrote to the alumni association."

"Was he in trouble of some kind? He made some fast moves in the last few months—closing his practice, accepting another job, getting married."

Sandy gave a sharp and short laugh. "Trouble? Frank? I couldn't think of anyone who would be less likely to get into trouble. Frank was a model citizen."

"His finances were in order, then?"

"I don't know anything about his finances, but if you think Frank would . . . what? Income tax evasion? Something like that? Is that what you're asking me?"

"Something like that," Jones replied.

"Frank would never bend a rule, much less break a law. More than anything, I caught him at the perfect moment, a few months before this young woman had stirred him up. I'd continued to nudge him, starting to think he'd never come around. Then I got a call out of the blue. He'd met Catherine and said that he'd fallen in love and his priorities had changed. He almost sounded giddy, which, if you knew Frank, isn't an emotion he expressed often. Love can get to anyone, can't it? I think the idea of marrying her and taking her to somewhere new sparked his interest."

Jones waited for more.

"Besides, I think he already missed practicing. Just like you, he was a detective. He seemed addicted to solving the mysteries of a patient's health. By coming down here, he could still be involved, still have patients, but also have plenty of time for research. *And* . . . he would have access to our alma mater in Gainesville, a far superior place for research than his options in the Chicago area."

Jones heard a cough on the other side of the door and saw a shadow move under the crack. Was Glenna listening in?

Though his eyes darted toward the sound, Sandy pretended not to notice. "I can be rather convincing when I want to be. Glenna was considering selling her house, so he had the perfect spot. We had exactly what appealed to him: a place to do research, a job to keep him in the field, enough free time to allow for writing, and a house on the water to start a new life with Catherine."

"Did he have any family? Did you ever meet anyone?"

"His rigid father, once or twice. He's long gone now." A light bulb came on in Sandy's head and showed through his eyes. "He did tell me he'd been married previously."

"What happened?"

Sandy shrugged. "He was a private man, and I came to respect his wishes. He would never have wanted to discuss his past. Take my word for it, you couldn't press Frank for details. He could shut you away like the closing of a vault."

"You're describing a rigid, humorless man, Dr. Westerling. Am I right?"

"On paper, he sounds terrible, but when you got to know him, you could really see his soul shining. He was just hard to know. I imagine that's what happened to his first marriage. I hoped it would be different with Catherine. She would have been good for him."

Sandy fumbled for a handkerchief and mopped his face. "I say, Detective, are we almost finished?" He leaned forward and rested his head on the desk. "I don't feel well."

Jones popped up, opened the door, and called down the hallway, "Miss Greely!"

Before her name was barely past his lips, Glenna rushed through the door.

"It looks like we need an ambulance," Jones said.

"No ambulance," the doctor muttered.

"This happens sometimes," Glenna said as she lifted his limp wrist and checked his pulse. "I know what to do." Jones stood uncertain until she said, "I think you ought to go now."

"Can I help you move him to the couch?"

"I can do it," she said firmly.

Before he left, Jones paused again in the waiting room. The walls resplendent with their brilliant, colorful paintings made the street outside seem like another world. The warmth and genuine affection of Westerling filled the very air.

I saw this before, Jones remembered. I saw him work this kind of magic comfort on Mrs. Overbrook. Sylvie had even called him a magician, a rescuer from her private dragons. That is what his magic is. He makes them all seem worthwhile. Even Glenna.

He can't be true. He's likely an illusion, and I must remember that. Could Sandy hate as much as he could love? Could he kill? An illusion was a trick, a smoke screen to distract from the truth. Sandy himself had admitted to being convincing when he wanted to. That skill was only one rung short of being manipulative.

Chapter 13

HER OTHER SELF

Catherine's body tensed when she saw Detective Jones pull back up to her house. Thunder like she'd never heard before rumbled in the distance, slightly terrifying for a Chicago girl.

There would be more talking, Catherine thought. That ceaseless, endless talking. She sat motionless, shrunken far into the cushions. Maybe he would go away. She was so tired. Bone weary. Assaulted with people and sound. It was unfathomable that only two days ago she welcomed such things.

"Mrs. Overbrook?" Jones pounded on the door. "Are you there?"

She was not there. There was no Catherine Overbrook, only Catherine Thomas of Chicago, Illinois. Go away.

He wouldn't stop knocking, and the racket ate at her torturously.

"Yes, yes, I'm here," she finally called out, unable to take even one more of those thunderous knocks.

As she cracked open the door, he asked, "Are you all right, ma'am?"

Her other self answered. "Yes, of course." She stepped aside to let him in, hiding the fragile part of her. It was a trick as old as her life, masquerading in an alien land.

Inside, she screamed to her faceless guardians, Tell me who I am! The answer, a collective response from all those who had ushered her in and out of foster home doors: You are who you are. Deal with it.

She was Catherine Thomas of Chicago, Illinois. She had tried to be someone she was not.

"Where is Miss Nye?" Jones asked.

"She's gone home. The other officer took her. Did he not call you?" Catherine was almost amused by the tranquility in her voice.

"I tried him on the radio but wasn't able to connect. Is she okay?" Jones seemed overly concerned, and Catherine knew he'd wanted to be the one to take Sylvie home. They were so unguarded, these strange people, showing all the world their every thought.

"She was anxious to go," Catherine explained, then thought to herself, Not nearly as anxious as I was to have her go.

He unfurled a hand toward her. "I'd like to talk to you again, if you're feeling up to it."

Whom would he like to talk to? The woman who'd lost her husband was no longer here. The other Catherine led him into the living room. She wasn't sure why she felt a need to hide, but her instincts had taken over.

They sat in two Gulf-facing chairs that flanked a lamp. She pulled the chain, illuminating Jones's face. The mustache made him look far older than he probably was.

The detective seemed incredibly comfortable in the awkward silence between them. Catherine couldn't take it another moment. "Officer Challa was nice enough to clean up after himself," she said, looking toward Frank's study. "There was powder everywhere."

～

Detective Jones glanced at the phone on the small table in the corner. "Do you mind if I try to catch him?"

"No, that's fine."

Standing back up, Jones dialed the station and waited to be connected to Challa. After three minutes of watching several boats race away from more dark clouds, he heard, "Jones, that you?"

"Yeah, I just got back to Mrs. Overbrook's. How's Miss Nye?"

"She's back at her place, doing fine. I didn't find one print other than the vic's. I checked every page. Whoever it was used gloves; I'm sure of that. It's what Mrs. Overbrook says it is: a medical book that's way over my head, detailing anatomy, offering cures to common illnesses. Then there was a stack of letters between him and his publisher in that folder. Nothing out of the ordinary."

After a few follow-up questions, Jones ended the call. Dammit if this wasn't a troublesome case. The killer had a calculated mind, a cunningness that reached far beyond the garden variety of those he'd sent to prison in the last few years.

Easing back into the chair by Catherine, he slid a glance her way. This was the toughest part of the job. In his kindest voice, he said, "The medical examiner completed the autopsy. He confirmed murder."

Jones watched her for tells. She seemed rattled for only a moment before raising up her walls. He wanted to believe she wasn't a killer. She seemed genuinely heartbroken and to have truly liked—or even loved—the man, despite his odd ways and lack of good looks. Sometimes a person is seeking more than a physical attraction. They're looking for a partner who makes them whole. Perhaps that was the case here.

"Someone stabbed him with a sharp object shortly after midnight, killing him quickly. The murderer then attempted to dispose of his body by dragging him out into the water."

Other than a nervous scratching motion with her right pinkie, Catherine sat still. She was less taken aback than he'd expected, Even broaching the topic with loved ones could send them reeling.

"I'm sorry," Jones added.

Catherine eventually looked toward him, though it felt more like past him. "We had something that could have become much more than it was. No matter how he appeared to people, he was a good man and would have made a good husband. He did not deserve to die."

"I can't imagine that he did."

"Please find the person who did this," she said, breaking out of her trance. "Find them and put them in jail and . . ." She shook away the rest of what she was about to say.

"I'll do my best, Mrs. Overbrook." He'd learned the hard way not to make difficult promises. Some elusive cases on his desk grew colder by the day. Either way, he was glad to see she had some chutzpah. Was it an act, or was she truly hopeful for a resolution?

Jones scratched an itch under his mustache. "I am still so surprised at the speed of your engagement and marriage. Wasn't it hard to walk away from your old life? I would assume the same of Dr. Overbrook."

Catherine lifted her hand to push absently at a tendril of hair that had escaped from the tight knot at her neck. She wore no cosmetics, and the pallor of her face was stained by the shadows beneath her eyes. "I have no family, no friends. I was as isolated as if I had taken a vow of silence. I worked at home, so I had no office acquaintances. I didn't socialize. When I left Chicago, there was no one to notify except the rental agent. Frank was somewhat similar to me."

"What kept you so isolated?"

She smiled darkly. "The way I was living was the way I'd learned to survive."

Jones paused to consider her statement. Though she might be hiding something, the truth rang in her words.

As it grew darker outside, Jones questioned her childhood and pried deeper into her short time with Frank. Did they stop anywhere on the drive down from Sarasota? Did Frank make telephone calls along the way? What other topics did they broach? Did he seem anxious to arrive?

"On the trip," Jones said, "did he discuss his former practice?"

"Not really. He said he missed it more than he thought he would."

"He never mentioned relatives, family in Burbank?"

"Nothing." The sky rumbled, and she peered out the window with what looked like fear.

"How about Dr. Westerling? Did he mention him? What were their arrangements?" He was shooting in the dark, seeing if he might hit something.

Catherine lowered her gaze to where her hands were gathered on her lap. She twisted her wedding ring. "He said that Dr. Westerling had been nagging him for a while, trying to get him to move down, but only after meeting me did he consider the offer."

Jones noted the word *nagging* in his mind. Sandy had used differently phraseology.

"How did meeting you make him reconsider?"

She lifted her head to look at Jones before dropping her chin back down. "I'd mentioned wanting to escape the Chicago winters, and he took it to heart, coming up with a plan before he'd even proposed."

"That is indeed love."

As if it required prying, she lifted her head again. "Believe me, I was as skeptical as you, regarding the haste of the whole thing, but we had something. Our own kind of romance."

"I appreciate that." Jones let a few beats pass by. "If there was a connection, then you surely had more to talk about. You went out on dates, sat next to each other on a plane, and then drove down to Sarasota. It couldn't have been spent in total silence."

Twisting her ring some more, she said, "You'd be surprised. We could go a long time without saying a word. It was kind of nice in that way. But we talked some about the trial going on in Chicago . . . and about the president. Frank did *not* like Nixon. Actually, he was opposed to the war and the draft and said that Hubert Humphrey would have gotten us out by now had he won the election. I got the sense that Frank could be extremely opinionated if you wound him up."

Catherine let go of the ring and searched the ceiling. "He told me about his hopes for his book and that he looked forward to fishing—as it was where he escaped to brainstorm. He mentioned that he'd grown up on the South Side of Chicago and that his parents were both gone. He'd been married before but didn't elaborate. I didn't interrogate him; it didn't feel like my business. I hoped that someday he would tell me about it, but that was all. Couldn't Dr. Westerling tell you anything?"

Jones shook his head and kept pressing. "I'm sure Frank's made some good money in his life. Probably has a good fortune in his bank account, especially after selling his practice. Other than this house, what else will you inherit?"

Catherine pulled her hands apart and pressed fists into her thighs. "I have no idea."

Crack! A bright light flashed through the window as a near-simultaneous boom shook the house. The light bulbs of the two lamps flickered. Catherine jumped, and her eyes shot open.

"First Florida storm?" Jones asked, unfazed after growing up around them.

Her face had lost its color. "They're horrible."

"After a while, you get used to them. Might even start to like them. Back to your husband: Did you kill him, Mrs. Overbrook?"

Her face tightened as she ripped him with an angry look. "Why would I do that, Detective? He's the first man who's ever acknowledged my existence. He's the only person I've ever cared for."

Jones wondered if her words were true. A woman with her looks would have to work hard to avoid men's advances. "You've never dated before?"

"Not at all."

"I'm sure you've been asked out."

"Until Frank, I avoided men. They might have asked me out, but I had no interest in a relationship of any sort. He changed that." She crossed her arms at her chest and found a spot on the floor at which to stare. "I was abused throughout my childhood, and I'd found the best way to avoid any further suffering was to limit my contact with others. I worked and ate and slept. That was it. Then Frank came into my life and somehow found a way to get through to me. I found him sensitive, shy, and disarming."

She was telling the truth, as she'd suddenly come alive, speaking from her heart.

"I could not care *less* about money." Her shoulders slumped wearily. "I have money of my own anyway. I had a good income and saved most of it, as you will likely discover when you check on me. I never wanted anything except . . ." She stopped and looked hard left.

"Except what, Mrs. Overbrook?"

"Nothing."

"That's a provocative statement. You ought to finish it."

She stood and walked to the windows, watching the light show out over the water, a woman facing her fears. "Except what I had this past couple of days."

Jones sat back, wondering if he could crack her—or if there was anything to even crack. "Let's go back to the end of the night, after the Arnetts had gone home."

She took a calming breath, clearly trying hard to tolerate him. "Sandy asked Frank to stay. They went into his office, and I fell asleep in a chair. Miss Greely came in and woke me, and then Frank and I walked home." She winced. "Frank must have put me to bed. I don't remember. I recall stumbling home and that's it."

There she went again, turning into someone else. It was in the way she seemed afraid of eye contact, afraid that he'd see her skeletons.

"Dr. Overbrook must not have gone to bed. He was fully dressed, you know."

"Oh, I know."

Another bolt of lightning shot across the sky, lighting up the house as the clouds rumbled.

~

The detective patted the air, attempting to calm her. "The bark is worse than the bite. All my years, I've never known anyone to suffer an injury from lightning."

"It happens," Catherine said, thinking that maybe it wouldn't be so bad if a lucky strike electrified her.

The detective seemed skeptical as he studied her. She hated this silence that he seemed to lean in to. It didn't help that this horrific storm was coming down on them. Could he just leave her alone?

Her mind wandered back to the night of the murder. If Frank had gone to bed, found he couldn't sleep, and decided to walk to the beach, he wouldn't have gone out in his nightclothes. He would have made his side of the bed and dressed again exactly as if it were morning. But she had said enough about Frank's idiosyncrasies. Each detail Detective Jones pulled from her made Frank seem stranger. Enough! It was unfair.

"You say Dr. Overbrook and Dr. Westerling had a meeting after the party. Do you know what they talked about?"

"As I told you, I had too much to drink. I couldn't have concentrated on anything if Frank had told me, much less remembered it. I assumed they were going over what they would do the next day, something like that—or that Sandy was telling him more about the practice."

"You say Miss Greely was with them when they went into the office?"

"Yes. Then she woke me up and told me Frank was ready to go."

"Dr. Westerling didn't come out to say good night? Didn't that seem odd? You were the guests of honor."

"If I thought about it at all, I would have thought he'd said good night to Frank and that was enough. Truly, I can hardly remember leaving." She *could* remember, though. She'd been singing on the way home. She'd clung to Frank's arm, and he hadn't liked it. Even now, she could feel the sharp pressure of his fingers on her elbow as they'd moved along the path. Yet she was so happy that even making Frank angry had not bothered her.

Frank had steered her firmly into the bedroom and told her with a frown that she mustn't fall asleep in her party clothes. She had stumbled about, somehow managing to undress. At the last moment, she saw her shoes flung carelessly to one side. She'd bent to pick them up and put them away, but the room spun crazily, and they seemed too far away to bother. She had giggled, thinking she would have to wake up before Frank in the morning and get them into the closet. He would never tolerate slovenliness.

"Frank?" she had called as she laid her head on the pillow. He was still at the door, watching her with hard, cold eyes. "I'm sorry," she said, knowing that they should be consummating their marriage, knowing that even a reserved and quiet man like Frank would want to sleep with his new bride.

But the room was spinning, and her eyes fell closed, and the night was gone.

Back in the present, Jones asked, "Y'all didn't talk after you came home? Didn't discuss the party or the people or what you would do the next day?"

"No," she lied. "I don't think so. I don't even remember saying good night to Frank."

"That must have been quite a celebration. Did anyone else have too much to drink? Dr. Overbrook? Dr. Westerling?"

"Frank would never drink too much." She had done it again—made Frank sound so rigid. Everything the detective asked made her answer seem critical or hostile. She hurried on. "They were used to Champagne. I'm not. They kept toasting. No, no one but me . . ." Her brain told her to stop talking so much.

Jones lifted his head. "No one else?"

Miriam. David had had to take Miriam home and she was crying. But that had nothing to do with Frank. There was no reason to repeat such things.

"Just me," she said firmly.

His nod was caked in doubt. "Random question: Do you sleepwalk?"

"What? No."

"Just curious."

After a few more queries, Jones stood to go, and it felt like Catherine could finally take a breath after holding it for far too long. The sky was dumping rain, and Jones raced out into the darkness under the cover of an umbrella.

Once he'd gone, Catherine moved restlessly from room to room, trying to focus her attention on something, anything at all. On other days, she would have gone to her drawing board. It would have blotted out every thought. Now there were people to crowd her mind, and their faces floated in and out: Sandy, Sylvie, Miriam, David, Glenna. All right then, she decided. Think of them, one by one. Exorcise them away so I can retreat into that secret room inside my head.

Another explanation crept by her, a suggestion both absurd and . . . possible? Could she have blacked out and sleep-*killed* her husband? That wasn't such a thing, was it? Sleepkilling? She wasn't capable of such an atrocity, was she? She couldn't have hurt the one man she'd ever loved. If only she felt fully convinced. The Champagne had done a strong number on her. To answer the detective's question of whether or not she'd been known to sleepwalk, it was an unequivocal yes.

Ever since she was a child, she'd risen from her bed and wandered down the hall, sometimes made her way outside. Once, in one of the foster homes she'd lived in during her teenage years—long after she'd given up hope to ever find a real home—the mean old lady who smelled of cigarettes and body odor had caught Catherine on the porch well past midnight and had accused her of sneaking out. Catherine couldn't remember how she'd gotten there, but she would never forget the beating she'd taken.

Chapter 14

DIGGING DEEPER

Detective Jones drove back to the clearing as the angry rain pounded the windshield. Florida rain could escalate in a hurry. The wipers swished back and forth, and he had to squint to make sure he didn't hit anything. It was a hell of a day to track down a murderer.

He parked, opened the umbrella, and ran down the overgrown path to the Carters' place. He went up to the front door this time, another rickety set of steps, and took respite from the downpour under the porch roof. He folded the umbrella, shook it dry, and rested it against the wall. A chair rocked lonesome in the wind, creaking on the forward motion.

Levi took a long time answering. Through the window, Jones saw him fiddling with the rabbit ears on the television. He was barefoot and shirtless, in cutoff jeans. Jones knocked again, thinking the kid hadn't heard.

"Levi," Amber called from somewhere unseen. "Someone's here."

Levi twisted around and saw Jones peeking through the window. He cursed, let go of the rabbit ears, and went to the door.

Running a hand through his long, shaggy hair, he said, "Had a feeling I'd see you again."

"We're investigating a murder. I'll be here every day till I have some-one in cuffs. May I invite myself in? I need to get your wife's statement, and some more from you too."

Levi shook his head. "Amber's about to pop, sir. I'd rather not—"

"I'd rather not have to take you both to the station. I have to talk to you one way or another. Why don't we get it over with?" Jones kicked the water off his boat shoes and dragged them against the doormat.

Levi was smart enough to give in. He swung the door open and yelled, "That cop's coming in, Amber! Put on something decent."

There was a scramble of footsteps running away from the tiny living room. The place was surprisingly clean, aside from a pile of dishes in the sink. Not much on the walls, simply a fading watercolor of palm trees waving in the wind. Static played on the television. The floors creaked as they walked toward the center of the main room. The faint scent of marijuana was unsuccessfully covered up by incense.

"I was trying to get some news about the storm," Levi said, "but the reception is terrible out here."

Jones was checking out the place, looking for reasons, clues, expla-nations. "You're out in the middle of nowhere, that's for sure. I'm still trying to figure out why a young couple like you would want to live in a place like this." Jones was trying to ease into the conversation. Of course he understood the desire to live out here.

Levi pointed through the window to the Gulf. "Who wouldn't want to wake up to that? It's even prettier in the rain. I told you, we're trying to stay away from her parents. I'm sure they're looking for us . . . And her daddy, he's got money. Probably has a private investigator on the hunt."

"Why don't we take a seat?" Jones suggested.

"Yeah, suit yourself." He pointed to one of the chairs facing the television, then plopped down on the couch himself. All the furniture had seen better days.

Jones crossed his arms and stared at Levi. The rain grew louder, and he had to raise his voice. "Seems to me you'd do a better job in a city somewhere, disappearing as opposed to sticking out in Paradiso. Especially on this island. The others are more than curious about you."

"Yeah, well, they need to mind their own business."

"Do you know any of 'em?"

He copied Jones, crossing his arms too. "Do we really have to do this now?"

"We do, indeed. The looks of your wife, it would be best if I get to the truth now before the baby comes. It's not safe here until I find who did it."

"The world's not a safe place, Detective." He looked right toward where Amber had disappeared, revealing some scarring under his ear—maybe a burn. Considering his young years, the man had lived a hard life.

Jones reached in his bag for the microphone and held it up for approval. Levi shrugged in defeat.

"You been in jail before?" Jones asked.

A shake of the head.

"Here's the thing, Levi: If you make it easy on me, I can be more discreet. Give me a hard time, and I'm happy to knock down your world with a bulldozer. Choice is yours."

He chewed down hard on his jaw, meeting Jones with an icy look. "We had nothing to do with it."

Jones watched everything—the way he was fidgeting, the way his eyes kept easing down. "I can be discreet, but you can bet I'm going to ask around till I have a grasp of what's going on."

Levi wanted to play ball, from the way he was shaking his head and giving up the fight. "Okay, okay. Her name's Amber Kentworth, but she's adopted. That name's as good as nothing. She doesn't have a lick of family."

"No one's coming after you?"

He shook his head, looking like a puppy who'd gotten caught chewing something it shouldn't.

"Why'd you lie to me?"

"I don't like cops. Don't like being pinned against a wall, man."

"Fair enough." Jones considered his play. It was doubtful that a man about to be a father would kill someone—unless Amber had been in danger.

"How about *your* family?"

"I'm from Rogers, Arkansas. Haven't seen my kin in years."

"You're about to raise this kid on your own, then?"

"We wouldn't be the first."

"Where'd you two get together?"

"Atlanta."

Jones kicked out a smile—a charming one too. "You see? Doesn't it feel nice to tell the truth? I know when you're lying, anyway."

"How's that?"

"Something deep within me. The truth has a way of resonating, almost like when you're tuning an instrument. The truth chimes right. I don't know much about anything, but I've always had a handle on the truth."

"Pretty good at tooting your own horn, too, I see."

Jones acknowledged the comment with a subtle smile, then paused to redirect. "You've been here about three months, right? Who have you met on the island? Who do you know?"

Levi's eyes went toward the kitchen for a second before he brought his look back toward Jones. "I've run into them all, I guess. Some of them say hi when we pass."

"Did you know Frank?"

"Who's Frank?"

"The victim. Dr. Frank Overbrook. Don't play dumb with me. Even if you didn't kill him, you know his name."

"I did not know him."

"Did Amber?"

"No." His answer came too quickly.

"I'd like to talk to her. Can you call her back out?"

He looked toward the hallway, which presumably led to a bedroom or two. "Amber!"

The floors creaked and a door swung open. She appeared a moment later. Despite her tan, her face had gone sallow. Her belly hung out of her white shirt. She wore bedroom slippers and moved slowly, making a shuffling sound as she came.

"Hello."

Jones stood. "I'm glad to see you're feeling better."

"'Feeling better' is a stretch." She rubbed her belly.

"Must be an exciting time," Jones said.

She plopped down on the couch next to Levi. Didn't say a word.

Jones returned to his own seat. "You sure you don't need to be in the hospital? Looks like you're days away."

"Maybe hours," she said, turning to Levi, resting a hand on his bare thigh.

Her husband put his hand on top of hers. "I helped my sister deliver a baby back in Virginia. It's a piece of cake. It'll slide right out."

Amber struck him hard in the chest. "Piece of cake? Why don't you try pushing this thing out? God, men are so clueless sometimes. Why do you even open your big fat mouth, Levi?"

He looked like his face had become a target, his nose a bull's-eye. "Oops," he said to Jones.

"Oh, I'm not bailing you out," Jones replied.

Levi tried to comfort her. "You know what I mean, baby."

She pushed him away. "The hell I know what you mean—*baby*." Turning to Jones, she said, "Dr. Westerling is helping. He's such a sweet man, visits every afternoon. We'll call him when the time comes."

"I don't think we need him," Levi said.

"Why don't you go make yourself useful? Go scrub a toilet or something."

"You know I was just being—"

"An asshole?"

All was not copacetic in the Carter house. Jones let it play out for a while, the two of them bickering, Levi begging for forgiveness. Finally, she relented and let him hold her hand, though she looked down at his like it was a tarantula.

Jones asked her if she was okay with him recording, then got right into it. "Your husband said yesterday that you were running from your parents. Now he's saying you were adopted and don't have anyone else out there. No kin."

She glanced at Levi, who scrambled to give an explanation. "Detective, I told you that because . . ." He sighed.

"Nope, don't do that, Levi. You were doing so good. What do you want, a treat? Let's stick with telling me exactly the truth. The nice detective was here yesterday. You get the impatient one today. Now, take a deep breath and come clean—unless you want me to think you did it. I doubt Amber did it. Aside from her physical barriers, I can tell she's a good person. Which gives me hope for you. Don't screw that up."

Levi let out a smirk. "Everybody has something to hide, Detective."

"Oh, is this where you teach me about the ways of the world? No, thank you. Look, I'm okay with what you're hiding, as long as you didn't jab Dr. Overbrook with that awl your wife keeps with her for her jewelry making. Or with whatever else it is you could have drummed up."

"I didn't kill him."

"That may be so, but I wonder if the thing you're hiding might shed some light."

"It won't, trust me."

Jones knew a brick wall when he saw one. "Trust is something you have to earn with me. Tell me where you both come from, how you met."

Amber spoke up. "I grew up in an orphanage in Georgia. When I was eighteen, I followed a friend to McLean, Virginia. She'd gotten a job in DC working as a clerk for a representative, and she let me crash with her. I started working at a diner, and one day, in comes Levi. He didn't have a beard or long hair back then, and after about five days in a row, I relented and said I'd go out with him. The next thing we know, we're getting married and . . ."

She looked at Levi quite curiously, as if asking him to bail her out. Jones spent a minute wondering if the fact that both Amber and Catherine had been orphaned was anything more than a coincidence.

"Yeah," Levi said, "we got married and decided we'd hit the road, thumb our way south to find the Gulf. That's when we found the sign."

"You mentioned the property owner's name last time. Barry Gatt. Could you share his telephone number with me?"

Levi sat up reluctantly. "Yeah, I guess I have it somewhere."

"There you go. Oh, while I'm thinking about it, did you happen to leave your house late last night?"

"Oh man, what happened?"

"Amber, did he leave last night?"

"No, sir."

"Detective, I would not leave my wife right now."

"I believe you, Levi," Jones said, though he only half believed him.

Amber winced in pain and clutched her belly.

"You okay, Mrs. Carter?"

"I should go lay down." She started to press up, and Jones went to help her. She thanked him and apologized.

"I understand. I'll talk more with Levi. If something comes to mind, please track me down. I'm trying to make this island safer for all of you."

"We appreciate that."

"You'll be a good mama," Jones said. "I can see that."

"I'm going to try."

Levi produced a piece of paper with Gatt's number. "I understand that you want to check things out, but please don't get us kicked out of here. You asked why we're here and not some apartment in a city where we can be anonymous. Because we like the water, Detective. We might not hang out with all the old folks, but this is a dream, being out here. A heck of a place to raise a kid."

There was still something missing, but Jones decided not to go hard on him. "Yeah, I agree. And I get your point, Levi. Just do me a favor and get in touch if something else comes up."

Levi followed him to the door, and Jones opened his umbrella and stepped back out into the rain.

⚊

Next, Jones thought he'd ask some questions at the general store, which he hadn't been to in a while but remembered they made a good sandwich. He slid the patrol car to a stop right outside, and a handful of locals turned their heads toward him. He offered a friendly wave as he stepped out. The rain had turned to a drizzle.

The Paradiso General Store was the kind of place that made its money from the tourists passing through. You'd think the locals would be more welcoming, considering. Stands outside the wooden building featured jewelry like what Amber was making, along with fins and masks, postcards, anything a tourist might find useful.

A bulletin board under a neon beer sign featured a messy display of advertisements stuck to it with pushpins. Boat and scuba rentals, moving companies. Restaurant menus. Inside, you could buy any groceries that you needed. The next closest place was twenty minutes toward the highway. They even had some decent produce. He wandered his way to the back, where a generous woman with curly hair spilling out of a hairnet asked, "What'll you have, honey?"

"You got some egg salad back there?"

"Best you've ever had in your life."

"That's what I'm talking about. On some rye, if you have it. Lettuce, mustard. Just hold the onions, if you will."

"Give me about five minutes."

"Thank you. Is the owner around, by the way?"

"Charlie? Yeah, he's at the register right now. You'll pay over there anyway."

On the other side of the store, Jones introduced himself to Charlie.

"I didn't do it," the man replied, holding up his hands like a victim in a robbery. He was a heck of a character—a shirt unbuttoned more than Jones's, a tan that was going to give him problems one day, and a gold tooth that shone off the fluorescents above.

"I'm not here to cause any trouble. Just looking for lunch and an answer to a quick question."

He gave a look out the big window. "You guys come in here and the locals will stay away for a week."

Charlie must have seen the patrol car pull up. "They need to lighten up a bit. I'll be quick. Give me a pack of those Marlboros while we're talking." As Charlie reached up above him, Jones said, "We had some trouble on Lollipop, as you know. One of the couples that live out there, the Carters—they say they do some business with you."

"Oh boy. I have nothing to do with all—"

"No, they seem like decent people. Just want to make sure their story checks out. I'm doing it to everybody. Levi said you sell some jewelry for them."

"That's right. Busy season right now, you know. I can't keep enough of that crap in stock." He slapped down the pack of cigarettes. "You need matches?"

Jones shook his head. "They said they came across a sign on the board offering up the place on Lollipop. Free to someone willing to watch over it."

"Could have been. I don't know. You want anything else other than the cigarettes?"

"She's making me an egg-salad sandwich. Throw in an Orange Crush too. Levi says he's been asking for a job."

"Damn near every week."

"You're not hiring?"

"Not right now. He seems okay, if he'd clean himself up. We'll see what happens."

Jones slid him a fiver. "Do you know the owner of the place they're renting, this Barry Gatt person?"

Charlie pecked some digits on the cash register and fed Jones back his change. "Can't say that I do."

"All right, thanks for your help. I'm gonna get my sandwich and get out of your hair."

"Thanks for stopping by, Detective. Hope not to see you for a while."

"If I like your sandwich, it'll be hard not to come back tomorrow."

"You call in and I'll deliver it to you, okay?"

The egg-salad sandwich was good. Once he'd polished it off, he radioed into the station and then headed back to Osprey Isle.

Miriam Arnett had taken to the bottle early today. Perhaps that was the norm. She let Jones in with a wobble. "Welcome back, Detective. Come right in." Her words melted into one another.

Their front door opened up into a giant living room with well-appointed furniture. A wealth of sunlight poured in through oversize windows and glass double doors that led to the deck. The sofa and chairs faced the water. The kitchen was to the left, all part of the main living space. A bouquet of dying flowers sat in the center of a circular breakfast table.

"Your husband around?" Jones asked, thinking that, with the booze on her breath, he better not light a cigarette too close to her mouth or he'd blow the place up.

"He can't go anywhere without me taking him, so yes."

"That's a heavy burden, I'd guess."

"You'd guess right." Between the Carters and these bozos, the case for a man to get married wasn't being presented too well.

David Arnett came screeching into the room from the back. "I thought we answered all your questions."

It was a wonder how Jones had become the enemy out here. All he wanted was to catch a bad guy. "Just trying to keep y'all safe, Mr. Arnett. May we talk?"

"Sure," Miriam said, eyeing David. He grunted disapproval but relented.

Jones sat down at the breakfast table, and Miriam did her best to be hospitable. "I'm sure you won't say no to a drink. What is it I can get you, Detective Jones?"

"I'm an orange juice guy. That, or some water. You mind if I record again?"

"That's fine. You don't ever drink?" Miriam swung wide a refrigerator spilling over with goods.

"Not on duty, ma'am."

"What's with this *ma'am* stuff?" she asked, drawing out a gallon of juice. "You sound like you're from Savannah."

"My dad was from Charleston, so you'll get a *y'all* from me from time to time, and I'd eat a ton of boiled peanuts or fried okra if you put it in front of me."

"David could learn a thing or two about being a southern gentleman from you." She drew out the last part in a perfect southern accent. "You were born in South Carolina too?"

"Sarasota, Florida. But how about I ask the questions?"

David had wheeled up to the table but was staring at the wall and doing his best to be inhospitable. "Get on with it," he said. "I've got a busy day."

"Okay. What put you in the wheelchair?"

You would have thought Jones had asked him to drop his drawers. Both Miriam and David stopped breathing. You could have heard a fly fart.

"Now, that seems invasive," Miriam said, turning a tad icier as she slid a glass of OJ in front of Jones.

"That's what they do, Miriam. They pry every last bit of information out of people. Like a citrus squeezer. You know all about those, don't you?"

"Living with you would drive anyone to the blender for another margarita."

Jones wasn't going to argue. "I have to paint the whole picture in my head. I'm sorry if you feel offended. My questions are direct and invasive and cut right to the chase. The way I see it, you're all in danger until we nab this person."

Miriam sat a little too hard on her seat. Part of her fizzy drink spilled on her lap. "We all want that." It sounded more like *Weewaahhhwanhhdaaat.*

"Dammit, woman, how many have you had today? Barely past noon and you're a wreck." David had a bite to his tone, clearly having issues he needed to work through.

Miriam fought back with "Barely past noon and you're still an imbecile. I'm still one drink away from you being tolerable."

"You're always one drink away."

"Yeah, well, whose fault is that?" She took a big gulp, as if proving her point.

David turned to Jones. "We're working on drink management in this house."

She set her glass down hard, more of it spilling out. "I bet I could manage to get one more down and still see straight. Now *that's* drink management."

David seemed to be holding back from unleashing on her and looked like he might explode.

Jones jumped in before he had another murder on his hands. "Where were you two last night?"

"Why is that?" David asked. "Was someone else murdered?"

"Because of the house invasion." Jones had all his senses firing, seeking evidence that these two knew more than they were letting on.

"What invasion?" David asked. His surprise checked out.

"Someone broke into Mrs. Overbrook's house looking for some-thing. They didn't realize Sylvie was there and knocked her over in a rush to escape."

"Is she okay?" Miriam asked, showing true concern.

"She'll be fine. Just a bump on her head."

David's eyebrows curled. "What were they looking for?"

"You can leave that to me. And we're back to . . . where were you two last night?"

David disappeared inside his head. "I was . . . we were both here." He lifted his gaze to Miriam, who jumped in.

"I was with Sylvie and Catherine for a while. Being supportive, you know." Suddenly her speech wasn't as slurred. Being afraid can do that to you.

"You took her some food, right?" David asked.

"That's right."

Jones already knew that. "What time did you leave?"

"Around nine?"

"Did you happen to see anyone else out and about? See anyone else's lights on?"

She shook her head.

"When you visit others on the island, do you go via the beach or through the clearing?"

"The beach, typically."

"David, you saw her return?"

"Naturally."

Jones let the silence take over for a while. Both Arnetts shifted in their seats.

Miriam sighed. "Look, we didn't know him and had no reason to hurt him." She was back to slurring.

"In fact, my wife was quite cordial to him the night of the party. I think you're looking in the wrong place."

Jones took a big sip of juice. "Where would you look, Mr. Arnett?"

He thought about the question while fiddling with the joystick on his chair. "My guess? It wasn't anyone who lived here. Sandy was the only one who knew him, and Sandy couldn't hurt anybody. You know, some people are born with evil in them. Sandy is not one of those men.

If you're sure it's an islander, I'd be looking at the Carters. Something doesn't sit right about them."

"What's wrong with the Carters?" Miriam asked. "I think they're perfectly nice people."

"So you know them?" Jones asked.

"Well . . . I . . . They live next door to us. Of course I've encountered them."

"Have you spent time with them?"

"Not really. Just passing by, being neighborly." She took in an abrupt breath and blasted it out with exasperation. "I don't like being questioned."

"You'll have to get used to it. I'm a curious guy." Jones raised a finger. "Before we continue, could I use your restroom?"

David looked surprised but said, "By all means." He pointed through the hallway. Jones took his time, looking around. He'd noticed video cameras outside during his visit yesterday. There was another out front, two more in the living room, hung high in the corners. What was it with these people?

Jones shut the door to the carpeted bathroom and first looked to make sure there wasn't a camera. Then he pressed his ear to the door. He heard bickering but couldn't make out the words. Before doing his business, he pulled back the shower liner. The metal rack was full of fancy shampoos and conditioners and soaps. Apparently, they didn't share the master bath. Perhaps it was set up for his handicap and she preferred the ease of this shower.

Next, he turned on the sink to mask any noise and opened up the medicine cabinet. A few perfumes occupied the top row. Below were some first aid items, including a roll of bandages and a bottle of rubbing alcohol. A bottle of Valium prescribed to Miriam stood next to a bottle of aspirin and a few packets of Pepto-Bismol. Valium and alcohol all day . . . The poor woman was killing herself.

When Jones returned to the living room and sat back down, he said, "What's with the video cameras?"

The couple looked at each other with unease. David finally spoke up. "I'm slightly paranoid since my accident. I can see everything going on in and around the house from my study."

"What's the point?"

David let out a churlish grin. "They make up for where my legs fall short."

What a strange guy, Jones thought. "What I'd like to do is back way up. To where you met, what brought you together . . . what led you to Paradiso." He eyed David respectfully. "What put you in the chair. The less I have to feel like a dentist prying it out of you, the better."

David chuckled at that, as if he'd spent his life since whatever had happened trying to be more than his chair but it was the chair they always asked about.

"We met in Coral Gables—what, almost twenty years ago?" Miriam said, the past giving her a ripe smile. If Jones looked closer, though, he thought he saw some decay in that smile of hers. "A friend of a friend and a blind date."

"She was the prettiest girl I'd ever seen."

"You didn't have any children?"

"It was never part of the plan," David said. Miriam fidgeted at that, as if it was still a sore subject.

"How about you, Miriam? Have you ever been married?"

She squirmed. "One's enough for me."

David enjoyed this apparent inside joke.

"Okay," Jones said, "you met and married. What led you here?"

"Miriam's idea. After the car crash."

She stifled a burp. "David didn't want to go back to Miami. It was too painful for him. We looked around. It was my job to find us a new place to live. I'd heard of Paradiso before, can't remember how. The listing caught my eye. A secluded place on the Gulf. Those Atlantic waters are too shark-infested for me anyway."

"I prefer the Gulf side as well," Jones agreed. "You didn't know anyone on the island before moving here?"

They both shook their heads. "No," David said. "Bought the place and then Sandy was quick to introduce himself, and we got pulled into the group."

"Was Barry Gatt living here?"

David's ears perked up like a dog's. "Barry Gatt? We haven't seen him in a couple of years. He was here at the time. Glenna was, of course, living where the Overbrooks . . . well, where Catherine lives now. Jerome and Hilda Tyner were in Sylvie's place."

That was the first Jones had heard about the Tyners. He scribbled their names down. "So Sylvie came after you."

"I'm the one who lured her onto the island," Miriam said. "We met at the hospital shortly after the crash. We'd had our accidents days apart."

Warning flags rose in Jones's mind. "That's auspicious timing. Tell me about the accident."

"We were staying on Saint Pete Beach," Miriam said, "a getaway from Miami. After dinner downtown, we ran off the Pinellas Bayway."

"What caused it?"

David faked a drink in his hand, tossing it back, then fired a finger at his wife.

"Sure, we'd had some drinks, but it was late at night. David didn't want to drive. We didn't know the area well. I lost control. I ended up with a broken arm, a few scratches, and David lost everything."

They both bored holes into the table as the memory percolated the air.

Jones asked several more questions about the accident, then: "How did you meet Sylvie?"

"She'd been in the hospital for almost two weeks when I met her. We hit it off. Misery loves company, you know."

"How'd she get here?"

"We kept in touch after we left. Spoke on the phone on occasion. I went to see her and saw how tough things were on her. A lot like how they were on David, dealing with old friends who were no longer friends."

Jones was having a hard time keeping this news at a distance. He hated thinking of Sylvie hurting so.

"And family who didn't look at them the same way," Miriam continued. "When the Tyners announced that they were selling, Sylvie was the first to come to mind. A small island like this, you want to make sure you know who's moving next door."

"Sylvie just up and moved?"

"Yeah, she didn't have much to lose at that point."

It was a silly thought, but he wished he could have been there for Sylvie. He thought he'd better go check on her, make sure everything was okay. He lobbed a few more questions to the Arnetts and then rose from his seat with his bag.

"I thank you for your time. I'm sure I'll be back. Please don't leave Paradiso."

They spoke nearly in unison. "Anytime, Detective."

Chapter 15

THE DAYS AFTER LOSING

Catherine finally had some quiet. As she sat alone in their cavernous house where Frank's ghost lingered, the last of the rain falling all around her, she wished herself away, back to a time before Frank. It wasn't right that she'd been plucked out of her trance and shown what life could be only to then have it taken away.

If only they'd never met. If only he'd found someone else to help him with his book, or if she'd rejected his abrupt proposal. If only she could return to her old life, working during the day, having her soup at night, and going to sleep without expectation of anything more exciting the following day. No, thank you, to the wild swings, the ups and downs of a spirited life. She was fine settling into the pocket of . . . what was it? Mediocrity? No. Realism? Yes, simply realism. Why paint this distorted picture of what life could be?

Beyond the blue water and the palm tree facade was the real world—where children were often discarded, where people used you for their own means.

Another thought had been working its way out: Had Miriam put something in her tea last night? How else could she have become so drowsy? The sedative Sandy had given her had to have worn off by then. She'd felt fine while she and Miriam and Sylvie sat together. Why in the world would Miriam want to break in and search through Frank's things? Besides, she was more focused on keeping a martini glass glued to her finger pads. Perhaps Sylvie had drugged her and hurt herself, making up the story about the attacker. But what could she have been looking for? She couldn't even see!

This was what Catherine did: shutting people out, not trusting them—her modus operandi.

Look at her pointing fingers when she herself could be the guilty one! If she had killed Frank, why should she be surprised? She'd had murderous thoughts before. She'd lain in bed countless times dreaming of wrapping her young fingers around the throats of the foster parents who'd treated her like a caged animal. What was perhaps most revealing was that she still was yet to shed a tear. One miserable tear. The rain had come and gone, the tears of the heavens splashing down with remorse, but not the desert that was Catherine. That was how little of a person she was, how unemotional and detached. Frank deserved someone who would at least grieve the way a spouse should grieve.

Catherine sighed as the emptiness consumed her.

The rain came to an end, leaving the leftovers dripping from the sides of the roof in a soft continuous rhythm. She lost herself in the *dut, dut, dut* of each drip.

What am I going to do? she wondered. My apartment couldn't still be available. That life feels over. This one does too. How could I possibly put together the puzzle pieces that Frank left scattered? Did he have a will? Is it right that I take his money? I should give it all to charity and go walk out into the water and disappear. That's what I want to do: be taken away by the waves.

The thought was strong enough to pull her up from the couch, as if someone had grabbed her arm and tugged. The darkness had fallen away to a lighter shade of black, and near the horizon, a patch of cerulean blue had broken through the clouds. It wasn't a hopeful sight, though. It was . . . the last of Catherine Overbrook, drifting away.

In her robe, she left the house and moved toward the water as if she were on a moving walkway like the one at O'Hare. Had it been a day with Frank, she might have delighted at the ripe smell of the beach after a rain, at the darkened sand, the seagrass glistening with rivulets of water.

The cool breeze raised goose bumps on her skin as she strolled across the sand toward the Gulf. It was in between tides, and she'd never seen such a still body of water in her life. There were no boats, only a canvas waiting for her to paint herself away. It was here, and out there, where her husband had become nothing. No matter who'd done it, he was gone. So was she.

The cool water swelled around her ankles and took her breath away. She looked left and right. The late-afternoon sun was trying to sneak through, but it was still masked by dark clouds, consumed like Catherine was consumed.

None of it matters. I once knew love and now it's gone. Now he's gone and I'm gone too.

Catherine pulled off her robe and let it fall into the water. It puddled and expanded and began to sink. She walked away from it, nude, lost, and eager to find the end. Eager for her pulse to stop, for her lungs to fill with water. For her life to expire.

She came to her waist, the chill a welcome distraction. The Gulf spooled out forever, a glassy abyss that seemed like the only answer left. She couldn't deal with life, not now that she'd seen what was possible. *No, no, no. Go to sleep, my little Catherine. Go to sleep and fall away from these feelings that feed on you.*

She went farther, the water rising over her belly button and her chest and soon her shoulders. A rising wave lifted her off her feet and she was floating.

"Take me away," she said, her lips now barely above the surface.

The seawater slipped into her mouth, and she didn't fight it. Catherine sipped the saltiness down, relaxing her throat muscles. She exhaled everything in her and fell back, her legs rising above her head.

The current swished her back and forth, and she breathed in the water like air. *Take me away, take me away from here. I don't want to live any longer.* She heard the music of a peaceful place calling her . . . singing to her. *Take me away.*

━

A few stray drops of rain fell on Sylvie's head. She could feel them through her hair, but the rain was mostly gone now. A mild warmth came from the sun. The wet sand was firm under her feet. She'd found a nice patch on the beach where there were no seashells, only sugary sand slipping in between her toes. Some days, the Gulf screamed angrily, crashing her waves onto the shore. Today, after the rain, the Gulf gave nothing more than a whisper.

Were it a normal day, this would be such a pleasant walk, a reminder of why she'd come here, a reminder of the woman she'd become.

It was all different now. Everything had changed.

Life would never be the same.

The sound of these waves and the gentle rain dancing on her roof would never lull her to sleep again. This island. Their island. Her island. No matter how things shook out, she'd never feel like this was home again.

Quentin, of all the men in the world, how was it he who had been the one to arrive on the island to investigate a murder? The only man for whom she'd ever had feelings—and yes, that was silly. They'd barely ever touched, but she would go home after school and lose herself in daydreams about him, wishing he were her age, wishing he weren't a student and she a teacher. She would touch herself and imagine that it was his hands exploring her. What it might have been like if they had a life together—if he were there waiting for her when she got home from work.

Waking up in the hospital without her vision was more terrible than a nightmare; it was a black hole of such horror that she would have far preferred death. Maybe she should have killed herself. She'd thought of it. She'd come close, too, more than once opening the hospital window that looked out over the parking lot and imagining what it might be like to disappear. One morning, she'd even climbed up onto the sill, one step away from ending it all.

She should have jumped. Then she wouldn't be in this mess now.

The sound of footsteps invaded her ears, and a chill ran through her. She put her hand on the scalpel that she always carried with her on these walks. "Is that you, Mir?"

No answer. Sylvie removed the cork from the blade and readied herself. "Mir?" She was whispering this time. Then she listened hard.

"Put the blade down," Miriam finally said.

"Why didn't you say anything?"

"I am saying something. You called me and now I'm here."

"What took you so long?"

"The detective wouldn't leave."

Sylvie took a long breath and put the cork back on the blade and stuffed it into her jacket pocket. "I'm afraid, Miriam. Everything's falling apart."

"You did the right thing, don't forget that."

"I know, it's just . . . why did this have to happen? I feel like I dragged you into—"

"What is that?" Miriam interrupted in a sharp tone.

Sylvie put her senses on high alert. "What is what?"

"Someone's out there."

"Out where?" Sylvie tried to see through her blindness, imagining her surroundings put together by the clues of sound and what she remembered of beaches before she'd lost her sight.

"In the water."

"Are they okay?"

"I don't know."

Jones pulled into Sylvie's driveway. How hard it must be to not have a car, to be so locked down by her disability. It couldn't have happened to a nicer person, losing her sight. Wasn't that the way the world worked? Jones had seen it so many times. No matter who you were, how much good you did, there was no insulation from the bad things that were always out there, hiding in the thicket, ready to strike.

Even sweet and wonderful Sylvie wasn't protected. He wished he could have been there, first to stop whatever had happened in her accident and then to help her afterward. The poor thing, so all alone, trying to find a way to see in the black. What that must be like. He closed his eyes and tried to envision being Sylvie, wishing that some form of light could come back.

It never would, though.

It *never* would.

He stepped out of the car. His shoes splashed into a puddle. Coming up the steps, he kicked off the water. He might look for lights to be on in a normal house, to wonder if a person was home. But she didn't use lights. She didn't have a car. It was as if she lived in the shadows.

There was a stillness that scared him, though. He hurried to the door and knocked. "Sylvie?" He checked the door, jangling the knob. It was locked. "Sylvie!" He peered through the window. Nothing.

Jones circled to the back. That door was locked too. Maybe she was asleep. It was always nighttime in her world. Still, something wasn't sitting right. He'd learned to follow his gut. As he was about to kick in the door, he heard something on the beach.

He looked over and saw figures out near the water. Squinting, he made out two people carrying someone, feet dragging. Holding his pistol to keep it from bouncing out of the holster, he jogged down the boardwalk and into the sand. They were about a hundred yards away, coming toward him. He ran faster, hoping to God Sylvie was okay.

To his great relief, it wasn't Sylvie being dragged. It was someone else. Wait . . . It was Sylvie and Miriam dragging a naked woman by the arms. It was . . . Catherine Overbrook, limp as a dead body.

Jones ran as fast as he could and, when he'd reached them, lifted Catherine up in his arms. "I got her. I got her."

He took her to the sand and laid her down. She was out cold, her body deadweight. Her legs folded outward, her breasts fell to the sides. She lay there naked and unashamed. Miriam and Sylvie cried to him, "Help her!"

Jones scrambled to do what he could. He checked for a pulse. Nothing. Without another thought, he began pressing her chest down, one, two, three. He felt his heart reeling in overdrive, and he worried he might break her ribs. *One, two, three.*

He tilted up her head and pressed his lips to hers, pushing in breath. *One, two, three.*

Nothing.

He went back to her chest. *One, two, three.* "Come on, Catherine." The other women remained motionless as they stood over him.

Jones went back to her lips, performing CPR. He'd never had to do it before but had been trained in the academy. *One, two, three.*

He turned to Miriam. "Call for help, dammit. Call for help!"

She took off in a sprint. Jones did another round on Catherine's chest. The water rolled up around her body. She lay flat and still.

He was about to blow more breath into her when he saw her lips shake. He moved away as salt water came rushing from her mouth. He flipped her to her side, and she heaved over and over, and her body convulsed. He patted her back, helping her reject all that water, which pooled on the sand below her head.

"She's alive!" Sylvie yelled. "Oh dear, thank God!"

Catherine finally opened her eyes, revealing dilated pupils. She tried to speak but was unable.

"You're okay," Jones said, brushing hair from her face. Then to Sylvie: "Can I have your jacket?"

She pulled it off, and he laid it over Catherine's privates as best he could. "You're okay. Let's stay here a minute. I'm going to go get you a blanket and we'll take you home."

Catherine gave enough of a nod to show she was alive and somewhat okay. She seemed to understand him, and that was a good thing.

Jones stood and took Sylvie's hand. "Stay with her. I'll be right back." He guided her down and helped her find Catherine's hand.

As Jones stood to go, he heard Sylvie comforting her. "You're alive, dear one. You're alive."

～

"What a day," Jones said to Sylvie as he opened the patrol car door. She'd slipped her sunglasses on during the drive from Catherine's house. The ambulance was still parked over there, and the medics were tending to her. Miriam, Sandy, and Glenna were there too. As Jones had been leaving, Catherine was insisting that she was fine and was refusing to go to the hospital.

Sylvie took his hand and climbed out. "What a series of days. I moved out here for some peace, and now I'm wondering if there's any place on Earth where such a thing exists."

"I don't know," he said. "Wouldn't that be nice. Big step up."

"I know." She lifted her foot and set it precisely in the center of the board.

Jones found himself once again impressed. "How . . . ?"

"I could feel you slowing. Enough people have stood where you are, stuttering at the first step. That's when I know to lift my leg."

"You're simply amazing."

She smiled a smile that stirred his soul. If anything, she'd become more beautiful in her thirties.

As they reached the top, he said, "I don't . . . I'm not exactly sure how you'd like me to help. I know you can get around on your own. Do I need to tell you as we reach the threshold? Feel free to smack my hand."

Sylvie patted his arm. "It's nice to have you leading me, even if I don't need you." She chuckled as they went into the foyer, where one of her pieces—a perfectly spun and elaborately decorated vase with glazed navy-blue handles—stood on a small turquoise table.

"I feel like you can see me even though you can't. Can you tell what I'm thinking?"

"I can hear breath. I can tell when it turns slow or if it escalates. You wouldn't believe me, but I can hear smiles too."

"What does a smile sound like?"

She spun her head up to the ceiling. "A smile sounds like a shimmer of leaves in the fall, or the lull of the waves after a rain. I can feel it too. The energy in the room vibrates differently."

Like the truth, he thought.

Stillness settled in the room.

"Ah, you see." She raised her finger. "You're smiling, aren't you?"

He'd only just let his lips curl. "I . . . I . . ."

"I remember your smile as if it were yesterday. May I feel it?"

He stepped closer to her and took her hand and guided it to his face. He shivered as her fingers glided from cheek to cheek and then to his lips as they turned even wider. "It feels like I remember it looking, mustache excluded. I imagine you've seasoned wonderfully."

"Not as well as you."

She drew back her hand.

Just as quickly, the moment washed away. A wave that comes in always goes back out.

Jones shook it off. "Okay, Miss Nye, could we take some time to talk further?"

She directed her head at him. "Back to business, are we?"

"Every minute wasted makes my case harder to solve."

"Is that all this is to you—a case?"

"None of them are just cases."

"What are they, then?"

"They're everything. They're why I get out of bed."

"To solve murders?"

"Did you feel me nodding?"

181

"Not necessarily . . . but I could feel your answer."

Jones turned to the rest of the house. "Shall we sit down?"

She stuck out her arm with a cunning morsel of a smile. "You lead the way."

They sat at the same table as they had when he'd first talked to her. An apple and a tangerine decayed in the fruit bowl. The murder had stripped many of the pleasantries from the island, like fresh flowers and fruit.

"Do you mind if I record?"

"Go right ahead. Do you think I killed Frank?"

"I don't know who killed Frank." He could see his reflection in her lenses.

"You must have an idea. Isn't that what you do? Build hypotheses . . . ?"

"I try not to jump to conclusions."

"You're putting together a puzzle. At some point, you start to see the larger picture. Are you there yet?"

Sylvie was right: it was a puzzle, and he took a moment to imagine the pieces coming together. "No, I don't see the larger picture yet, but I'm getting there."

"You're good at your job, aren't you?"

He drummed the table with his fingers. "That's why I'd like to focus on you. I don't think you're guilty, but I think there's a chance you know something that might help me."

"I think you work too much."

"Miss Nye, please. A man was murdered in cold blood. You were attacked. The killer is likely still on the island. I want to put them in jail."

"Or all won't be right in the world?"

"Tell me again. What happened today? Why were the three of you on the beach?"

Her smile faded. "I was walking the beach and ran into Miriam. We were talking, and all of a sudden, Miriam saw Catherine out in the water."

Jones stopped himself before asking if Catherine was swimming . . . or drowning. "And . . . ?"

"Miriam ran out to save her. She called to me, and I raced into the water, following her voice."

"What were you and Miriam talking about?"

Sylvie could have flinched, but he couldn't tell from behind the glasses.

"Would you please remove the glasses?"

"You think I'm lying to you? These aren't poker glasses, Quentin."

"Miss Nye, I don't take sides in a murder investigation. I simply look for the truth. Please don't be offended, but I'd like you to remove your glasses."

She did so. "Very well, then."

"Thank you." He stared into the whites of her eyes, the flashes of blue like sky breaking free of clouds.

"You're assuming whoever attacked me was the killer. Doesn't that take me off the hook?"

Jones had seen people injure themselves in an attempt to throw off an investigation, so the answer was an unequivocal no. But he decided he'd keep his cards close to his chest and ignored her question.

"Let's go back to you and Miriam and your conversation."

Sylvie shook her head with exasperation. "Yes, let's forge ahead. Miriam said you'd just left. We talked about who the murderer might be and—"

"What was the consensus?"

Sylvie scratched her hand. "I don't like to draw conclusions either. I'd hate to put the wrong person behind bars." Jones waited her out until she continued. "I don't like David Arnett. He's a bad man. If bad men are the guilty ones, then perhaps he did it. He might be disabled like me, but he's crafty and cunning too. Perhaps he paid someone to do it."

Jones noted the idea. "Why would he want Frank Overbrook dead?"

"That *is* the question, isn't it? Perhaps he didn't like how Frank was speaking with Miriam at the party? He's a jealous son of a . . . Excuse me. I don't curse. Or he had wanted to buy their house himself? I don't know."

"Who does Miriam think did it?"

"She'd just mentioned that Glenna seemed different that last few days when she saw Catherine."

Glenna . . . Jones had more questions for her too.

"Any idea why Catherine was in the water?" Jones asked.

"We both know the answer to that, don't we?"

Sylvie made a good point; he changed course without acknowledging the comment. "Let's leave today alone and go back a ways. Forgive the intrusion, as I imagine it's sensitive, but could you talk more about the accident that left you . . . ?"

"Yes?"

"You know . . . um . . ."

"It's nothing to be afraid of. Say it, Quentin."

"Blind?"

"There you go—but what does my accident have to do with anything?"

He had this sense of wanting to tiptoe on glass but being unsure how. "I have no idea. I'm asking everyone about their past. I was just at David's, learning about his accident. Miriam mentioned yours was about the same time. It seems relevant to know what brought you here."

"Scallop diving. Did you ever meet Mr. Turner, the history teacher? Or did he come after you left?"

Jones saw a quick flash of himself in high school. He scrolled through his former teachers as if they were mug shots. "No, I didn't have Mr. Turner."

"He was a nice man, and we became friendly. Platonic, though. I think he might have been gay. Though I have aged and lost my eyes, there was a time when I was beautiful. I do remember looking in the mirror. A few men had validated that. Not Corbett Turner, though. I could have stripped on that boat and he might not have noticed."

Jones sat back and crossed one leg over the other.

Sylvie kept going. "Corbett liked to dive for scallops on Crystal River, and he asked me to join. I was single and always looking to have fun. We brought his boat up on a trailer and put it on the water near Jay's Pass. We found a few scallops and were taking a break, drinking Mountain Dews and munching on chips. It was a gorgeous day, really. So nice to get away from what was going on in the world. Several of our former students had recently died in Nam. Others were promising to enlist right after graduation."

She paused to take a long breath. "I remember thinking that everything was going to be okay, despite all the turmoil of the war. Then a boat comes out of nowhere, taking the bend really fast. They were students from Florida State, all drunk and loud, louder than the motor. It all happened so fast; they crashed into us. The driver never saw us."

Jones felt sick.

"Everyone was knocked into the water. I hit the dead tree trunk that we were tied to, a fact I learned later in the hospital. Corbett swam over and pulled me out of the water, then carried me to the boat landing. I was the only one seriously hurt and didn't wake up for two days. When I did . . . voilà . . . I learned I had seen my last sunrise."

Her story hurt far more than stories usually did, and Jones had heard some tough ones. "I'm so sorry."

She slowly inclined her shoulders. "We're all sorry, all the time. What do you do? Statistically speaking, people are bound to go blind. Just like the drafted men on their way to Vietnam, my number was drawn."

"You impress me, the way you've climbed out of it."

"I can't quite shake the cynicism, but I do think I've recovered my attitude well enough."

A knife jabbed into Jones's heart and twisted. "You inspire me."

"I have the people here to thank. Miriam. Sandy and Mary Elizabeth. Glenna. They were so good to me."

Though he'd already heard it once, he asked, "How did you end up here?"

She patted the table as if it were a dog. "Miriam had me over for the weekend and casually mentioned that there was a house for sale. The Tyners' place. I had money. The one thing I got out of the whole mess was money. The driver of the boat went to prison, and my parents sued his family . . . and won."

Sylvie retracted her hand back to her lap. "I had the time of my life that first weekend on the island. Miriam was the *only* person in the world who didn't pity me . . . or at least make me feel less than. She promised me that she'd help me get on my feet."

"Why would she do all that for you?"

"Because she's a good person. They're out there, you know. Good people. You're one of them too. Some folks do good for goodness' sake. Miriam is one of those. To this day, she takes me to Naples for clothes—she's my stylist. Even drives me to the grocery store every week. She won't let me pay her for her troubles. She's a friend like that. I try to be a friend back when I can, always being there for her. Listening, at least. I still have my ears." She pinched and wiggled both of her lobes.

"I'm glad you have someone like that, Miss Nye."

"Will you *please* stop with the 'Miss Nye'? I'm five years older than you, Quentin. You're treating me like an old lady."

"Okay, Sylvie. I will try. It's best when I distance myself from the . . ." He stopped himself.

"From the suspects?"

"You're not a suspect."

"Of course I am. We all are."

Jones ran through a few more questions, then clicked off the tape. "I need to go into the station. If you need me, call and they'll track me down. Lock your doors tonight. I'll have an officer driving around. Please, if you think of something, tell me."

Sylvie leaned in, resting her elbows on the table. "Have a nice rest of your day, Quentin. I hope to see you again soon."

There was longing in her voice, and it jumped right into Quentin's bones. A wave of what-could-have-been ran through him. Had he had the nerve to talk with her after he'd graduated, to tell her how he felt, she never would have been scalloping with Corbett Turner.

Chapter 16

Confessions of Affection

February 23, 1970
Day 3

Jones only caught two hours of sleep before his worry over Catherine pulled him out of bed. Getting there shortly after midnight, he checked in with the night officer who'd been sent to patrol the island. Though he'd been walking around most of the night, the guy hadn't seen a thing. Jones wished he could have a whole team here, but the department was short-staffed. It would have to be one lone rookie making sure there were no more house invasions.

The first stop was Catherine's house. Her lights were off, but he meandered around anyway, eventually deciding he better let her get some sleep after the day she'd had. He walked the entirety of the island before returning to the clearing, where he climbed back into his vehicle. Next, he drove down Sylvie's driveway and parked as the house came into view. It was a good place to get some work done.

Lighting up a smoke, he pressed play on his recorder and started through the stack of files on the shotgun seat. A clean and chilly breeze pushed through the open windows, blowing back the papers. He pulled on his Marlboro, his mind ablaze. At the station earlier, he'd called the medical examiner with some follow-up questions and to get a couple of recommended funeral parlors for Catherine. Then he'd tried to call Barry Gatt, the owner of the house where the Carters were staying. Turned out he was a PI up in Sarasota. His secretary, Pam, had promised he'd call back when he was free. Apparently, that would be tomorrow. Jones had also collected the requested reports for each of the islanders. There wasn't much to work with. Not one of them had ever been arrested.

He opened up the file with Frank's information. His office had reached out to the Burbank Police Department and taken pertinent notes. Frank had been married before, to a Zelda Smith in 1945, the same year Jones's father had been shot down over France. Their relationship had ended in divorce in July of 1949. No reason stated. He'd bought a house in '48 and the building for his practice in '53, both of which he'd sold recently.

"Why would you come down here, Franky?" Jones asked out loud. "I know it's cold up there. Was that it? You got worn out on the winters? Or was it really all for your new bride? Closing down a practice after twenty-five years . . . That's a big decision. Did something run you out of town?"

Jones jabbed the butt of the cigarette into the ashtray and flipped back to the medical examiner's report. Who on the island was skilled enough to have found his carotid artery in the dark? It hadn't been a surprise attack if he'd been lying on the ground. That person would have had to have been strong enough to pull him out into the water, too, which perhaps anyone could do with the right amount of adrenaline running through them. Could one of the women on the island do that? Glenna could. She was still such a mystery to him.

Sometime after three, Jones decided he'd take another walk around. He started with Sylvie's house, pausing on occasion to listen. There was nothing but crickets sawing out a song and the lullaby of gentle waves washing over the sand. He went back to the beach, close to where they'd found Frank's body. The water was up high.

He set loose his imagination. Had Frank gone out to the beach after Catherine had passed out? Perhaps he'd seen something he shouldn't have. Or had someone been waiting for him specifically? Were they hoping for cash? Levi Carter seemed like the kind of guy who could use some extra dough. There was cash in Frank's wallet, though. Maybe something went wrong. Maybe Frank fought back.

Had the killer been after something else? He or she had returned the next night to search Frank's office. Levi Carter again looked like the kind of guy who would go after a doctor's drugs. He was focused on Amber having a baby. Had Levi tried to force him to help with the baby? Nah, that didn't check.

Sylvie had admitted to going for a walk. Why would she lie about it if she'd heard something? Jones hated to jump to conclusions, but imagining Sylvie attacking the newcomer was pretty difficult. It was hard for a woman to kill a man with a sharp object, let alone a woman who couldn't see.

Don't count her out, a voice said to Jones, reminding him that truly anything was possible. He'd learned that the hard way.

As Jones moved farther north, Sandy's house came into view. He and Glenna were the two wild cards, the two who had interacted with Dr. Overbrook before he'd arrived on the island. No one was as good of a person as Sandy appeared. No one was that perfect. In a lot of ways, the doctor was the leading suspect. He'd known Frank for thirty years. They may not have kept in touch, but he was the only one who could have a strong reason to kill him. They'd possibly argued that night in Sandy's house; then Sandy had gone down to find Frank, maybe stop him on his way home.

Then it would be Sandy who had broken into Frank's last night to retrieve any paperwork that might suggest a row between them. As kind as he seemed, he wouldn't have hesitated to push Sylvie to the ground if it was his only way to escape undiscovered.

A light popped on in Sandy's house. The good doctor was having trouble sleeping. Had a bout of guilt set in?

Jones crossed the dunes and worked his way toward the house, moving slowly. Through a westerly facing window, he could see Sandy, dressed in boxers and a white T-shirt, making his bed.

"Up for the day already?" Jones said to himself.

The guy slept less than he did. Or was Sandy going to try to break back into Catherine's house? Jones could almost taste the victory of putting the man behind bars. All it took was hanging around the suspects long enough; he'd eventually hit pay dirt.

Sudden movement from farther around the house caused him to drop. Someone else was out there. Jones lowered to his stomach in the tall dune grass. A snake or maybe an iguana moved away from him. Hoping it wasn't a rattler, he crawled toward the disturbance.

"What do we have here?" Jones whispered, watching a figure cross the yard to the main house. It was Glenna. Jones looked for a weapon, but the lack of visibility denied him access.

She's going to kill him. He must know something about the murder. He knows that she's guilty. Or is it something deeper? Is she trying to take over the medical practice, killing all the doctors on the island? Jones cracked a grin, thinking he should write fiction. It couldn't be that hard.

He moved closer, ready to race that way if necessary. But he needed to see how events played out. The night was so quiet, the Gulf so still after the rain, that every movement seemed to echo out over the island. She had a shuffle to the rhythm of her walking, and Jones moved when she moved, creeping closer to her intended target of the front porch.

As she climbed the steps, the moonlight caught her. Her hands were empty. Perhaps she was hiding a weapon underneath her robe. She tapped on the door lightly, removed the belt from her robe, and let it fall open.

Jones's jaw hit the sand.

A second later, Sandy was standing there with a face that looked like that of a kid stumbling out of Willy Wonka's place with a chocolate high.

~

"Is that you, Mary Liz?" Sandy took in the half-naked woman standing at his door, and his loins stirred as he gave way to his fantasy.

"It is, my love," she said.

His wife had returned to him—or was the closest he'd ever get to again. He reached out his hand and guided Mary Elizabeth inside. There was a part of him that knew it was only Glenna, but he shut that part out, almost pushing it down like a jack-in-the-box who'd escaped prematurely. For now, his wife was back in his life, and that was all that mattered.

Sandy pecked her lips, and she pulled him in closer, pressing her body against him, absorbing him. "Oh, Sandy, how I've missed you."

He nearly broke into a cry. "Oh, me too, my love."

In the living room, she slipped out of her robe, and it drifted down to the floor like a kite falling from the sky. As it settled at his feet, Sandy raised his eyes inches at a time. He poked out of his boxers, causing him embarrassment. This type of fantasy wasn't something he'd done in the past.

Only in the last few months had they let something happen between them. Had it been her idea or his? Perhaps it was more mutual, that first time being in the office when she had dropped a folder and they'd both bent down in a synchronized fashion to retrieve it. When their eyes met, Sandy had recognized a longing in her that he'd had himself. Not for Glenna, but for his wife, who was long gone. Perhaps Glenna had other motives. David Arnett had insisted Glenna had a tremendous crush on Sandy, despite Sandy brushing it away.

Those doe eyes had filled with lust that day, and their lips had gone to one another for a million reasons. Once they'd touched, it had become so easy.

Even now, after breaking the initial barrier of leaping into role play, it was like cooking a recipe one knows by heart. A few days after their first touch, he'd accidentally called her Mary Elizabeth. "Mary Liz, we're out of gauze, could you find some in the main closet?" Seconds later, he'd caught what he'd said. "Forgive me, I didn't . . ."

She'd approached him and put a finger to his lips. "You can call me Mary Elizabeth."

Like now, she'd lowered her hands below his waist and taken him in her warm fingers. Sandy trembled at her touch. With the lights on, she was no beauty, but she could set him on fire in the dark.

He relaxed as she led him deeper into this new fantasy, saying, "My dear husband. I never left. And, oh my, you're as big as ever down here."

As she touched him, the talons of grief that typically clawed at him lost their sharp edge. They moved to the bedroom, and he guided her onto the side where Mary Elizabeth once slept. The broken piece of him became restored, and he made love to her like when they'd first met in the thirties, he a young and strapping doctor and she an intellectual unsuited for her hometown of Beaufort, when they were young and healthy and had no idea that cancer would one day take them both.

Only after they lay together in the postcoital aftermath did Sandy's eyes leak a few tears.

Glenna turned over to him and set her hand on his waist and kissed his cheeks. "I told her I would protect you. That I would keep you from being alone. Rest, my love. I will always be here for you."

Sandy smiled through the tears. "You're a special woman, Glenna . . . the reason I can still get up in the morning."

She touched his chest, dragging her fingers through the pelt of hair that had turned gray years ago. "You are the bright light of this island, and such an inspiration to us all. We, and I, would do anything for you." Her concern showed itself in the wrinkles of her brow. "I know you're tired of hearing it, but Mary Elizabeth would want you to start treatment. With your energy and positivity, you can make it through."

Sandy gave a crooked smile, then frowned. "We'll see, Glenna." He took her hand. "We'll see."

Glenna pulled away and sat up on the other side of the bed, just as Mary Elizabeth might. It seemed his use of her real name had awakened the dragon of her guilt. Standing abruptly, she hurried across the room in her nakedness.

"Glenna . . . ," he whispered.

She stopped but did not turn back.

"You're a treasure. Thank you."

"Good night, Doctor."

Two minutes after Glenna entered the door to give the doctor a late Valentine's Day present, Jones decided he needn't intervene in fear of the doctor's life—as long as his fragile heart could take what she seemed intent on delivering. A twist he'd not been prepared for had taken place instead. Glenna and Sandy were sleeping together, and before they'd closed the door, he'd heard him call her *Mary Elizabeth*.

Jones had crept back out to the beach and sat on a washed-up log, which was where he was now, ruminating over what this new information meant. Out on the horizon, a tanker ship glided by.

Had Frank discovered what they were doing? It was possible. If so, what a thing to hide. Sandy was the pillar of the community, the keystone. No one could have imagined that he was sleeping with Glenna, let alone role-playing with her. Had he been so ashamed that he'd extinguished Frank before he could tell anyone else? On that note, what if Frank had told someone? Did Catherine know?

Maybe Glenna was the one who didn't want things coming out. There was something so incredibly strange about her. Her subservient nature to the doctor now had taken on new meaning. What else would she do for him? Would she kill for him? Judging by what Jones had seen, she'd probably lie for him. Maybe even cover up murder.

Or maybe she'd killed Frank because she was demanding she get her house back. Sandy had forced her to sell, and she'd regretted it afterward, that house being the last one in her family's name. She *had* been in the water when Sylvie discovered the body.

More than one person on this island was burying the truth, and if he kept asking questions, kept hanging around, somebody would make a mistake.

He checked his watch. It was almost 4:00 a.m. now. The sun wasn't far from popping up its yellow head. He better get some sleep. Returning to his patrol car halfway down Sylvie's driveway, Jones lowered the seat back and lit a cigarette, enjoying the sweet tobacco as it filled his lungs. Through the windshield, the stars danced and spun in the black sky.

The first thing he wanted to do once morning came was go see Barry Gatt, who wasn't returning his calls. That didn't feel right. Why in the world would you let two drifters stay at your beach house for free? With that real estate, there had to be a boatload of midwesterners who'd pay a fortune to escape the winters up there. There was something as fishy as three-day-old mackerel going on there.

Thinking bigger picture, how did it all piece together, the thing with Sandy and Glenna and how Levi seemed to be holding back?

"It's a little early, isn't it?" a voice asked, someone coming his way.

Jones was so lost in his thoughts that he dropped his cigarette just as he saw that it was Sylvie. Before he could snatch it, it tumbled in between the seat and the center console. He cursed as he squeezed his hand into the tight space, trying to nab it. The smell of burned carpet rose up into the air.

Finally locating the cigarette, he stubbed it out in the ashtray and turned to Sylvie. "You scared the heck out of me."

She was wearing her dark glasses and held her cane in her right hand. "You dropped your cigarette. Is that the smell? Maybe a sign you should stop that nasty habit."

"I read the other day that it was good for you. Almost like a daily vitamin. Anyway, what are you doing out here this time of night?"

She shook her head at his bad humor. "It's not easy to sleep with a killer walking around."

He looked down the driveway. One couldn't see his car from the house—not that it mattered in her case. "How'd you know I was out here?"

"The cigarette. Your smoke."

"You'd make a hard woman to stake out."

"It was either you or the killer. I hoped it would be you."

"What would you have done if it was the killer?"

"I wouldn't have seen him coming."

Jones looked at her, trying to interpret her meaning. A wonderful smile curled on her face, bringing one out of Jones too.

"You didn't just say that."

She flashed a one-sided smile. "If I can't make fun of myself, what would I do?"

"You're one of a kind, Sylvie Nye."

"Glad to hear we're off the 'Miss Nye' train." She rested a hand on the car door. "Why don't you come in for some breakfast? It's about that time."

Her invitation brought a certain intimacy for which he wasn't prepared. "I . . . I don't . . ."

"You have to eat, you know. I'm sure you have some more questions for me. Make sure I'm not the killer and all. Now, take me back home. I'm not sure I can find my way."

"Somehow I doubt that."

She tapped her cane on the ground. "You're still wondering if I'm faking it?"

"You'll have to forgive me. Skepticism comes with the job."

"That sure makes for a lonely life." She took his hand this time, her warm fingers slipping into his. "Take me home, Detective."

Every part of him knew it was a bad idea. It didn't feel professional, how and what he was thinking. And yet the strongest parts of him insisted on going with her.

Once inside, she hung her cane on the coatrack. "I have eggs and bread. Why don't you make us scrambled eggs and toast?"

"I'd be happy to."

In the kitchen, he found her refrigerator surprisingly organized. She bounced up on the counter. "Mixing bowls are two cabinets right of the sink. You'll find the whisk in the first drawer left of the fridge."

As he established his bearings and collected ingredients, she said, "I get the sense that all you think about is work."

"There's some truth to that."

"Why? What went wrong that you've become so focused on catching bad people?"

He opened up a half-full container of brown eggs. "I just think it's what I'm good at. There's a sense of urgency when a case is open. It has an addictive quality to it."

"What happens when there are no killers out there, when your chalkboard is empty? I'm guessing you have a chalkboard somewhere. Some kind of command center?"

He cracked the first egg into the bowl. "I have a wall in my office with open cases."

"Am I on your wall?"

"You are."

"What picture is it?"

"One that Challa took the day we arrived on the scene."

"Oh, I must look a hideous wreck. I'd barely slept."

Jones turned his head to that. She hadn't mentioned not sleeping. "You don't sleep well?"

She forced a smile. "Not always."

He dropped another cracked egg into the bowl, the yolks floating like dead bodies in the white. "To what do you attribute that?"

"You have a masterful way of avoiding questions about you, Quentin."

"I've been told that." In fact, Angie—the woman he'd last dated—had told him that he ran from question marks.

He finished cracking the eggs, poured in some milk, and whisked it all together. What was on her mind right now?

As he moved to the stove, she said, "Insomnia is quite common with blind people. I still have headaches. Still think about my accident. It makes me sad that I won't see what my family looks like again. I won't see another sun set over the Gulf. Never once another handsome man. The things we take for granted."

He glanced over at her. She looked childlike up there on the counter, with her hands on her thighs, her tanned legs poking out of her dress, her bare feet resting against the cabinet door below. "I can't imagine, Sylvie. You asked what I do when there are no killers out there. You wanna know something I've never told anyone? I don't know what to do with myself. I don't want someone to die, but I stand by waiting, you know."

"Because you've found what you're supposed to do."

"Yeah, maybe."

"That doesn't mean you should let other parts of your life die. How is it that you're not married? You were such a charismatic young man. I wouldn't have guessed you'd turn out to be a detective at all. Maybe a salesman."

Jones tested the level of heat in the pan over the fire. "A salesman? I think I had you fooled."

"Isn't that what salesmen do?"

"Some of them, yes. My uncle's a cop back in Sarasota and introduced me to his world as a teenager. Something about chasing bad guys played well for me."

"You never told me that."

I didn't tell you a lot of things, he thought. "I was set on the police academy by my senior year."

Their shared memories distilled into the room a quiet void, the edges of which were sharp. Jones had always wondered if there was something between them then. Like her, though, he'd known it wasn't right, and so he'd avoided entertaining those alluring thoughts.

As if she'd been swimming through the neural passageways of his mind, she said, "I wonder what would've happened had you been older.

If you'd been another teacher or . . . or someone else in my life. Would you have asked me out?"

Jones poured the eggs into the pan and dropped two slices of bread into the toaster. He was really just delaying his answer. It was a slippery slope, opening up to her so.

"Let me say this," he said. "I thought about you long afterward and wondered the same thing. What could have happened between us? *If* you'd been interested."

A smile stretched on her face. "Really? Then who was Brooke? Who were those poems about? There wasn't a Brooke in the whole school. I thought you might be dating another older woman. The poems . . . they were so rich and artistic. Sensual. I'm going to blush telling you, but I imagined you were a wonderful lover, the way your hands worked the clay and the way you understood your feelings."

He folded the eggs over and turned down the flame. "Now *I'm* the one who's going to blush."

A complicated laugh escaped her. "Quentin Jones. It's fun to imagine the different lives we could have had. I don't know what I'd be doing if I could still see. Everything changed that day. Perhaps I'd still be teaching in Sarasota. It was a fine life, though lonely. The men were boring to me, all the Ohioans and Michiganders and New Englanders who came down for the season and escaped before it was hot."

"My mother married one of those. A guy from Cleveland."

"She did?"

"Shortly after I got out of the academy. I think she realized she was done with me and wanted someone in her life. They race out of Florida before Easter every year."

"Wait, didn't your family own a motel?"

The eggs were almost done. The toast had popped up and was waiting for him. "No longer. She sold it when she left."

"Things change, don't they?"

"That they do." He cut off the burner and looked over at Sylvie on the counter. Her head was twisted his way. She'd removed her glasses.

He could have kissed her right then and there. What was it that mesmerized him so? She'd always been so easy to talk to and had always been so curious.

He prepped their plates, shaking some salt and pepper over the eggs. "After all this is over, I'd like to see you again. Maybe we could have a drink?"

"Detective Jones, are you asking me out?"

"I . . . I don't know what I'm doing. I do like talking with you. Breakfast is served; shall we take this to the table?"

"Saved by the eggs." She hopped down. "When all this is over, a drink would be nice."

"For the record," he said, "I should come with a warning label."

She found her way to her seat without any difficulty. "Shouldn't we all, Quentin. Shouldn't we all."

Chapter 17

CAGED BIRDIES

It was barely 7:00 a.m. when Jones pulled up to Catherine's house. She could still be sleeping, but he was willing to wake her. The birds were chirping like they'd had too much coffee. An iguana slid into the brush, leaving a trail in the sand. Up on the porch, Jones knocked and listened for movement. The rising sun warmed his back and shot a splinter of light through the window and into the foyer.

After a few more knocks, he called out, "Mrs. Overbrook, it's Detective Jones. I'll knock down the door if I have to."

"I'm fine," came her voice from inside.

"I'd like a word."

"Not now."

Jones dropped his head. These people were making his investigation unnecessarily difficult. "When?"

"This afternoon. Can you please come back?"

"Okay. Are you feeling better?"

"Somewhat."

"Good. I have a list of funeral parlors the medical examiner recommended. I'll slide it under the door. I'll be back in a few hours."

Next, he swung down Sandy's driveway. The doctor came out dressed for work with a big smile on his face. Jones might have thought he was just a happy guy all around—but there was more to it than that, wasn't there?

"Good mornin' there, Detective. Tell me you've come with good news." The jolly guy was speaking like he was about to ask what Jones wanted from the North Pole. Either his sickness came in waves, or he had an extraordinary ability to be cheery despite the symptoms.

Or he wasn't sick at all.

"Oh, I wish I could," Jones said, noticing a pair of wooden pelicans staring down at him from the railing.

Sandy leaned against the railing at the top of the stairs. "Any good leads?"

"A few things are coming to light." Like your secret affair with your nurse. Jones didn't say that, though. "I was hoping to speak to Glenna this morning. Thought I'd sneak over before you open your practice. I know it's distracting to have me over there."

"That's kind of you. I'm sure she's around." He nodded toward the villa, which stood at the end of a short sandy path bordered by tall grass.

Deliberately leaving his recording device in the car to appear more friendly, Jones headed that way, feeling Sandy watching him. What else was the man hiding? Best way to know had to be through Glenna herself.

On the small veranda, two chairs faced the Gulf. The water looked like one big sapphire out there, so glassy that you could skate on it.

Glenna came to the door in sweats. She looked as cheery as Sandy, though perhaps a shade skeptical as well. Some strange games these two were playing.

"Yes, Detective?"

"Good morning, Miss Greely. I was hoping you had a few moments before you headed into work. May I come inside?"

She glanced back. "I'd rather you not, if it's all the same. Why don't we sit outside?"

Jones peered past her shoulder. "I'm sorry. Is there someone in there? I didn't mean to interrupt."

"No, no one is here. You know what, just come in." She backed away as he entered.

It wasn't much more than an efficiency apartment inside. A tiny kitchen with a two-burner stove and enough counter space to fit a shoebox-size cutting board. Pictures of her mom and dad on the fridge. In the living room, a pair of wicker chairs and a sofa rested on an orange shag rug. A wooden desk pushed into the corner hosted an antique globe and several towering stacks of paperback books and magazines. There was a faint musty scent—the downside of living so close to the water.

"Nice place you have," Jones said as they sat in the wicker chairs. "I bet you never get tired of this." Maya Angelou's *I Know Why the Caged Bird Sings* rested on the table beside him. A bookmark with tassels poked out of the top.

"I sometimes forget how lucky I am," she said. "Forty-eight years on this island, things lose their sheen."

"I can understand that. You've never left?"

"Never left."

Other than their voices, it was dead quiet in there. "As good as this is, I can't blame you for wanting to get out of here, then. Where will you go when you do?"

She glanced back at the globe. "I've always had the pyramids on my mind."

"The pyramids? In Egypt? You're full of surprises."

"There are times when I feel like I missed my youth, taking care of my parents. A friend went to see the pyramids during high school, and it stuck with me. I cut out a picture from *National Geographic* and kept it on my wall."

"This is a small place to grow up, huh?"

"Osprey or Paradiso? They both are. But maybe I'll be disappointed when I leave. Everyone who comes here tells me it's the greatest place on Earth."

"They're not too far off," Jones said with conviction. He waited a moment and then jumped right in, just to see how she'd take a blindsiding question. "How long have you been sleeping with Dr. Westerling?"

There had never been a head that swiveled so quickly in history. Had she been swinging at a golf ball, she would have knocked it halfway to Cancún.

"I don't know what you're talking about." A venomous look zapped any kindness she might have been showing.

Jones tapped his fingers on his lap. "I'm not here to pass judgment. You two are adults. I imagine the secret's not out, and I'm not looking to expose you. That's not what I do. What I'm looking for—"

"I told you, I don't know what you're—"

"Here's the thing, Miss Greely. My job is to take every lie and break it down to the truth. Eventually, a murderer appears. If you're straight with me, and if you didn't kill Dr. Overbrook, then you'll come out of this okay. In a way, it's always bad luck for those in the circle of a murder victim. No one comes out with their secrets intact. Like I said, though, I'm not in the gossip business, and I'm not a judge."

Defeat painted her face. "Are you going to tell the doctor that you know?"

"I'm not sure yet."

Her bottom lip quivered. She looked like she might make a run for it.

"You didn't kill Dr. Overbrook, did you?" Jones asked.

She shook her head, now terrified and fidgety.

"Do you know who did?"

Another shake of the head, this time slower and less convincing.

"I wonder if Dr. Westerling did it. Would he tell you? Seeing your . . . how do I say . . . closeness? You might consider helping him get away with it, wouldn't you?"

Her fangs nearly showed. "I don't like the way you're speaking to me."

Jones raised his hands. "I don't mean to scare you. What I know, Miss Greely, is that the murderer is likely still on this island, and someone else could die if I don't get to the truth. That means I'm no longer playing nice. You understand?"

"I didn't do it, and Doctor didn't do it. That's all I know."

Jones pressed harder. "So you were with him the night of the murder?"

She nodded, avoiding eye contact.

"When did this all start?"

"A few months ago. I was trying to be a good friend, to both of them. He's dying and lonely, and I wanted to be there for him. How do you know, anyway? Who told you?"

Jones ignored her question. A magician doesn't give up his secrets. "Last time we spoke, you said you were under the impression that someone else knew Dr. Overbrook. I'd like to revisit that topic."

She tilted her head to the right. Her breathing went shallow. "I don't remember saying that."

Was she really going to make this more difficult than necessary? Despite his lack of sleep and patience, he dug deep. "Fair enough. Let's start from scratch: Who else knew Dr. Overbrook? Even a guess."

She spun her head up and around, like she was prepping for a swim. "I . . . I don't know. David and Miriam seemed strange around him. That's probably who I was referring to. But David can be strange around anyone."

"When you say 'strange,' what do you mean?"

"David kept eyeing Dr. Overbrook, almost like the alpha would when a new dog comes to town. He was being protective of Miriam. He doesn't like men talking to her. He's worried she's going to leave him. She *should* leave him, by God."

"Why doesn't she?"

"Because she thinks she's to blame. Told me once that she'll never leave him." Glenna swatted at a fly with impressive force. Nonetheless, she missed by a mile.

"It would be an impressive feat for him to make his way to the Overbrooks' place and kill Frank, wouldn't it? Considering his disability, of course. It's not like his chair can skate across the sand."

"I don't know about 'skate,' but I've seen him on the beach in his chair."

Jones wasn't surprised. "Why would he do it, though?"

"Maybe Dr. Overbrook made a comment about Miriam. Or made a pass at her. I'm telling you, David doesn't like that sort of thing."

"Has he exhibited any tendencies toward violence?"

She closed down, returning to the devoted employee who reports directly to her doctor. "I'm not at liberty to talk about our patients."

Here we go, more walls rising. "That excuse takes you off the hook from anything, doesn't it? Like diplomatic immunity. Isn't everyone on the island your patient?"

"I'm not at lib—"

"You're not really doing this, are you? I can get judges involved, subpoena the records."

"No, you cannot."

Ah, she'd caught him there. He felt liked Rod Laver had knocked a tennis ball right by him, delivering a spectacular ace. Jones tried a few other angles, but she'd turned to stone.

About twenty minutes later, he stood and thanked her. "You think of anything else, you let me know, okay? A lot of you seem to be holding back, but like I said, I'm trying to make sure everyone is safe."

"We appreciate that, Detective. I wish I could be of more help."

Do you now, Miss Greely? he thought. I'm pretty sure you could if you'd stop all the lying.

⁓

"I don't know anything she doesn't," Sandy said a few minutes later, having invited Jones into his home—albeit reluctantly. They stood around the kitchen island. Several different bottles of medical prescriptions stood beside the coffee maker.

"Sometimes we know things that don't seem relevant. That's what I'm looking for today. I'm going to ask again: You're sure no one else knew the Overbrooks? Nobody else spent time in Burbank or Chicago? Or Illinois? Or the Midwest? Give me something to work with."

"Not that I know of. I told you, Frank and I knew each other from the University of Florida. I decided I needed help, and he was the first person I called."

"Why is that?"

"Because he was the smartest doctor I knew. Maybe awkward, but that can be forgiven. When I go, I want to know the people of Paradiso are in good hands. Frank would have done well."

"Did he do well in Burbank?"

"I imagine so. According to him, he had a tough go after the divorce years ago, but he climbed out of it and ran a good practice. I looked into him some before offering. His patients were sad to see him go."

Jones chewed on his bottom lip, debating his route. "How did you even end up here in the first place? Right after med school?"

"No, I was in Savannah, Georgia, for my second residency—surgical. Was looking to stay up that way. I liked the lowcountry. Took a job at a clinic north of there in Beaufort, South Carolina, which is where I met Mary Elizabeth. We married and had a good life . . . But her family wasn't the healthiest, emotionally speaking. We started wondering what it would be like to make a change. One day, I was scrolling through the news from my alma mater. The College of Medicine puts out a quarterly magazine of sorts. One of the openings was for a job here. Another doctor by the name of Hemworth was retiring."

"That's a handy magazine. So you jumped on it."

"That's right. Mary Elizabeth had wanted to go north, but she let me win that one. Dr. Hemworth had this house for sale. All was well until she got sick shortly after we moved."

"I'm sorry, Doctor." Though he'd planned on it earlier, Jones decided it wasn't the time to bring up what he'd seen the night before with Glenna. He'd use that secret weapon down the road.

"Okay, Detective, is there anything else? I want to check in on Catherine and Amber Carter before I go into work."

"You didn't mention that you were helping with Amber." Jones braced himself for an *I'm not at liberty to discuss my patients* excuse.

Sandy didn't hide behind his oath, though. "They wanted a hippie midwife but got me instead."

"And Catherine . . . how is she?"

"She's lucky Miriam found her." Sandy put his mug in the sink. "She's fine now, considering. Grief is a horrible thing. I definitely want to keep an eye on her."

"Had you met her before?"

"Not before that day, no."

Jones bit his lip and wondered what he was missing. Catherine and Sandy could have been working together, scheming. They might have known each other long before she met Frank. Despite what she had told him, her hasty marriage was still bothering him.

～

Jones called a former colleague in Sarasota and asked about Barry Gatt. "Oh, you know him, the shady PI up here. *We Gatt 'em right where we want 'em.* He got a lot of press last year for catching the mayor's brother with his pants down. He's living the good life, making all kinds of money. A big golfer. He throws a charity event at the Sara Bay Country Club every Christmas."

Jones drove the hour and a half up, burning three cigarettes on the way, splitting his time between thinking about Sylvie and wondering who the hell killed Dr. Overbrook. He wanted to get Sylvie off the island. He'd let her crash at his place, but there weren't capital letters big enough to spell the TROUBLE that would cause.

Funny how taking her to his house would both protect her and hurt her. Not that funny, though. He just wasn't cut out for the things women wanted: the long-term stuff, the kids, the marriage, the white picket fence. Jones liked reeling one in, having fun, and then moving along—a humane catch and release that was safe for all parties involved. He was best dating women who felt the same way, and there were plenty of them.

None like Sylvie, though.

Gatt's office was right off the Tamiami Trail, the long stretch of road that goes all the way up the coast. The big sign above the sidewalk read:

GATT INVESTIGATION SERVICES, INC.

WE GATT 'EM RIGHT WHERE WE WANT 'EM.

His car had to be the fancy polished Cadillac near the entrance. The building was nondescript, a brick affair that could have been a post office or a vet clinic. Jones pulled back the glass door and found a chipper blonde with a glossy smile and a perky bosom looking back at him from behind the desk.

"You must be Pam. We spoke on the phone. I'm Detective Quentin Jones, Collier County Sheriff's Office."

She eyed him up and down. "You don't look like a cop."

"Oh yeah? What do I look like, then?" Jones stepped toward her and offered her his badge and ID.

"Like a surfer, maybe, but we don't have waves."

"There're a few waves out there, you catch 'em on the right day."

After a look at his credentials, she asked, "Did Barry not call you back?"

Jones shook his head. "He around now?"

"I think he's busy at the moment." Pam answered like someone had wound her up and pulled her string.

"He needs to get *un*busy. Shall I walk back there?"

Pam picked up the handset of her phone and mashed a button with a shaky finger. "Mr. Gatt, a Detective Jones is here to see you." Once she'd hung up, she said, "He needs about five minutes."

Jones crossed his arms. "He owns a place down on Osprey Isle, right?"

"I don't know. I've only been here a few days."

"He good to work for?"

"So far. He pays well."

Jones backed up and found a chair next to a table of magazines. Johnny Carson was on the cover of *Life*, and the look of the guy made Jones smile. He didn't watch much television, but he could watch Carson all day long. Jones crossed his legs and made small talk with Pam: Where you from? Pennsylvania. What brought you down here? The sunshine. That sort of thing.

Gatt finally came in, swinging his big belly with a swagger that should only be reserved for Hollywood. His suit looked like it had been worn a few days in a row.

"Detective Jones . . . I was going to call you today. Wanna step on back?"

Gatt didn't offer a hand to shake. He ushered Jones down a hallway, the first door on the left. The office looked like he was still unpacking, boxes everywhere. A putter leaned up against one of them. His PI license and some photographs of him and his golf buddies hung up on the wall. A half-smoked Cuban burned in the ashtray on his fancy wooden desk. A fan failed miserably at blowing the smoke out the cracked window.

He plopped down in his chair and reached for the cigar. "So . . . you have a dead man on Osprey and you're wondering what I have to do with it."

The guy had definitely been around the block. "Among other things." Jones slid into the chair opposite the desk and resisted the urge to light a cigarette himself.

"I didn't know him," Gatt said.

"How'd you hear about it? I understand you haven't been back to the island in a while."

"Yeah, that place got small for me. I've thought about selling but haven't had the time to even think about it. Busy the past couple of years." He pulled on the cigar; the tip glowed orange.

"Mainly I'm curious about the young couple staying there. How'd you end up with them?"

Gatt blew out his puff and chewed on the question. "I don't mean to be complicated, and I hate to disappoint you, but I'm not interested in sharing the details of my arrangements. They're looking after the place, plain and simple. Better than having it sit there collecting dust."

"Yeah, but you could get paid for it if you wanted to. Somebody with money."

"What do I need more money for?" He set his cigar down and looked around as if the visual of his office proved the point. It did not. "I'd have retired by now, but I'd be bored as hell. My wife would chase me off."

"Yeah, you've done well for yourself." Jones waved smoke from his face. "The Carters said they found a flyer at the general store, seeking someone to watch over the place."

"Then that's what happened."

Jones didn't have time for this shit. "Look, Gatt, I get that you're a good PI and know the rules. I can't force you to talk . . . yet. Do me a favor and don't make me play hardball. I just want to know the truth of why two young drifters are staying at your place for free. No offense, but I know it's not because you're kind to strangers. You're getting something out of it."

He raised a hand, palm up. "What, a guy can't have a heart?"

"You can have a heart. But there's more to the story, and I won't stop until I have every last detail of it."

Gatt chuckled. "You've met your match, buddy. Let me save you some trouble. Whatever I got going on at my place is my business, and it has nothing to do with your dead doctor over there. You understand?"

Jones slapped his legs and rose to stand. "Sorry to bother you. I guess you *are* going to force me to play hardball. You'll hear from me soon."

"We'll see about that." Gatt didn't even bother getting up as Jones left the room and went back the way he came.

"Hey, Pam, mind if I borrow your phone?" he said, returning to her desk, jolted by her unwelcoming boss.

"Sure."

He came over to the side of her desk and dialed a number he knew by heart. "Hey, amigo. Do me a favor: see what you can find on Barry Gatt. Guy's a dirtbag and has something to hide. I'm asking for his help and he's not giving it, so I need to put some pressure on him."

Another PI whom Jones had traded favors with over the years was on the other end. "Sure thing, Q. I'll get back to you."

Jones hung up the phone. Pam was looking at him funny.

"Yeah, he's not so nice after all," Jones said. "Have a good day, Pam."

Chapter 18

CATHERINE OF CHICAGO

Catherine lay on the floor in the bedroom. She'd been sweltering in the bed, as if Florida were rejecting her, so she'd climbed off and had been lying there on the wooden planks for hours, sifting her way through her muddy thoughts, recalling the events since the murder, wondering what in the world she might do now.

She'd heard Sandy knocking but refused to answer. She'd spied him through the bathroom window and called out, "I don't want to see anyone right now."

"Are you okay, dear?"

"I'm feeling much better, thank you. Just need to sleep."

Somehow she'd managed to collect herself enough to contact a funeral parlor and have a conversation about the transfer of the body and a potential date for the funeral. She'd said she wanted to push it off a few days, as she still wasn't herself and hoped to find a will once she took delivery of their belongings.

It was close to lunchtime now. Catherine felt weak and knew she needed to eat something. What was the point, though? No matter where she searched, she didn't have the answers to the questions relating to her future. It would have been easier if she'd drowned yesterday.

Damn Miriam for seeing her and swimming out there, tugging her back to the shore, tugging her back to life. All she wanted was for this to go away, these feelings, pinpricks of pain that wouldn't stop, the demon that grew in her chest and belly.

What was the point?

Frank was gone. No man would ever love her again. She didn't even love herself. For some reason, he'd thought she was beautiful. Perhaps only because he'd been looking at the mirror for so long. He didn't know what beautiful was.

Catherine lifted her gaze as if there were a heaven.

What am I to do now, Frank? Stay here in this tropical paradise and sleep in the bed where we had yet to make love? Walk the beach where we were supposed to stroll together, the Gulf waters where we were supposed to swim? Attend another party, knowing it would only be a reminder of the last time I saw you?

I understand that ours was a different relationship, but I do believe we met for a reason . . . that we were going to bring each other out of our shells. God had other plans. Oh, God, are you really out there? I don't think so. How could something as beautiful as this piece of paradise be created only to eventually become the setting for such terror?

Something Sandy had said to her pried its way into her mind. He'd suggested she write a letter to Frank. Catherine wasn't one to write letters. She'd never written one that didn't have to do with her work. But she'd been talking to Frank all morning. Maybe a letter could solidify thoughts. Sandy had said his letter made a big difference.

Feeling desperate, she dug through Frank's desk, found a notebook and pen, and settled in to try.

> Dear Frank,
> Do I go on without you? Or do I go back to my old life? As if it could ever be tolerable now. I cringe thinking that your last breaths were spent agitated at me for drinking so much. Had I to do it over again, I wouldn't

have had a drop of Champagne. I was swept away in the joy of it all, our new house, new friends, new life. I'd never been to Florida before, remember? I'd never even seen a beach other than Lake Michigan's, and it's not the same, is it? Please, please forgive me. You can't, though, can you? You're not out there watching me. You're long gone, a mere memory.

If I killed you, then I don't deserve to continue this life that we set out together. I've thought of the possibility a thousand times since Detective Jones brought it up. I do sleepwalk, very badly. I fear that the ghosts of my past could bring something out of me. If I did hurt you, though, it was not intentional. Despite our short time together, I loved you. I was prepared to give you everything.

I think of all the things I didn't have the courage to say. How I never told you that I loved you. That you were the best thing that ever happened to me, that you breathed life into me. We didn't even get to consummate our marriage. Dumb me, I got too drunk. Oh, how I wish I'd kissed you a thousand times more.

If there were a button that I could press to stop existing, I'd press it in a moment. But there is no button, and it is not easy to take your own life. The alternative is scary, though, Frank. It's overwhelming, the idea of going through your belongings, making sense of our finances. I guess they are our finances, right? We're married and did not have any agreement otherwise. I don't know anyone in your past life. You haven't mentioned a soul—except your ex-wife, of course.

Do I need to find her and let her know of your passing? What am I going to say?

Nearly meeting the end yesterday did seem to awaken a sleeping part of me. As scary as living is, the idea of not living seems like a white flag I do not want to wave. When I came to yesterday, I felt grateful that it wasn't over. Perhaps I need to grow that seed. That's what you'd want of me. That's what I should expect of me. If only it were that easy.

Truthfully, I just want you back. I want to see what could have become of us. I want you to have answered when I called out to you in the morning. We would have had breakfast and talked of the day. We might have taken a walk, our feet splashing in the water. You would have taken my hand and glanced at me shyly with the love that I want to believe you felt for me. Damn you for leaving me, for closing the door on all the possibilities . . .

A car coming up the driveway tore Catherine away from her concentration, and she realized she'd been right on the edge of tears. She pressed up from the chair and entered the bathroom and peeked through the small window. It was a patrol car. Detective Jones was back.

~

"Mrs. Overbrook, please answer the door. I wanted to check on you . . . and I do have more questions." He'd seen her head appear through a window, so she was there, no doubt. He knocked again. "Mrs. Overbrook, I will bust open the door if I have to."

"Fine, fine!" she called.

When she appeared, her hair was all over the place. No trace of makeup. Her shirt looked slept in. And yet there was something still attractive about her, the pale skin and polished face, such a foreign look in this world of bright sunshine, palm trees, and windswept dunes.

"Would you mind if we talked more? I know you're going through a lot, but . . . I have to continue my investigation. It's best for everyone on the island."

"I don't know how else I can help, but that's fine."

They took seats around the circular table on the deck. Jones had once again left his recorder in the car, as he'd already gotten official statements, and he'd found the microphone changed people's responses and reactions. Along with the nice weather came a rolling and steady Gulf. A shade of gray marred the innocent baby-blue color, as if even the water reflected the gloom of a murder gone unsolved.

"Are you sure you don't know anything more of Frank's life before you? Why he sold his practice. Why he'd up and move to Florida. Or his ex-wife. Did he ever mention her? Zelda was her name."

"Zelda? He'd never told me."

He nodded. "Zelda Smith."

"It's strange to think of him as being married before. I got the sense that she hurt him."

"How's that?"

"He mentioned her with a kind of . . . melancholy tone . . . and then raced away from the topic, making me feel like it would be awful to pry."

As they continued to speak, Catherine managed to hide any sign of life. Zero joy or hope, barely a pulse in the timbre of her voice. There was no harder part of his job than coming to know those grieving after a murder. Because it was random, wasn't it? In most cases, a victim did not deserve to die and most certainly those around that someone didn't deserve to be thrown into the black lake of loss.

Jones decided to give the interview a rest and attempt to offer some kindness. "You don't have anyone to talk to you, do you, Mrs. Overbrook? It appears that Sylvie and Miriam are your new friends, but I sense you're feeling . . . Well, I can only imagine what you're going through. Is there anything I can do to help? I'm assuming you're starting to wade through your husband's things, trying to put together the pieces of what will be next."

"I don't even know where to begin." The way she met his eyes showed that she could use some assistance.

They talked about her conversation with the funeral home, then Jones said, "You're right. See if he has a will when the moving truck gets here. And see what you can learn about the rest of his life, his finances and all that. It's important you figure out if he had insurance, that kind of thing. You're sure he didn't mention life insurance?"

"Look at me, Detective." An angry scowl grew on her face, showing she was quite alive after all. "Do I look like I was after his money? Do I look like the kind of person who would kill him to get his life insurance policy? I was fine financially, and I told you . . . I don't care about money. I don't buy things. This is all foreign to me—going to a lobster boil, drinking Champagne, having a house on the water . . . being the object of someone's desire . . ."

Jones paused, making sure she'd gotten it all out. He thought of Sylvie being alone too. Good people getting knocked down hard.

"Mrs. Overbrook, I can't pretend to know how you feel, but I have known enough spouses who have lost their partners. I know what you're going through on some level. It's a chilly time of year to go swimming. You didn't even have a bathing suit on. Do you want to say anything about that?"

She steepled her fingers together and looked away, possibly wondering how open she should be. When her eyes locked on Jones, she seemed to have made her decision. "Would you want to live after losing the one person who'd ever loved you?"

Jones considered her question. His father had died too young to even get a chance to love his son. His mother had loved Jones in her own way. Sure, there had been women with whom he'd had relationships, maybe a couple who'd been serious enough to keep it going for a year or so. But no, there had never been anyone other than Sylvie, and that was a pile of longings and what-ifs.

If he was going here, he needed a cigarette. Once he'd lit up, he said through a haze of tobacco smoke, "I can't say I know what it's like to be loved in that way, but if I could even imagine it, then I can only assume what it would be like to lose them." He started and stopped a few times. "I see a whole island of people who have faced tragedy. A few of them, I see fighting back. Why? I don't know. I suppose everyone has to find their reason. You might have walked out into that water hoping you wouldn't come back, but I think there was something inside that was keeping you from giving up. Even if Miriam hadn't—"

Her face suddenly morphed into a wilting flower. All the air in her seemed to leave her body and she collapsed, like a dahlia broken at the stem, folding in on herself and breaking into a cathartic sob.

"Oh God, oh God." She let go of something she'd clearly been holding for a while.

Jones felt compelled to be there for her and stood and crouched next to her. It wasn't what he normally did, but these were never normal circumstances. He lifted an arm and tried to wrap it around her shoulder.

She pushed him away. "Please don't do that. I'm not good with being touched."

He pulled back faster than an eel poking out of a patch of seaweed. "I'm so sorry."

"No, it's . . . it's okay. Thank you." She peered up from her misery, showing wet eyes. "I'm not good with people. Not good with connecting."

"You don't have to be." Jones sat back in his chair.

Catherine retreated back into herself and wept hard. "What is wrong with me? Do you know this is the first time I've cried since . . . since I heard Sylvie's scream? I'm so lifeless that I didn't even cry when my husband died."

"It takes a while for the body to process grief, Mrs. Overbrook. Most people fall into shock, and that can take hours or days. Years, sometimes. It's okay to cry now."

That she did, weeping hard for several minutes while Jones sat there in respectful silence. Eventually, she composed herself and took a series of deep breaths.

Jones sat up. "Do something for me, Catherine. Close your eyes."

She looked at him with a giant dose of skepticism.

"Just do it, trust me. I'll close mine too."

After they did so, he asked, "What do you sense?"

"This feels like a game Sylvie would make me play."

"It does, doesn't it?"

"You're attracted to her, aren't you?" Catherine asked.

Jones chuckled. "Let's leave me out of it."

"You two make a cute couple."

"Mrs. Overbrook, you're embarrassing me. Now, close your eyes and use your other senses like Sylvie would. No peeking."

"Fine, fine." She followed his instructions.

"Tell me, what's out there?"

"Salt in the air, the wind."

"That's it. And?"

"Birds."

"Ah, the song of birds that visit us in the winter. What else? Do you feel something?"

She shook her head. "I feel alone, Detective. Dead inside."

"What else?"

"I feel ugly. Afraid."

He chose not to contradict her. "Fair enough. Keep going? What do you feel against your skin?"

"The sun."

He looked at her and hit the table, too hard in hindsight. "Ah! That's where I was going. Sometimes that sun is all you need. Feel that warmth, that burn? I've been a loner for a long time too. Something about the sun and salt water, you know? You could go back to Chicago or go find a new life. But I'll tell you this: There is healing to be had down here. Even the most broken can find peace."

"What do you know about being broken?" she asked, opening her eyes.

A flash of all the bad he'd seen out there came to him, almost like a video reel, but it was more a feeling than a visual. "We live in a broken world, Mrs. Overbrook. My job is poking around in such a world."

"Still, you get to go home at night, back to a safe place." She looked at him with piercing eyes now, more beautiful in her aggressive state, her blue ovals reflecting light like a glacier might.

"I suppose you're right about that."

Catherine nodded, point made. "Have you ever lost someone personally?"

Jones wasn't one to spit out all his issues, but she needed some honesty now. "I lost my father. He was shot down in the war."

"I'm sorry."

"I barely remember him, little bits and pieces—like him holding me up and trying to make me smile. Kissing my mother goodbye when he left for training." It was disgusting how a death from so long ago lingered within him. "It hurts all the same. More than twenty years has gone by, and there's the missing piece inside of me, always wondering how my life could have been."

The look on her face warmed, the skin softening. He got the sense that she was a far deeper woman than anyone had ever given her credit for.

"Thank you for telling me that," she said.

"None of us can avoid the ugly stuff. We're all survivors on some level. Some have it worse than others. I'd say you have a tough road ahead, but you have what it takes to find the other side."

She chewed on what he'd said, watching a gull pass by. "You're a good man, Detective."

He almost made a joke about how that was taking a big leap, but he held back with reverence to the moment. "Thank you, ma'am."

"Would you like something to drink? I'm being terribly rude. Maybe a sandwich. Frank and I went to the store. What am I going to do with it all? I can't eat right now."

He was still full from earlier, and he had work to do, but this might be good for her, letting her make something. She did look like she hadn't eaten in days.

"You know what," he said, "I'd love a sandwich."

She lit up. "Oh, good! I'm a terrible cook, but I can make a good sandwich . . . with chips and soda."

"I'd love all of it, Mrs. Overbrook. The works."

Damned if there weren't days like this when Jones felt like maybe he was useful, maybe he did have something to contribute. If nothing else, he'd always be there to eat a sandwich if needed. Detective Q, sandwich man for hire.

Catherine passed Jones a plate with a pickle spear, chips, and a ham sandwich bursting over with iceberg lettuce. Posted up at the kitchen island, he'd been talking to her while she worked.

He took a bite and moaned with pleasure. "As good as the general store."

She sat across from him. "Detective, aren't you supposed to be the one person on the island not telling lies?"

Jones smirked and then hid behind another bite.

She picked up her own sandwich; a drip of mustard fell to her plate. "It's nice to take care of someone else and get out of my own head for a minute."

They ate in silence for a while before Catherine asked, "What would you do if you were me?"

Jones finished chewing. He'd almost cleaned his plate. "If I were you . . . I'd sit tight for a while. You can't run from the pain. Let it beat you up; try to throw a few punches back. Spend time soaking up the sun. When the time's right, you'll know whether you want to start over or stay here. Or maybe go back to Chicago. I've heard it's a lovely city."

"You've never been?"

"I haven't. I haven't left Florida much."

"Why's that?"

He wiped his hands with a napkin, wanting to be real with her. "After my dad died, my mom took on everything, as you can imagine. They'd been running a motel together, and after he was gone, she had to pick up his slack. Being a mom on top of it was a lot. Traveling wasn't an option. I had a chip on my shoulder growing up, so I didn't care to think about going to college or going out and seeing the world. I had an uncle who was a detective, and I jumped right into the academy."

"Don't you get days off?"

"I do, of course."

"What do you do?"

"I get out on the water. Sometimes play poker with some guys at a dive near my house."

"You really are a loner. No girlfriend or wife?"

"Not at the moment." Even as he said it, he was reminded that he was married to his work.

"No interest in being a father?"

"You'd be a good detective, Mrs. Overbrook."

"I've spent a lot of my life without much human interaction. It's nice to ask questions sometimes, learn about people. I don't mean to pry. I just . . . I've been thinking about what life might have been like for Frank and me. If we'd met when we were younger, we might have had children. He told me over dinner one night that he wished he had." Her eyes crinkled into sadness.

Jones knew better than to comfort her this time. He let the grief do what it had to do.

When she returned to him, she asked with less emotion, "Who do you think killed him, Detective?"

"I don't know yet."

"You have an idea."

"Nothing I'd want to share yet. Everyone seems to be holding back. Once I get through the shell to the center, I'll have a far better idea."

"What if it was me?" Catherine asked. "What if I was sleep—"

"It wasn't you, Catherine. I know that much."

Relief seemed to wash over her. She didn't think so either. "How do you know? I do sleepwalk."

"Because I know."

Her eyes reddened. "I hope you find him soon, and I hope they go to jail for the rest of their lives."

"I'll do my best to make sure he or *she* finds their way there."

"Good," Catherine said. "Very good."

Jones said goodbye to Catherine and meandered back down to the patrol car. He was so in his head that he didn't even see it till he'd sat down in the driver's seat. Tucked under the wiper was a folded piece of paper. He climbed back out and pulled it open, careful to make sure he left plenty of room for Challa to find fingerprints.

Someone had cut out letters from magazines and glued them together to make a short statement: *David Arnett is the killer.*

"Well, that settles it," Jones said, shaking his head. "I'm sure this will be admissible in court." He looked around, wondering who might have left the note. Could have been any of the islanders.

He studied the tracks around the car. Not much to go on. Had it been sand, it would be another story. It *was* time to see David again. He was the one guy who definitely hadn't left that note, but he sure did keep popping up in conversations.

Chapter 19

IN THE DARK, A FLAME BURNS

Jones flashed a big grin, all teeth and charm. "Mr. Arnett, do you have a few minutes?"

A scowl carved its way into the face of the man sitting in his wheelchair. "Would it be best if I prepared a room for you? I'm seeing more of you than I'd like." He wore another leisure suit, this time a coffee-colored brown.

"Trust me, I'm working hard to wrap things up."

"Then you have things under control, someone you're suspecting?"

"I'm getting close." Not exactly the truth, but Jones knew someone was getting close to making a mistake—or breaking. He just had to keep shaking the tree.

David nodded in what almost seemed like a retreat. "Well, come in, then. Miriam's gone shopping, though. You'll have to wait an hour or so to speak with her."

"I mainly came to see you this time."

"Lucky me."

Jones sat in the same place as before, one of the chairs at the breakfast table. David wheeled his chair to the opposite side. The *Tampa Bay Times* was folded open to the crossword puzzle. Jones assumed David was the one who'd nearly completed it, as Miriam didn't seem like the puzzle type.

Jones set his recorder on the table. "This okay with you?"

"I think you've gotten enough of me on tape, Detective. I'm not guilty, but I don't want to fall prey to your entrapment."

"That's not what I do."

"Nevertheless, you're welcome to take me in, but I don't feel like recording today."

"Fair enough." Jones dropped the recorder back in the bag. "Why did you tell me your wheelchair wouldn't go in the sand?"

David's head kicked back. "How do you know I lied to you?"

"It's my job, Mr. Arnett. You asked if I have suspects. You are one of them. All of you are. Help me clear your name. This investigation is as much about ruling people out as it is zeroing in on the killer. Miriam seemed to connect with Frank in some way. Multiple witnesses saw them speaking. Did you take her home, put her to bed, and then go back out into the night to wait for him?"

David gripped the arms of his chair. "You really think that I could go chase down an able-bodied man on the beach in the middle of the night and kill him with a . . . with a knife, or whatever it is you say?"

Jones leaned in. "What I know is that I will not exclude you because you've lost the use of your legs. The fact that you lied to me points a finger in your direction. Could you have driven your chair all the way to his house without a problem?"

"If the sand is hard after a high tide, I would assume so. I haven't gone that far before."

"What happened to you after the accident? Have you always been angry at the world or . . . ?"

"'Angry at the world.' Is that how you put it?"

"Did I stutter? I see a man who is punishing his wife because he can no longer walk. Sure, he might blame her for driving the car, but even if *you* had been driving—even if *you'd* been hit walking—you would have found a way to blame her."

"How am I punishing her?"

"You tell me."

"I'm not the threat you make me out to be."

"Perhaps not, but I suspect the way you treat her—and speak to her—is not what she or anyone deserves." Jones watched his eyes. "I think you're afraid of her leaving you, right? You're terrified that you won't have anyone to help you dress, to get showered, to cook your meals. So you pound her guilt into her, never letting her forget that she was driving the car." Jones let out a laugh. "I bet you're afraid she's getting bored too . . ."

"Bored?" His skin seemed to sizzle.

A nerve hath been struck!

"She's a young and beautiful woman. Do you sleep in the same room? Can you even . . . ?"

David was getting riled up, which was exactly the point.

Jones pressed harder. "She's beautiful. I'd bet there's someone back on the mainland who's eyeing her right this moment. Or is she meeting someone? I keep wondering that. What is the purpose of your surveillance equipment when it stops at your driveway? She can do whatever she wants when she leaves. Would you even know?"

An element of confidence came over him. "Oh, I'd know."

"How's that?"

Wham! David's fist crashed down onto the table, nearly knocking over the empty vase in the middle. "I'd know, goddammit."

"That's all it takes," Jones said. "Some fire, like what I'm seeing right now. Anyone is capable of murder. She's been rubbing you the wrong way, maybe ignoring you. Then there's a new man on the island. *Fresh* blood for Miriam. You knew she was eventually going to sleep with him, and you thought you'd stop the idea before it blossomed. It's almost too easy, David. May I call you David?"

David pulled back his anger. "I did not know the man, but he was not terribly attractive. Believe me, I wasn't worried that she was going to start making late-night visits his way."

"He might not have been attractive, but he clearly had some charm. Catherine Overbrook's a good-looking woman. She could have had her pick. Perhaps what Frank lacked in looks, he made up for in charm . . . or other ways."

"I wouldn't know about that."

Jones didn't want to lose momentum. "Has Miriam cheated on you before?"

David's beady eyes traced the wall, then came at Jones like the guns of a firing squad. "Absolutely not. She has always been faithful."

"How would you know that? Do you have someone watching her?"

David shook his head, apparently refusing to answer that one.

"Do you think she crashed the car on purpose?"

"Of course not."

"Then why? Why have you chosen to make both of your lives miserable? I see Sylvie over there fighting to bring joy to herself and those around her. Her accident was at the same time, right? Sure, you may never walk again, but she can't see. Tell me why you think anyone deserves to be punished for your bad luck?"

Arnett's lips didn't even part.

Jones was the one to hit the table this time. "Can you imagine losing your vision? You'd feel like you were the most vulnerable person in the world. There she is all alone over there with a killer on the loose, and she wouldn't even be able to see 'em coming."

Mr. Arnett leaned in and said through gritted teeth, "I'd trade my eyes for my legs in a second. Talk about feeling vulnerable. Maybe I can see someone coming, but I can't do anything about it. At least she can walk the beach or go for a swim. You know what I can do? Nothing. I can sit in this chair and wheel around. You're right: I can't have sex again. I can't swim. I can barely change myself. Does that make you feel better, Jones?"

The two men weren't backing down now, their eyes tied to each other like boats in the bay.

"It sounds to me like you have a good woman who has stuck by you, but you treat her like shit. I have no pity for you, Mr. Arnett. The poor lady is drowning herself in booze because you've stripped her of happiness."

"You don't know anything."

"What don't I know, Mr. Arnett?"

He shook his head.

A car came down the drive.

"What were you going to say, Mr. Arnett? What don't I know?"

He stayed silent.

"Tell me."

The car door shut, and David kept his mouth closed. Footfalls sounded from the steps leading to the front porch.

"Did you kill Frank Overbrook, Mr. Arnett?"

A heck of a scowl came over him. "This interview is over. You want to talk more, you take me downtown."

Jones turned as the door swung open.

Miriam stood there, sober and curious. "What's going on here?"

"He was just leaving."

"Where are your bags?" Jones asked her.

"What bags?"

"Your husband said you'd gone shopping for provisions."

She looked down at her empty hands. "Oh, I . . . I was just poking around on Marco Island, looking for a bathing suit."

"You came up empty?"

"Clearly."

She circled the table and kissed David on the forehead. "Everything okay?"

He patted her on the buttocks. She recoiled, wincing as if she was in pain. There was no attraction there.

"The detective is getting desperate, that's all," David said.

Miriam looked over to Jones. "I can tell you've raised his blood pressure. I'd like you to leave now."

"Very well." Jones stood and studied the couple. What was going on between them? They were both guilty of something. Did it have to do with the murder of Dr. Overbrook, or was it something else entirely?

⌇

Catherine realized she was barefoot and hadn't even thought of putting on her shoes. How wonderful the sand felt on her feet. Even amid all the terrible things going on, the sand really did feel nice.

It took twenty minutes to reach the Arnetts'. She'd never actually visited their house and was surprised to see a pool—a pool right on the Gulf. Who could have even dreamed of such a thing?

Her giddy mood faded and died when she saw Miriam there, stretched out on a lounge chair, her long legs sticking out of a sarong that wrapped around her waist. She was on her stomach, the back of her bikini unstrapped, showing not a bit of a strap line from the sun. Her tanned skin was nearly enviable. Perhaps Catherine could look like that one day, though her white skin would likely turn the red of a lobster in a pot.

"Ah, darling Catherine," Miriam said. Almost shyly, she popped up and fastened the wrap tighter on her waist and pulled it down to cover her legs. "I was going to come see you later. How are you feeling?"

Catherine tried to smile, tried to give Miriam the benefit of the doubt. "I'm doing better, thank you. Very dehydrated and—"

"Let's get you a drink. In fact, I need one as well."

Miriam waved her over to the cooler and reached in and took out an ice pick. "Vodka or gin?"

"Oh no. I'm fine, thank you."

"Suit yourself."

They took seats in neighboring lounge chairs. "First, I wanted to thank you," Catherine said earnestly. "You saved my life."

Miriam sipped on a drink she'd already worked halfway down. "I'm just glad you're okay."

Catherine was glad Miriam didn't push for the details of why she'd been in the water in the first place. "I wanted to ask you something," she said. "Please don't take it the wrong way . . . though I don't know how else you'll take it." She propped herself up, as if preparing for battle. The new Catherine had to look out for herself.

Miriam took another long gulp, readying herself. "Am I going to wish I'd had another?"

Catherine ignored her. "I can't help but wonder why I felt so groggy after you left two nights ago."

"Two nights ago?"

"When you and Sylvie and I were having tea, remember? You brought over your delicious food. I was so out of it after that, long after I'd woken from whatever Sandy had given me. Someone must have put something in my tea . . . or . . . in the food."

Miriam let her jaw fall. "You think I drugged you? Why would I ever do that?"

Catherine inclined her shoulders. "That's what I'm trying to figure out. Whoever broke in assumed I was drugged . . . or maybe they wouldn't have risked it."

Miriam ran a hand through her hair. "Darling, whyever would I drug you? I'm hurt, honestly, that you would insinuate—"

"I want to believe you, but—"

"Why would I do that?" Her head was shaking.

Catherine wished the detective were there to read her face. She didn't know the first thing about that. She held eye contact for a long time, until Miriam looked away.

"I think you're lying," Catherine said, "but I don't know why."

"I think you were just tired."

Catherine shook her head. It didn't feel right. Miriam sat up and took Catherine's hand. "I am far from perfect, Catherine, but I'm not a terrible person. I want to be your friend. I want all of us to get along. This is my only home, the only place I'll ever live. Why would I do something to mess that up?"

"I don't know."

Miriam leaned forward. "I don't blame you for not trusting anyone. I get it. But I'm your friend. At least, I want to be."

Catherine muttered a thanks.

—

Miriam could tell Catherine didn't believe her, and she so wanted to tell her the truth—about everything. Wouldn't that make this so much easier?

"I brought you a meal, for God's sake."

"Maybe only so you could drug me and go into Frank's things later. Were you looking for his black bag, for his medicine? Tell me the truth."

Catherine was so hardheaded, unforgiving in the way she wouldn't break her stare. Miriam gritted her teeth and stared right back. "You can't come onto this island and bring all this on us . . . on me. I wanted to be your friend, but you will not come into my home and accuse me of something so absurd. As you said yourself, I saved your life yesterday. I'm not going to—"

Miriam heard the sound she'd come to loathe: David's wheelchair motoring her way. He seemed ready to scold her for something but held back upon seeing Catherine. As he came to a stop, he said, "I didn't realize we had a visitor."

"She came over for a visit. Poor thing." Miriam tossed back the rest of her drink. "I think I'll have another."

"You're full of surprises," David said sarcastically, eyeing her empty glass. For Catherine, he put on some charm; he was a pendulum that could swing from one person to the other with ease. "How are you, dear girl? I heard what happened in the water. The Gulf doesn't always play nice."

"I'm learning that."

If only to quell her anger, Miriam considered what would happen if she pushed him into the pool. The thought was almost as appeasing as the idea of another drink. The deep end was right there. His arms had grown so strong, with all the weight lifting. Could he swim out? Wouldn't that be terrible, to have him survive such a thing. He'd make her life even more miserable. He probably wouldn't even tell the police, choosing instead to take matters into his own hands.

Miriam looked at her husband, who, now making conversation with Catherine, was pretending to be the charming man he once was. "Please let us know how I can help. I'm sure there are all sorts of business affairs to attend to."

"Yes, I think I'll fly back to Illinois soon and try to make sense of it all."

"That's a grand idea."

They continued to talk while Miriam made herself another drink. Make it go away, she thought. All of it. Please. How can our lives ever return to normal? Damn David, and all he's done to me. Damn all that I've done to myself!

Miriam raised her glass and stared into it, a circular and transparent vessel that was at once her lighthouse and buoy, her safety net. Right here. *Right here* in this glass was the only ticket to peace. She took it to her mouth as if she were chugging water from the Fountain of Youth, and the liquid began to wash away her troubles.

Chapter 20

The Command Center

After leaving the Arnetts', Jones stopped by the Carters' house. Sandy's truck was parked in the driveway.

Before Jones even reached the steps, Levi raced onto the porch. "This is not the time, Detective. Amber's in labor."

"Can I take her to the hospital?"

"We got all the help we need."

Deciding he wouldn't impede such an important moment, Jones backed away and returned to his car, hoping that she and the baby would be okay.

Jones drove the rickety bridge off the island, then back through Paradiso and onto the highway. He was frustrated with himself. He should have a better idea by now of who the killer was. At this rate, it could be damn near any of them, including Catherine.

He'd told her she was off the hook, but he'd been bending the truth. She was clearly navigating some heavy emotional issues. Was she mentally ill? He'd seen it before, someone who could play delicate but then turn on an entirely new persona when it suited. All for the sake of survival.

An hour later at the station in Naples, Jones stifled a yawn. He could feel his thirties looming. There used to be a time when he wouldn't sleep until he'd put somebody behind bars—even if that was days.

First, he had to deal with his supervisor. After chatting with a few officer friends, he wound his way to the back of the station and knocked on Wycoff's door.

"That better be Jones."

Before Jones had even gotten two feet inside the office, Wycoff let him have it. "What did I say about wearing those damn Hawaiian shirts?"

"I'm undercover. Trying to stay below the radar." Wycoff was a tough guy, but maintained a row of healthy ferns along the wall with meticulous watering. A picture of his wife and two boys sitting around a dinner table hung next to a picture of him from his army days. His arms still showcased the muscles he'd earned in the service, but his belly had grown from countless hours of sitting behind a desk.

"There's nine people on the island; you're not undercover. I swear, Jones, I don't know whether I'm your babysitter or your boss. Sometimes I feel like you were sent down here from Sarasota like a Biblical plague. If you weren't so good at your job, I'd send you right back. For some damn reason, though, you think like a killer and keep making me look good."

Jones plopped down in the chair facing his boss. "Then you're okay if I don't dress up."

"It's a uniform; you're not dressing up for church. For God's sake, wear it when you come see me, at least."

Jones loved that he won that one. Back in the old days in Sarasota, his uncle had never worn a uniform, and Jones had picked up the habit. A man works eighty-hour weeks, dedicates his whole life to solving crime, and gets paid like he's scrubbing floors. At the least, he shouldn't have to dress like a clown.

He bit his tongue, though, deciding to show respect. "Thank you, sir."

Wycoff started to roll a cigarette. A tattoo showed from under his sleeve. "You know, Jones, just because you're a cop doesn't mean you don't have to follow the law. I know your uncle would say differently, but I don't run it that way down here."

"I hear you loud and clear."

A big sigh escaped Wycoff's mouth. "Now, tell me the latest. Somebody got clipped on the other side of the highway, and I'd love to put you on it, but I need answers with Paradiso first. You still think it was one of the islanders?"

"I'm leaning in that direction." He told Wycoff about the note. "I'll drop it off for fingerprinting, though I'm not sure I believe it's Arnett. His disability makes murder difficult."

"Who do you like for it, then?"

Jones shook his head. "I hate to guess."

"Humor me."

"Well, it's not Amber, the pregnant one. She went into labor this afternoon. Her husband, Levi, could have done it, though I'm coming up empty for a motive." Jones told him about Sandy and Glenna and discussed their potential motives.

"You really got a soap opera over there, huh?"

"That's about right," Jones said. "Then there's Sylvie Nye."

"She found the body, right?"

"That's right. But I can barely dream up why she'd do it, other than Frank trying to take advantage of her. I've spent some time with her, though. I'm not getting murder vibrations."

"Who else?"

"Could be a psychotic break with the victim's wife, Catherine. I can't figure her out. Then Miriam and David Arnett . . . Whether the message of the note is true, I'm wondering what they're lying about." Jones expounded on his issues with them. "I've still got a few angles. The guy renting to the Carters, Gatt—there's more to that story. If I keep asking questions, something's going to turn up. They can't all keep lying to me forever."

Wycoff crossed his big arms. "This one has you stumped, doesn't it?"

"It's not as easy as some, that's for sure. The whole lot of them are lying."

"Maybe they're all working together to hide something. Don't rule that out."

⁓

Ten minutes later, Jones stepped into his own office. There wasn't a fern in sight. The only photos on the wall were the ones from open murder investigations, including pictures of Frank's body sprawled out on the sand.

Jones sat down in his chair, spun it toward the photos, and looked at each of them. What the hell was he missing? Maybe a couple or even a few of them *were* working together. Could Sandy and his loyal posse have lured Frank Overbrook to the island for some reason? Something had gone wrong, a plan that went awry. Extortion . . . or blackmail. It could be simpler. Sandy could be holding on to a grudge from their medical school days, and he'd finally found a way to exact revenge.

After picking up the phone, Jones got the operator to connect him to the Burbank Police Department, then asked to be transferred to homicide.

A gruff midwestern accent barked through the receiver. "Jerry Baxter here."

"Good afternoon," Jones started, "I need some help and thought I'd call one of my own over there." He introduced himself and shared the pertinent details, including what little he knew of Overbrook's first wife. "Could you look into it when you have some time?"

"I'd be honored."

A sense of blue pride rose up out of Jones. It was nice to think there was still some camaraderie out there among cops.

⁓

At nine, Jones jumped into his Boston Whaler and rode out into the night. The moon was about half-full and painted the water a fuchsia color. Other than the boat's motor purring, it was quiet out there.

He stopped about a hundred yards out from Osprey, cut the motor, and watched for a while. The beach was deserted. All the houses were dark but the Arnetts' and Carters'. An officer was out there somewhere patrolling.

Coming in on the south end between Sylvie's and Catherine's houses, he raised the propeller and slid into the sand. He hopped over the side, and his bare feet splashed into the cool water. Once the Whaler was secure, he scanned the beach. Not a soul in sight. Anyone could easily have done what he'd done, sneaking up here. What if Frank came upon a drug smuggler who'd lost his way? A smuggler would have a gun, though.

Jones looked over at Sylvie's house. It was a long shot, but she did say she walked at night. Like Jones had told Wycoff, what if she came across Frank? He could have had one too many and tried to take advantage of her. But Catherine had said he wasn't drinking. Maybe he'd come across her sober and decided he'd have his way with a blind woman who would have a hard time fighting back.

Why wouldn't Sylvie say something, then? If he'd attacked her, she had every right to protect herself. It was time to have a more serious conversation. What he knew in his gut was that he couldn't let his feelings for her get in the way of the investigation. The thing that didn't track was that Frank had a new bride in the bed. Why would he be out on the beach going after another woman?

Jones didn't want to scare Sylvie, so he waited outside the house for a while, looking for signs that she was up. Moving closer, he ascended the deck and peered through a back window. That's when he heard jazz music playing—Charlie Parker, maybe.

He tapped lightly on the door. "It's Detective Jones, Sylvie. Can I come in?"

Appearing a minute later, she unlatched and pulled open the door. She wore khaki shorts and a white button-up twisted at the waist. "It's a heck of a thing to sneak up on someone when there's a killer on the loose. Had I a gun, I would have shot you."

"Sorry to scare you," he said, entering her house and switching on a light. "I should have called."

Sylvie offered a beer, and there was no way he was turning it down, on or off duty. In the kitchen, she popped the top off two Miller High Lifes and handed him one. "Why the back door?"

"I came over by boat."

She smothered a smile. "To check on me? This feels like an unofficial visit."

"To check in on everybody."

"Oh, I see."

They sat a few feet away from each other on the couch in the living room. Quiet ensued. He dug his toes into her rug. Of course he'd come to check on her, but he couldn't tell her that. There they were again, stuck in this intimate space where they'd last left off ten years ago. She seemed far more comfortable than him right now—as if it were a game.

He took a long pull of his beer, then broke the silence. "We better soak up this nice weather while we can. I can already feel summer coming."

She wasn't having weather talk. Twisting his way, she asked, "What are you doing, Quentin?"

"What do you mean?"

"Coming back into my life like this."

Are we really doing this? Jones thought. Warning signs flashed in his head.

"Cat got your tongue?" she asked. "I'm still wondering why you're alone. How many girls have you had to turn down? I can see you're still shy."

"A few here and there."

"I bet."

Sylvie inched closer to him, unashamed of what she was doing. "What are you afraid of?" Her voice had turned to a whisper, if a tiger cub could talk.

He looked down at her thigh, the lovely stretch of skin coming from her shorts, a map to desire. "You mean, other than sitting dangerously close to a suspect in my investigation?"

"Yes, I mean other than that. Look at it this way: if I'm the killer, no one else is going to get hurt tonight."

"That's not funny."

"I'm teasing you." She reached and found his arm. "Seriously, why no one since then?"

Jones gave her the respect of thinking about it. "Because I work all the time. Because the world I see doesn't make much room for love . . . and all that."

"'All that'?"

"I wouldn't make much of a husband . . . or a dad."

What was Jones doing? It was becoming increasingly difficult to be a gentleman. And to be a police officer. He could hear Wycoff yelling at him: *You slept with a suspect, Jones! Couldn't you have waited till after you closed the case? I'd fire you, but then I'd have to hire you right back because you have an uncanny ability to sniff out murderers.*

"Am I being too forward?" she asked. "You're giving me the cold shoulder. But I can feel you looking at me." She moved even closer and touched his chest. "Your heart rate is escalating. What's going on behind those pretty eyes of yours?"

"I'm trying to control myself." It felt like ten years of longing wasn't going to wait much longer until it came screaming to the surface.

She smiled. "Ah, you don't want to take advantage of a blind woman?"

"Don't do that," Jones said.

Sylvie stared at him without really staring. "Look, Quentin. Get up and go home. Or take me into the bedroom."

"Just like that?" His loins stirred.

"Life is too short to pussyfoot around. I missed a chance with you years ago. I won't miss another because I was too afraid to tell you how I feel."

She was speaking his language. Life was indeed short and could be taken away at any time, without warning. His craving was starting to burn inside, an absolute desperation to pull her toward him and . . .

But he couldn't.

He couldn't do her like that. He popped up as if someone had dumped a bucket of icy water on him. "Don't take this the wrong way, but I'm going to leave."

Her face flattened as he fought back the urge to cast his worries aside. He remembered getting home after school and being completely unable to shake her from his mind, wondering if she felt the same way. Part of him *knowing* she did. He'd wanted to tell her, but instead, he'd written about her. Calling her *Brooke* so that no one would know, so that his nosy mother wouldn't search through his things and know that he had a crush on his teacher.

"Suit yourself," she said, trying to act less hurt than she was.

Sure, he didn't want to blur the lines during an investigation, but there was more. He didn't want to mess up her life. She'd been hurt enough. The best he could do was protect her from himself. If he told her that *she* was Brooke, it would all come crashing down.

He moved toward the back door. "Sylvie, trust me, you don't want me to stay here with you."

"I'm not going to beg, Quentin. You don't want to step into my world now. I get it. Just go."

"It's not that."

"You don't need to lie to me."

"Dammit, Sylvie, I'd dive into your world if I could. It's just not a good idea, okay?"

Sylvie shooed him away this time. "Goodbye, Detective Jones."

Jones put his hand on the knob, knowing he better get out of there if he was going to escape this temptation. "I'm going to wander around the island. Be back in the morning to check on you."

"Don't bother. You've successfully put me in my place. Should the murderer come calling, I'm not sure I'd care that much."

His heart broke for her. "You're really laying it on thick, honey."

"Don't you dare call me *honey*."

"Sylvie, you're too good for me. If I carried you off to your bedroom, we'd have a hell of a time. You'd unlock something in me. But I'd mess it up down the line, and I couldn't bear it. You've endured enough already."

Something he'd said struck a chord. She stood and faced him, speaking loudly across the room, her finger pointed at him. "You're not the only one in the world who has seen the devil. The devil makes me tea every *goddamn* morning when I wake up and see black. He makes us all goddamn tea. At least I'm showing up." A cry escaped her. "I might have made it all worse by moving here, but at least I'm getting out of bed." She fell back onto the couch. "Why are you still here?"

The answer was complicated. He didn't like running out on her. And he hadn't gotten to his questions about the investigation. He drew in a long breath, let go of the knob, crossed back across the room, and stood over her. "Did you get it all out of your system?"

She looked mad enough to hit him. "I don't know."

Watching her closely, he asked, "What did you mean, you made things worse by moving here?"

Judging by the way she fired off a response, it was almost as if she knew Jones would circle back to her statement. "Oh, you mean during my diatribe?"

He didn't say anything. She wasn't good at playing dumb.

"Don't worry about it," she finally said.

Jones sat back down. "Sylvie, I'm going to know every single thing about all of you. I won't stop until it's all laid out in front of me. Did you kill Frank Overbrook?"

"What? No!"

"Then tell me. I can help you, but you have to tell me the truth. I can make sure you get a fair trial. Did he go after you?"

"I far preferred the part when you were rejecting me."

"Did he?"

"No! I told you . . . I was asleep."

Jones felt bad for pushing, but this was important. "I'm not going anywhere until you come clean. What are you keeping from me?"

Her chest sank; words tumbled from her mouth. "David's a bad man. He's awful to her."

"In what way?"

"The way he speaks to her, treats her. She just takes it . . ."

"What does all this have to do with you?"

"I confronted him about it. Not that I could threaten him much, but I told him we all knew and that he'd get what was coming to him if he didn't stop."

"How did that make it worse? What does this have to do with Frank?"

"It doesn't have anything to do with Frank."

It had to, Jones told himself. "How did you make it worse?"

"He was furious that Miriam was talking about it to me and made her life a living hell for it, speaking even worse to her, locking her out, making her sleep outside."

Though he sympathized with Miriam, Jones was glad to hear this was Sylvie's confession. A smile even rose on his face. He wasn't quite ready to put a woman he cared about in prison. For a minute there, he thought she might be on the verge of a murder confession.

"Well, Sylvie, you put the 'oh' in *Paradiso*."

"Oh, is this when funny Quentin rears his head? After he rejects a girl and forces a confession? Maybe you're right: no one is that dark."

"I told you." He wiped the smile off his face, wondering if she could tell. "I'm going to look into David more. Whatever is happening between them will stop."

"I hope so. She's such a good person, Quentin. Faithful. I do think she should leave him. So she was driving the car; she doesn't deserve to live the rest of her life in hell like this."

"I agree with you."

What a night, Jones thought. He wasn't sure he was any closer to the truth. Maybe he was. Maybe David was hiding something. Glenna too.

~

Jones hiked the pine-needle-laden path to the clearing to find the officer who'd been assigned to watch the island. Sergeant Tacker sat in the patrol car, smoking. He didn't see Jones coming till Jones reached into the window and plucked the cigarette from his hands.

"A lot of good you're doing, Tacker."

He jumped so hard, he about hit his head on the roof of the car. Probably whizzed himself. "Dammit, Jones! You scared the shit out of me."

Jones leaned down, well aware that Sylvie had surprised him smoking in the car the night before. Some might have called him hypocritical, but what the hell. They were all overworked and short on sleep.

"You need to get your ass out of the car and go walk around. This is no joke. There are good people on this island who need to be looked after."

Tacker's face reddened. "I just got done with taking a round. Came back for a smoke."

"Well, do your job, Tacker. Keep your eyes open." Jones handed him his cigarette back. "Especially keep an eye down that road for Miss Nye. You see a light on, there's a problem."

"Why's that?"

"She can't see. Doesn't use lights." Jones hit the guy's shoulder. "I'm serious. There's a killer on this island. I'm going to find him, but first I need some sleep. Been short on it."

"How'd you get here, anyway?"

"My boat's dragged up to the beach. Stay awake and I'll be back early."

"Yes, sir."

Chapter 21

KNOCKING DOWN THE PINS

February 24, 1970
Day 4

Catherine hadn't gotten out of bed yet. Having been too hot during the night, she'd shucked off her nightgown and tossed it and the covers aside. Now that the sun was up and shining harshly through the windows, she'd slipped on sunglasses and was sitting up against the headboard. The fan spun lazily overhead, casting down a welcome breeze.

Detective Jones was right: all the healing she needed was stored in the rays that now warmed her skin and filled her soul. Something about writing that letter to Frank, and certainly Jones's kind words, had helped lift her out of despair. She also kept thinking of how she'd been saved from killing herself. There was a reason for that. She'd been given a second chance.

No more feeling sorry for herself. No more wondering if she should return to where she'd been. She was now Catherine Overbrook, a woman who would never again look back over her shoulder. A woman who knew only how to press on.

I will pick up the pieces of this broken heart, she thought, *and do what we set out to do when we said our vows to one another. That day,*

I shed the skin of Catherine of Chicago and became this woman that I am now. When I get out of this bed, I will only forge ahead. I will find a way to make this life work. I will go barefooted into the sand and swim in the Gulf and find joy in those warm waters. I will do all the things that Catherine of Chicago wouldn't have imagined doing. I will do the things that Frank and I had promised each other on the drive down.

Even though he'd been subdued, he'd let out moments of excitement in his own Frank way. That drive had been more special than she'd known, even in the silence that lasted sometimes an hour.

I will not worry about being alone. I've been alone all my life. This time, I will have Frank tucked into my memory, his energy flapping my wings.

Ready to face the day, Catherine removed her glasses and slipped off the bed and stood at the window for a while, watching the tiny waves slide onto the shore and spread out in pools over the powdery sand. The sun shone even brighter, tingling her skin and calling to her.

I am dreaming, she mused. It couldn't be so easy to climb out of grief. I know that I have a long road ahead of me, but I also know that I am able. I will remember this feeling I have in my heart, the way that I know who I am and what I'm capable of. No matter how I feel tomorrow, I am alive today.

A smile stirred, one she'd not known since the night of the lobster boil. It felt real and fresh and full of . . . what was it? Full of life. She had a long stretch of life spread out in front of her, and Frank would want nothing less than for her to live it wildly, colorfully, richly. Surely he'd loved her. Maybe he hadn't been the best at showing it, but he had to have loved her. Why else would he have married her and swept her away to Florida?

She retrieved the letter she'd written to him from her bedside drawer. Rummaging around, she found a lighter and padded into the bathroom. "This is me trying, Frank. This is me letting go." She kissed the letter and lit a corner, holding it until the spreading char threatened to singe her fingers. The smell of burned paper filled the room. She dropped the last of the letter and watched it disappear in the sink.

Finding herself in the full-length mirror mounted to the bathroom door, she nearly shied away but held strong. "This is me," she said. She opened her arms outward, as if on display. "This is me."

Back in the bedroom, she became transfixed by the view west. The sun had turned the water into a kaleidoscope of color. The sun and the water called to her. Uncaring that she was nude, she walked through the house and right out the back door. Past the deck where she'd heard Sylvie scream and down the walkway to where she'd first seen Frank's body.

In the place where they'd found him on the beach, Catherine knelt and drew a heart in the sand and gazed at her handiwork.

"You made me Catherine Overbrook, and I will not return to Catherine of Chicago. I am yours forever, Frank; the woman you woke inside, the woman who you gave wings."

She stood and went to the water and let it swirl around her feet. The sun warmed her chilly skin. She stood tall and proud and raised her arms and gazed out to the horizon. Flashes of a new her, wearing a new painting smock and tackling new projects, flashed before her, a future ripe with possibility and hope.

"I am Catherine Overbrook, and I will be okay!"

～

Detective Jones stood before Sylvie's door at seven on the nose. He'd gotten little sleep but felt ever so slightly refreshed. Enough to keep going.

She cracked the door. Her tightened cheeks glowed red with anger. "How'd you know it was me?"

"Because, Quentin, no one else knocks on my door at seven in the morning. I can smell you and your cigarettes, anyway. What a nasty habit."

Jones laughed. "You're telling me. May I come in?"

"What for?"

Had he supported the war, he could have bottled that attitude and sold it to the US Marines fighting over there in Vietnam. Oorah!

"I wanted to check on you," he said.

"You checked on me. No one killed me in the night. Unfortunately. I can go on to live another day. Now, if you'll excuse me, I'm starting on a new project."

Only then did he notice the clay on her hands. "Sylvie . . ."

"I'd like you to go."

Jones blew out a frustrated blast of air. He'd already screwed things up, and they hadn't even gotten started. It hadn't taken a crystal ball to see it coming. Best to quit while he was behind. "I'll come back and check on you later."

"I won't hold my breath."

Damn, she could cut deep when she wanted to. He turned and went back down the steps. It might hurt now, but it would hurt worse if he let anything come between them. Forget his professional duty. He wasn't that tied to the rules. Had she been another girl, perhaps he would have been open to messing around.

Not with Sylvie. He came loaded with far more trouble than she deserved.

⌇

Sylvie was torn apart, roadkill being eaten by the vultures. She'd almost told him the truth, every bit of it, last night. She'd felt so vulnerable. Had he kissed her, her walls might have come down in a way that wouldn't have let her keep the secret another moment.

Even in his light contact, as he guided her with his arm, she could sense something so powerful in him. His touches were lightning strikes, strong and confident. Protective.

Yet there was a fragility too. A fear, even. It was that beautiful balance in him that made her crave him, crave his touch. How could she keep lying to him?

After he'd left, Sylvie lowered and curled up on the tile floor, terrified of what was to come, her last days of freedom. Because Jones would soon come for her.

He was good at his job. Good enough to eventually get at the truth. If she confessed, he might help her. Might even let her go. She couldn't ask that of him, though.

She was torn because she loved him, and she couldn't bear the idea of lying to him. And he seemed like the kind of man who believed in the law. Had she opened her mouth, he might have been forced to take her in, to slap cuffs on her wrists and throw her into the back of his patrol car.

She wasn't ready to face the inevitable yet.

Sylvie pressed up, went into the kitchen, and reached for a glass in the cabinet, ignoring the clay still on her hands. She started to fill it with water from the tap but then turned around and slung it as hard as she could.

"It's over! Everything is over!" As the glass crashed into something hollow on the other side of the kitchen, she yelled, "What a waste of life you are, Sylvie Nye!"

It wasn't enough, throwing one glass. She threw another and then reached for the porcelain vase she knew was there. Miriam had usually kept it filled with fresh flowers, but she hadn't been over since the murder. Sylvie flung the vase toward the refrigerator, and it smashed into pieces, splattering all over the floor.

She followed that with an outburst of screams and slammed her fists down onto the counter. Her life was over. Quentin was going to find out, and she would live the rest of her life in a cell somewhere. Stale food. Loud noises. A hard bed. A shared toilet. A life not worth living. She collapsed into a chair and dropped her head to the table, the one where he'd first interviewed her.

If only she hadn't woken up from her accident. It would have been so much easier . . .

A sudden sense of not wanting to give up rose within her—likely her desperate survival instinct. The only way she'd survived so far was by pushing away the memory of that night and the thought of a life behind bars. She remembered slashing in the air with her scalpel and finding flesh. That grunt he'd made as his life began to leave him.

No. Stop. She couldn't revisit that night for another second.

Maybe Quentin *would* understand. It wasn't cold-blooded murder. She hadn't set out to kill Frank Overbrook when she'd gone walking.

Jones caught Glenna on the way to her car. He was surprised that Sandy didn't come running out like he had the day before, as if he were Glenna's protector.

"Hello, Detective." Glenna didn't look particularly pleased to see him. Her scrubs were folded up at the ankles to accommodate her short stature. She had one hand on the door handle.

"I thought I'd grab you before you head in. Do you have a few moments?"

"Just one or two. Doctor's not feeling well and will be coming in late today, so my plate is full."

"I understand. Let's be fast. Wanna take a walk?"

They headed out toward the clearing, their shoes crunching shells. "Firstly," Jones said, "a note was left on my car identifying the killer."

"Oh." Glenna's voice chimed like a bell on a beach cruiser.

"I'm not the sharpest crayon, but it seems to me it might be someone with access to a lot of magazines, like the ones in a doctor's office or perhaps the stacks in your villa. I wonder if I might find a few with pages missing in the trash."

She let her shoulders rise in bewilderment.

"Uh-huh." He waited. "You wouldn't know anything about it, would you?"

Glenna rolled out her bottom lip and swiveled her head back and forth.

"Something you said about cutting out travel articles, pinning them on your wall. That stuck out too. Makes me think you left the note. I'm not upset about it. I'd like to know why. And . . . Officer Challa is examining the fingerprints. I'll know exactly who left it by nightfall. Just thought we could skip all that and jump straight into why you left it."

Glenna slumped. "I just want the killer caught and things to return to normal."

"Any particular reason why you think it's him?"

She looked left and right, checking her surroundings. "Because I've seen how he treats Miriam. He has the potential to be a violent man."

After a few more questions, Jones changed direction. "I want to understand why you sold the house and moved to your little place now," Jones said. "Seems like such a dream you walked away from."

"I told you. These views . . . I've known them all my life."

"That's what you said. Why not go now?"

"Because I have a duty to Doctor. He needs me."

"Oh, isn't that the truth?"

She cut him a look that could have come with a slap or a punch. "Don't be inappropriate. We have been working together a long time, and we know how to help people. The least I could do is wait until he retires."

"Why didn't you wait and sell the house then?"

"Well . . ."

"Because you were moving in with him? Because he was luring you into some kind of relationship that would be much easier to hide with you on the property?"

"No."

"Why, then?"

"Because this was a perfect opportunity to find someone great to live there. A way to bring Frank out here. A way to make sure that Lollipop was populated by good people."

She was holding strong, not giving any signs that she was lying. Dammit, she was good. "Did Sandy make you sell your house to Frank?"

"No."

"He told me he did." That was a lie, and Jones felt bad about it, but not for long.

"Well, he . . ." Her tongue turned into a bag of jelly beans. "He didn't exactly make me."

"What happened then?"

"He . . . he told me that—"

A door swung shut behind them. Sandy had exited the front of his house and was coming down the steps.

"Tell me," Jones said to her under his breath.

"He was just trying to help me."

"Help you by forcing you to sell the only thing you have left? They've stripped it from you, haven't they? Not only Sandy, but all of them. There was a time when your family owned this *whole* island. That has to eat you up."

"I don't know your point."

"Oh, I think you do. Sandy pushed you. You relented. Because you'll do anything for him . . ."

Sandy was about fifty feet away now, moving slowly.

"When you met Frank, something snapped. Was it the price? Did he pay you cash? How did that work?"

"Yes, he paid cash."

Sandy was on them a few seconds later. "Am I interrupting?" He moved slowly, almost limping.

"I was asking Glenna if she'd felt obligated to sell her house."

"*Obligated?*" Sandy said, clearly not liking Jones's word choice.

"You know, for the good of the island. To make sure you could bring in someone of Frank's quality."

Glenna jumped in. "The doctor was encouraging me to leave the island."

"That's my point. I don't think you liked the deal. When you saw Frank, and you saw his happy wife drinking Champagne, talking about her new house and life on the beach, it hit you. That night, you confronted him and demanded he sell you the house back. When he said no, you stabbed him."

"I did not!"

Sandy went to Glenna, standing in between her and Jones. "Officer, it is time you leave. She won't say another word without a lawyer."

"Ah. We're getting somewhere."

"I—"

"Don't you say another word, Glenna. This man has crossed boundaries, and he's trying to force answers. Detective, I'd like you to leave my property."

Jones looked between the two of them. He wasn't done. "Sandy, I'm not saying you're off the hook in this case. Glenna didn't like you offering up her house to Frank. She may have killed him. What role did you play? Speaking of roles, this role-playing . . . how long have you two been sleeping together?"

That caught his attention. Sandy looked like he was about to lose his bowels. "What are you talking—"

"He knows," Glenna said through gritted teeth.

"That's right," Jones said. "He knows."

"There's nothing to—"

Jones cut him off, slicing his hand through the air. "There is no sense lying, sir. I am good at what I do, and I'm getting closer. It's a sad thing when a murder investigation happens. All the little lies come out. Turns out you two have quite a few. So tell me . . . did you manipulate Glenna? She's loyal to you and was a faithful friend to your wife. She sleeps with you, sold her house for you, what else? Did she murder for you, too, Doctor? I don't think you're completely innocent in this whole thing."

"This is preposterous! Come with me, Glenna." He grabbed her arm. "Look, Detective, what we do in the privacy of my home is *none* of your business . . ." His face had gone cherry red as he escorted her away. "It has nothing to do with the murder of Frank Overbrook."

"Are you sure?" Jones couldn't help but smile as he followed after them, speaking over their shoulders. He was finally getting somewhere. He still had layers to peel back, but this was a good start. The dominoes were finally starting to fall.

Sandy stopped. "Glenna and I have had a relationship since my wife died. It happened naturally. I very much like her company. She's kept me from . . ." He suddenly reached for his side. "She's kept me from . . ."

"Doctor," Glenna said. She slipped her arm under his.

Sandy's eyes closed, and he began to fall. Jones raced over, and he and Glenna caught him. But only barely. He was a heavy man. They lowered him to the ground, and Glenna went to work checking his vitals.

She finally looked up. "Help me get him into the house."

Chapter 22

LONELY FITS THE BILL

Once Sandy was in his bed with the nurse by his side, Jones went to check on the Carters. Baby or not, he needed more answers.

As he parked, he wondered what Frank's belongings from the moving van would reveal. Hopefully, Catherine would let him search without a warrant. There had to be something in his papers that indicated an issue—perhaps something specific with Sandy or a hiccup in his real estate deal with Glenna.

Jones climbed the steps and did a double take. The first thing he saw through the window was Miriam. She was holding the baby with a big smile on her face.

He stood there, puzzled, watching her tease the baby, making sounds and smiling. She'd indicated that she'd met the Carters but hadn't mentioned being friendly with them. That aside, Jones hadn't pegged her as the motherly type. Maybe that's what a baby did to all women.

Jones knocked on the door, and Levi pulled it open. "Detective." He looked less hostile than last time.

"It seems congratulations are in order," Jones said.

"They are, thank you."

"Boy or girl?"

"A big healthy boy. He must be nine pounds or so. That's what Miriam thinks."

Jones scratched his head, thinking that sly Levi and sweet new mother Amber might have pulled the wool over his eyes the same as Miriam. He'd been given the impression the Carters didn't know anyone on the island other than Sandy and perhaps Glenna, who had been helping with the pregnancy.

"I'm glad you have some help," he finally said.

Levi turned back for a second. "Yes, it's nice to have Miriam around. She's a kind woman."

Jones stepped forward. "I know it's a bad time, but I need to ask more questions."

The man didn't even put up a fight. He swung the door open. "The detective's coming in."

Amber lay on the couch, covered in a blanket, bags under her eyes. Miriam looked over from where she stood, rocking the baby in her arms.

"Good morning, everybody," Jones said.

They echoed the greeting.

Jones wasn't much of a baby guy, but he thought it might behoove him to recognize its presence. "Hello, little one."

The baby had a churlish smile. Miriam was apparently good at this sort of thing. Jones still couldn't believe she was the same woman whom he'd come to know by her pool. She was as sober as a preacher at the pulpit.

"He looks like a budding detective," Jones said.

"Let's hope not," Levi said, plopping down next to Amber.

"What's his name?"

Amber spoke from her comfy spot on the couch. "Silus."

"Silus," Jones repeated. "That's a good name."

"Would you like to hold him?" Miriam asked.

Jones raised his hands faster than Muhammad Ali under attack in the first round. "Oh no. I'm afraid I'm not good with babies."

"No one is until they have one," Miriam said. "They're more durable than you think."

Jones looked at the durable baby. How would childless Miriam know that? "He's cute, but I'll let you do the holding. Actually, I was hoping to talk more with—"

A movement out the window stopped him. David Arnett was perched at the end of the boardwalk, staring at the house with the scowl that had proved to be his resting face.

"What's your husband doing out there?" Jones asked.

Miriam took the baby to the window.

"He's doing what he always does: being angry, watching me, following me." She had some rancor in her voice, but it softened in an instant when she looked back down at the baby. "Don't you grow up to be a bad boy, okay, little Silus? I think you're going to be a gentleman."

"You seem pretty close to your neighbors, Miriam. Closer than you let on."

She kept her eyes on the baby, shaking his little hand. "I've been coming by to visit from time to time. Other than Sandy stopping by, they don't really have anyone."

"That's nice of you."

"It's my pleasure. I love babies."

"I'd like you to watch the baby while I talk to his parents. Could you give us a few?" Jones redirected his attention to Levi and Amber. "Just twenty minutes or so." He wasn't asking this time. Four days and still no arrest. The nice guy had left the island.

Miriam bounced Silus down the hall, and Jones pointed a chair toward Levi and Amber.

"No complications. I'm glad for that."

"Not a one," Levi said.

Jones waited for Amber to reply. "No, we were fine. Just like the old days."

"Okay . . . ," Levi said. "Can we get this over with?"

Ah, there was the old Levi.

"I think I told you last time. I'm trying to eliminate possibilities. How long has Miriam been coming over?"

Levi gave a quick look to Amber. "What, maybe a couple of months?"

"She just walked up one day?"

"No, we . . . Well, yeah. She brought us a cake."

"A cake? What kind?"

"What kind?" Levi echoed.

Jones clapped his hands and smoothed them together. "You know . . . it's all in the details. And I like cake."

"A pineapple thing, wasn't it, Amb?" He touched his wife's knee.

"Yeah, an upside-down cake."

"So she saw that you were pregnant and jumped right in to help?"

"She comes by from time to time to check on us."

"Why didn't you mention that before?"

Levi took back over. "You didn't ask."

"I'm sure I did. I asked who you knew on the island."

"Well, we know Miriam."

Jones was about to start pulling his own hair out. "You don't have to turn into a brick when I talk to you. I'm trying to help. Unless you killed Frank Overbrook. Then maybe you should turn into a brick. If you killed Frank, tell me now and save us all the trouble. I know you're a new dad and killing isn't the behavior of a good role model, but it would be so much easier if you told me now."

"I didn't kill anyone, Detective."

"How about you, Amber?"

"You're joking, right?"

Jones raised his hands. "Did you?"

"I didn't kill anyone."

"Then what are you two hiding? You're not here running from her parents. You're not here for the weather. You have some sort of an agenda. Something brought you to Paradiso."

Levi cut a glare at him. "We didn't like Virginia, and the idea of the tropics was appealing. I already told you."

Jones amped up the speed of his questions. "How do you know Barry Gatt?"

"Our landlord?" Levi asked. "We've been down this road, Detective."

"We have, but you were lying. You said you found an ad at the general store."

"That's right."

"Forgive me, but I'm not buying it. Nobody hires young kids to watch over their beach houses. No offense, but you look like a man who likes to catch a buzz, cause some trouble. I smell the grass in the air. I wouldn't even let you borrow my boat for ten minutes."

He shrugged. "Maybe some people are better at seeing the good in people."

"Fair enough. But you're still lying, and Gatt's going to tell me sooner or later. You sure could save me some time."

Amber reached for his hand—an act of solidarity.

"Okay, so I have to assume that one of you is the murderer or that you know who is. Otherwise, why are you hiding? I don't care why you're here. Just give me something to work with. You got money I'm not aware of? You rob a bank up in Virginia? I'm not going to tell anyone. I only want to know who stabbed Frank Overbrook in the neck."

"We don't know."

Jones looked for tells, letting the air buzz with Levi's words. The baby started to cry in the other room. Amber turned in that direction. "I need to go check on him."

"Amber, why are you lying to me?"

She sighed. "I don't know what you're talking about. We came down here and saw the sign—"

"I know your story."

"Then there you go."

She stood and followed the cries.

"Levi, last chance. I'm gonna have to start digging deeper. Way I see it, Gatt will tell me exactly what's going on. Does he know you? He owes you a favor? Did he know Dr. Overbrook?"

"You're really fishing now." He started tapping his foot to a beat only he knew.

"I'm a pretty good fisherman, Levi. Somebody's going to bite my hook before too long."

He scratched at the material of the couch. "It's not going to be me."

"No?"

"I'd like you to leave. My kid doesn't need to be around you and your investigation. We're over here minding our own business." He stood and waited for Jones to follow suit.

"Okay, then," Jones said. "Always nice seeing you, Levi. Something tells me whatever secret you got hiding is going to come out real soon. I look forward to it."

"You do that, Detective."

Jones looked out to where David had been stationed. Boy, did he have some more questions. "I'll take the back way, if that's all right with you."

"Whatever, man."

Catherine sat in the chair by the phone. She held a notebook and pen in her lap. Once she got to an operator in Burbank, Illinois, she said, "I recently lost my husband, and we were in the midst of a move."

"Oh no. I'm so sorry."

"Thank you. I don't know which mover he was using. I'm in Florida now and will have to call them all. I suppose we start in alphabetical order. Could you please help?"

"Of course. One moment, please."

Catherine heard some chatter in the background while she waited. This was a start, she thought. One day at a time, one step at a time, she would pull her life back together. Not only for Frank but for herself too.

"Hello, are you there?"

"Yes."

"Looks like there are about seven different moving companies. Want to start with A-Plus Moving?"

"Yes, please."

A series of clicks followed. Catherine drew her breath. *This is where it all begins. One step at a time. Don't think about the past.*

"A-Plus Moving," a cheery male voice chirped a moment later.

"Good morning, my name is Catherine Overbrook. My husband's name was Dr. Frank Overbrook. He passed away during our move, and I don't know who the moving company was that he enlisted."

The man offered his condolences.

Catherine thanked him, then laid out the facts. "Would you mind checking to see if he was working with you?"

The man left Catherine on hold. She gazed out the window. A shrimp boat bobbed in the water offshore. How had she made it her whole life without seeing salt water? The Gulf ebbed and flowed so differently from the lakes back home. She'd always found comfort when she walked along Lake Michigan, but this was different—far more satisfying.

Hold on to this feeling, Catherine. You're getting there. Recovering.

"Yes, Mrs. Overbrook, I'm sorry to say we don't have any records here with your last name. You might try Cantrell Moving . . . or Silhouette. They're the two that likely would handle a cross-country move."

"Oh, thank you. I didn't even think to narrow it down."

"You got it. Please let me know if I can help further. I'm sorry about your husband."

"You're kind to say so."

Catherine hung up and then found the operator again. She repeated the steps and came up dry with Cantrell. When someone from Silhouette answered, Catherine gave her the spiel. The woman, who sounded like she'd just burned through a Pall Mall, said, "Let me check for you, sweetheart."

Oh, please let this be the one. Please make it this easy. I need a break.

"I have you right here, Mrs. Overbrook. A shipment to Paradiso, Florida, right?" She gave the zip.

Catherine nearly jumped out of her chair with excitement, which would have been something Catherine of Chicago could never do. "When is it supposed to arrive?"

"I'm not quite sure. We work with United, and I see it's been transferred down to their Tampa office. You'll have to call them."

"I sure will, thank you very much!" This was progress, and it was a relief.

Back to a local operator, Catherine asked to be transferred to the United Van Lines office in Tampa, and in four minutes she had them. "Yes, Mrs. Overbrook. We've been trying to call you about scheduling a delivery and haven't heard back."

"My phone hasn't rung once in days."

"Let me see here." He gave a number.

"That's an Illinois number. We're already down here."

"That would explain it. I can get this out to you quickly. How about tomorrow? I'm sure you're anxious to get your things."

"You have no idea." She imagined what she might find. She'd learn more about her husband in those boxes than she had in their conversations.

"How about between eleven and twelve tomorrow? Osprey Isle, right?"

"That's right."

"We'll see you then, Mrs. Overbrook."

Catherine thanked him and put the phone back on the receiver. "That's right, Mrs. Overbrook," she said to herself. "Life isn't always impossible. Difficult, yes. Impossible, no." She had an urge to tell the detective the news. Mrs. Catherine Overbrook was not letting the darkness win.

Chapter 23

Wheelchairs on Sand

Once Detective Jones came over the dunes, he caught sight of David Arnett trucking it back to his house in the wheelchair that he'd said didn't move well on sand.

Jones jogged up to David just as he bumped up onto the boardwalk of his own property. "That thing moves mighty well, doesn't it?"

Arnett stopped with a jolt, his body jutting forward before settling. "What do you want, Detective?"

Jones came around to face him. "What are you so angry about? I get the accident. How about today, specifically? Kind of strange, you hanging out, watching your wife like a voyeur. Are you really that distrusting or paranoid? It's a bit creepy, my man."

Arnett started to move farther.

Jones put his hand on the back of the wheelchair. "Are you paying their way? The Carters, I mean. Does he do your heavy lifting? How much would a man like that charge you for murder? He'd probably do it for free, you pay Gatt his rent. Or was all this arranged spur of the moment? You didn't like how Miriam was talking to Frank, so you had your man put him down. What's Levi normally do for you? Run drugs? What went wrong? He after your wife?"

"You're insulting me now."

"No, I'm asking questions. I get the feeling that someone else knew Dr. Overbrook, and I'd like to know who that was. The sooner you all stop lying, the sooner I'll stop bothering you. Simple as that."

"Nothing is ever that simple, Detective."

"Not on this island, that's for sure. So, you don't like Miriam going over there. Is it a baby thing? You mad she likes that baby? Why aren't the two of you parents?"

"I think we've already told you. It wasn't something we wanted to do."

"You really hate her because she was driving the car that did this to you? That was a long time ago."

"Not easily forgotten." David looked away.

"Let me be clear about something. You're done treating her the way you do. Now that I know, I'll be checking in. No woman deserves that."

David pressed his joystick forward and the chair started moving. "Have a good day, Detective."

Jones didn't reply. It was time he head back to the office and do some more digging. Time to shake some apples off the tree.

⌇

Jerry Baxter, the homicide detective in Burbank, had left a message for Jones to call him. It took him thirty minutes to track Baxter down.

"Jones, sorry for the delay. Busy day."

"Tell me about it." Jones put his feet up on his desk, glancing at the pictures of the suspects adorning his wall.

"I did look into things. This Zelda Smith, I don't think she's in Burbank anymore. Born in twenty-three, only child. Parents are both deceased. Married Frank Overbrook in 1945. Divorced in forty-nine. Not much more to go on; the records were terrible back then in Burbank. I stopped by their former residence. As you know, he just sold the house. Place is empty. The neighbors on the left have only been there about five years. Said that Frank was a quiet man, kept to himself.

Neighbors on the right, the Williamses, were there longer than Frank and Zelda. Said they remembered her—pretty girl. More bubbly than Frank. They said he was a different guy after she left him."

"They didn't know where she might be?"

"I didn't get the sense they knew them more than passing by each other at the mailbox."

"Yeah, okay. Please keep me posted. And I might need more from you."

"Happy to help, as time allows."

"I appreciate you."

~

Jones went to a Mexican place near his house. He drank two strong margaritas, quickly. A man can't have tacos without tequila. The world seemed to bend into view, and he thought more of the islanders, probing into their psyches.

He shouldn't have been driving, but it was a straight shot to his place. He hit the bed hard, with barely enough energy to pull up the covers.

The clock read 9:04 p.m. when he came to. He wiped his eyes and went into the bathroom to splash water on his face. He felt refreshed despite the time. Four hours of sleep would buy him another day or two. He stripped and went down to the water for a dip. A manatee eased away as he slipped in.

Back inside, Jones showered and shaved, then cracked a beer and dialed a number he knew he shouldn't be dialing. "Sylvie, it's Quentin."

"Yeah." Her tone lacked any sense of excitement. He really had a way with women.

"I was calling to check on you."

"I'm still breathing."

He sipped his beer. "There's an officer walking around."

"Yeah, he came by earlier. What do I need you for?"

"Good question. I wanted to hear your voice. Always so warm when you speak to me."

"Quentin, you're not funny. Either come see me and let's see what we've been missing, or leave me alone. I'm not comfortable anywhere in between."

If she kept talking to him like that, he'd have no choice.

"Sylvie, it's complicated."

She didn't say a word.

"You there?"

"Make a choice, Quentin."

His brain and heart ran in opposite directions.

Sylvie sighed. "I'm sitting here with nothing on and wondering what to do." He'd detected a slur in her voice, and her brazen words confirmed that she'd been drinking.

"What's going on? Why are you drinking?"

"Who says I'm drinking?"

"Lucky guess."

"Well, take a guess at why I'm drinking. You're the detective."

"Sylvie, put a cork in it and go to bed."

"What's the point? So I can wake up bright eyed and bushy tailed?"

"I'm coming over."

"Oh, is that right? For what reason?"

"Because you don't sound okay."

"I'm perfectly fine. Another martini and I'll be flying."

"Sylvie, I'm hopping on the boat. Be there in twenty, all right?"

He slid up onto the sand and walked the anchor up to the beach. She sat at the kitchen table with a bottle of vodka in front of her. The whole room smelled of alcohol. Some slow jazz crept out of the record player.

There was a crunch at his feet. Glass and porcelain shards littered the floor. "Sylvie, what did you do?"

"Oh, that?" she said. "A little tantrum."

He looked at her and back at the floor. "Yeah, I'd say so. Where's the broom?"

"You don't have to."

Jones ignored her and went to the pantry, found the broom and dustpan leaning in the corner. He went to work sweeping up the mess, going after the big pieces first. "You could have really hurt yourself."

"Would that be so horrible?" she said.

He emptied the last load of the dustpan into the garbage and reached for a bag of white bread on the counter. Removing the twist tie, he said, "My mom had an old trick to get up the last bits of glass from a break. A piece of bread." He knelt down and sponged up the slivers of glass that he'd missed with the broom.

When he was finished, he sat next to her. "What has gotten into you?"

Her head turned his way, her eyes directed over his shoulder. "You ever wonder what the point is?"

"I think we all do."

She shook her head for a long while. Much longer and it might not stop. "I'm not sure there is one."

He took her hand. "Don't say that."

"You better not touch me unless you mean it."

Jones wasn't sure what to do. He pulled back slowly, eyeing the bottle of vodka and empty glass, the ice melting. "I wouldn't have pegged you as much of a drinker."

"I think I'm pretty good at it."

"This been happening a lot lately?"

She laughed under her breath. "No, but I think I might start."

"I can't imagine what you've gone through, but I see no reason why you can't have a fine life ahead of you."

"A 'fine life'? What does that mean to you, Quentin? What am I good for now? Lord knows there's not a man in Florida who'd want to take me on."

"I'm sure that's not true."

"Yeah, where is he?" Her lips thinned into a fine line as she let one eyebrow rise.

Jones had a lot to say but held back.

"I'm waiting . . ."

"Sylvie, you're still the same woman I knew way back when. Whatever happened doesn't make a difference."

"Yeah, just older and blinder. You would have done something about it, otherwise."

"If I didn't care so much about you, you're probably right. Trust me, I'm no good for you."

She shook a finger at him. "Isn't that a line of bullshit? I keep wondering, was it only me having those feelings back when I was your teacher? Was it only me that went home at night and got angry that you were my student? That I'd fallen in love and couldn't do anything about it?" She seemed to want to continue but stopped and let her curiosity fill the air.

She was really doing this, wasn't she? He'd asked for it, coming over here. He was pretty sure he'd be in trouble no matter what he said now.

"Of course it wasn't just you."

"I don't believe you."

He was caving, ready to tell her more than he should. "Sylvie, I would have dropped out of school had I known you felt the same way. I couldn't *stop* thinking about you." He drew a few lines on the straw place mat with his finger—a nervous habit. "You know those poems you found of mine? You *are* Brooke. I would go home and write poems about you . . . but I didn't use your name. In case my mom found them."

Her mouth slowly closed, the slowest motion in the world. "I see." All of her drooped.

Jones looked at her lips. He wanted to kiss her. Tell her she was still everything to him.

"You're looking at me," she said. "What are you thinking?"

Considering he didn't tell lies—according to him—he felt backed into a corner. "I'm thinking that I want to kiss you but well aware how poor of a choice that would be."

"Why would that be a poor choice?" Her voice changed, growing sensual and quiet.

"For one, you've been drinking."

"What's that have to do with it?"

"I don't want to take advantage of you."

She licked her lips, and he narrowed in on them. "I give you permission to take advantage of me. I would do the same thing sober."

He kept looking at her.

"Apparently, we're at a crossroads, Quentin."

"Isn't that the truth," he muttered.

What in God's name was he doing out here with a suspect during an investigation? She was right here, the missing puzzle piece to his life, the only woman who'd ever kept him up at night. Maybe he wouldn't hurt her. This could be the real thing. Either way, there was no denying how desperately he wanted her right now. Had he been a bull, he'd be pawing the ground.

But he kept pushing back. With this kind of discipline, he might even be able to quit smoking.

Thoughts about the brevity of life wedged their way in like a crowbar, prying back his fear of losing another chance, tasting the bitterness of regret in his last breaths. Don't miss another chance with her, Jones . . . Not after all those years of wondering what had come of her, what might have been had he reached out . . .

"It's all about the choices we make, isn't it?" Sylvie said, interrupting his thoughts. "The crossroads of life. I've been living right at that point where the road divides. And I don't—"

Jones couldn't take it another second. He sat up and drew closer to her. So much for quitting smoking. Touching her chin, he guided her to him, and she accepted a kiss with pursed lips. It was just what he'd imagined all those years ago, an overdue reunion shaking the walls of his soul.

Sylvie smiled as they pulled apart. Jones could have sworn she was looking right at him. "That was nice." She didn't exactly look happy, though.

"What's wrong?" he asked, noticing tears collecting in the rims of her eyes.

"I don't know . . . I don't know."

⌐

Sylvie did know. His kiss was as sobering as an ice bath. She'd wanted that for so many years and thought about him every day since he'd reappeared in her life.

"Well, there you go. I can make a woman cry with my kiss," Quentin said, knocking her from her thoughts. "Don't say I didn't warn you."

"No, it's not that. I . . ." How could she tell him the truth? She wanted to. Needed to. What a wretch she was to take advantage of him so, luring him in.

What in the world could she possibly say, that he'd kissed the lips of a murderer?

Later.

She would tell him later . . . if it came to that.

Flawed as it was, she still wanted this moment to last longer.

Though her chances were dwindling, Sylvie *still* could get away with it. It wasn't only her life that a confession would destroy. Others would be affected if the truth came out. She had to hold strong.

⌐

Sylvie finally looked at him with an exhausted expression. "I just want to go to bed." With that, she stood and worked her way to the back door, where she pulled it open. "Have a good night."

Jones was so bewildered that it took him a moment to find his legs. "Ohhhh-kay. I feel like I'm getting some mixed signals here."

"You're right," she said coldly. "It's not a good idea."

It was as if someone else had inhabited her body.

No matter what the explanation, Jones knew when he was no longer wanted. He stood and headed toward her and the open door. He was about to ask her what the hell was going on but stopped himself. It really was for the best if he got out of there.

"I'll be walking around the island, should you need anything." He could hear the bitterness in his own voice. But what the hell? She'd busted his heart wide open, but as soon as he started going with it, she'd shut him down.

"Be safe out there," she said.

He didn't bother even looking at her. Now he was the one with hurt feelings.

She closed the door after him, and he headed back toward the beach. What a mess he'd made now.

As he was about halfway down the boardwalk, he heard a crash. He turned and raced back to her door and found it open. Sylvie stood amid the pieces of a shattered vase that she'd made.

"You okay?" Jones asked, noticing she was out of breath. She'd clearly had another tantrum.

"I don't know." She dropped her head.

Avoiding the pieces of the vase, he stepped closer and pulled her into his embrace. "I'm here." He nuzzled his head up against hers, smelling her hair, feeling her body pressed to his.

"It's okay," he said. "Everything is okay."

She opened up to him and squeezed him tight. "I don't know," she said again.

"What in the world has gotten into you?" he whispered.

"I'm lost, Quentin."

"Aren't we all?"

"You don't understand."

"What does it matter, anyway?"

"It does."

She placed a hand on his chest and looked even deeper into his eyes. "You're a good man, aren't you? Just like I always thought." She was speaking more coherently now. The alcohol had worn off.

"I don't know about that."

"Just kiss me again, dammit. Good man or not, kiss me."

A flash of how wrong it was tried to block him, but his heart wouldn't have it.

He kissed her, and his knees nearly buckled. Her hands started moving, pulling him in, tearing at him. Back in the far and deep regions of his mind, he knew he shouldn't let this happen, but it was happening, and there was no stopping it. He'd waited too damn long . . .

He tugged at her shirt and lifted it over her head, exposing a pink bra. She went after his shirt buttons. "You're awfully liberal with your buttoning. Why even button at all?"

He smiled. "I was just making it easy on you."

Whatever had happened earlier—all the mixed signals, the confusion, the resistance—it fell away.

Sylvie ran her fingers along his chest and dragged them south, taking his breath away. As she unbuttoned and unzipped him, she pushed him up against the counter. She was damn hungry, and good at what she was doing.

She lowered his pants to his ankles, where he kicked them off, and there they were pressing against each other. Jones lifted her up onto the counter and pulled down her underwear. Then he unhooked her bra and kissed the bare skin of her breasts, then her stomach and thighs.

Sylvie pulled at his hair as he buried himself in between her legs, tasting her sweet essence and coming to know her body in the most intimate of ways. She soon moaned in explosive pleasure as her body kicked and pulsed.

"Take me to the bedroom," she said, reaching for Jones in all the right places.

He did as commanded, lifting her up and carrying her across the house, thumping his shoulder on a doorjamb along the way but managing to keep her safe from any bumps in the dark.

"Aren't I supposed to be the blind one?" Sylvie asked, causing them both to giggle.

Once in bed, she became animalistic, shoving him up against the headboard. "My turn," she said, and she had her way with him, taking him places he didn't know existed.

Afterward, Sylvie moved to the shower.

"I can feel you looking at me."

"I sure am." He analyzed her curves, savoring the view.

"I hope ten years has left you with more than that," she said before disappearing behind the wall.

The shower came on.

"You don't have to ask me twice." Jones rose and followed her into the bathroom as if she were tugging him with a rope.

Chapter 24

Running Like There Was No Yesterday

February 25, 1970
Day 5

When Jones awoke later, he felt her side of the bed. She was gone. It smelled like Sylvie everywhere—the sheets, the pillow. The air. He could get used to it, a scent like that.

As he stretched out and felt the comfort of her bed envelop him, he wondered what he'd been afraid of, anyway. He could get used to lying in bed with her. They'd made love and laughed and made more love and then talked late into the night, showing Jones the possibilities of a life with her.

He could get used to this, knowing all he had to do was get up and fight crime, then race back to her. Could he be the man she deserved? She had overcome a terrible accident and had been finding her way. That was more than one could say of Jones. It didn't take a shrink to know Jones still harbored a lot of pain over losing his father and what it had done to his mother and how it had carved a giant hole in his childhood. His work had become the only way to heal such pain. Or was it healing at all? Maybe it was just filling the void, one murder investigation after another.

Things seemed so clear, lying here in Sylvie's bed.

Jones swung his legs over to the side of the bed, eager to see her. He caught himself whistling. Jesus, Jones, what's gotten into you?

"Detective Quentin Jones, at your service," he said to himself. "Flipped upside down by a woman."

Shirtless and in shorts, he came out of the room calling her name. "Sylvie . . . where'd you go?"

Certainly no smells of bacon and eggs, no pitcher of fresh-squeezed orange juice. Maybe that would be his department. He could get into that, letting her sleep in and taking her a tray. Lying there with her and talking life, planning a day off that didn't include going over to the Salty Pearl and taking advantage of Larry, Curly, and Moe in poker. A day off that was about connecting with someone else, the simple pleasures of taking long walks, having picnics, sharing silly stories, exploring each other's minds. He wouldn't know what to do with himself.

She was out on the deck, wearing gray shorts and a thin top.

"No bacon and eggs?" he asked, coming out the door.

She didn't turn from her position facing the water. It was as if she were looking at the water, but she wasn't. Maybe listening to it, smelling it. Jones closed his eyes to imagine what that would be like. In a second, the waves were louder, even as small as they were. The breeze sang a song of its own, a tease that pushed by and tingled his skin and rustled the dune grass. And the birds, all of a sudden they were everywhere, chirping and cooing like a symphony. The smells came rushing in, too, the salty tang of the Gulf hitting him on the tip of his tongue and in the back of the throat.

He opened his eyes and approached the table. "What a morning, huh?"

Still nothing from Sylvie.

"Anyone in there?" he asked. He squeezed her shoulder, sensing incredible stress beneath the surface. "Hey, you okay?"

Sylvie finally turned. Her face was painted with agony. Heartache, pain, terror. Something. All of it. He wasn't sure.

He lowered to his knees and took her hands. "What's going on?"

She shook her head.

"Tell me."

Another shake of her head: cold, lost, empty.

"I need to tell you something," she finally said. "Sit down."

Jones had no idea what she was about to say as he took the chair next to her.

"I . . . Oh God, am I really doing this?" she started. "Why do you have to be who you are, Quentin?" She swallowed back a mess of emotions. Then it came like a tsunami appearing out of nowhere. "I know what happened to Frank."

Jones had opened himself up to a lot of options. Maybe she was going to tell him that it was over with them before it started. Or that she was leaving Florida.

But not that.

Not that . . .

"Okay," he said. "It may come as a surprise to you, but I'm interested."

She wasn't in the mood for his humor.

"You're not going to like it," she said. "Or me."

"I'm all ears."

He had to wait a long time before she spoke again. Then finally: "I *was* out walking that night. You guessed right when you'd asked me that earlier. You were right about a lot of things . . ."

"Take a breath, Sylvie."

She nodded and took his advice, gathering herself. "Frank attacked me," she said.

"What?" Jones sat up and leaned in. His heart nearly fell out of his chest.

"I was strolling along the waterline, and the next thing I knew, a man's body was on top of me in the sand, pulling my shirt apart, ripping my shorts off. Forcing himself on me. I didn't know who it was, just a strong man grunting as he forced himself on me."

"Oh God, Sylvie." Jones had gathered that Frank was an odd duck, but he'd missed the clues that he could be such a violent animal.

"I carry one of my scalpels when I walk," she said. "I reached into my pocket and drew it out, took the cork off the top. And stabbed him."

"Sylvie . . ."

"I know."

"Why didn't you tell me? Why didn't you report it?"

She shook her head as tears spilled out. "I was ashamed, I don't know. He'd nearly stripped me and rubbed all over me and kissed me and felt me and then he was dead. I still didn't know who it was. I was . . . I don't know."

She began to tremble, her fingers and her lips. "I didn't think people would believe me. I wanted it to go away. I dragged the body out as far as I could go, way past where I could touch, and I gave him one last push."

"Where's the scalpel?" The detective in him was already back to work.

"I . . ." She tripped over what she was about to say. "I tried to find it, but I couldn't."

Jones remembered how she had said she hadn't gotten much sleep that night. Now he knew why.

Sylvie lowered her head. "It didn't occur to me that the body could float back up. When the sun came up, I went back out onto the beach and walked the waterline . . . and heard a disturbance. The way the water circled around something, like a manatee. I've found one washed up before. I heard birds tearing at flesh. I shooed them away and felt down; it had to be the man I had killed the night before. I wasn't sure what to do, Quentin, but I didn't want to go to jail. I pretended like I'd stumbled upon a random body."

She wiped her eyes. "I didn't know who it was until Glenna ran up and said his name."

Jones stared at the wood plants for a while, scrambling to put it all together. "You were defending yourself. Why didn't you report it? Why didn't you tell me earlier?"

"I was afraid. I thought . . . I wasn't thinking clearly."

"Even in the days afterward?"

"By then, it was too late."

"How did you know where to stab him? It was a perfect kill." He wished he hadn't said it so coldly, as if he was speaking to Challa.

"I got lucky—or unlucky. I stabbed into the air a few times." She made a jabbing motion. "He was trying to block me, but I landed one. I'll never forget what it was like, feeling the blade sink into flesh."

She shook her head, seemingly recalling the moment. "He kind of . . . his body went limp . . . and I dragged him out into the water."

"That's not easy."

She shrugged. "I had so much adrenaline going through me."

His insides went to pieces. "Dammit, why didn't you tell me sooner?"

"I'm telling you now."

He lit up a Marlboro as his mind shot off in a million directions. According to the coroner, Frank had still been alive, but Sylvie might not have known it. "What did you do with the clothes you were wearing? Did they have his blood on them? Of course they did."

"I'm sure." She paused. "I . . . I burned them in a bucket. Then I threw the buttons that didn't burn into the Gulf."

"How about the bucket? Where is it?"

"In the water somewhere."

"What did you do with your shoes?"

"I was barefooted."

"It was cold out."

"Not really."

He sighed out a puff of smoke, thinking she had all the answers that he'd been looking for. He'd completely let her get in the way of his process, a fact that hung heavy on him. It was the biggest mistake he'd made in his career.

"Had you called it in, you would have been fine. Now you look like you're hiding something."

Fury took her over. "Have you ever had someone force themselves on you? You can't imagine what I've been through." Her words had a cutting edge to them.

"I'm not blaming . . . Sorry. I'm . . . scrambling to figure out what to do . . ." Admittedly, despite the bigger issue here, he felt used. Couldn't she have shared this revelation before ravishing him throughout the night?

"Can you help me?" she asked.

"What do you want me to do?"

"I don't know."

With a flash of hope, he imagined a world where he carried her back to the Boston Whaler and they took off, running like there was no yesterday, two people off for a fresh start. Or he could push the investigation in the direction of a suicide. That was the real ticket, make it look like the bastard Frank had stabbed himself and then walked out into the water. Quentin could make it happen. No question.

Jones could put the evidence in place. Even come up with a suicide note if he had to. Nobody back in Naples would question him. He could testify and make a jury believe whatever he wanted them to.

He didn't live in that world, though. The world of Detective Quentin Jones had only one building block, and that was the truth. He couldn't look himself in the eye ever again if he abandoned justice. He only had one choice, and he sent his mind in that direction, like a school of fish going to work on a dead animal floating in the sea. There had to be a way to protect her.

"I have to take you in," he said.

Her shoulders slumped. "No."

"I don't have a choice."

"Can't you just . . . ?"

"I don't do that. If you told me because you thought I'd help you get away with it, you made the wrong decision."

"Fine, then. Take me in. I deserve it, anyway." She stood up and crossed her hands out in front of him, brave and exhausted in equal parts. "Take me in!"

Jones stood and pulled her into a hug. She didn't resist. "It won't be like that," he said. "I mean . . . I can help you, but I do have to take you in. You'll go in there and tell the truth. You'll have to sit in a cell, but we can get you out on bail. I'll connect you with the best attorney in the state. We'll dig up dirt on Frank. Guys like that don't do this kind of thing only once. I'll find his ex-wife. She'll know. We'll prove that he was going to rape you and you defended yourself."

"What about how I didn't fess up? How I didn't tell anyone until now?"

"How you attempted to make the body disappear?"

"That too."

"I'll testify, if it goes to trial," Jones said. "I'll tell them how messed up you were, how you didn't trust anyone. How you eventually told me, wanting the truth to come out."

"Will they believe it?"

"We can make them buy it." He sounded surer than he really was. You never knew with Florida juries. They could be unforgiving. That's what scared him.

Jones squeezed her tighter. "You're going to be okay, but I have to take you in."

She nodded into his shoulder, sniffling.

"We'll talk more on the way in. But the sooner we get you to the station, the better."

He let go of her and found her eyes. "Sylvie . . ." He wanted to kiss her, but that felt wrong. Fuck it, who cared. He kissed her. "I'll protect you, okay? Everything is going to be fine." Tears collected in his eyes now, daring to run down his cheeks.

He stubbed out his cigarette. "We have to go."

Chapter 25

THE MERMAN TAKES HER AWAY

Though he was still a rebel at heart, Detective Jones was bound by his devotion to justice. He did this thing, upheld the law, not because he was some Boy Scout but because it had to be that way. His uncle had burned the idea into him. Bending a few rules was even okay, as long as it was in the name of justice. In the end, balance had to be restored.

There was no other way.

Jones drove Sylvie toward his place, the motor whirring, the boat slicing through the water. Sylvie was riding a boat for the first time since the accident that had taken her vision, her mind likely being torn apart by the past and the future.

He knew these waters well and kept the speed up as they rode the shoreline, only pulling back the throttle once he cut inland. The day grew brighter as the boat crept through the narrow creek surrounded by mangroves.

"We're here," he said when the dock came into view.

She twisted her head forward. "Paint the picture for me."

"It's not much."

"It's on the water?"

"We're as middle of nowhere as you can get in Collier County. Little dock leading up to a house that I've been renting from a guy who used to use it as a fishing cabin."

"Suits you," she said.

"Yeah, I guess so."

He hopped onto the dock, tied the Whaler up, and helped her step off the boat and toward the house.

"Can we wait a little longer?" Sylvie asked as he led her toward the patrol car. "Do we have to go right now?"

The whole thing could wait a few more minutes. "Why don't you come inside?"

As he opened the door, she said, "Tell me what I'm seeing."

"Not much."

"It smells like you."

"What's that like?"

"Like a merman would smell."

"A *merman*?"

"That's how I picture you. A man who retreats back to the water to recharge. You go around flapping your tail under the surface, maybe going to see the other mermen. Hopefully, there's no mermaid down there."

He chuckled, more out of a courtesy than anything else. "There are no mermaids down there, trust me."

Enough of that, he thought. He took her hand and led her to the couch. She had cold, fearful fingers. "I'm not going to let you go, Sylvie. I'll be by your side. I'll help you. We'll find a way through this."

She sat perfectly still. "I don't want to drag you into it. I did it; I tried to hide it. They'll decide what to do with me and I'll accept my punishment. Maybe I'll sell the house. I won't need it where I'm going. You can have it if you like."

"You'll be back to Osprey before you know it." At least, he hoped so.

She smiled. "I'm not sure I'll be welcome. Never mind the other islanders—imagine Catherine. She'll hate me forever. I ruined her life."

"Her new husband ruined her life," he said. "How could she have known better? She didn't know him at all."

Jones imagined what it would soon be like to walk her into the station. What a tragedy.

Sylvie patted the couch around her. "What an indentation. You sleep here?"

"I've been known to."

"You're a mess, Quentin. You really do need a good woman. All you messes of men do. I would have been good for you . . . before the accident."

Jones sat next to her on the couch, slipped his arm around her, and moved his head to hers, cheek to cheek. "You're good for me right now."

"Yeah, but it's different now, isn't it? I'm more of a burden than a partner."

"Will you stop talking like that? It's the other way around."

She felt his face. "That's ridiculous."

"I'm worried I'd hurt you."

She kissed him. "I'd be willing to take the chance."

He pulled his lips away. "I . . ."

"What, Quentin? What's on your mind? What are you afraid of? I'm the one going to jail."

Her decision to sleep with him before her confession gnawed at him. Was she manipulating him? "I'm sorry for this, sorry I have to take you in. I wish there was another way."

"I wouldn't expect anything else. You're a good man, Quentin. Good men do good things." She slapped her leg. "Let's go get this over with."

"Yeah."

Quentin was torn apart inside. Manipulation or not, he would do everything he could to make sure she got a fair trial and was able to return to her life.

She rode up front, and they didn't talk much. "When we get to the station," he started as they drew close, "I'm going to find you a lawyer. You don't talk to a soul. I'm serious. You don't open your mouth until a lawyer says that I sent him. Got it?"

"When will I know more?"

"Arraignment will be later today or tomorrow morning. I'll be back to take your statement, but the lawyer comes first."

Things were just getting moving at the station, the morning round of cops going in and out through the swinging doors. Jones got out and went to her side, pulled open the door. "I have to cuff you."

She nodded and stuck her hands out. He put the cold steel around her wrists and Mirandized her in a near whisper, then escorted her up the steps and into the station. It took five minutes to book her. After she'd changed into an orange jumpsuit, they took her away. She looked so helpless, being ushered through the steel doors that led to the jail cells.

He left her to go find Wycoff. "The Osprey Isle thing," Jones said as he busted in, "it was Sylvie Nye who did it. Overbrook was trying to rape her. She had a sculpturing scalpel that she carried for protection."

Wycoff had his elbows propped on his desk, those tattoos swollen against the muscles. "Jesus, what has this world come to?"

"Exactly what I just asked. I didn't pick up that the vic was violent. He and his wife had only known each other a short amount of time. She thought he was charming in his own way, despite being strange. The other doctor felt the same way."

"You know as well as I do," Wycoff said, "the really bad ones are the best at fooling people."

"I guess so." Jones pinched his mustache. "I'm going to go find Milton, see if he can take her. Don't let her talk, otherwise, please." Milton was the best lawyer in town.

Wycoff sat back. "You can finally go home and get some rest."

"Yeah, I'll do that once I get Milton." Jones didn't want to tell Wycoff—or anyone, for that matter—what Sylvie meant to him. Not yet. "Do me a favor: make sure she's taken care of in there."

"You're such a bleeding heart, Jones. She'll be fine."

"Just say something, will ya? Make sure they treat her like a lady. She didn't do anything wrong other than hold back what happened."

"Yeah, that's not exactly the right thing to do, Jones. She'll have to pay for that."

"She was afraid. Hurting. He'd wrestled her to the sand and pulled her clothes off. A woman can't get past something like that. She didn't know what to do."

Wycoff picked up the phone. "I'll take care of her. Just get her Milton and she'll be okay. Then go put your head on a pillow for a while, for God's sake."

"Will do," Jones lied.

꙳

The moving truck was thirty minutes late. Catherine had been watching the window with anticipation, wondering what might arrive. A whole house worth of furniture? A few simple items? Frank might have been boring to the outside eye, but he was full of surprises, even in death. She couldn't believe she hadn't asked him what he was bringing with them on their journey south. They'd bought Glenna's house furnished, but it was an outdated collection of wicker and weatherworn wood. Some new pieces could really spruce up the place—not that Catherine was materialistic now. But she did like the idea of making her place more presentable, a home of which to be proud.

Aside from the furniture, what else? Was she about to discover his secrets? Had he written any other books? Would there be pictures, photo albums?

When she heard the shells crackling under the wheels of the truck, she raced out the door. Heavy rock 'n' roll blasted from the speakers.

Two guys returned her wave through the windshield of a medium-size moving van. The driver got out. He was as big as a refrigerator. The ground shook when he stepped down.

"Good morning, ma'am. I'm assuming you're Mrs. Catherine Overbrook?"

"That's me." She was barely a *Mrs.*, she thought, but the correction didn't seem necessary.

The other guy was as scrawny as the driver was hefty. He had a missing tooth up top and was sucking on a cigarette. He gave a smile but didn't say anything.

"I don't know what to expect," Catherine said. "It's all my husband's things. From his house in Burbank."

"We have a full load," the big one said. "You want us to take it all inside?"

"I think so. Let's take a look."

They went around to the back, and the big one unlatched and pulled up the door. Catherine was shocked by the number of items before her, a heap load of furniture and boxes stacked floor to ceiling all the way to the back.

"Oh, goodness. I . . . Yes, I suppose everything goes inside. If it's okay, I'll direct you with each piece. I need to do some rearranging."

In a way, she felt a sense of joy. Frank had come back to her. This piece of him she hadn't known. She eyed a nice recliner edged with gold trim. Was that chair where he used to read and relax? Oh gosh, did Frank ever relax? She hadn't seen it, but she'd only spent a few hours in a home with him.

"Let's put that right by the windows, facing the water . . . We'll start there."

The men moved the chair up to the house and set it right where she wanted. She plopped into the recliner and smiled. This was him, my husband. This was his chair. I can feel him sitting here, smoking his pipe, maybe sipping a bourbon, thinking about his book.

"What a view," the big one said.

Catherine barely heard him and only registered his comment a few seconds later. "Thank you. It really is a treasure."

As the movers continued to unload the van, Catherine pulled the lever and rested back in the recliner. It smelled like him. Like an old library with leather and wood and pipe smoke. That was the way she'd always seen him in her imagination. His mind must have looked that way, too, a library with shelves full of musty books, all the wisdom in the world. Was it any wonder that he was always watching from the outside? He wasn't much of a participator—more an observer, taking it all in and shelving it where he could access it later.

The men brought in several more pieces of furniture, two bedside tables that were far more attractive than what had been there previously. She had the men swap out Glenna's tables for Frank's. They brought in a gorgeous corner cupboard. Catherine had never thought she'd ever own a corner cupboard, let alone such an exquisite antique example. There just so happened to be a spot in the dining room for it. She wasn't sure what she'd put in there. Maybe he had some fine china too.

Catherine sent a few more pieces of furniture into the guest bedroom, and then it was on to the boxes. The movers kept going out and coming back in with more. An hour after they'd arrived, she was staring at a stack of cardboard boxes in the living room that would take hours, if not a couple of days, to go through. What a wonderful task to have, though. What a gift—a chance to get to know Frank even more. It was the greatest gift he could ever have given her.

As she followed them back out, she gave the nice men ten dollars each and waved at them as they drove away. Returning inside, she approached the pile of boxes. It was time to get to know the only man she'd ever loved.

⌇

Detective Jones sat at his desk, staring at pictures, wondering how he hadn't pieced this together sooner. Dammit if he hadn't shaken up the island, all the while completely missing Sylvie as the killer. He scrolled through the islanders in his mind. Sandy and Glenna, having their . . . whatever it was. Miriam and David's abusive relationship, the way he was punishing her. The Carters . . . Don't even get him started. Sylvie was right. If she found a way to walk, she wouldn't be able to live next to Catherine Overbrook. One of them would have to leave the island.

There were other laws being broken, secrets being kept. They weren't his job anymore, though. The murder had been solved, no thanks to him. Unless he counted sleeping with the accused to get her to confess. He'd done that well enough.

He called Milton, the public defense attorney, and left a message asking him to call him back. While it was fresh on his mind, he banged out a report. That way, Wycoff wouldn't ride him later. Two pages. He kept it short and sweet.

Milton returned his call twenty minutes later. "Sorry, Jones, I was in court."

"I got a favor to ask." Jones told him about Sylvie, asked him if he'd make sure to take the case. Milton promised him he would.

Jones stopped for a burger and beer on the way home. Had another beer or three once he was showered and shaved. Sometimes drinks multiply like rabbits, especially when the truth that comes to light isn't the truth you'd hoped for. Poor girl was sitting alone in a cell, waiting to know whether she'd spend time in prison, and there wasn't much more Jones could do.

A few things kept bothering him, though, splinters that he couldn't dig out with tweezers. Catherine had said that her husband had acted differently after seeing the Carters. He must have known them beforehand. To back up the theory, Glenna had even insinuated that someone else on the island other than Sandy knew Frank. He could have been the one paying Barry Gatt for their rent, but why?

Jones took the picture of the Carters and set them next to the photo Challa had taken of Frank's body. Amber and Frank did have similar sharp features: a skinny frame, a slightly pointy nose, and cheekbones that rode high up on the face. It was a stretch, but she could be related to him. Maybe a niece.

That line of thinking didn't add up, though. If Frank was there to be with family, he would have spoken to the Carters. Catherine would have seen the reunion. What would Frank the family man be doing raping a woman the first night on the island? On his wedding night, for God's sake?

Frank had escorted Catherine home. Maybe she'd been too drunk to sleep with him. Their first night as husband and wife. As she'd passed out, he'd gone out of the house in a sexual fury, and then he'd stumbled upon Sylvie walking by. There was some sense to that idea.

What was Jones doing still thinking about it, though? He should finally get some rest, but something wasn't feeling right. The case might be closed, but his curiosity was still on fire. He picked up the phone and got his guy in Sarasota.

"Jerry, you still got nothing on Barry Gatt? I need something."

"Nothing, man. There're rumors that he sleeps around on his wife, but he's walking a straight line right now. Almost like he knows he's being watched."

"All right, thanks for looking. Keep me posted."

"You got it."

Jones lay down on the couch, closed his eyes. A snooze would be good for him. After three minutes, he sprang to his feet, grabbed the keys, and climbed into the patrol car.

An hour later, he was in Sarasota, sliding back into the same parking spot at Gatt's place on the Tamiami Trail. *We Gatt 'em where we want 'em.*

Jones entered the office and cast a quick look right to Gatt's secretary. She was filing her nails. "Pam, right? It's me again. He in his office?" Jones didn't wait for a response. Busted right through the door into the back.

Jones found Gatt sitting in his chair with his feet up and picking his teeth. The office carried the tang of a recently smoked cigar.

"What the hell you doing back here?" Barry Gatt asked, sitting up and setting the toothpick down.

"I need to know who's paying rent on the Carters." He wasn't exactly sure how it linked up, but he couldn't rest till he had the facts.

Gatt set his hands on his belly. "Back to this again?"

"Yeah, we're back to this. I got a handful of problems down there that need cleaning up. The thing is, I'm not going to stop until I know. That means I'm going to turn your life upside down. I hear you run around on your wife. I will make it my life's mission to make sure she knows that. In fact, I think I might just go find her now. I bet she's at the club. Knocking a few tennis balls around . . . knocking back a few martinis. Maybe she's porking the tennis pro. She *will* be, soon as I tell her what's going on."

Gatt wasn't easily backed into a corner. "Jones, I'll eat your badge if you start threatening me. I played golf with the DA last week. He'd love to help me straighten you out. You'll be writing parking tickets to moose in Anchorage."

"About now, I'm not sure I'd give a shit, Gatt. You know what they say about a man who has nothing left to lose. I'm that guy. And I'm telling you . . . I want to know who's paying rent, or I'm going to cause problems in your life. A whole shit ton of them. I might even be willing to risk my badge over it. There are things going down on that island, and if you're going to keep hiding them from me, then I gotta assume you're neck deep in whatever it is."

Gatt looked away.

"Oh, did I touch a nerve? How do you know the Carters? How about Frank Overbrook? Did you know him? There's a reason he came down to Osprey Isle. What did you have to do with this whole mess?"

Turning back, he said, "You better leave my office right now, or I'm on the horn to your boss's boss. My final warning."

"I don't think you heard me. I'm not walking out of here without an answer. Who is paying the Carters' rent?"

Gatt went for the top drawer, and Jones assumed one thing: he had a firearm in there. Jones moved fast and reached over the desk just in time. He grabbed the end of the gun and jerked it away.

"You're going to pull a gun on me, Gatt? This secret you're protecting is that important. No, sir." Jones went around the desk and backhanded the guy. Gatt dropped hard. Jones unloaded the bullets onto him, shiny gold raining down on his chest, and then set his foot on Gatt's neck.

"Two minutes, I walk out of here and go find your wife."

"I can't breathe, Jones."

"That's the whole idea, asshole."

Spittle came out of Gatt's mouth.

"You got one minute now. And you know cops: we don't do math that well." Jones pressed hard. Gatt's face turned blue. He couldn't get out a word, but it looked like he was trying.

"Talk to me. Ten seconds left."

"I'm . . ."

Jones let off the gas pedal.

"Miriam Arnett. She's the one paying me."

Jones smiled and took his foot away. "That wasn't that hard, was it?"

Gatt flipped sideways like a fish gasping for water. He heaved for a while. Jones was already thinking about what he'd said. Miriam Arnett. What was that all about?

When he could finally talk, Gatt scratched out, "You're done in this state, Jones. You mark my fucking word."

"Yeah, well, I told you. I'm not sure I care. Good thing is . . . I'm not going to go find your wife right now. But I'll tell you this: I got a guy up here who's going to keep an eye on you. You ever run around on her again, you'll have some big problems."

As Jones was leaving, Pam was standing in the hallway with a smile on her face.

"He deserved that, didn't he?"

"Every bit of it." Jones cruised by her. "Have a nice day. Go get yourself a better job."

Back in the patrol car, his head spun. Miriam Arnett, paying for the house. Sure, it could be the saintly thing to do, help some drifters. But that wasn't the case. She knew the Carters before they'd come to the island. They could be related in some way.

Why did he even care so much?

Because something was off.

Chapter 26

A Baptism in the Wreckage

Catherine felt like she was putting together the missing pieces of Frank. It was late afternoon, and she'd been going nonstop, slicing through tape and peeling open boxes, revealing bits of her husband, one item at a time. She'd also found her art supplies, and a surprising eagerness to attempt making art that wasn't work had ignited inside her. Mary Elizabeth's watercolors had really inspired her.

Of everything she'd opened so far, she'd been particularly excited that Frank was a collector of spoons. She couldn't quite believe that. Spoons! Had clients given them to him? He didn't seem like much of a traveler, but he had spoons from all over the country. A spoon with potatoes from Idaho. One with a wagon on it from Kansas. Another with the Gateway Arch in Saint Louis. Catherine had spread them all out on a table that had come with the movers.

Pulling open the sides of a particularly heavy box, Catherine found Frank's typewriter wrapped in between two pillows. She set the fancy Smith Corona down on the floor in front of her. It was a lovely blue, somewhere between the sky and the sea in color—perhaps robin's egg, though Catherine had never seen one of those. This was what he'd been using to transfer his handwritten words, chasing this dream he'd told her about on the drive. A chance to leave a legacy. She placed her fingers on the keys, sensing him there with her.

Next, she found a box with photocopied articles from medical journals and also stacks of notes with information destined for his book. Getting Frank's project finished felt even more possible; all she had to do was find another doctor with writing skills. Maybe the publisher could help.

A record player and a stack of albums surprised her from the next box. She'd never owned a record player in her life! Her—Catherine Overbrook—a lover of music. Was it really true? She knew nothing about music at all, but she could learn. She flipped through the albums. The Kingston Trio. Woody Guthrie. Bob Dylan. Peter, Paul and Mary. Pete Seeger. Simon & Garfunkel. Come to think of it, she and Frank had listened to the radio on the way down. He'd patted his fingers to the beat, but she'd thought he was lost in his head. He could have been lost in the music.

Pulling the record player from the box, Catherine set it up on a table by the window. She delicately placed the Peter, Paul and Mary album on the player, then lowered the needle. She'd never once played a record before, and the needle scratched as she fumbled around, but she eventually got it to work.

"Where Have All the Flowers Gone" filled the air.

Catherine stood back and closed her eyes, imagining Frank listening to this song. Feeling him come alive, seeing him against her eyelids, she raised her arms and let him lead her in a dance, their first one together. She could almost smell him, almost sense him smiling in his Frank way, a subtle joy rising out of his stern demeanor.

How wonderful this is, she thought. My Frank coming back to me, if only for a song.

Back to work, she was on the tenth box now. Christmas over and over again, the *Miracle on 34th Street* coming alive on Osprey Isle. The box was heavy, and even as she pulled back the flap, she knew it was important. An entire box of files, carefully organized in exceptionally clean handwriting, revealed itself. She thumbed through. This was it, labels that read

BANKING, KEEPSAKES, HOUSE RECORDS, TAXES, CLIENTS, ESTATE PLANNING. And on and on. She would have no idea how to read, interpret, or make sense of it all, but at least she had it.

The KEEPSAKES file first drew her eye, and she began to pull out stacks of photographs. Shots of who had to be Frank's parents, holding him upside down, pushing him on a bike, tossing him a baseball. Judging by the smiles, his mother and father looked like they were in love. Catherine wished she could have met them. There were more pictures, of Frank as a toddler and teen; of their house; of other happy people, some of whom had to be relatives. As she drew out a baby bracelet, she decided he truly was a sweet, sentimental soul.

Then she saw her name on something—what was it? Oh, the pamphlet for the conference where they'd met. He'd drawn a heart around her information.

Catherine nearly fainted. What a doll. He really had been in love . . . and a romantic, too, saving this lovely memory.

Her eyes watered. This was why she would press on, because she was loved. Loved so much. In his own sweet way, he'd adored her. Had he lived, she would have loved him back with all of her and made him laugh again and again.

She returned to the photos, wondering where some of these people were now. He must have cousins or aunts or uncles. Someone she should notify, someone she could connect with and learn more about her mysterious husband.

She flipped through the photos, thinking, These are my people, too, through marriage, of course, but they're my family. I finally have a family, and I will find them. I will go to Burbank and tell them they all have a place to stay in Osprey Isle. I will tell them that Catherine of Florida loves to entertain, with my china that I keep in my corner cupboard, with my house that faces the Gulf.

She picked up the next stack of photos, introducing herself. "My name is Catherine Overbrook. I'm related to you. We're all one big fam—"

Something else caught her eye. Gasping, Catherine clutched her heart. It couldn't be. Her throat tightened and she . . . she grew dizzy.

David wheeled out to the pool and found Miriam sitting up in her lounge chair, eating a bowl of berries. Beside the bowl stood a fizzy drink she'd been sipping on.

His heart collapsed. In so many ways, he'd done this to her, and he hated himself for how he kept treating her. If she could only know how much he loved her. Damn Detective Jones for challenging that fact. The imbecile thought he had David figured out, but he didn't. He could never understand how much David loved Miriam.

Perhaps Miriam didn't know either. He'd tried to express his love, but his broken body wouldn't listen. How many times had he wheeled out like this to the pool with every intent of being sweet to her, being the man he used to be? Only to fall back into the wretch he'd become. Sure, he hadn't always been a saint, but they'd had a good run before the accident.

How could he show her how he loved her now? Okay, by being kinder, and he tried. But he couldn't hold her, bring her in and protect her. Protect her! Who was he kidding? How could he show her that she still was the love of his life, that he'd do anything for her? He could never make love to her the way he used to, and he knew she craved that. Perhaps he should let her go, let her find a man who could satisfy her.

While he'd grown uglier over the years—his skin sallow from a lack of physical movement, his legs turning more grotesque by the day— she'd grown even more beautiful. It was as if the sun were only good to her, not cooking her skin like it did so many other Floridians'. Her skin stayed a perfect golden brown.

How many times had he awoken in the morning and wished he hadn't? Then she could be free. Why couldn't he wheel up to her and say, "Miriam, I love you dearly, and I know that you've been there for me. I'm eternally grateful. You must go now, sow your wild oats. Find a man who can take care of you like I no longer can. Let me fade away from history without making a mark. Let me hide in my cave and wait to die."

He often opened his mouth to tell her he loved her, but only toxicity would spew out, a dragon breathing fire, when inside his heart longed for her touch, her love.

What would a second chance be like? It was preposterous to even ponder. It would take all of him. Sure, he knew that he could still be charming on occasion. He could even make her laugh sometimes. Especially when they were alone. But he found it almost a requirement to be mean to her in front of others. When he heard that part of him speaking down to her, he hated himself despite being unable to control it.

His heart was as paralyzed as his legs.

But he'd have to try harder. The way he'd been feeling lately, he might have it in him. Perhaps it was the death of Frank Overbrook and knowing what Catherine might be going through, in spite of it being a brief relationship. David couldn't imagine losing his partner. All he knew was a life with Miriam by his side. The way she took care of him. The beauty of her taking over every room. The joy of hearing her laugh out by the pool—even if it was alcohol induced. He couldn't bear not having that, and he couldn't shake what it must be like for Catherine. Or Sandy, for that matter.

The good doctor had somehow found a way to live after losing Mary Elizabeth. Even more, he had somehow found a way to smile again—and not just any smile. Bending the lips was easy; it was the meaning and feeling behind the facial muscles and deep in the heart that was hard. Sandy's smile came from the depths of him.

They were all that way, all the islanders. Sylvie and what she'd been through. Glenna struggling to find herself while putting her focus on others. They were all damaged, and David liked that about them. They were even able to see past his flaws and accept him. Where else could he find that?

It wasn't only the doctor dying that had begun to tug David out of the cesspool in which he'd lingered. So much of it was Miriam's own evolution. She'd become a different person since starting to visit the Carters. She'd tried to hide her visits with infinite excuses, but it had been months of sneaking over. The color in her face had changed. Her mood had perked up. Until the murder, she'd even been turning down the bottle, if even until the afternoon. She was walking on the beach and looking out over the horizon more. Smiling wider.

Witnessing her growth, David realized he might not be able to hold on to her forever. She was waking up, climbing out of her own coma. Soon she might walk out the door and never come back. If she would stay with him, then he really would change this time. He'd fight with all of himself to find the good inside.

"Miriam, may I speak with you a moment?"

His wife jumped at his voice. She must have been lost *deep* in her own thoughts to not have noticed the sound of his wheelchair's motor.

Her head turned halfway toward him. "I'm in no mood today, David. You can tear me up any other day, but not today."

He wheeled closer to her. "I don't want to tear you up today. I want to . . ." He stopped. What was he going to do, apologize? A little late for that, wasn't it? How could he possibly make up for how he'd treated her for so long? Blaming her. Hurting her.

"What is it?" She gave him a look of compassion, a rare one.

He played the part like a baby comforted by his mother. "I've been thinking a lot. The loss of Overbrook, what it's done to this place."

"Don't tell me you're ready to leave."

"No, no. Quite the opposite. I'm ready to try again." He gathered himself. This was not easy. Perhaps his heart truly was as broken as his spine.

"It's too much to ask, especially now, but I'd like another chance with you. I think all this . . . the way I've treated you . . . is because I'm terrified of losing you. I can't lose you. I've been a terrible man, a terrible husband. It has to stop. I want another chance."

He couldn't tell what kind of look she carried on her face. Probably one of disbelief, a look he'd earned. Could this really be the end of the David who had awoken from the accident? He should tell her he could walk on water next. Though she'd probably prefer him to turn water into wine.

"I know my words can only go so far," he said, "and it's action that's required. Perhaps it starts with a promise, dear Miriam. I love you, and I want to change. I want to find a way to be the man you need." He sighed. "If I can't, or if I am no longer that person to you—if you don't think I can be that person—I understand. I want you to be happy . . ." His words cracked, his shell, all of him, the yolk of him spilling out into the hot sun. "If you need to go, go. You are set free from the blame of what happened. These things happen, and Lord knows you've suffered enough."

Miriam's face changed colors, a prism of bright fragments coming together, settling on a scarlet red, but only a faint hint of it. If he could see through her body, he imagined her heart had gone still.

Her eyes, her gorgeous brown eyes, flickered up and down. What he'd said was doing something to her, but he didn't know what.

"There's more," he said, sensing that maybe they did have a chance. Perhaps somewhere deep inside her, a cinder of love still glowed, one that could come back to life with some focus and effort.

"I see the way you look at the Carter girl. I saw the way you held the baby, your glow after your visits with them. Yes, I follow you. Of course I do, Miriam. I'm not mad. Who could blame you for wanting to escape?" Was that a tear in her eye, a lonesome puddle collecting at the rim?

"What I'd like to say is that we could give it a go, my dear. Having a family. I know I resisted. I was wrong."

She seemed to have lost her tongue, but she kept her eyes on him. He'd caught her on the right day. She was listening . . . and sober. What was going on between those ears, behind those pretty eyes?

"We're old, but we could adopt. You could be a mother, if you'd like." In his mind, he saw her holding the baby next door, how it had lit her up.

Miriam finally shook her head, as if someone had removed the spell that had turned her to stone. Then, like a bottle of Champagne that had been shaken before uncorking, she spilled over into a burst of emotion.

Her mouth flew open, and she squeezed down on her eyes as they splashed out tears. Almost as quickly, her hands rose to her face, and she folded over and started into a cry like David had never seen before.

He nearly stood from the chair before remembering he wasn't able. His brain told his body to move, and for an instant, it almost did. Then it didn't. He pushed forward the joystick and went to her and reached out his long arms, unsure if she wanted him or not.

But she did.

By God, she *did*.

Miriam slid closer and opened to him and let him hold her. It was awkward, the way he was in the chair, and she rose to climb on top of him. She'd never done so before but accomplished the feat with seasoned grace. She sat on his lap and wrapped her arms around his shoulders and wept and wept and wept. From her mouth escaped sobbing and gasps and attempts to talk that fuddled into more crying.

"Dear, dear, it's okay. It's okay."

"I'm sorry," she finally said.

"Why would *you* be sorry, dear?"

He'd never felt so much love in his life, and if in fact his heart had been paralyzed, it was back to work now, pumping all the love he'd forgotten, feeling for her the way he'd first felt for her when they met.

"You have nothing to be sorry for. Any pain you have, it's all because of me, and that changes today. Can we start all over as if we had just met again on that porch in Coral Gables? Can we start all over and I do my best to be the man you married?"

His words landed like more logs on the fire of her emotions, and she wept harder, nestling deeper and deeper into him.

"I'm so sorry . . ."

David could be so clueless sometimes, couldn't he? Perhaps that was what she adored about him. Behind that mass of mean, he was a teddy bear, a clueless teddy bear that she'd put in that chair. What kind of monster had she been to do that to a man? Was she that sick?

Yes. Because she was the same monster who'd ruined her first marriage—a marriage no one on this island knew about—and later abandoned their blue-eyed little girl at the hospital.

So much guilt and frustration and utter rage had been running through her when she'd decided to yank the wheel hard right and drive them off the road, and the memory was as fresh as if it had happened yesterday.

For years, they'd been arguing about having a child. He'd been up front with her from the outset about his preference to never have children, and she'd been okay with it until the guilt of leaving her daughter, Jessica, started eating at her. She couldn't tell him why she wanted a child so badly, as he'd never forgive her. But she needed one—*had* to have one. How else could she make up for her past mistakes? Having given up on finding Jessica, she could only try again, a last chance to prove herself, a way to fill the void that played out like an echo chamber in her womb and heart.

All their arguments had come to a head on that road in Saint Pete, both of them fueled by too much to drink. Condos with bright-blue swimming pools stood on either side of the Pinellas Bayway. The evening couldn't have been more stunning, another warm tropical night.

But Miriam was full of desperate rage, white-knuckling the steering wheel. "You can't take this away from me!"

David had slapped the glove box. "From the first time we met, I made it abundantly clear that I never wanted to have children!"

Something had snapped inside Miriam. She knew that she'd lost the battle. She'd been good all her life at manipulating people, convincing them to do things they didn't want to do. Not this time. Not when it counted most of all. This was her last chance to bring another child into this world, one last chance to redeem herself for the awful person she'd become. And he'd not given it to her. The pain had started smashing into her, blinding her, and drowning her to the point that it wasn't even difficult to turn the wheel hard right. It was the only answer.

First, though, she'd nonchalantly pulled on her seat belt. He was so frustrated with her that he didn't notice. If she survived, she'd get his money, and she'd go start a new life, maybe find her lost child or find someone new willing to let her try again.

When she'd awoken in the hospital, guilt pounded at her like a relentless migraine—if migraines could hurt that badly. How could she be capable of such madness? Then the doctor delivered the news that David would likely never walk again. It was all too much.

The following hours and days were a purgatory. It felt like someone had grabbed a handful of her hair and was pushing her down into the toxic abyss of her own awfulness. As much as she hated her father, she'd turned out just like him.

But her purgatory had served as a wake-up call. Perhaps what had been the pinnacle of this awakening was Sylvie, the newly blind woman who sat across from Miriam at exactly the right moment.

There, in the cafeteria, the whole world was crashing down on Miriam, cascading down her back and hammering her to tears, when a soft voice first asked to join her, then asked if they could cry together. During the following days in the hospital, they'd become friends. The start of a new Miriam. Her compassion toward David and her sense of duty grew every day. As she saw him struggle with his disability, accepting that his life would never be the same, she'd promised him, *I will never leave you, David. I will be by your side to the bitter end, and that still won't be enough.*

Sitting on his lap now, wrapped around him and weeping, she realized she'd been nothing but a fraud. Here he was, saying he would change, saying he was sorry. But she hadn't changed at all.

Oh, the poor man. She'd tried to kill him, and then she'd only devolved from there.

Miriam lifted her head and finally looked at him. He was still handsome in his own way, and in those eyes, she saw love and kindness and compassion, the traits she'd never deserved in the first place. She pressed her forehead to his, their noses and lips touching.

Not having known such intimacy in a long time, he turned tense and unsure.

She'd put him in this chair, and . . . what could she do now? Could she really tell him all the truths she'd been hiding?

"I'm so sorry," she whispered, kissing his lips, her tears wetting his face. "You were my protector, and I failed you."

"What are you talking about?"

"I have to tell you something," she barely got out, "and I need you to not hate me. I feel so afraid of you, afraid of telling you . . ."

He touched her ever so gently. "I never want you to be afraid of me."

"David, you can be terrifying."

"I know," he admitted, nodding with eagerness. But also with kindness. Understanding. "I don't want to be that way, not anymore."

Out with it, she decided. "I've been keeping so many things from you . . ."

Chapter 27

THE LADY WRAPPED IN RED

Jones was thinking, I'm coming after you, Mrs. Miriam Arnett, as he opted for the steps over the ramp to reach the Arnetts' front door. He hadn't quite put it all together, but he was getting there. Usually when he arrested someone, he felt a sense of accomplishment and finality, even before a conviction. This case had lingering fires he needed to extinguish.

He'd considered a lot of possibilities. Miriam didn't seem like a kind Samaritan who would pay someone else's rent simply out of the goodness of her heart. What he kept going back to was how he'd seen her hold Amber's baby. Sure, she had motherly instincts, but it felt different. Miriam had an attachment to this couple, as evidenced by the fact that she was paying for them to live there. She wanted the Carters close by.

When suspects held back facts, they were often hiding something much larger. Perhaps Mr. Arnett knew the details of the relationship. It could explain his creepy voyeurism.

An image of Sylvie figuring her way through her jail cell flashed in his mind. Was it that he didn't believe her or that he didn't want to believe? The way she'd talked about the murder still didn't sit right. He had to admit, though, their relationship complicated things. Perhaps the lack of balance he detected was simply because love had gotten in the way. Ten years on the force, he'd come to know the power of love in its wickedest ways.

What sounded like crying from behind the house stopped him from knocking. His fist had been only inches from the wooden door. He jogged back down the front stoop and made his way around the right side of the house, slowing as he drew near the brick steps to the side entrance of the terrace.

Ascending quietly, Jones found Miriam sitting on David's lap with her arms around him. They were face-to-face. Her tears glistened like diamonds in the sun.

Jones tried to interpret what she was saying, but it was muffled.

Then David spoke up. "I know. I don't want to be that way, not anymore." He squeezed her tighter, and she seemed to melt into him.

Jones cleared his throat, alerting them of his presence. David's shoulders pumped up into the air as Miriam leaped out of the chair. Her sarong fell to the pool deck as she clutched her heart.

"Oh God, you scared me."

She looked so fragile then, standing in her bikini, her hair a mess, her eyes watery. There was something else, too, something that stood out to him.

David spun toward him. "Dammit, Jones, don't you know how to knock? We don't want someone sneaking up on us any time of day."

Jones pulled his eyes away from Miriam, who was quickly tying her sarong back around her waist. "Pardon me. I thought I heard someone in duress and ran around the house."

Miriam went to work mopping her face with her hands as Jones continued, his mind working to make sense of what he'd seen all the while. Flashes of Sylvie protecting herself from Overbrook played in his head, distracting him, breaking up his words.

"I'm letting the residents know that I've arrested Sylvie Nye for the murder of Frank Overbrook."

Jones opened up all his senses, ready to interpret any sort of expression or movement from either of them. Something was terribly wrong now.

"Really?" David said. "Sylvie Nye? A blind woman is the murderer?"

Jones shrugged. "I'm not at liberty to discuss the details, but I did want the residents of the island to know that they're safe. I was hoping I might talk to Mrs. Arnett for a moment."

That caught her attention, and she threw up her hands. "Why do you need to talk to me?" Fright painted her face. Jones was onto something.

"Oh, not a big deal. Just tying up loose ends. You two were close."

She seemed to calm at his assurances. He watched her, wondering what he was missing.

"Why can't I be there?" David asked.

"Standard stuff. Sometimes I prefer to ask questions without others present."

"If we say no?"

"I'm afraid I'll have to insist. If we can't come to an agreement, I will take Miriam downtown. But that's not necessary. Just some harmless questions to understand Miss Nye better." Jones was really pulling out all the stops now. Paul Newman would be proud.

David turned back to his wife. It didn't take a detective to see that she was trembling. He reached for her hand, and she took it in a show of affection Jones had not yet seen from this couple. Even abusive relationships could thaw and morph into passion . . . perhaps even into love. The world was a strange place. Jones had seen couples who could love and hate in equal measure.

"It's fine," David said, "if you're up for it, Miriam."

"Sylvie murdered Frank?" Miriam said, suddenly finding her tongue. "Are you sure?"

"Again, I can't discuss the—"

"She wouldn't hurt a fly."

Probably not a fly, Jones thought, but she'd run a scalpel through the neck of a rapist. Jones didn't respond further to her inquiry, and instead gestured behind him. "Shall we go inside or . . . ?" He let the question linger.

David waved a hand. "No, it's fine. I'll go inside and let you two talk. Miriam, don't answer anything you're not comfortable with. I'm sure he's right, just tying up loose ends, trying to make sense of his former teacher being a murderer. Anything is possible these days." He shook his head, as if bewildered by what the world had come to.

"Crazy times," Jones said, thinking that was the perfect response. But he was more concerned with what he'd seen when Miriam had jumped to attention upon his surprise arrival.

David wheeled by him. "I'll be right inside."

"Don't bother trying to listen in. We're going to walk down the ramp to avoid all your cameras and listening devices. They give me the creeps."

"I had no intention of listening in. Miriam, I'll be right inside. If you feel uncomfortable, ask him to leave. I'll get a lawyer over here."

"No need for lawyers. This case is a wrap. I'm just doing due diligence."

David bounced his look from Jones to Miriam and then back to Jones. "Fine, then."

As the man wheeled inside, Jones pointed to the ramp that led down to the beach. "Shall we?"

Miriam led the way, saying, "I still can't believe it."

"You and me both . . ."

Once they were halfway down, Jones said, "We should be good here."

Miriam turned and leaned up against the railing. A flock of seagulls soared overhead. She crossed her arms. "So . . . what do you want to know? She's a good person. My best friend. She didn't do it."

Jones leaned against the opposite railing and chewed on the comment. An idea had come to him, and he had to set it up with finesse. "She told me she did."

Turned out there was a whole collection of actors on the island. Miriam spread her eyes open so wide that Jones could have taken a jump shot and knocked a ball right into one of them. "She told you she murdered Frank Overbrook?"

"A full-on confession."

"My God . . ."

Trying to focus on the surprise she should be feeling over Sylvie's confession so that Jones couldn't read her mind, Miriam wondered what exactly Sylvie had told the detective and why he'd come with more questions.

"I had a visit with Barry Gatt this morning. You know that name, right?"

She kept an even face. This guy was good, and he was looking for clues. Miriam played it calm. "Sure, he used to live here."

"That's right."

Then there was silence. This must be his trick, waiting for her to say something. Nope, she wouldn't play the game. The incoming tide brought gentle waves that splashed onto the sand. A seagull squawked from somewhere down the beach.

"He still owns the house next door, right?"

"I think so."

"Uh-huh. Strange you're not sure. I usually know what's going on with my neighbors."

"Not that house."

"Oh, c'mon, Miriam. I'm tired. Let's get to it. Let's dance. You're the one paying the Carters' rent."

"I am not—"

Jones tsk-tsked. "I can't dance with you if you're going to lie to me. That doesn't make a good partner. Gatt told me you're paying the Carters' rent. Are you going to make me guess why, or can you go ahead and tell me the truth? I told you a few days ago that I'd get to the bottom of things. I'm mighty close now. Let's tango together, what say you?"

Even if Miriam had wanted to talk, she couldn't. Her whole body had locked up.

"You sure went from talking to not talking in a hurry. Did I strike gold?"

Miriam opened her mouth, but it was as if she'd eaten a spoonful of sand. She had thought she at least had that hole covered. Barry had promised he'd never say a word, and he'd owed her big. She'd slept with him even though she hadn't been attracted to him. She'd done so because David had hired him to watch her, and what better way to control the information being sent to her husband?

The deception lasted several months, until David started to get suspicious and Miriam had called it off. But she'd kept Barry on the hook, making him feel like he might get another chance. As long as he kept telling David she was behaving like an angel when she left the island, they'd give their relationship another go once it calmed down.

The truth was that she'd gotten tired of sleeping with Barry Gatt. Men were uninteresting. Men were toys that were meant to be discarded after use. Almost disposable. Yeah, that was the word. Even this detective. He'd been disposable to someone. Come to think of it, he might have to be disposed of now.

When she'd called Barry, he'd been happy to help her and, being so loyal and admittedly obsessed with Miriam, didn't balk when she'd made him promise not to tell a soul.

"Darling," he'd said, "I have fond memories of you. You ask a favor, I'm happy to help out. Maybe one day you and I can see each other again. What do you say about that?"

"When the timing is right, Barry. Let's hold on to hope." Of course, *she* wasn't holding on to hope. She was using him to keep David off her back and to find a way to visit her daughter and experience the birth of her grandson.

"Miriam, you in there?"

Get it together, Miriam. Hold on a little longer. The detective needed some truths, so she better give them.

"Okay, you want to cut to the quick. I didn't want you to know because I'm hiding a serious secret from my husband."

"There we go. Isn't it fun to dance together?"

"Don't be a jerk," Miriam said, gaining some confidence back. All she had to do was give him this morsel and move on. Sylvie was already in jail, already confessed. Miriam was so close.

Jones stepped forward and clapped his hands. "I don't have much patience left in me, Miriam. Let's get to it."

She remembered at the last moment to say, "You can't tell David. I have to be the one who tells him, and I'm going to. I always was. I don't see what this has to do with you, anyway, but fine. I used to be married. David doesn't know that. I had a child that I put up for adoption. No, that's not the truth. A child I abandoned because I didn't think I'd be a good mother. That child came to find me recently. Her name's Amber."

The detective raised his head. "Aha."

"You already knew that, didn't you?"

"I was leaning in that direction. I guess congratulations are in order. For being a new grandmother and finding your daughter."

Miriam smiled. Actually smiled. Because Amber coming back into her life was the best thing that had ever happened to her. This new part of her that had climbed out of the wreckage of her accident with David had been ready to become a better person. Amber's reappearance was confirmation, proof that second chances were possible. Miriam could now be a mother *and* the grandmother she always wanted to be. Before Frank's murder had screwed everything up, all she'd had to do was figure out David.

The old Miriam would have run off on him, but she was trying not to do that. She'd already done that to her first husband, sneaking out in the middle of the night and never turning back. This Miriam wanted to come clean and see what happened from there. She didn't want to abandon David. She'd tried to kill him but only paralyzed him instead. The least she could do was stay with him. What was the worst that could happen when she told him the truth?

Jones started back up toward the house, the planks creaking underfoot. He seemed to be wrapping up. "That's really all I was trying to figure out. I hope you get the life you deserve—a big happy family, all that."

"Are you going to tell him, Detective?" she asked in a whisper as she started to follow him. "Please . . . I need to find my own way to say it. He's . . . he's volatile and . . . you know . . ."

Jones stopped and turned back to her. "Nah, I won't spill the beans. I do have one more question: What happened to your leg? Forgive my wandering eyes, but the wound jumped out at me earlier."

The whole world came crashing down on Miriam, and she nearly became faint. It was all she could do not to run.

She reached for the railing and almost missed it. "My leg?" He'd figured it out, hadn't he? She looked past him, over the terrace to the sliding doors, wishing David were there.

"Looked like a pretty nasty gash in your upper thigh. Again, I wasn't exactly looking, but it stood out."

Miriam followed his gaze. She'd covered back up but knew exactly to what he was referring. "Oh, that? I was making a drink the other day and chopping ice. The darn ice pick got me. I missed the block and hit myself." Her lie was so damn good that she perked up, feeling her spine straighten. "Oh God, it hurt like hell. I suppose I'd already had too much to drink. Then, wham, right in my leg."

She forced herself to find his eyes. He looked like he was buying it. Still, he let a long few beats of silence go by before finally letting her off the hook.

"What an injury," he said, walking backward. "You might want to get that looked at. Could leave a scar."

She shrugged, feeling an uninvited bout of sadness. "What do I care? No one's looking at me anymore."

"I was."

"Yeah, I guess so."

A sly smile rose over him.

Jones waited for her to catch up with him as they descended the ramp. "Well, I think that's it. Don't worry, your secret's safe with me. But be careful. I don't like how he treats you. He won't take this well."

"I know. Thanks for caring." Just a few more seconds and she'd be free. Don't break now, Miriam.

Back on the terrace, Jones passed the pool and headed for the exit, saying over his shoulder, "I'll leave the way I came. Have a nice one. You know where to find me."

"Thank you." Miriam moved toward the lounge chair she'd occupied earlier and straightened the towel. Her tension began to fall away. The detective was right. She did deserve this, a second act that involved family and a new life.

With every step he took toward the side exit, she felt better and better, a priceless easing of tension. Poor Sylvie. She didn't deserve what was happening, but someone had to pay. If Miriam went down, then Amber and the baby would suffer. Miriam couldn't have that. Sylvie had to be the one to fall.

"Hey, Zelda."

Miriam had been lost in her own head, but her name being called felt like she'd been underwater and someone had grabbed her and tugged her out.

She lifted her head. "Yeah?"

Only after she'd replied did she realize what she'd done. An entire life thrown away in a second, a four-letter response to end it all. Her shoulders shot up and wound tight.

Jones watched her with a confident smirk. "That's your name, isn't it? Zelda."

Miriam shook it off and jumped back into defensive mode. "What are you talking about?"

The detective approached her again. "Oh, c'mon, I won't tell David. Zelda Smith Overbrook, right? That's a mouthful, you know."

Her eyes watered and started to burn. He knew everything.

"This is fun, isn't it?" He came within a few feet of her.

Miriam stared down at the tile, refusing to look up and meet her fate.

"What's even better," he said, coming to within arm's distance of her, "I finally feel all right inside. It's like Earth has rejoined the right axis. All because of your reaction just now. You couldn't have hidden it if you'd been preparing to all your life. Even if you had, I would have gotten you. That cut on your leg made me start to wonder. Well, I was onto you before that, the whole thing with Gatt. You had Amber with Frank, didn't you? Is that what you were fighting about?"

Miriam looked to the ramp leading to the Gulf.

"Oh, you're not thinking of running, are you? Don't do that." Jones wagged a finger at her. "Let's keep this civil. Why don't you tell me what happened? He came upon you and . . . Gosh, why don't you take over?"

Anger swelled like an incoming tide. He was making a game out of it. This was her life, her fucking life! Her daughter's life! Silus's life! Where was David? There had to be something . . .

Jones pulled handcuffs from his waist and jingled them at her. "Mrs. Overbrook-slash-Arnett, you are under arrest for the murder of your ex-husband, Frank Overbrook. You have a right to an attorney, and if you can't afford one, the state of Florida will provide one for you."

The cock of a gun shut him up.

Chapter 28

ALWAYS AND FOREVER DANCING

Catherine stared at the picture of Frank and Miriam. It had been taken at least twenty years ago, and suddenly, everything made sense. His first wife was Miriam, and that's why they'd engaged at the party and why he'd been so disturbed. He must have been astonished to see her. Or was this his ugly way of rubbing a new marriage in his ex-wife's face?

So many questions . . . How did they both end up on Osprey Isle? Why hadn't he told Catherine? Why had they both kept it a secret? Why had Miriam still not said anything?

Catherine's eyes opened wide. It *was* Miriam who'd drugged her. She must have been looking for something Frank had, like this picture. She might have been looking to remove evidence!

Because Miriam had killed him.

Chills ran up her spine.

Oh God, Miriam killed him. The reasons weren't clear, but it was obvious that she was the missing piece. This was what Detective Jones had kept wondering: Had Frank known anyone else on the island?

Catherine pressed her eyes closed. She still hadn't let go of the feeling of Frank's arms wrapped around her waist—of Peter, Paul and Mary playing to the beat of their heart, her husband coming back to say that he was still with her—but this photo threatened everything.

Why hadn't he told her? She would have understood. Unless it was all part of the plan. Frank wasn't like that, though. Somehow he must have been surprised. That was why he'd been acting so distracted. She'd thought it had started when he saw the Carters, but he must have caught a glimpse of Miriam before the party.

Catherine raced to find the detective's card. She called the number, and a dispatch person answered. "Hi, I'm looking for Detective Jones. This is Catherine Overbrook on Lollipop . . . or Osprey Isle. He'll want to talk to me. It's an emergency."

"Please give me a few minutes."

Catherine sat impatiently for three long minutes before a reply came. "I'm sorry, he's out in the field. Would you like me to get a message to him?"

"I think I know who murdered my husband. Please tell him to come find me. Quickly. I'll be at my home."

The response that came back was unhurried. "I'll send a unit out. Stay where you are and lock the doors. Okay, Mrs. Overbrook?"

Catherine hung up and raced to the windows, wondering if someone was watching her. She looked out to the Gulf and remembered Miriam saving her from the water. Why would she do that if she was a murderer? Maybe Catherine had it all wrong. But Miriam was definitely lying to her.

I have to do something. I have to find him.

Deciding to ignore the dispatcher's advice to lock the doors, she slipped into her shoes and went out the front door. No more being scared and small and feeble. Feeling a stir of danger, she ran down her shelly driveway to the clearing. A light breeze swished through the sea oats and stirred the sand, a scene as eerie as the opening of a spaghetti Western.

First, she raced to Sylvie's house. She didn't see a patrol car, but she ran up the steps anyway and knocked on the door.

"Sylvie, I think I know who did it! Let me in. We're in danger!"

No response. She ran around to the back. "Sylvie!"

Her pulse had turned to popcorn crackling on the stove. With each second that passed, the sense of something bad happening, the island falling apart, someone else being hurt, intensified.

If Sylvie wasn't there, where could she be? The only person she ever left the island with was . . . Miriam. She had to find the detective.

~

"Take the gun from your holster, Detective. Set it down on the ground and kick it toward me." David wheeled through the back doors onto the tiles of the terrace, holding what looked like a Beretta 70 in his hand.

"Now, hold on, Mr. Arnett," Jones said, raising his arms. He hadn't seen this one coming.

"You heard me."

Jones saw the worst of the guy now, the Arnett who abused his wife. Mean and evil eyes glowed out of his skull. He'd likely shoot if pressed. Come to think of it, why hadn't he already?

"What are you doing, David?" Miriam asked.

"Come over here, honey. He's going to kick his gun, and I want you to pick it up."

She did as she was told. Jones thought he better obey and reached for the sidearm tucked into his shorts, just two fingers extended, nothing aggressive.

"Slow it down," David said.

"You sure you want to go any further?" Jones was scrambling for a way out. "Stop now and let me take her in. We can pretend like you never pointed a gun at me. Or . . . we go further and you're going to have trouble."

"The only trouble we're going to have is if you don't shut your mouth. Do as you're told."

Jones wondered if David would shoot him.

"Three seconds, Jones. Don't test me."

He looked dangerous enough to actually pull the trigger, so Jones drew out his revolver, holster and all, and gently set it on the ground.

"Kick it."

Jones did so, and Miriam picked it up and set it on a table. He was in some trouble now.

"What are you going to do now, Arnett? Take your criminal wife across the country? You can't hide."

"Miriam, go get the rope from under the house. The one we use to tie up the tarp." She ran off, and David kept the gun trained on Jones.

Jones thought now would be a good time to practice his negotiation skills. "Did she tell you what all she did, David? I'm guessing you've figured out that new mom over there is Miriam's daughter. Actually, Frank Overbrook and Miriam's daughter. She went by Zelda Overbrook when she was married to him. Yeah, that one was hard for me to believe too. Do you know she killed Frank? Yeah, another scorching fact comes to light. It's like playing bingo, getting all the right calls. I didn't put it together until I saw the stab wound. It made me think of what Sylvie had said, how she had stabbed the scalpel through the air, trying to get Frank." Jones made the motion that Sylvie had shown him. "The problem was that the wound didn't reflect such a motion. It was more a downward jab, holding it like a vampire slayer would hold a spike. Or like Miriam would hold an ice pick. I have so many questions for her once we get her downtown—"

"You're not taking my wife."

"Ah, is that what this is about? You need her, don't you? You treat her like hell, abuse her, but when you realize she might not be coming back home, it hurts, doesn't it? She's still a killer, though. God, I have some questions. What it seems to me is, she made Sylvie think she did it. Somehow all three of them were out there. We'll get to the bottom of it. Miriam will talk soon enough."

Jones saw a flash of someone sneaking onto the terrace from the side entrance. At first, he thought it was Miriam. But it wasn't. It was Catherine Overbrook. She carried a stick in her hand, a piece of driftwood the size of a baseball bat. He didn't like the idea of her getting shot, but he did like the look in her eye—almost the way Mickey Mantle used to look when he stepped over the plate. She had fierce eyes that made Jones feel like she might be capable of stopping this madness.

"What I'm most curious about," Jones continued, "is how Miriam and Frank both ended up on the island. Do you know? If so, you have to tell me before you go. Don't go over to Mexico and drink your margaritas without sharing that crucial bit of information. I don't sleep well with lingering questions out there."

Catherine crept toward him and raised the bat. David was too preoccupied with watching for Miriam in the other direction.

Jones kept going. "Did she know he was moving? Had they kept in touch? I don't see it being some sort of surprise. The world is a small place, but not that small. Frank and Miriam didn't happen to pick the same island, did they? Nah, I think they'd been in touch. You're really going to forgive her for that? What a partner you are. I mean, I'm forgiving. I once had a girlfriend—"

Whack!

While Jones was talking, Catherine had made it all the way up behind David and then she'd swung—quite hard—and struck him. His head jolted sideways, and he gave off a grunt as his hands went limp, the Beretta falling from his fingers.

Jones was on the move before the gun hit the ground. He swiped it up and went to retrieve his own. Catherine was looking at the bat and at the bloody gash she'd left on David's head, back and forth, back and forth, like a kid holding a smoking match who'd just lit a puddle of gasoline, shocked by what she'd done.

Jones had to think quickly. Miriam was still out there. "That was a brave move," Jones said to Catherine. "You okay?"

"I found a picture of Miriam and Frank. They were married." She was out of breath.

"Yeah, I figured that out."

David was in his chair, holding his head and moaning.

"That'll leave a mark," Jones said. "Catherine, I might go see if the Yankees are interested in you when all this is through. That was a hell of a swing. Now, do me a favor: go inside and call the police."

"I already did. She said they're on the way."

Jones unholstered his revolver and got it ready for her. "There we go. What a team we make. I'm going to give you this gun. Safety is off. You keep it pointed at his shoulder. He tries to leave, you show him what it feels like to have a .38 Special embedded into his flesh. I'm going to find Miriam."

Catherine nodded as she raised the weapon in David's direction, and Jones ran off the other way after Miriam. He went down another set of steps, and as he came around the south corner of the house, she was coming his way, holding a neatly coiled strand of rope.

"Jig's up, sweetheart. You ready to take a ride?"

Miriam stopped dead in her tracks, looked this way and that, debating her next move.

"No, don't you do it. Don't make me chase you."

She dropped the rope and started running in the opposite direction.

"There she goes . . . ," Jones muttered to himself, right before taking off after her.

Her sarong once again fell from her waist as she picked up speed. She was surprisingly fast, considering the bare feet, her leg wound, and the fact that she was quite a bit older than Jones. It took him a good two minutes or so to get close to her.

"Don't make me tackle you, Miriam. That's going to hurt."

She kept going.

Sirens sounded in the distance. The clearing came into view as they broke through the tunnels of overgrowth.

"You hear that?" He tossed the gun to the ground and picked up his pace. Finally catching up with her, he grabbed her up high on the arm. They slid to a stop, both panting. She struggled, swatting at him. He bear-hugged her until she finally relented in a desperate release of crying.

He took her by the arm and started to walk her back, grabbing the Beretta on the way.

"Wipe that smile off your face, you asshole," she said as the sirens grew louder.

"Don't start calling me names. I'm just doing my job."

Back on the terrace, Catherine still had the revolver on David, who looked like he'd been frozen in a stage of rage. As soon as he saw Jones, he started yapping about wanting his lawyer.

Jones set Miriam on the ground next to him. "Oh, Mr. Arnett, you'll get plenty of your lawyer soon enough. I suspect he'll tell you pulling that gun wasn't the wisest of moves." Then, to Catherine, he started to say, "You'd make a good police officer if Major League Baseball doesn't—"

Catherine wasn't listening. She was now pointing the gun at Miriam's head. Which was too close to Jones's head.

"Now, hold on there." Jones reached out a hand and hoped this wasn't how he would meet his end. "Why don't you give that to me?"

"You killed my husband." Catherine stepped closer with a trigger-happy attitude. "You lied to me. Pretended to be my friend. And killed him in cold blood."

While Catherine was spitting words, Jones took a chance and was able to grab the gun and peel it from her angry fingers. "There's been enough murder on this island. She'll pay for what she's done."

Catherine brushed by Jones and gave Miriam a slap that could have been heard in Key West. Miriam's head jerked sideways.

Jones set down one of the two guns and seized Catherine by the arm before she could take another swat. "Where she's going, she'll get plenty of that."

As she was pulled backward, Catherine glared at Miriam like a bull staring down someone who'd gotten into his ring. "I'm counting on it."

Chapter 29

The Last Card Is Drawn

"Sylvie, you're frustrating me," Jones said two hours later in one of the interview rooms. "You didn't kill Frank Overbrook."

"I did." She wore the same orange jumpsuit he'd seen her in earlier and sat on the other side of a white table that had coffee stains all over it. Up behind him was a closed-circuit TV camera that Jones had unplugged. Her lawyer wasn't there, but he wasn't worried about it.

"No. Miriam made you think you did. You stabbed her in the leg. I'm guessing she stabbed Frank at about the same time. I don't know why, but I know that she was there. I know that what you're saying isn't the truth. Why are you covering for her? Sure, she's done a lot for you after the accident. I get that. But she was going to let you go to prison for murdering Frank. You didn't. She's a manipulative person, and I need help keeping her locked up. I'm asking again: What really happened?"

The handcuffs clacked together as Sylvie buried her face in her hands.

"Sylvie, don't throw your life away. She manipulated you. She knew you couldn't see what was going on. Just tell me why the three of you were on the beach after midnight."

She finally sat back up. "I don't think Miriam would use me like that."

"Sylvie, you have to stop protecting her. We don't always know who our friends are. She lied to all of us about being married to Frank. There's a reason she wanted him dead. I don't know what that is. It all starts with you helping me see what happened that night. Don't let her manipulate you. She might have been there for you, but she was going to let you rot in prison for the rest of your life. Give me something to work with."

Jones hit the table, causing it to shake.

Sylvie gasped. She was on the brink of falling apart. "I thought I killed him. You don't think I did?"

"I know you didn't. The wound doesn't add up. I told you. She must have been thinking fast and stabbed him at about the same time."

"I was walking the beach and heard her screaming. I ran toward the noise and figured out it was Miriam in trouble. She was begging for help, screaming that she was being raped. I pulled out my scalpel and rushed that way."

"Did you know who the attacker was?"

Sylvie shook her head. "I could hear him grunting and breathing, that's all. Enough to pinpoint his location. I went for him. I felt the blade go into flesh. I'd never done anything like that in my life, and I froze up, dropping it. A moment later, Miriam started yelling that I'd killed him. I heard him take his last breath and then . . . she said that we had to get rid of the body and our bloody clothes and that she'd cover for me. I didn't even know it was Frank until she told me afterward. I was trying to help. You're saying she was lying to me?"

"That's exactly what I'm saying. Pretty impressive, actually. She orchestrated everything in that moment. I don't know why they were fighting. Or how they ended up on the island together." He paused, collecting his thoughts. "You helped her with the body?"

"We dragged the body out as far as we could. Since the tide was coming in, we knew the evidence would wash away. We agreed we wouldn't say a word, no matter what. I swear, I thought she was being raped and helping me cover up what I had done."

"That's why you kept her out of it?"

Her shoulders slumped. "I didn't want her to go to jail too." Sylvie wiped away a tear. "What now?"

"For starters, you're getting out today. Just give me some time. Let me get all the answers. Then I'm going to take you home."

"But I . . . I broke the law. I lied. I got rid of a body."

"We'll get you out on bail, and I'll talk to the DA—the district attorney. The way I see it, you were framed, Sylvie. I'll do everything I can to keep you from coming back to this place."

Sylvie dropped her head.

Jones took her hand. "I know. I know."

~

In the other interview room, two hours later, Jones was on his third round with Miriam. The camera was capturing all of it, and a few of Jones's colleagues watched from a small room on the other side of the wall. The air-conditioning wasn't working well, coughing like it had the flu, and it was cooking in there.

"Look, Miriam, you're causing headaches. Sylvie told me you were there. We've put it all together. Tell me the truth. Was he attacking you? You defending yourself? Sylvie shows up and you see a way out? I don't know. Something's off. Why wouldn't you tell the truth then? Come to the cops?"

Miriam stared at him hard. Something told Jones she wanted to talk.

Her lawyer, Bill Rose, sat next to her, tugging at his lip. He'd done some work for David Arnett's family over the years and had come down from Tampa within two hours of the arrest. He was no Milton, but he'd helped more than a few guilty men and women walk free. Somewhere in his late forties, Rose was probably being told by his doctor that he needed to exercise more. He kept his thinning gray hair parted to the left in a desperate attempt to cover up a bald spot. A continuous wave of menthol aftershave wafted off him. A pink paisley tie hung loosely from the collar of his damp baby-blue shirt. Being suited up, the heat had really gotten to him. Puddles of sweat gathered under his eyes. His forehead was so shiny that Jones could almost see his own reflection.

He clasped his swollen fingers together. "She has nothing to say to you."

Jones ignored the mouthpiece, which was the moniker he gave to every defense attorney, and said to Miriam, "I'm the only guy who can help you now. Make it hard on me, I'll make things hard on you. Why pin this on Sylvie? What kind of example are you setting? You puzzle me, all the bad things you've done. Then you go and befriend Sylvie and, quite frankly, change her life. Then you go over there and try to help your daughter. What's going on in that brain of yours?"

Not a word. Rose chuckled to himself with obnoxious confidence.

"Here's the thing, Miriam: maybe Amber did it. She's the only other person I can put at the scene." Jones wasn't exactly being truthful.

"Amber?" Miriam exclaimed. "She was pregnant."

"Don't take his bait," Rose said, dabbing a stark-white handkerchief against his face.

Jones raised his hands, all friendly like. "Maybe Sylvie thought it was you. You two sound a lot alike. Did you stab yourself to protect Amber? Do I need to check her legs? Maybe I have all this wrong. I'd hate to do it, go drag her off the island right now. Can you imagine the trauma that would cause to Silus, losing his mom at his age? He'll grow up visiting her behind glass. Poor Levi too. I liked that guy. He'll have his hands full, won't he? Raising a kid alone. Unless you help him. You know, it makes sense. Something wasn't adding up with you killing someone. You're not that kind of person, but Amber . . ."

Jones clicked his tongue a few times like he was urging a horse to go. "Something was wrong with her from the get-go. I think she came to find you, to extort money from you, and then she realized the new islander was her biological father. Jackpot! She probably tried to take his money too. But he wasn't having it and—" Jones made one swift stabbing motion. "Lights out."

"Enough," Miriam said. "It wasn't Amber."

"What's that?" Jones perked up. That was some of his best work, all on the fly there.

Rose swiveled his head to his client. "Miriam, not another word."

"I was trying to change," Miriam said with fiery intensity, a release that made Jones hopeful. He'd broken through.

"Stop it," Rose said. "Let him run his mouth. Do not engage."

Miriam gave him a *fuck off* look. "I'm done lying." To Jones, she said, "You're right, Detective. I did kill him. I made Sylvie think she did it."

There it was. All on tape.

"Jones, you need to get out of here. My client is not in her right mind."

"Let her talk," Jones said.

Rose came alive, putting a heck of a lot of effort into springing from his seat. "We are done here!"

"It's my life!" Miriam yelled. "Put me in jail. I deserve it. I killed Frank." As if that wasn't enough, she said, "I killed him, I killed him, I killed him."

Three's a charm. Four was a slam dunk. He hoped the guys watching on the screen had made popcorn.

"Mrs. Arnett, I'm advising you not to say another word." A big drip of sweat fell from Rose's forehead and dropped onto the table. He'd just lost his first case in a while, and it hadn't even started.

Miriam cut a look at him that could have blown a hole in his head. "I'm advising you to keep your mouth shut." Then to Jones: "I'm done lying."

"Then let's go back to the beginning, Zelda. What happened?"

Bill Rose collapsed into his chair. "What a disaster."

"I wasn't happy," Miriam said to Jones. "Frank was too strict and boring." She lost herself for a moment, her head falling back, her eyes on the ceiling. "Our life was so . . . so boring. I demanded a change, and he wouldn't hear of it. So I withdrew a big chunk of money and disappeared. Only, a few days later, I realized I was pregnant. I was on my way down to Florida."

"Why Florida?"

A look of disgust passed over her face. "Frank wouldn't even go on vacation. He got this packet from his medical school, mentioning a job opening in Paradiso. This was, you know, over twenty years ago. It came with a brochure and some talk about the area. I found it in the mail and showed it to him, said we should move. I wanted to get out of Burbank. For God's sake, I didn't want to live in Burbank another minute. But he said he'd never go back to Florida. Said it was too hot and that his patients needed him. That was the tipping point. I couldn't take the flatline we were living for another day. I don't even know why I married him."

Jones was angry at himself for missing some of this.

"I stayed in Georgia to have Amb—well, she was Jessica back then. Then I picked Coral Gables almost out of a hat. I'd heard there were rich men there. And there were. David came along, and we fell in love. As much as I can fall in love. But he emphatically didn't want children, and I didn't fess up to having one. I kept leaving Jess with a babysitter when I'd go out. She was one at the time. As things got serious, I realized I had to either tell David about her or let her go. She was already too much on me. I was a terrible mother. Any other life would have been better for her. I was hypnotized by David and his fabulous lifestyle and the idea that it could all be mine—if only I was childless. So I made it so. I drove back up to Georgia to the hospital where I had her, and they helped me get her into the system."

Jones's throat tightened; nausea crept in. He was beyond disgusted, but also maybe a hair sympathetic. Whatever it was that had happened to her, Zelda was damaged goods.

A line creased her forehead as she disappeared into herself. "It's the worst thing I've ever done in my life." It took her a moment before she could keep going. "I went back to Florida and tried to forget about what I'd done, telling myself she'd definitely have a better life without me. David and I married, and it was good for a while. Until it wasn't."

A breath escaped her. "I was so messed up by abandoning my daughter that I let him treat me that way. Almost like I deserved it. I guess I did. Two years later, I went back to try to find her, but they wouldn't tell me where she was. The only thing I could think of was that we should have our own baby. I started pushing David, every chance I could get, and it started ruining our marriage. That's what led up to our accident. I intentionally steered us off the road."

A tear came that told Jones that she was indeed done lying. "Then I met Sylvie and tried to be her friend, my way of absolution. And I vowed to be there for David, to help him through. That was my punishment."

Jones had heard some confessions in his day, but this one topped them all. "Let's back up. The accident. You were hoping to kill him?"

Bill Rose muttered something to himself and dropped his head, probably wondering why he was even there.

Miriam had definitely forgotten about him. "I was okay either way, but I pulled my seat belt on. He had a good insurance policy. I thought that I could try again." She shook her head in shame. "I'm a bad person, Detective. Surrounded by good people, I'm the only bad one."

"So David knew that you intentionally tried to kill him? He had reason to blame you?"

"He suspected. He wasn't in my head, but he's always suspected it, and treated me accordingly."

Miriam closed her eyes and stayed that way for a while; then: "You want me to keep going?"

"By all means." Jones sat back and crossed one leg over the other. It would have been nice if his colleagues would share some of that popcorn. Butter if you have it, fellas.

Miriam got going again. "David didn't want to go back to Coral Gables, so I started looking at real estate. I'd always wanted to see the Gulf. Came across a listing here and recognized the name *Paradiso* from the alumni mailing all those years ago. That would be the last place Frank would ever go. He'd even said so. It turned out the doctor before Sandy was the one who had taken that advertised job."

These revelations were a symphony of glorious sounds to Jones. An ice-cold Coca-Cola with that popcorn would be nice.

"What about Amber coming along?" Jones asked.

"One day, I was at the general store, and a young woman came up to me, told me she'd been searching for me, that I was her mother. I didn't believe her at first. She didn't really look like me. Then she showed me her adoption papers, showing the exact date I left her."

"How'd she find you?"

"When I went back to get her, two years after I'd left her, they wouldn't share where she'd gone, but they let me leave my information. Anyway, I told her I wanted to be a part of her life but that I had to find a way to tell David first. In the meantime, I called Barry Gatt, and he let me rent the place from him. That way, I could go and see Amber whenever I wanted to. All I had to do was make up an excuse to David."

"Why was Gatt so insistent about covering for you? Why'd he have any skin in the game?"

It took her five seconds of debate to finally answer. "I used to sleep with him."

"Ah, that'll do it." *Days of Our Lives*, be damned! Jones thought. There was a new soap opera in town.

"Shortly after we moved, David hired Barry to look into my background and track me when I left the island. Barry had introduced himself and mentioned that he was a private investigator. With all his paranoia, David hired him, thinking I wouldn't figure it out. But I caught on pretty quickly. I decided that sleeping with Gatt was a perfect way to control the information."

"So Gatt was feeding David whatever you asked him to."

Miriam smiled with deranged pride. "Barry reported that I was an angel."

Jones had to acknowledge her sinister efforts. Considering David's actions, some of what she'd done could almost be justified.

"I got to know my daughter—and Levi too. He's a good boy. Life was getting better. I was going to tell David, I swear I was, about everything—most everything. Everything was fine until the party. Of all the flipping people in the entire world, Frank had to be there."

Miriam sat back and crossed her arms. She was looking so light now that Jones might have to tie her down before she floated away.

"I couldn't believe it," she said. "Last person on Earth I thought I'd see. I started scrambling, not knowing what to do. I snuck away and wrote him a note, told him to meet me later, that I could explain. I thought he might out me right then, but he read the note and walked away. We didn't speak the rest of the night. I faked being happy the best I could. All the Champagne helped."

"Okay, what else?" Jones leaned in, eager to hear about the night of the murder.

Miriam was there first, waiting at the tide line directly down from the entrance to the Overbrooks' new house. The nearly full moon and the bright stars shed enough light to see the entire beach. She held an ice pick in her right hand, hidden under a silk throw. Frank had never hurt her before, but she wasn't sure what to expect tonight.

Her ex-husband appeared at the edge of the dunes and descended the steps. He looked so out of place when the moonlight lit him up. He hadn't even rolled up his sleeves or taken off his shoes. Fury lay on his face like a veil, a look she'd not seen before. He was a strange man, but never an angry one. Until now.

As he searched for words, his head twisting back and forth, Miriam said, "Before you say anything, I need you to know . . . I've changed. It's been so long. I know you hate me, but I've changed."

"Oh, I'm sure."

Miriam didn't even have to pretend to be desperate. "Please don't tell anyone, Frank. My husband doesn't even know that I was married before."

"The jig is up, Zelda. David's the first person who needs to know."

"No, please." Miriam thought of Amber. That was how she knew she'd become a better person. "I'll pay you back. I'll do whatever it takes."

"Can you imagine," he started, "what it's like to wake up and realize your wife has run off on you? A note that says nothing more than *I'm sorry*. Then to find out later in the day that she'd taken a big chunk of your money?" Frank was not one to cry, but his voice cracked. "I let you go then; didn't even bother reporting it. I was too distraught to even put up a fight. And I didn't expose you earlier tonight because I wasn't sure of the right thing to do. Especially in front of my new wife. But I can't bear to think you're fooling someone new, some poor guy who has no idea who he's married."

"If you only knew the truth, you wouldn't feel so bad for him." Miriam's mind searched for a way out. "Your wife doesn't have to know. Let's keep our secret. I'll pay you back as soon as I can."

"And we live on this island in some sort of harmony?"

"Exactly."

The Frank who'd barely laughed in his entire life did so then. "Not a chance, Zelda. Or what is it? Miriam? Do you know how many years I was hurting? I didn't even care about the money. I loved you, Zelda."

"You didn't love me, Frank. You never wanted to be with me. It was work, work, work, work, work. When that job here came up, I brought up the idea of moving to Florida, and you said it was the last place you'd ever go. You wouldn't even take me on a trip! You barely recognized my existence."

"Don't make this about me. I loved you the best way I could."

"Which was *not* enough."

She could tell her words stung. Maybe she'd found his weakness. Leaning in to those emotions, hoping she might tap her own tears, she said, "You hurt me. Long before I hurt you."

"No. I won't let you do that. You should have talked to me. Instead, you did the unimaginable."

Miriam tried another direction. "Why now, Frank? Why would you come to Florida, of all places?"

His face stretched in bewilderment, as if that was his biggest question too. "After twenty years of living in the house where you'd faked your love for me, wallowing in heartache, I finally found the courage to close down my practice and start my book. Twenty years, and I was finally over you. Then I met Catherine, the blessing that I thought you might have been. Sandy had been nudging me for months to come down. I kept saying no. But Catherine changed everything."

Miriam heard a tenderness in his voice, and she wondered if she might be able to appeal to him. It would start by listening.

"We'd only just met," he continued, his voice calming, "but I felt renewed, even more so than when I'd closed my practice. It was quite uncharacteristic of me, but I called Sandy and told him that I'd take the job. Even before mentioning it to Catherine. I didn't want to take her to Burbank. I didn't want your memory entering into our relationship. I wanted something new."

Frank's disposition changed. "Everything was perfect until I saw you."

"I was in the *one* place you said you'd never come, Frank." Miriam tried to stay calm but gripped the ice pick tighter. "Please. Let me make this right. You can still have your perfect life. I will leave. We'll sell the house."

"It's not that easy."

Miriam only had one more angle. "There's something else I need to tell you . . ." This could go badly, but she was ready. "I was pregnant when I left you."

A dumb look took over his face. His eyes drooped.

"I . . . I had our child a few months later. A girl."

"You what?"

Miriam tried to smile. "A beautiful girl."

It took him a while to respond. "Where is she?"

"I put her up for adoption but . . ."

Through gritted teeth, he said, "You gave away our child?" Moving fast, he seized her left arm, gripping down hard. "I am taking you to David now. You can explain everything to him."

Miriam was out of options. She raised the ice pick up in the air and went to stab him. He saw it and caught her forearm and shook the ice pick loose. Miriam broke free and clambered on the ground for the weapon. He landed on her, though, and attempted to pin her to the sand. She thought her life was over until she heard Sylvie screaming.

Thinking quickly, Miriam cried out, "He's raping me. Help!"

Sylvie raced into the melee with the scalpel she always carried, swiping it wildly in the air. Miriam pushed Frank up toward her, hoping Sylvie could get her blade into him.

But Sylvie missed Frank entirely and stabbed Miriam in the thigh, then dropped the scalpel to the sand in horror. Pain shot through Miriam's leg, but she clung to her need to survive and covered her mouth and kept from crying in pain. Never had she been able to think so clearly in her life. In a flash, she saw an opportunity.

Miriam grabbed the scalpel and thrust it into Frank's neck. "You stabbed him, Sylvie!"

Frank slumped off Miriam and down onto the sand, a gurgling sound rising up from him. Sylvie stood staring blankly. Miriam drew in a deep breath and sent her mind to work, devising a plan that would save her.

⌒

"You know the rest," Miriam said. "I lied to Sylvie. I didn't want her brought into this. I really do love her, but I was worried she'd confess. Not if she thought she'd done it, though."

Jones let her finish before jumping in. "On the fly, you masterminded a murder. You tricked Sylvie. Somehow you didn't so much as let out a peep when she stabbed you. Made her think she was a murderer. You nearly ruined the life of someone who called you a friend. You convinced her to lie to everyone, convinced her to help you drag a dead body out into the water."

Rose couldn't stifle his laugh this time.

Miriam turned to him. "I don't want you here. Please leave."

She didn't have to ask him twice. Rose retreated without a word.

Once the door clicked shut, Miriam said, "I didn't want to ruin her life. We were both going to get away with it. I knew the rising tide would wipe away the evidence."

Jones set his elbows on the table. "Where's the murder weapon, the clothes you wore?"

"Once we got Frank out there, I found the scalpel and threw it into the water. I made Sylvie strip off her sweater and sundress. I knew she wouldn't be able to get rid of them. I put everything in a garbage bag and stuffed them into the tire well of my car, then took them off the island the next morning before the body was found."

"Where'd you take them?"

"A dirt road down Alligator Alley. I burned them." Alligator Alley was the nickname for the stretch of I-75 that crossed over the Everglades to the East Coast. She'd chosen well.

"I'll need your help locating what's left of the fire. Could you help me with that?"

She offered another nod.

"How much did you steal from Frank?"

"About fifty thousand." Her mouth had gone dry. He could hear it in her voice.

He inclined his eyebrows. "That's big money. It was you who broke into the Overbrook house the night after the murder, right?"

Miriam wiped her eyes. "I crushed up a few pills of my Valium and put it in the tea so that I knew they'd be asleep." She looked down, seeming to age more and more by the second.

"How'd you get in? Wasn't it locked?"

"Glenna had given me a key a long time ago, in case she got locked out."

Jones couldn't think of anything else. He stood and knocked his knuckles on the table. "Thank you, Mrs. Arnett."

"That's it? A thank-you?"

"What do you want, a cookie? You're a killer. You destroyed people's lives."

"I know . . . and I'm sorry."

Jones held eye contact until she broke away. Then he turned and went to find Sylvie.

⌒

A police deputy pulled open the heavy door that led to the holding facility and escorted Sylvie out into the waiting room. She'd changed back into civilian clothes. Her blond hair was pulled into a ponytail. The look on her face was stoic. She held her white cane in one hand and a plastic bag with her belongings in the other. Never had Jones seen anyone who fit less in this place.

He stepped forward. "I'll take it from here."

As the deputy nodded and turned away, an angelic smile rose on Sylvie's face. "Your voice is music to my ears."

Uncaring that some of his coworkers were milling about, Jones slipped his arms around her waist and got in close. "All of you is music to my ears."

"That doesn't even make any sense."

They both laughed despite the circumstances and *all* the shit that had gone down. As their chests pressed against each other, their hearts found the same rhythm, ten long years and two lonely hearts finally finding the healing they deserved.

Looking into her unseeing eyes, Jones caught a glimpse into her soul and let out a sigh that carried the weight of the world with it. "I thought I'd never . . ." He damn near teared up.

She pulled back. "Are you getting emotional, Quentin?"

He was too torn up to answer. The idea of her being a killer. The idea of her spending her life in prison. The idea of them missing their second chance . . . It was a lot.

Leaning into his ear, she whispered, "Let's get you out of here. We don't want all these cops to know you're a softy."

A smile came over him—the kind that rises from deep within. "Yeah, I guess you're right." Jones stuck out his arm and wondered if she'd realize it.

And she did.

And. She. Did.

Jones led her out the front doors of the Collier County Sheriff's Office. The sun was taking it easy on the good people of Florida today; it couldn't have been more than seventy-two degrees. A few unmenacing clouds passed by. Men in blue came and went.

"First step down," he said when they reached the steps that led down to a parking lot half-full of patrol cars. She found it gracefully, and they descended in silence.

Once they'd reached the car, he popped open her door. "You're not curious what happened?"

"I'm guessing you found the truth and paid my bail."

"Exactly that. I spoke with the DA. If you agree to cooperate, he'll work with you. They'll likely drop any charges. Things will get back to normal."

Sylvie gently pulled him forward by the shirt. "I'm happy to cooperate, but I hope things don't get *too* back to normal."

"What's that supposed to mean?"

She touched his face, her delicate fingers gliding along his cheeks, his mustache, his lips. "My normal didn't have you in it." As his heart swelled, she added, "As if there was anything normal about you anyway."

He chuckled. "You picked up some 'tude while you were on the inside, didn't you, Miss Nye."

"You don't know me well enough yet, Detective Jones. I might be the one mystery you never solve."

He looked her over. They might still have some getting-to-know-each-other ahead of them, but he couldn't be surer of what he wanted. It was nice to know she shared a similar vision of the future.

Jones moved in for a kiss, and a missing piece of his heart slid into place. The whole world could be watching and he wouldn't care. Something so bone deep was telling him that she was the one who held the keys to the kingdom. She was the one who could break him free. It was time to let go and see what happened, to take love for a spin and see where it went.

It was time to put less focus on the dead and more on the living.

Epilogue

LOOSE ENDINGS

January 11, 1971
Eleven Months Later

It was one of those nights that made Jones feel like he might never leave Florida. There was something special about the air, how it carried the perfect amount of humidity, crisp but still fluffy. The way the tropical breeze blew in, offering a taste of the Caribbean. The birds were all down from the north, too, heaps of them, every color and size and species. They must have been glad to be a long way from the snow.

Just like the folks who were clogging up I-75 and all the restaurants and every road in between. Naples was as much of a disaster as Sarasota, he'd found in the three years he'd now been down here. Paradiso was different. Osprey even more so. Where else could you break away from all the madness of the world? Hopefully, the remainder of the seventies would be a bit tamer than the sixties. It had to be.

In the meantime, Jones would be hiding out on Osprey as much as he could. It didn't feel right that the burdens of life on the mainland had made their way out here. Maybe they wouldn't again.

But, hey, Jones wouldn't have been sitting on a chair with Sylvie on the sand leaning up against him had a murder not taken place. Sure, he might have run into her one way or another. Heck, he might have even looked her up one day. But that was the way the world worked. Dr. Frank Overbrook had been murdered, drawing Jones to the island, putting Jones and Sylvie together at the proper age. Damned if a life or a love didn't pop up when another faded away.

Jones had turned twenty-nine and was still kicking, thinking he might finally be coming to grips with how his childhood had played out, the hole his father had left and how his mother had never quite recovered.

Levi Carter stoked the driftwood fire. Amber rocked her baby. It had been a year of ups and downs for them. For everyone, really. Amber had had it tough, though, losing the father she'd never known, then watching her mother go to jail for the murder. Miriam had been sentenced to twenty-five years, no parole. David had done six months for holding a gun to Jones and was now carrying out two years of probation back in Coral Gables, where his family was taking care of him—reluctantly, Jones supposed.

Despite all that had happened, David apparently couldn't stop loving Miriam and would still do anything for her. He'd agreed to let Levi and Amber move into their house on Osprey Isle. Warrior that she was, Amber could still put on a smile for their baby. She glowed now, clearly determined to give Silus what she never knew growing up: unwavering love. Wasn't it amazing what mothers could and would do for their child?

And even what grandmothers who weren't actual grandmothers would do. It turned out that Levi and Amber and their son, Silus, inherited an unexpected family member in Catherine Overbrook. Since Miriam and David had left the island, Catherine had stepped in and assumed her proud roles as a mother figure to Amber and grandmother to Silus.

Catherine had found Frank's will in the box where he'd packed most of his important documents. She shouldn't have been surprised to find that the ink had barely dried. He'd visited his lawyer two days before he'd married Catherine and left her everything. After a funeral in Burbank, attended by a few distant family members and an army of his former patients, Catherine had held a small ceremony of life with her new friends on the island and then walked Frank's ashes out into the Gulf, hoping that he would always be part of this dream they'd started together.

Frank had also taken out a large life insurance policy, setting Catherine up as the sole beneficiary. More important than the fact that she'd never have to work again was that these efforts were further proof of his budding love.

It didn't sit right with Catherine that Amber hadn't been part of the will. She surely would have been if Frank had known of her existence. So Catherine had written Amber a large check or two. Jones didn't know the amount, but he'd gotten the impression that Amber and her family would live a comfortable life, even if all they ever did was sell trinkets, which didn't turn out to be the case.

With some of Frank's money, Catherine had bought a gallery space on Fifth Avenue in Naples, where all the artists on the island could sell their wares. While also continuing her work as a medical illustrator, both in finishing Frank's book and with new clients, Catherine had also begun to explore other forms of art. Her paintings of sunsets adorned an entire wall. Sylvie's pottery graced the shelves of the opposite wall. Amber's jewelry filled the glass display case that Levi religiously polished with Windex, because he might have been the proudest of them all at this new venture they'd taken on.

It was he who drove the convertible Pontiac GTO that Miriam had left them into Naples five days a week to man the shop. He'd cleaned up his act and, from what Jones had heard, turned his poor lying into impeccable sales chops. Catherine had joked one time that Levi could sell sand to a beach bum. As Sandy had told Jones, something about becoming a father had growed him right up.

Catherine did not know her way around the kitchen but was doing her best to learn, and she had her new family over for dinner twice a

week. Jones and Sylvie often joined them as well. Even Sandy stopped
by when he was up for it. On Tuesdays, Catherine watched Silus so
Amber and Levi could ride into town for a date.

Jones was learning a thing or two about family as well and still trying to wrap his head around the little being Sylvie was carrying in that
belly of hers. They'd intended to marry first, but that was how it went.
He told everyone it was her fault . . .

Taking her hand, he noticed the clay around her fingernails. In
some ways, life was getting back to normal. Thank goodness the DA
had let Sylvie walk—and she hadn't even had to testify, as Miriam's case
never went to trial. Divers were unable to locate the scalpel, but Jones
had gotten Miriam out of jail one morning and followed her directions
to find the dead-end road off Alligator Alley where she'd burned the
clothes. Though most of it was gone, he'd been able to photograph the
burn site and recover remnants of the women's clothes, including a zip-
per, several buttons, and a few strips of material with blood on them.
The prosecution had been fully prepared for Miriam to back away from
her confession, but she'd never flinched from her guilt and accepted her
sentence with her head held high.

Apparently, the three stooges—Mac, Hugo, and Salvaje—missed
losing their money to Jones since he'd stopped going to the Salty Pearl.
Once a week, they came out to Osprey Isle for an afternoon of Texas
Hold'em. Lately, there'd been a new winner in town, though. Jones had
ordered a braille-marked playing deck manufactured by a company up
in Poughkeepsie, New York, and now Sylvie was the one taking the pot.

In other ways, life was only getting started. Jones hoped for a girl,
but he'd be happy with either. He and his mom were talking a lot now.
She'd said that she might be interested in Barry Gatt's house, which had
come up for sale recently. Jones loved his mom dearly, but that island
was far too small to bring her onto it. If she wanted to be around her
only grandchild more, maybe a condo in Naples or Bonita Springs
would work just fine.

Thankfully, someone else had swiped up Gatt's house. The new residents had only taken it up earlier in the day, a doctor named Gladys Willoughby and her husband, Mark. Of course, Dr. Willoughby was taking over Sandy's practice. At this moment, everyone waited for the doctor and her hubby to arrive.

Sandy stood by the lobster pots. He'd lost a lot of weight, but he was still fighting. It turned out that the only way Glenna would agree to leave Paradiso was if Sandy consented to treatment for his lymphoma. Right about now, Glenna was landing in Egypt to go see the pyramids. Of course, they'd enlisted the help of Frank and Sandy's alma mater to find a replacement, and the new nurse was en route from Boise, Idaho. She'd live in Sandy's guest villa till she found a more permanent residence. Meanwhile, Sandy was set to begin radiation therapy in three days.

All really did feel right in the world. Jones had moved in with Sylvie a few months prior, and they'd obviously been rapidly successful at trying to have a baby. Who could blame them? They both felt like they'd missed out on some years, and something about the sunshine and a beautiful woman and the Gulf out the window . . . it stoked the libido. As he liked to tell her, he'd do it again in a heartbeat. She always shook her head when he said that. If it ended up being a girl, they'd agreed to call her Brooke. Boy names were still up in the air.

Sitting next to Sylvie, Catherine was barefoot and tan—tan for a midwesterner, at least—and looked like she was exactly where she was supposed to be. Frank would have been proud of her resilient attitude and the way she'd taken in Amber and company as if they were her own. He'd also be thrilled that she'd found a younger doctor in Tampa to join her in completing his medical treatise.

"Catherine," Jones said, "how's Frank's book coming? What a challenge it must be to finish someone else's work."

She turned back to him, radiating an infectious inner peace. "It's all coming together as if it were meant to be. The drawings are almost done, and Dr. Easley says he'll be finished in time to meet the publisher's dead—"

"Here they come!" Sandy yelled, stealing everyone's attention.

The new couple came onto the sand, waving and smiling and saying their hellos. Everyone stood from the fire to greet them, showering them in hugs and kisses. On Osprey Isle, you had to be part of the community. You just had to, or it didn't work. That was why they were all there to welcome the new couple, intent on making this night far different from the one a year prior when Frank and Catherine had arrived.

Dr. Willoughby looked young to be a doctor, Jones thought, but maybe he was getting older. Thirty was looming. Back problems and sleeping issues would likely plague him before long. Then he'd be thinking about joining the AARP and playing thirty-six holes of golf every day. God bless him.

"What do they look like?" Sylvie asked, tugging at him.

"Well, she looks like she's about fifteen. I wouldn't trust her to give me aspirin. *He* is handsome. Not as handsome as me, though. Don't worry, you still have the pick of the litter."

"Oh, I know that."

He took in the sight of his soon-to-be bride, falling in love all over again.

As usual, she sensed him staring at her. "What? What is it?"

"How did you know I was looking at you?"

"Because I can see you. If I can see anyone in the world, it's you."

He raised a few fingers in the air. "How many fingers am I holding up?"

"You still think I'm fooling you?"

He smothered a smile. "I'm flirting with you, darlin'."

"It's a good thing you keep a clean house, because you're a terrible flirter. Now, let's stop being rude, and take me to meet the doctor. It'll be so nice to have a new friend out here."

He stood and held his arm out. "Let's go."

As they approached, Dr. Willoughby broke away from speaking with the others. Her raven-black hair fell to one side in a french braid. Thin gold hoops hung from her ears. She had a nice smile and a sharp yet youthful disposition. Hopefully, she was old enough to have gone to medical school.

"Hi, I'm Gladys Willoughby. So nice to meet you."

Jones took her hand, noticing a slight hint of a flowery perfume. "I'm Quentin. Welcome to the island. This is Sylvie."

Gladys turned her attention to Sylvie. "I'm so looking forward to getting to know you. We might be partners in crime before too long."

Sylvie looked reticent to take her hand. Her words came out shaky. "I recognize your voice from somewhere. Do we know each other?"

Dr. Willoughby shook her head. "No, I'm . . . I'm sure I'd remember you."

A crease of concern and doubt marked Sylvie's forehead. "How strange. I could have sworn we've met before."

"Oh, here we go again," Jones muttered, thinking that everyone had their secrets. Hopefully, whatever this one was wouldn't lead to murder.

~

Catherine of Florida, barefoot and sparkling, stepped toward the fire, feeling the warmth of it as she clinked her glass.

"I'd like to give a toast." Once everyone had gathered around her with their drinks, she said, "First off, welcome to the island, new friends. We're so excited to have you."

The newcomers raised their glasses.

To the rest, she said, "I wouldn't have survived the last year without you guys."

"It's *y'all* down here," Jones corrected.

"That's right," Catherine replied. "I wouldn't have survived the year without *y'all*. Losing Frank was . . . horrible. But today, I feel more hope than sadness. Today, I feel more part of a family than I ever have in my life. I'm sure Frank's right around here somewhere. Probably over in the corner sulking—but sulking with joy, if you know what I mean."

Catherine felt another wave of warmth and wondered if Frank was even closer to her than that. "Anyway, here's to stepfamilies, and newcomers, and drinking moderate amounts of Champagne, and to belly dancers, and—speaking of—to Glenna and her adventure, and to new babies, new lovers, and to this island that I don't ever want to leave."

"Hear! Hear!" Sandy said, waddling his way to the center as he cleared his throat. "And to Mary Elizabeth, my one true love. I'd like to think there's another Osprey Isle on the other side. I'll be there soon enough, dear one, but don't worry. I'm not rushing."

"You better not be," Catherine said, slipping her arm around him. He was a fine man, the cheerleader of the island, the humble mayor who held them all together. Had anyone truly been surprised when Sandy admitted that he knew Amber was Miriam's daughter? He'd not known that Frank was the father, but he'd been well aware Miriam had been harboring her daughter with the intent of eventually telling David the truth.

What a good and loyal man.

Catherine dreaded the day when they would say goodbye to him. What she'd promised herself, though, was that she'd do her part to keep this island going. She might not be Sandy, with his big bursting smile and joyful demeanor, but she could shine her light in her own sweet way and, in doing so, keep Sandy's and Frank's going too.

Not many people find a home, the place where their souls vibrate. Her journey had hurt, but she'd made it, nonetheless. Bad things had happened in her world. Bad things that she could never properly forget. But there were good things ahead and good people here, and she was honored to know them. It was in her power to choose where to put her focus. Catherine of Florida's focus would not be on the past. It would be on the here and now, where the sun shoots healing golden rays and where bare feet meet the sand and where palm trees stretch toward the clouds.

Author's Note

The circumstances of how this story came to be still blow my hair back every time I think of them. In August 2020, I hosted a release party for my latest novel, *An Unfinished Story*, at a friend's restaurant called Grace in Pass-a-Grille, Florida, where my family and I were living at the time. If you haven't read it, *An Unfinished Story* is about a widow who tries to convince a well-known and washed-up author to finish her late husband's book. It's how she faces her grief.

A day later, I received an email from a woman named Leigh Shainberg Howe, mentioning that she'd attended the dinner and happened to be in possession of her mother's unfinished manuscript, an Agatha Christie–style murder mystery set in 1970 Florida. Leigh asked if I'd be willing to take a walk with her on the beach so that she could bounce a few questions off me, as she was intent on finishing the book. We connected a few days later and had a lovely chat about what it would take to bring her mother's story to fruition.

Her mother, Peggy Shainberg, was no stranger to the written word, as she'd written for newspapers all her life. She also lived next to Walter Farley, the author of *Black Stallion*. Equally cool to me, her sister typed out most of the novels of John D. McDonald, who was the creator of Travis McGee and one of my biggest inspirations. In fact, I've even visited the marina in Fort Lauderdale where McGee kept his boat, *The Busted Flush*. (Yeah, yeah, I know it's fiction.) As you can imagine, my walk on the beach with Leigh stuck with me afterward.

Fast-forward to June 2023. I'd relocated from Spain to Maine and was in the process of coming up with a few new story ideas. Leigh came back into my life. She'd reached out to my agent, Andrea Hurst, and convinced her to read what her mother had written. Andrea called me and said, "I know cowriting's not exactly what you do, but you should give it a read." Though I'd written a few mystery/thriller books back in the old days—stories now under the pen name Benjamin Blackmore—a 1970s locked-room mystery was far from what I was writing now. Not to mention, I wasn't interested in finishing other people's manuscripts. That just wasn't my bag. Or was it?

I'll never forget the day I sat down to read what Peggy had written. It was super early, long before the sun had come up, and I was drinking coffee in my little writer's cottage on an island off the coast of Maine and thought I'd go ahead and read a few pages and find a polite way to say no. The next thing I knew, I'd finished every word she'd written—all forty-five thousand of them. I tore through it, I tell you! The writing was exceptional. The characters jumped off the page. And I was hooked from the first sentence. Not only all that, but I felt absolutely compelled to finish what Peggy had started.

Leigh and I began chatting, and as the project became more real, it got scarier, especially for Leigh, who had put a ton of work into this book, typing her mother's written words, coming up with ideas for the plot, convincing my agent and me to take a look, and most importantly, making the decision to put her trust in one particular writer: me. We kept talking, and as we continued to hash out the details, she asked me to speak with her sister, Lynn.

It was clear that their mother meant a great deal to them and doing this project the right way was paramount. All I could do was promise that I'd give them my all. The fear on my part started stacking up, as I didn't want to disappoint them or anyone else in their family.

Then a cherry on top came to light, an incredible connection that solidified that we'd come to this point for a reason. As I was getting off the phone with Lynn, she said, "I should tell you about my parents.

My dad, Norman, was a Jewish podiatrist and became a fighter pilot in World War II. In August of 1944, he was shot down over France and endured a bad leg injury. Thankfully, he was rescued by French resistance fighters, but his leg was in such bad shape that they told him he needed to turn himself in to the Nazis so that they could amputate. Otherwise, he would not survive. The Nazis amputated his leg and put him in a prison camp, where he miraculously survived the rest of the war. Returning to Memphis, he met Peggy, the love of his life. In 1948, they won a contest on *Bride and Groom*, a radio show based out of Los Angeles that was the start of 'reality shows.' The show paid for Peggy and Norman to fly out to California and enjoy a world-class wedding, including a wedding dress fit for a queen."

I stopped Leigh's sister there. "Wait, that sounds familiar. Can I call you right back?" I hung up and called my dad in Flat Rock, North Carolina. "Hey, Dad, didn't Grandma Betty and Papa Hacky win a radio contest and get married in California?"

"That's right. *Bride and Groom*."

"No way. Do you remember what year?"

"1948."

Peggy and her husband were married the *same* year and on the *same* radio show as my paternal grandparents! Any creative talent that I have comes from my grandma Betty. She will always be my biggest hero. My grandfather, Hacky, was also an amazing human and, like Norman, fought Nazis from an airplane in World War II—but as a tail gunner. I tear up every time I think about the link between my grandparents and Peggy and Norman.

Once I'd confirmed the story, I called Lynn back and then connected with Leigh, and we all teared up together. If that connection wasn't a green light, I don't know what would ever be.

Even how the title came about was a sign. I've had this title for years, and knowing it was a winner, I've tried to squeeze a few stories into it. I even pitched a previous novel idea to Lake Union using this title. But the other stories never seemed to fit. As I was reading Peggy's story, though, I had this lovely feeling that the title had been patiently waiting for Peggy's story to find me. I hope she likes it.

By the way, did you notice there was an unfinished book (Frank's medical treatise) inside an unfinished book that was completed because of *An Unfinished Story*? This is too much fun. I'm tempted to end this paragraph with an unfinished sent—

Peggy Shainberg was a wonderful writer, and it was an honor to jump into this world that she created. I hope I did it justice. I can tell you this: On the wall next to my desk, I have a lovely picture of Peggy at her typewriter. She's staring right at me, and often, as I was writing, I could feel her urging me on, whispering to me, encouraging me, and making suggestions.

This has been one of the most challenging yet fulfilling and enjoyable projects of my life. To you, my readers, thanks for allowing me to take a chance and write something far outside my comfort zone. I hope you found yourself fully entertained, as I was, right from the get-go.

Most of all, here's to Peggy, who had a lovely mind, an incredible imagination, a daring voice—*especially* for her time—and a sensational sense of humor.

I thought it might be fun and interesting to share where Peggy left off. Though a few gems of her writing can be found in chapter thirteen, her part essentially ends with chapter twelve, where Jones drives into town to interview Sandy and Glenna at the doctor's office.

In the original manuscript that I first read, the last scene was actually the one where David goes to his super-creepy office and then into Miriam's bedroom to watch her sleep as he recalls their time together before the accident. What I knew from reading that brilliant scene was that Peggy was a daring writer and had plans to keep pushing boundaries, and I took it as a message that I was allowed to do the same. To make the timing work better, I moved the David scene to an earlier section.

The finished novel is about 110,000 words long. I had 45,000 of Peggy's words to work with. Though I had to delete and rearrange parts, and change a couple of names, I tried to alter as little of her foundation as possible. Of course, a fair amount of editing and additional writing was required. I inserted a few new sections in the first chunk, including the introduction of Detective Jones, his investigatory work, and his meeting with the medical examiner. In fact, Jones was the only main character who hadn't been developed. Also, I did what I needed to do to create a consistent voice throughout and had to tweak a few bits to get to my desired ending. But the concept, the heart and tone of the novel, and the lovely characters are all hers. All I had to do was figure out how to bring it together.

Acknowledgments

First and foremost, thank you to Peggy and Peggy's daughters, Leigh Shainberg Howe and Lynn Shainberg Sass, both of whom entrusted me with their mother's special manuscript. I hope I've made you both proud. It's been an absolute honor to get to know Peggy. What a creative force.

Leigh, thank you for your incredible devotion to bringing this story to fruition. Not only were you the one who typed out your mother's handwritten words, but your edits and suggestions proved invaluable, especially making the baby Frank and Miriam's. That idea became the foundation for the rest of the book.

My editor, Danielle Marshall, has had my back from the day we first connected. She didn't even flinch when I mentioned that I wanted to finish Peggy's murder mystery, a genre that isn't exactly in line with my oeuvre of book club fiction. How lucky am I to have a publisher who is open to my ideas and willing to take a chance on letting me follow my heart? Danielle, your developmental edits were priceless, and I can't wait to see what we do next together. Something tells me you and I are just getting started. Thank you for giving me the ability to do this for a living and for supporting me as an artist.

To the whole Lake Union team: I'm the luckiest writer in the world. Y'all are a class act and have introduced me to so much of my audience and paved the way for me to chase my dreams.

Andrea Hurst, it is not lost on me that you're the one who encouraged me to read Peggy's manuscript, suggesting that it might strike a chord. You were so right. It's also not lost on me that so many of the good ideas in this story came right from your imagination. Creating with you is an absolute pleasure. Thank you for your incredible love and support in all walks of my life. You're not only one of the good ones, you're one of the best ones.

Katie Reed, you have found your voice as an editor. Thank you for sharing your talent with me. No doubt you've made this far better. I can only hope we can continue to work together.

To my beta readers, the unsung heroes who are always here for me, always pushing me to do better, always finding ways to elevate my manuscript: Thank you for making art with me. My books would not realize their potential without you. Lauren Cormier, thank you for being willing to read early drafts before anyone else—and for consistently making me laugh. Your ideas and edits are *priceless*, and I'm lucky to have you in my life. Kristie Cooley, your edit on this one was spectacular. You're one of my secret weapons. Please don't go anywhere!

Donald Maass, it was a dream come true to spend time with you in Salem. I was struggling with how to get going with this one, specifically how to introduce Detective Jones, and your ideas and encouragement sent me running in the right direction. I'm grateful for both our time together and your extraordinary books and blogs on the craft of writing. You have done so much for my abilities.

Alan Janney (Alan Lee), master of the mystery, thank you for helping me understand your genre and giving Detective Jones a bit of that Janney charm. I'm a big Alan fan.

To my Tiki writing crew: James, Lucy, Nathan, and Cecelia, thanks for always being there for me. I have a deep respect for each of you and am honored to call you friends. When are we going back to Ocean City?

There is no way I could have gotten even close with this story had I not had the help of three men directly involved with real-life crime: Detective Mark Dorval, Officer Chief Joseph K. Loughlin, and forensic death investigator Kent Holloway. Gentlemen, thank you for your help, and more importantly, for what you do and have done to keep us safe.

Drew Grissom, thank you for helping me understand lymphoma. Your story is remarkable, and you are such an inspiration.

Mikella and Riggs Walker, my loves, my squash partners, my best friends, my core, my heart, my soul, my everything. I'd be lost without you. Thank you for supporting this wild passion I have for the written word. Living with an artist is no easy job, but you do it so well. I cannot wait to see what's next in this lovely life we're living.

Oh, and Mikella, I guess here's where I'll reluctantly give you credit for coming up with the brilliant twist. Ugh, that was hard to type, but it's true. You are the mastermind behind anything great that comes from my fingers.

To all my family and friends, near and far: I'm so darn lucky to have you in my life.

And to the librarians, booksellers, book clubs, and readers: you grant me the honor of making art for a living. Please keep reading and spreading the word. In turn, I'll continue to bleed my soul onto the page.

My love to all of you who make this possible.

Book Club Questions

1. How did you feel about the collaboration between Boo and Peggy? Have you ever read such a book?

2. Were you able to detect where Boo took over? If so, how would you compare the two styles?

3. Did you notice there was an unfinished book (Frank's medical treatise) inside an unfinished book that was completed because of *An Unfinished Story*?

4. Were there any story questions left lingering?

5. Catherine turns her life on a dime when she meets Frank, and then again after her suicide attempt. Do you think people are able to make such radical changes? How?

6. What could have caused Miriam to be the way she is?

7. Detective Jones crosses a big line when he gives in and sleeps with Sylvie. What was your reaction?

8. What do you think of Sandy's arrangement with Frank in medical school? Was it ethical? Do you think this ever happens in real life?

9. Is Glenna in love with Sandy? Why is she so devoted to him?

10. Is it more than guilt that makes Miriam stay with David? Do they love each other? Discuss.

11. What makes Detective Jones take the high ground when he discovers his love may be the murderer?

12. Halfway through the book, who did you think did it? Did you figure out who killed Frank before the reveal?

13. If Frank noticed the resemblance in Amber at a glance, do you think that the other islanders would have noticed it too? Have you ever met someone who reminded you of someone else? What was your experience?

14. How do you feel about Sylvie's life at the conclusion of the book?

15. How did you feel about Catherine's ending? Did you want more from her?

16. How would you compare this novel to that of a classic mystery?

17. Was there a love in your life who got away?

About the Authors

Photo © 2018 Brandi Morris

Photo © 1948 E.H. Jaffe

Boo Walker is the bestselling author of *An Echo in Time*, *The Stars Don't Lie*, *A Spanish Sunrise*, *The Singing Trees*, and *An Unfinished Story*, among other novels. He initially tapped his muse as a songwriter and banjoist in Nashville, but a career-ending hand problem sent him scrambling to find another creative outlet. After a stint as a day trader in Charleston, he bought a farm in a wine-growing region of Washington State, where he found his voice. Always a wanderer, Boo has lived in South Carolina, Tennessee, Florida, New York, and Valencia, Spain. He now resides in Cape Elizabeth, Maine, with his wife, son, and two troublemaking dogs. He also writes thrillers under the pen name Benjamin Blackmore. For more information, visit www.boowalker.com and www.benjaminblackmore.com.

Peggy Shainberg graduated from Baylor University in 1948 with a degree in journalism. After she and her fiancé were married on the radio program *Bride and Groom*, Peggy embarked on an award-winning career writing for television and radio in Hollywood. In 1965, they moved with their two daughters to Venice, Florida, where Peggy wrote for the Florida Press Association and *The Venice Gondolier*, and began her first, only, and sadly unfinished novel. With the help of her daughters and, serendipitously, author Boo Walker, it has finally found its way to print. The fact that Boo's grandparents were also married on *Bride and Groom* in the exact same year was perfect confirmation that the coauthored *The Secrets of Good People* was meant to be.